NO ONE WILL HEAR
Joel Hames

Praise for Joel Hames

"In *Dead North*, Hames' lawyer turned accidental sleuth, Sam Williams, finds himself far from home and neck deep in Manchester's seamy gangster scene. But what stands out in this intelligent, intricately woven crime procedural - with a plot to make your brain hurt - is the undercurrent of slick and highly enjoyable humour reminiscent of Raymond Chandler, updated for the twenty-first century. Loved it."

S.E. Lynes, author of *Mother, Valentina,* and *The Pact*

"I really enjoyed [Dead North]. The characters spring off the page with such natural ease. I was gripped by the story – I love a book that takes turns where you least expect. It's going to leave me with a thriller hangover for some time."

John Marrs, author of *The One, The Good Samaritan* and *When You Disappeared*

"Hames is such a talent that he has created a white-knuckle, breathlessly-paced read that also has heart. Beautifully written and thrilling, Dead North deserves to go to the top of any chart."

Louise Beech, author of *Maria in the Moon, How To Be Brave* and *The Mountain in my Shoe*

"A pacy thriller, rich in voice and with a gratifying degree of complexity. Hames knows how to deliver."

John Bowen, author of *Where the Dead Walk, Vessel* and *Death Stalks Kettle Street*

About the Author

A Londoner in exile, Joel Hames lives in rural Lancashire with his wife and two daughters.

His works of fiction include the novels *Dead North, The Art of Staying Dead* and *Bankers Town,* as well as the novellas *Brexecution, Victims* and *Caged.*

When not writing or spending time with his family, Joel likes to eat, drink, cook, and make up excuses to avoid walking the dog.

You can find out more about Joel and sign up to his mailing list through social media or his very own website:

Facebook: facebook.com/joelhamesauthor
Twitter: @joel_hames
Website: http://www.joelhamesauthor.com

Also by Joel Hames

Dead North
The Art of Staying Dead
Bankers Town
Brexecution
Victims
Caged

NO ONE WILL HEAR

BY

JOEL HAMES

Cover art by John Bowen

For My Wife

CONTENTS

Still my revenge shall take its proper time,
And suit the baseness of your hellish crime.
My self, abandon'd, and devoid of shame,
Thro' the wide world your actions will proclaim;
Or tho' I'm prison'd in this lonely den,
Obscur'd, and bury'd from the sight of men,
My mournful voice the pitying rocks shall move,
And my complainings echo thro' the grove.
Hear me, o Heav'n! and, if a God be there,
Let him regard me, and accept my pray'r.

Ovid, Metamorphoses

PART 1: TONGUE

1: The Reading of the Will

A LARGE, DARK room. Elegant. Brown. Wood panelling on the walls, a huge wooden desk, and a woman in a smart grey suit serving tea and sparkling water who might as well have been made of wood herself for all the expression on her face.

Not that the rest of the quietly-muttering vultures had tears coursing down their well-moisturised faces.

The man behind the desk held a glass of something that definitely wasn't tea or sparkling water. Whisky, I thought, and took a sniff as I strode up to the desk. Not whisky. Brandy. Cognac. VSOP, no doubt. Very Special Old Preserve.

He frowned as I stepped forward and reminded him who I was, and then he nodded and smiled. If cats could smile, fat, murderous, evil cats, if they could smile before they sunk their claws into their prey, that was the smile they'd use. Christian Willoughby's smile. VSOP. Vile Smug Obnoxious Prick.

Christian Willoughby cleared his throat, and the dull murmur died out. Still seated – the rest of us were standing, but that was Willoughby's style – he slowly surveyed the room, cleared his throat once more, and began his speech.

"Elizabeth Maurier is dead," he said. The vultures nodded, and I found myself nodding with them. This wasn't the time or the place to say that she wasn't just dead, she'd been murdered. "Elizabeth has passed, but she has left much to remember her by. She has left a legacy of justice, of noble service to the law, she has left memories of the battles she fought and won and those she helped."

Willoughby paused, surveyed the room again. I followed his eyes. Of the thirty-plus people in the room I hadn't recognised a soul, when I arrived, but now I found myself locking eyes with David Brooks-Powell, which didn't count, because he probably didn't have a soul anyway. Same face, same hair. He hadn't changed in a decade. I'd seen him at the funeral; I'd seen him a year or so back, when I'd shredded his professional reputation in a public courtroom, each event greeted with the same sombre scowl. The years, Elizabeth Maurier's death, his own humiliation, nothing had got to him. He tilted his head in a barely-perceptible nod of civilised enmity, and went back to staring at Willoughby. After everything that had come out in court, the devil alone knew what he was doing here.

Mind you, the devil alone knew what I was doing here, too.

"She has left memories of her professional life, her cultural life, her personal life," continued Willoughby, warming to his theme. "She has left memories as a lawyer, as a friend, as a mother." He paused, again, nodded towards a woman standing directly in front of him, and I gave a start.

Lizzy Maurier. At the funeral she'd been anonymous among a mass of hats and black veils. The last time I'd seen her face, she'd been halfway through her twenties. She was shaking, slightly, drawn in, old before her time. The same ten years that hadn't aged Brooks-Powell a second had done a job on Lizzy Maurier.

Perhaps I was being uncharitable. Her mother had recently been murdered, after all.

Willoughby held the pause to allow the restless fidgeting of his audience to subside. It was a cold wet December outside, but I couldn't see the window for all the gathered vultures, and in here it was hot, close and still. He smiled into the newly-restored silence, and returned to his monologue.

"Of course, Elizabeth also left a legacy of a more tangible sort, and it is that legacy that falls into my modest domain."

The vultures chortled, quietly, obligingly. I didn't know Willoughby well, but I suspected modesty didn't feature amongst his various vices.

Another pause. So many expectant people in the room. I wondered what they were expecting. For the most part, something simple, no doubt. Money. A house or a car. Shares and bonds and interests in complex offshore arrangements. A painting. A favourite tea service.

I wasn't expecting anything like that. As for what I *was* expecting, I could no more have answered that than I could have decapitated Willoughby and Brooks-Powell with my bare hands.

And that *would* have been interesting.

Willoughby had "called on me" three days after the funeral. That was how he'd put it, when he rang the doorbell at nine in the morning and forced me from my bed. "I apologise for calling on you without notice," he said, "but we really must discuss your attendance at the reading of the will."

Willoughby was wearing a suit and tie, and went on to address me as "dear fellow". I was in a dressing gown. Claire was in the kitchen hammering angrily at her laptop, so absorbed in whatever she was doing that she hadn't even noticed the doorbell. I gaped at him, and stepped aside to allow him into the flat.

"I won't keep you, dear fellow," he continued. He smiled out of a face shining with oils that probably cost more than I made in a year. "It's just that I do rather need a response, and the late Mrs Maurier did make it clear that she very much wished you to be present."

He'd said as much in the letter I'd received two days earlier. *The late Mrs Maurier requested your presence*, and the date, and the time, and the address, and nothing else. The late Mrs Maurier had been my first employer, had raised me to the edge of brilliance, and fired me (at the urging of my colleague and nemesis, David Brooks-Powell), had ignored me for years, even after I'd sued Brooks-Powell and her firm, had tried, belatedly, to contact me in the week before she'd been stabbed to death. I'd had next to nothing to do with the woman for close to a decade, so I'd assumed Willoughby's letter was either a mistake or something half of London had received, and thought no more about it.

Clearly I'd been wrong. Half of London wouldn't have Christian Willoughby in their living room, smiling and gazing appraisingly at the furniture. I'd conceived an instant dislike for the man, and I wanted him out of my flat.

"I'll consult my diary," I replied, hoping for a break in the smile, but he nodded and "took his leave" with an exaggerated courtesy that deepened my dislike still further. I'd never liked probate lawyers, but that was a prejudice even I knew was unfair. Just because they harvested the dead like jackals didn't make them bad people. But Willoughby was smug, and, by the look of him, unfeasibly rich. I'd have given good money to lock him in a room with Brooks-Powell and a single spoonful of caviar, and leave them there for a week or two.

I walked into the kitchen and sat watching Claire hammering away at that laptop for five minutes before I said a word, and when I told her what had happened and what I was inclined to do with Willoughby's invitation, she finally stopped typing and turned to me with a sigh.

"It's not like you don't have the time," she said, with a gentle smile that did little to moderate the sting of the words. "And what have you got to lose?"

She'd been right, of course. I didn't want to see Brooks-Powell and I didn't want to be reminded of Elizabeth Maurier and the past and what I might have been, had

6

things not gone the way they did. But that wasn't reason enough to stay away. Of course, Claire hadn't left it at that. She'd told me to stop running away and face things, she'd told me that something good might come of it, she'd told me that Elizabeth Maurier must have had a reason to want me there, and it must have been a good reason or Christian Willoughby wouldn't have trekked all the way from Mayfair to North London to request my presence.

All good points, of course. But still, I wasn't expecting a Rolls Royce or a Rolex.

Willoughby was into his stride, now, declaiming loudly on "the estate" and "the beneficiaries" and "the various trusts which he was honoured to accept the responsibility of administering". All those expectant beneficiaries were nodding solemnly and keeping their expressions neutral as their expectations were met or dashed with each announcement. Lizzy Maurier got her mother's houses – the Holland Park townhouse, the Cotswolds manor, the gîte in the Dordogne, and most of the cash and other assets. Various items of artwork and jewellery went to nieces and nephews, cousins, old family friends, Willoughby himself. The items were shrinking in value as the list went on, and those who had yet to receive their wished-for boon were struggling to conceal their dismay. Nothing for me, of course. Nothing for Brooks-Powell, either.

A fly settled briefly on my collar, and I barely summoned the energy to sweep it away. On he went, the Volvo, the Nissan; her long-dead husband's collection of classic cars had been donated to the appropriate museum decades earlier. The fly landed on Willoughby's desk and hopped onto the rim of his almost-empty brandy glass. Perhaps it was bored enough to be contemplating suicide. It wasn't the only one.

"And now we come to a separate and somewhat unique part of the legacy," said Willoughby. "One which will be both an honour and a solemn duty to take possession of, should the beneficiaries choose to accept."

Solemn duty. I blinked and tried to refocus my attention. This sounded bad. This sounded like me.

"The achievements of the late Mrs Maurier have been celebrated in print on numerous occasions, but as is the way with these things, there has, as yet, been no consistent record of her work and her life. Whilst Mrs Maurier was not one to glory in her own victories or wallow in her thankfully rare defeats, she did believe that there would be a benefit to posterity in the presentation of her life in, as it were, the round."

I felt a sour taste in the back of my throat and swallowed. The fly remained motionless on the edge of the glass, and suddenly I found myself afraid to glance up and meet Willoughby's eye.

"To that end, Mrs Maurier has asked that three individuals take on the task of assembling a full account of her career, from the notes and diary entries she meticulously made and retained, from the information available in court records and the public domain, and, where appropriate, from their own memories."

From their own memories. Elizabeth Maurier knew what she was doing. Elizabeth Maurier always knew what she was doing.

The fact that I'd known Claire was right hadn't been enough to stop me having second thoughts right up to the moment I put on my coat and stepped outside. All that morning I'd been trying to come up with reasons to go, and reasons not to, and the reasons not to won every time.

"Just say Roarkes calls?" I asked Claire, and she shook her head at me, slowly, sitting on the sofa and watching me with a look of quiet disappointment.

"If Roarkes calls, you'll call him back. How long do you

think you'll be in there, anyway? Roarkes can wait."

"How do you know?" I snapped, and instantly regretted it.

"Are you an oncologist?" she asked. I breathed out, slowly. This was a fight I wasn't going to win. "Are you an expert in palliative care? A hospice director, perhaps? Are you any use whatsoever to your friend Roarkes and his wife?"

"No, it's not that," I said, for want of anything else. She stood, walked over to me, placed her hand on my arm.

"It's precisely that," she said, gently. "That's exactly what it is. Helen Roarkes is dying. There's nothing you can do about that, there's nothing any of us can do about that, and I'm sure Roarkes will want to talk to you about it some day. But right now he doesn't seem to want to talk to anyone, does he?"

I kept my mouth shut. She was right. Of course she was right. That didn't make it any easier to accept.

"Does he?" she repeated, and I shrugged at her and shook my head. It had taken her a long time to warm to Roarkes, I remembered, to push aside her distrust of the police, but she'd got there in the end. I should have been grateful she was looking out for him and for me. I should have been grateful she'd spoken patiently with me instead of snapping my head off.

I'd always found gratitude hard.

I left twenty minutes later, with Claire now shouting, but not, thankfully, at me. Someone had called, a Sergeant Jenson, and asked to speak to her about the case, which I'd thought might be something positive. She'd spent enough time trying to get someone in authority interested in it, after all. But now Sergeant Jenson was reaping the benefits of my mistimed words and silences. Sergeant Jenson would be wishing he'd waited an hour or two before making that call.

Silence had fallen, again. A roomful of vultures, all praying they wouldn't be one of the three.

I didn't even bother with the prayers. That line about memory had nailed me as sure as if Willoughby had said my name.

"The three individuals are perfectly within their rights to decline this bequest. I use the term bequest because, as the lawyer and confidante of the late Mrs Maurier, I advised her to frame it as such. The individuals will, if they choose to accept, receive a bequest of the records and rough memoirs Mrs Maurier compiled throughout her life, on the condition that they work together to create a full and proper account of her career. There will be a small retainer to compensate for their time and effort."

Willoughby paused, and gazed slowly and portentously across the room. I fought back a sigh of impatience. I'd worked with Elizabeth Maurier on one of her biggest cases, and a handful more that were noteworthy enough. I had a photographic memory, and Elizabeth Maurier was well aware of it. I was on the list.

"The individuals in question," Willoughby continued, finally, "are Lizzy Maurier."

All eyes turned to Lizzy, who nodded. She'd known this was coming.

"Sam Williams."

I stared at the fly on the glass on the desk. Most of the people there had no idea who Sam Williams was or what connection he could possibly have had with Elizabeth Maurier.

"And David Brooks-Powell."

To my credit, I managed to keep my gasp quiet enough that I didn't think anyone had noticed. I turned and looked at him and he was staring at me, his mouth open, as shocked as I was. Too shocked for one of those nods, at least.

The gathering broke up a few minutes later, with assurances from Willoughby that he would be in touch with each of the beneficiaries to discuss the arrangements regarding the various bequests. I'd managed to reach him before he vanished under a flurry of disappointed relatives, and learned that his phrasing had not just been a figure of speech: that retainer was, indeed, small. He would contact me in due course, he said, and not for the first time, I found myself wishing he didn't know where to find me. I didn't want Elizabeth Maurier's *records and rough memoirs*, I didn't want to delve into the past and turn it into a three-hundred-page eulogy, and I certainly didn't want to *work together* with David Brooks-Powell any more than he wanted to *work together* with me.

Lizzy Maurier had other ideas. I'd tried to escape as unobtrusively as possible, but evidently I hadn't managed to escape unseen. She caught up with me on the pavement outside Willoughby's office, December's rain and wind a welcome relief from the oppressive calm inside, and took my right hand in both of hers before I could think what to do. The street was empty apart from the two of us and a man standing on the other side of the road behind a tiny green motorbike. It was parked on a double yellow line. He was watching us, I thought, or the door behind us, but as I caught his eye he ran a hand through his thick wet hair and turned to his phone.

"Sam," said Lizzy, gazing into my face.

Lizzy Maurier. Little Lizzy Maurier, I remembered, that's what we'd called her, that's what her own mother had called her, *Little Lizzy*, though she was only a couple of years younger than I was. She'd always seemed somehow squashed, even her name a diminutive of her mother's.

"I'm sorry, Lizzy," I stammered. I meant to go on, to apologise for declining the bequest, because that was what I was going to do, no doubt about it, and neither Claire nor

Lizzy Maurier nor the long dead arm of her mother would stop me. Willoughby's audience were still drifting out of his office and casting curious glances as they passed Lizzy and me talking in the rain, a whole wake of vultures of power and influence who would expect me to do my duty by Elizabeth Maurier, and they weren't going to stop me either. Instead, I stopped myself. *I'm sorry, Lizzy*, I'd said, and she'd nodded. I'm sorry for your mother's death. I'm sorry I haven't seen you in ten years and have no idea what your life is, what you do, who you love, what you despise. We were friends, once – not close, not lovers or soulmates, but friends who shared a laugh and a drink and a wary complaint about that mother, and I'm sorry all that's over. Poetry, I remembered. That had been her passion.

"Do you still write poems?" I asked. It was a stupid question, a line from a film in black-and-white where people wore hats and spoke in clipped voices devoid of emotion until it swept through them in a squall. But there was nothing else. The rain had turned stronger and colder. Her mother had died. We were no longer friends. What could I ask?

She shook her head and laughed.

"Oh no, Sam. Not for a long time. I'm a scholar, now. A professor, no less."

Now I remembered. Elizabeth had been against the poetry thing. Too fanciful. She'd wanted a job for her daughter, with a salary, and Lizzy had turned to academia. What Elizabeth wanted, Elizabeth got.

"Of course. Renaissance literature, right?"

She beamed.

"You remember! How charming! Yes, that's right. I'm a Fellow of St John's College. Oxford."

"Congratulations," I said. "That's marvellous."

"I have to go, Sam, there are so many people I need to speak to. But I'm glad to have spoken to you."

She was still holding onto my hand. I smiled back at her.

"Goodbye, Sam. I'll be in touch about the memoirs. Won't it be wonderful? I'll get your details from Christian."

With that, she was gone, back into Willoughby's offices, and I was alone on the street with the wind and the rain and a bequest as unwelcome as the weather.

2: Life Coach

NEITHER THE WEATHER nor my mood had improved when I reached the flat. Islington looked no more appealing in the rain than Mayfair had done, although the thought of Elizabeth Maurier's bequest, of what I would be doing and who I would be doing it with, would have blackened the brightest of skies.

Claire was on the phone. I could hear her as I turned the key in the lock. "OK, Jonathan," she was saying. I thought I heard a note in her voice as she said the words, resignation, perhaps, or disappointment. The Tribune's new editor, I assumed. Jonathan Thorwell. She spoke quietly, but the door was thin and the gap at the bottom large enough to let the cold air in and spill private conversation into the corridor.

"I understand," she said, as I walked in. She ended the call, put the phone down, turned to me and smiled, and whatever she'd been talking about, whatever shit I was going to have to endure at the hands of David Brooks-Powell, that smile let me push it all to one side.

For about five seconds.

She walked up and kissed me on the cheek and asked me how it had been, and even though I'd resolved on the way home not to let it bother me, even though I started out laughing about Willoughby and the vultures, by the time I'd finished it was like it had all just hit me for the first time.

"So now I've got to work with that bastard and dig through Elizabeth Maurier's history, and I'm supposed to be grateful?"

I slumped down onto the sofa and looked at her. She was still standing, one hand under her chin and a frown on her face, our midget Christmas tree, thin on foliage and sparsely decorated, obscured almost entirely by her head. She didn't answer.

"I'm seriously thinking about just saying no, telling them I'm too busy or some crap like that."

Still nothing.

I wasn't busy and Claire knew I wasn't busy, and she hadn't shied away from reminding me of the fact in recent days. I'd just spent a fortnight in Manchester getting beaten up, watching people die, recovering from a nasty bout of septicaemia. I hadn't earned a penny while I was up there and the only client I had was a lying Egyptian named Hasina Khalil who wanted me to stop her getting deported and couldn't afford to pay me what she'd promised. Even Willoughby's small retainer was more than I was getting anywhere else.

She shrugged. She looked tired, I realised, paler than usual, dark pools around her eyes.

"What do you reckon?" I asked.

"What do *you* reckon?" she replied. "You've got to decide this yourself."

"I'm trying."

"I know. I know you are. Maybe you're just not very good at it." She sat down beside me and took my hand. "You've got to be honest with yourself."

"I don't understand," I said, because I didn't.

"Ask yourself why. Why you don't want to do it, why you don't want anything to do with Elizabeth Maurier and David Brookes-Powell and all that shitty past you've spent ten years hiding from. No, wait," she said, as I opened my mouth to protest. "I'm not saying you're wrong. Sometimes it's right to run. Sometimes it's right to hide. You might have a good reason. But you need to know what that reason is before you know if it's good enough."

I nodded, even though I knew I'd been right to get away from all that – not that I'd had much choice – and I'd been right to stay away since. "Thanks," I replied, and she patted my hand, walked into the kitchen, and sat down behind her laptop. I stared at her back for a moment, and shuffled into the bedroom.

That was the way we worked, when we were both at home, which we usually were, except on Thursdays, when Claire put in her weekly office appearance and trotted out an article or two. Me in the bedroom, feet up, laptop beside me, trying to keep my eyes open and focus on work instead of daydreaming or trawling the web. Claire at the kitchen table, straight-backed, frowning in concentration, neck deep in the story she'd been working on for two years already, and stopping only to raid the fridge or make us both a coffee. I'd surrendered the lease on my office a couple of months back, when it became clear I neither needed nor could afford it. Hours of silence could slip by, each of us lost in our work.

The trouble was, I didn't have enough work to get lost in. I checked my emails and sent a few myself, and made sure nothing surprising had happened to Hasina Khalil. Hasina Khalil had surprised me from the beginning, a self-proclaimed warrior for sexual equality who turned out to be a preening middle-aged woman who had no more interest in sexual equality than a sparrow, a pawn in a political power-game who turned out to be the wife of a petty embezzler, a millionairess who couldn't even afford to pay me. If it weren't for the fact that no one else wanted to pay me either, I'd have extracted myself from Hasina Khalil some time ago. As things stood, even a client who couldn't pay was better than no client at all.

I found myself checking up on David Brooks-Powell. Still a *consultant*, I noted, although from the various references to recent cases he'd been involved in it looked like he'd managed to bag himself a handful of clients.

Brooks-Powell had been Elizabeth Maurier's golden boy, edging out his rivals one by one, until I'd toppled him from that perch last year with a lawsuit against the firm and, by implication, its most aggressive partner. He'd gone from *David Brooks-Powell, Partner, Maurier & Co*, to *David Brooks-Powell, Legal Consultant*, and everyone in the business knew he'd been as good as fired.

I changed tack and looked up Elizabeth Maurier, just out of interest. The firm's website was choked with expressions of shock and sadness, ringing through all of them a clear message that the work would continue. Not just "work", but "*the* work". That was how they saw it at Mauriers. Less a business, more a crusade.

There were obituaries everywhere. The legal press, but also the national dailies and even the BBC, buried half a dozen clicks away from the main page. I scanned them, one after another, hoping for something that would tell me why she'd decided to say her goodbyes by inflicting this torment on someone she hadn't spoken with in years.

There was nothing new, nothing surprising. Childhood in Oxfordshire. Her brother, three years older than her, had died from a misdiagnosed bout of meningitis when he was only nine. Elizabeth had always said it was this that inspired her to fight for those who suffered, but she wasn't the only one. Her mother was a GP who went on to chair the General Medical Council. Her father was a respected intellectual and legal professor who mentored half a dozen cabinet members and a Prime Minister. She'd left the family home at eighteen – I remembered the house, which had eventually become hers, the drawing room and the smoking room and the gardens, plural – and gone on to excel at Cambridge. Then the early years making her name in the legal profession. Her marriage to an artist thirty years her senior, a man she had turned from alcoholic and serial philanderer to the very model of propriety, the perfect union of art and establishment. The birth of her daughter, Lizzy. The deaths of her parents, just one year apart. The establishment of Maurier & Co. The death of her husband . The landmark cases, including one I'd worked on. The lobbying to improve remand conditions and reduce the maximum time in custody before charge. The friends and connections among the great and good. The brutal and untimely death.

I knew all this. I'd known it for years. It was burned into my brain, and I'd have known it even without the photographic memory. Elizabeth Maurier was a great woman who made the mistake of hiring a smug, supercilious bastard and not seeing him for what he was until it was too late. If she'd seen it at all – she'd named Brooks-Powell alongside me, after all, and the will had been reviewed and tweaked just six weeks before she'd died, so she'd had plenty of time to cut him out after the revelations in court.

So if I knew all this, if I knew everything there was to know about the woman, if all that remained was the detail, the scraps from court records, the recollections of friends and colleagues – *if I knew all this*, then why the hell was I reading it? What was I looking for?

I folded down the computer and walked back into the kitchen, where Claire was sitting exactly where I'd left her. She looked up as I came in, rested her elbows on the table and her chin on her hands and gave me that look that meant she had something to say to me. I waited.

"Did you ask yourself?" she asked. "Did you get an answer?"

I shrugged. We bounced things off each other, in normal times. I didn't think we'd done much bouncing since I'd returned from Manchester. I'd been too caught up in Elizabeth Maurier's death to have anything much to bounce. Claire was still throwing everything she had at her story, a piece of journalism on a group of men who had been smuggling girls into England for a decade, and selling them to sadists who killed them for pleasure. It had been more than two years in the making, this story, and for most of those two years Claire had been sniffing for scraps. A name here, a location there – none of it really helped. The men who'd done the killing had been caught, and no one except Claire seemed to be interested in finding out who'd brought the girls to England and delivered them to their murderers. Five girls. Five deaths. Five killers behind bars, and a dozen more who'd "helped". Four of the girls didn't even have names. "Girl A, Blonde," the police called them. "Girl B, Brunette." Claire had given them names, not their real names, nobody knew their real names. But names more real than "A" and "B".

A few weeks ago, that had changed. I'd been back from Manchester, just for the day, and we'd been trying some of that bouncing. She helped me, I helped her. She'd made a little progress and come to the tentative conclusion that two of the girls had been brought to the same industrial site in Sussex when they'd first arrived in the UK. She'd run checks on all the businesses on the site. She'd listed the names of all their directors. It was one of those tiny steps that usually went nowhere, but it was all she had.

She'd shown me the list, and one of those names had chimed with something I remembered.

Jonas Wolf.

Buried deep in Claire's files was a set of photographs taken from the security system of the apartment block in which Rosa had died. Rosa was a real name, the first of the victims, the only one to be identified. The men who'd been present when she'd died were all in prison, but the person who'd brought her there had never been found. Every individual who'd been buzzed through the main door of the apartment block in the twenty-four hours prior to the murder had been photographed by the security cameras, and Claire had worked for weeks to get hold of those photographs and identify those individuals. All thirty-six had been questioned by the police, and released without charge. Rosa herself couldn't be seen on the shots, but Claire was convinced she was there, just out of sight, walking obediently to her death.

I'd remembered those photographs and dug them up, and sorted through them until I'd found the one I remembered. A young, dark-haired man with a winning smile and a couple of days' worth of stubble. Across his face, in Claire's handwriting, were the words "Jonas Wolf".

Jonas Wolf ran a business on the site the traffickers may have used to bring the girls in. Jonas Wolf had been in the apartment block in which one of the girls had died.

Jonas Wolf should have been the beginning of the end. Claire delved deeper. After years of dead ends, there were suddenly names and addresses and clear, if circumstantial, evidence. Certain people had been in certain places at certain times. I'd told her it was time to celebrate, but she'd shaken her head and said she wasn't celebrating until she was done.

She still wasn't done. Whatever she had, it wasn't enough for the police. They weren't interested. Instead of celebrating Claire was still sitting there, in that same spot, silent, typing and thinking, the way she'd been typing and thinking almost every hour of every day since I'd got back. No wonder she'd been so patient with me. My issues with David Brooks-Powell and the Mauriers were probably light relief.

She took my silence as a negative, and sighed.

"OK, then. I'll answer for you. I'll tell you why you don't want to work on this memoir."

"Go on, then," I replied, my voice more petulant than I'd intended. She ignored the tone.

"You're scared of David Brooks-Powell. That's all this is. You're scared of the man, even after what you did to him in court. I think you somehow imagined that would be the end of Brooks-Powell, that he'd melt away like the Wicked Witch of the West the moment you beat him, and you're bitter and disappointed that he's still around at all. I think you need to speak to him and realise he's just a person, even if he is a twenty-four carat bastard. He can't hurt you any more, but he's got this power over you and you'll never shake it as long as you think he's more than human."

It was a long speech, but it wasn't Claire's. I knew Claire. Those weren't Claire's words.

"More than human?" I asked, and back she came.

"Yes. He had something over you, once. He knew you'd been cutting corners. He got you fired. Well boo-fucking-hoo. That was ten years ago. You can't blame David Brooks-Powell for everything that's happened since then."

She'd raised her voice a little, that patience stretched to breaking point. She pushed back her chair and got to her feet, and now she was standing there with her hands on her hips waiting for me to say something.

I had nothing to say.

The silence lengthened and I tried to picture myself from her angle. My mouth was shut, my jaw tight. How did I look? Angry? Thoughtful? I couldn't even figure out how I felt. Maybe knowing what I looked like would give me a clue.

I shook my head and turned to go back to the bedroom.

"You can't just ignore this," she called after me. "We need to talk about it. We need to talk about things like this. Adrian says it's absolutely critical."

Adrian.

Adrian Chalmers was Claire's "life coach". She'd been seeing him for a couple of months, if seeing him was really the right word. They'd met just the once, back at the start, after she'd had a brief but intense crisis of confidence about her story and whether she'd been doing the right thing dedicating herself to it so single-mindedly for so long. She'd told me she needed help, professional help, not the sort of help I could provide, so I'd suggested she get some. "No point delaying," I'd said. She'd spent an hour or two online and next thing I knew, she'd come up with Adrian Chalmers. The crisis had ended a day or two later, but she'd carried on speaking to him, once a week or so, on the phone or by Skype.

I had no idea what Adrian Chalmers actually did for her, what he told her, whether he was any use at all. I'd tried not to be dismissive when she'd told me she was going to see him, and tried not to seem too surprised when she'd told me she was still speaking to him even after the original reason had faded away. I'd made myself as neutral as I could about Adrian Chalmers.

I wasn't feeling very neutral at the moment. *More than human.* That was Chalmers. It certainly wasn't Claire. So she'd been talking to him about me. I contemplated storming back into the kitchen and confronting her, but I knew what she'd say. Adrian Chalmers was her life coach. I was part of her life. If there was a problem, I was part of that, too.

I decided to call Roarkes instead.

He answered on the seventh ring, just as I was about to give up, with a weary "Hello Sam" that made me think I'd made a mistake calling him before I'd said a word.

"Hello Roarkes," I said. I didn't like calling him *Detective Inspector* and he didn't like anyone calling him Gideon. So Roarkes it was. "What's the latest?"

I could almost hear the shrug. I could hear the sigh that went with it.

"Nothing new, Sam. It's just a matter of time. At least she's comfortable. Still thrashing me at Scrabble. Still doesn't realise I'm letting her win. Still telling me I drink too much. We're working on getting her into a hospice nearby. She won't be able to measure what's left in the whisky bottles then."

I cut through the levity. "Is there anything I can do?"

I knew there was nothing I could do. He hadn't told me about the diagnosis until I'd left Manchester, but he'd only known himself for a week. In the few days that had followed, Helen had gone from a healthy woman with a persistent headache to a shadow hovering inches from death, and I'd asked him a dozen times whether there was anything I could do. Every time he'd told me no, he could handle it, thanks but no thanks. Claire had told me to leave it alone, that Roarkes would call me if he needed me. I couldn't leave it alone. He might change his mind.

"No, Sam. Really. I'll let you know if there's anything I need."

"OK," I replied. "Just remember I can come and see you if you want. Get you out for a beer. Sort out some paperwork. I might even drag myself out to Essex or wherever it is you live."

He lived in Kent. I knew he lived in Kent. He knew I knew he lived in Kent.

"Fuck off, Sam," he replied. "And thanks. Speak soon, OK?"

The call hadn't done much to lift my mood, but at least I was thinking about something other than David Brooks-Powell. I managed an hour on the Hasina Khalil case, and by the time I'd had my fill of her I was feeling calm enough to brave the kitchen again.

Claire smiled as I walked in. She was standing by the hob watching the pot boil. Two cups, I noticed. At least Adrian

Chalmers hadn't taken that away from me.

"I called Roarkes," I said. I didn't want to talk about Chalmers. I didn't want to think about Chalmers.

"And?"

"And nothing. Didn't have anything to say."

"I've told you to leave the man alone. He'll call you when he needs you. He trusts you, Sam – more than anyone. You don't have to keep testing him."

For all that it had taken time for her to actually like Roarkes, she seemed to have a better sense of the man than I did.

"I just want to help" I said.

"I know you do. I just don't think you're doing him any favours calling him up every day when he's got so much to deal with."

"It's not every day," I muttered, but my heart wasn't in it. She could have pushed me on that, but instead she just nodded and passed me my coffee, and we sat down on the sofa, in our usual positions, her on the left, me on the right, remote control in the middle. We'd been living together less than eight months but already we were falling into these patterns. I smiled to myself, and noticed Claire doing the same, having the same thoughts, no doubt. It wasn't all bad.

"Lizzy Maurier didn't look good," I said. Claire had turned the television on but the sound was on mute, images flicking from a power station to Westminster and back to a newsroom.

"Hardly surprising, Sam. I mean, she's just lost her mum. Can't imagine she'll get over that in a hurry."

I nodded. It had been a brutal killing, according to the police. Beaten with a blunt instrument in her own home, and then stabbed in the stomach until she was beyond saving, breathing out her last on the floor of her own bedroom. She'd been found by her cleaner the following day, which was fortunate, in a way, because if the cleaner hadn't found her it probably would have been Lizzy herself, and whatever state she was in now, seeing the body like that wouldn't have improved it.

"I suppose so," I said. "But it's not just that. She seemed smaller, somehow. Maybe I've just remembered her wrong. Less vibrant I can get, after what's happened. But, I don't know, it felt like something more than that."

They'd argued about the poetry, I remembered that. I remembered Lizzy sitting in the pub with me telling me her mother didn't understand, didn't see the opportunity, just didn't get that this wasn't a childish whim but a serious ambition. I remembered ordering another pint and nodding along with her but secretly agreeing with her mother. Elizabeth had won that fight. Elizabeth had won all the fights that counted, except her final one. If she'd fought at all.

"People change," said Claire. "It's been a long time, after all." She was looking at the television. The Central Criminal Court – the Old Bailey, people still called it. Lots of press, lots of police. A picture of a man with his face blurred out – a notorious defendant, no doubt, or a star witness for the prosecution. Boats in the Mediterranean, so full there was hardly space for the shivering passengers to stand. Back to the studio. Onto the next story. A map of London with a street in Chelsea inset. A house with police tape outside. Claire was still watching, in silence.

I reached for my coffee.

3: You Think You Know Someone

FOR MOST OF the weekend I'd struggled to find a good reason not to do this damned thing, and failed. I'd even tried to get Claire to find one for me. I'd failed there, too. Our relationship for the past two-and-a-half days had been pretty much failure all the way – in fact, looking back, that brief interlude sitting there in silence drinking coffee and watching depressing news stories on the TV had probably been the high point.

Fifteen minutes, that silence had lasted, that false paradise where we sat comfortably and companionably and drank in other peoples' misery. And then Claire had turned to me and announced that her mother might be coming to stay. On the seventeenth. For three nights.

I had no problem with Claire's mother. I quite liked the woman, as it happened, dull, dyed and dumb on the outside with a sharp bitter filling that only came out when you'd chewed an hour or two. She made me laugh, which was a good thing, because her husband made me want to shut my eyes and drop off the face of the earth, with his bow-ties and bonhomie and in-depth knowledge of every fucking topic there was. He wouldn't be coming this time round, Claire offered, like a concession that sweetened the deal, and it did, but still. I liked Claire's mother well enough, but not on home turf. She'd show up and turn all that bitterness on London, which was too expensive and too crowded and too fast and too loud and inferior in every possible way to her beloved Yorkshire. I'd laugh for the first half-hour, and she'd laugh with me, and then we'd both stop laughing but she wouldn't stop the complaining, and pretty soon I'd be wondering why the hell she didn't just hop on the train and disappear back up North. If we had to see Claire's mother, it would surely be better to see her somewhere else. And some other time, too, I thought, because if I was going to trot along to Elizabeth Maurier's whip, I'd be pretty busy for the next few weeks. And hadn't we agreed to spend Christmas up there anyway? A whole seven days later?

And then I made the mistake of saying all that out loud.

"What's your fucking problem?" asked the love of my life, and without waiting for me to tell her she'd picked up her coat and walked out of the flat.

We'd barely exchanged a word since. I tried to talk to her about Elizabeth Maurier, I tried to apologise, I tried to find out precisely which one of the words I'd used had spat so much venom at her. I spent much of those sixty-something hours turning those words over and over looking for an offence I hadn't intended. I got a handful of nods and shrugs in return, a couple of grunts, no real words and not one cup of coffee. I tried everything I had. I didn't complain. I let her watch television and ignore me. I made the same bad jokes that had made her laugh just weeks earlier, and she hardly stirred. I asked her about Jonas Wolf and whether the police had shown any interest yet, and she turned away from the television to look at me, but instead of saying anything she just shot me a look of disgust, a look for a fool who didn't understand the words he was saying and certainly wouldn't understand the reply. She hadn't left the flat since she'd returned late on Saturday night with a face colder than the weather. Her moods did swing, but rarely above the line marked *angry*, and I couldn't for the life of me figure out why. I didn't know if there was something wrong, properly, seriously wrong, or if I was imagining most of it and this was what happened to all couples after a while. I knew Claire, though. Whoever this woman was, she wasn't the Claire I'd hooked up with and fallen in love with and found a flat with and moved into it. And I couldn't handle many more hours stuck in there with her.

Which was why I found myself outside the front door of a large townhouse in Holland Park on a mercifully dry Monday morning, trying to still the small angry creatures swarming inside my stomach. There were four steps leading up to the front door. Every house on the crescent had the same general shape, but each had its own unique feature, too – an unusual curve to the bow, a stone wall fronting the street, a panel of stained glass on the front door. Some had steps leading down to basement flats, but not this one. Elizabeth Maurier had owned not a flat but a house, a grand, four storey house in one of the most sought-after areas in London.

Lizzy Maurier owned it now.

As I started up the short path a voice called out behind me, and I turned. There was a man standing on the pavement across the road. I recognised the little green motorbike. He hadn't shaved, and up close there were patches of grey in the hair I hadn't noticed outside Willoughby's office, but when he smiled there was a youth and eagerness to him that sat uneasily with the stance and the grey.

"Can I have a word, mate?" he said.

"Who are you?"

"Rich Hanover. *Real World News*. Can I ask who you are and what you're doing at Elizabeth Maurier's house?"

"It's her daughter's house now," I replied, and regretted it immediately. He stepped closer, sensing easy prey.

"What's your name?"

"No," I said. "Sorry, Rich. I'd rather not talk to the press."

"Come on, mate." He took another step towards me, and I edged back, closer to the front door. There was something else to that look. A mutability, an unpredictability. "How are you involved, eh? What's your role? Relative? Friend?"

I shook my head. "I'm sorry. I really can't say." I turned and rang the bell, and to my relief the door opened seconds later. There was Lizzy, nervous smile on her lips. Rich Hanover had retreated back to his bike, but I saw her eyes widen as she spotted him, saw the smile turn to a scowl. She ushered me in and pushed the door shut behind me.

"I'm so glad you could come, Sam," said Lizzy. She stood in front of me with her arms out, and I accepted the hug. It wasn't as awkward as I'd expected. Over her shoulder I could see Brooks-Powell staring at me.

"Williams," he said, by way of greeting. I nodded. Lizzy turned to him and back to me and shook her head in a manner that suggested she'd been expecting this – I tried to think of the word but all I could come up with was *frostiness* – between us.

"Follow me," she said. I waited for Brooks-Powell and stepped into line behind him.

Lizzy led us down a short corridor with a closed door on either side into a clean and spacious kitchen. There was an island in the middle, and to the side a large oak table with eight oak chairs around it. She sat at the head; we took a place either side of her and waited.

"Well," she began, "I suppose I should have expected this, but I must admit to being a little disappointed."

I glanced over at Brooks-Powell. He was staring at her with one eyebrow raised. I opened my mouth to ask what she was talking about, but she hit me with a glare – nudged me, really, because it was difficult to take a glare seriously when it was on Lizzy Maurier's face – and I stopped.

"I wasn't going to say anything, I'd hoped, given the task we're undertaking, I wouldn't have to, but it looks like I was wrong. And I don't want to get things off on the wrong foot and I absolutely don't want your problems to get in the way of the work we're doing. So we need to clear this up now. Right now."

Brooks-Powell was smiling. I remembered that smile, from many years ago, the smile I'd hated, the expression I'd used to gauge how my day was going to pan out. Brooks-Powell is happy; I'll be miserable. Brooks-Powell is miserable; I'll be happy. Lizzy had paused. I decided to jump in.

"I'm not really sure what you're talking about, Lizzy."

She sighed.

"Come on, Sam. Don't mess around. I know you've had difficulties. I know you don't like each other, or you didn't like each other, but for Christ's sake, that was more than ten years ago, and to be honest, I don't really care what issues the two of you had back then. I'm surprised you care yourselves. Isn't it time you grew up?"

Brooks-Powell chose this moment to interrupt, beating me to it by a split second. I knew what he was going to say, which was why I'd wanted to get in first. He was going to point out that it wasn't ten years ago that I'd gone for him in court, humiliated him, got him fired. It wasn't even a year. And sure, I'd been acting for other people, it wasn't my own case I'd been pressing, I'd been hired by my clients to do my job and I'd done it, but by God I'd enjoyed it. I'd wanted to jump in and say *yes, sure, you're right, bygones*, all that meaningless rubbish. He'd beaten me again.

"Lizzy, I think you're reading a bit much into all this," he said.

That surprised me. By the look of things, it surprised Lizzy, too, because she frowned and took a moment to collect her thoughts before continuing.

"Excellent," she said. "I hope that goes for both of you."

I nodded.

"If there's one thing I've learned from my grief circle," she continued, "it's the importance of moving on.

Forgiveness. Growth. They're not just words, you know. They mean something."

This was even more unexpected than Brooks-Powell's intervention. *Grief circle.* It was like Claire's life coach, I thought, it could have been the same words, only when Claire spoke them she at least had the decency to look slightly embarrassed. There was no embarrassment from Lizzy Maurier. The glare had gone, but she was so serious, so matter-of-fact, she might have been telling us the time of day.

I glanced across the table and caught Brooks-Powell rolling his eyes. Lizzy was still looking at me, so he got away with it, but for a second he turned my way, and we were looking at one another, and I might have imagined it, but there seemed to be some kind of understanding in that look, a shared recognition of the bullshit. You think you know someone, you think you've got them pinned down as the bastard you always knew they were, and then they go and act like a person.

I turned back to Lizzy before it got any deeper. I didn't want to share a moment with Brooks-Powell. It was bad enough sharing the bloody bequest with him.

"Are you on board with this?" she asked.

"Sure," I replied. "Fine by me. It's ancient history."

Brooks-Powell nodded, that smile back in place.

Lizzy took a deep breath and went on.

"Good. I'm glad. This is important work we're doing here. I don't want personal matters getting in the way of it."

I bit back my reply. What was all this if it wasn't personal matters? It wasn't like I was getting well paid for it. It wasn't like it would further my career.

Brooks-Powell didn't seem to be in the biting-back mood.

"Is it, though?" he asked.

"Is it what?" said Lizzy.

31

"Is it important? I mean, I can see it's got some personal value for you, for all of us, maybe, I get that. But really, what's done is done."

Lizzy mouth was hanging open. Brooks-Powell continued.

"Don't get me wrong, Lizzy. Your mother was a great woman. An inspiration. But we knew her. We know all that. Her achievements are a matter of public record and those of us who had the privilege of working for her will remember that to our dying days. Why do we actually need to do this?"

She turned to me, a confused look on her face. I couldn't think of anything to say, so I shrugged. Looking down at the table, now, she addressed us both in a voice that failed to supress a tremor.

"I can't agree with you, David. Memories fade – even the strongest of memories. And it's all very well saying it's a matter of public record, but who's going to look through that record? Who's going to go through it all and put it in one place together with all those memories, if we don't do it now?"

Brooks-Powell was watching her, head tilted slightly to one side, as though he were taking in her words, considering them with the seriousness she thought they deserved. She raised her voice, now, for the first time.

"Don't you see, the pair of you? Don't you see it? This is it. This is all there is left of her."

Another pause.

"THIS IS IT!" she repeated, even louder, and I had a sudden flash of understanding. *This is all there is left of her,* she'd said, but who was that *her*? Was it Elizabeth Maurier, famous lawyer with a legacy that would live on long after her death? Or was it Lizzy Maurier, her daughter? I couldn't put my finger on it, not precisely why, but something told me this was important not because Lizzy needed it for her mother but because it told her things about herself.

She was looking from one of us to the other, now, suddenly quiet, suddenly little Lizzy Maurier again. I shrugged and nodded and Brooks-Powell followed suit, and Lizzy seemed mollified. I couldn't help being a little impressed by Brooks-Powell. He'd always been a political animal. Even fresh from university, he'd never taken a step without a clear view of where he it would take him. But here he was acting blunt and to the point and apart from making it clear he didn't want to be here any more than I did, he had nothing to gain from his comments.

Perhaps this wouldn't be as bad as I'd feared.

4: The Writing On The Wall

TEN MINUTES LATER, cups of tea in hand (I'd asked for sugar; there hadn't been any), we were making our way through the house, pausing as Lizzy pointed out items of interest. The two doors I'd noticed earlier opened onto a morning room and a dining room, and as Lizzy gestured at the furniture I had an uncomfortable sense of dishonesty, as though I'd somehow tricked my way in here, as though I were being shown around a house I had no intention of buying by an earnest and unworldly estate agent.

There were portraits and family photographs on the walls, of course, among the fine art reproductions and (I assumed) the occasional original. Plenty of Elizabeth Maurier and her late husband, Reginald. Plenty of Lizzy, too: Lizzy's graduation; Lizzy at a conference, Lizzy receiving an award. She'd clearly made a success of Renaissance Literature, and there was nothing embarrassing about the photographs, but I was sure I'd caught her frowning at one of them as she led us from the dining room. It showed her standing outdoors under a tree, in a small green surrounded by old buildings. She was smiling and shaking the hand of an older man, grey-haired, with a cane in his left hand. There was a caption underneath, in a slanting, understated font: *Lizzy Maurier Becomes A Fellow of St John's College, Oxford*. Smiling in the photograph, but frowning now, however briefly. I heard Claire's voice in my head. *She's just lost her mum. Can't imagine she'll get over that in a hurry.* It probably didn't mean a thing.

As we turned the corner at the top of the first flight of stairs I heard voices ahead of us. I paused, and David Brooks-Powell, behind me, stumbled into my back. I turned and muttered "sorry", and he flashed that smile at me. I'd been haunted by that smile far longer than was good for me, it had stabbed at me by night, on trains or long drives, sitting bored at my desk while my brain threw up images from the past, but seeing it here, now, in real life, it didn't stab at all. It was just a man, smiling.

Lizzy had stopped, too, and was looking at us.

"Sorry. I should have said. The police are here."

So we were taking a tour through a crime scene. The murder had taken place fifteen days ago, but the police still hadn't finished. They hadn't arrested anyone, either.

The voices were coming from a room to the left of the landing; we veered right and into a wood-floored, white-walled space with a huge window looking over the communal garden which nestled at the centre of the crescent. There was a large oak desk right in the middle of the room, and oak shelves full of legal text books and legal biographies on all the walls.

"The study," announced Lizzy, somewhat superfluously.

"Are there any useful documents here?" I asked. If we were going to do this, we might as well start getting our information together. Lizzy shook her head.

"No. There was a fire, see." She pointed to the wall beside the door through which we had entered. A black stain spread from floor to ceiling. The police had mentioned it, in the press reports: a small fire in the study. Lizzy continued.

"It doesn't matter, as it happens. A few papers got burned, a few books, but nothing important. She'd given me everything significant a week earlier."

"She had?" Brooks-Powell turned to her, surprised. She nodded.

"Yes. I know it's all come as a shock, it *is* a shock, of course, but this work, this is something she wanted me to do while she was still alive. She gave me the documents to get started and a list of names to contact should I need any help. Yours were at the top of the list."

I bet they were, I thought, but Brooks-Powell, as usual, was thinking several steps ahead of me.

"So," he said, walking over to the window and carefully running a finger along the sill, "if there aren't any documents here, there isn't really much point in our being here at all, is there?"

Lizzy sighed again. She was doing a lot of sighing. She took two steps towards the window and stood there facing him.

"I thought it would be a good idea for you to see where she lived. Get a feeling for her. Get an idea of what she was really like. And I thought it would be a good idea to meet and establish an idea of how we could work together before we actually started working."

"I see," replied Brooks-Powell, looking at his finger and nodding at the absence of dust. "Does that mean we'll be taking a look at the Oxfordshire house, too? And the gîte? I mean –"

He stopped, suddenly pale, staring horror-struck at the tip of his finger.

"What's wrong, Brooks-Powell?" I asked. "Not up to your standards?"

He ignored me, still staring at the finger, and stammered out a question to Lizzy.

"The police. They've dusted, haven't they? They've taken all the prints they needed?"

She nodded and I stifled a laugh. That would have been priceless. Brooks-Powell arrested for murder, and all thanks to one of his superior gestures. He relaxed and Lizzy answered his original question as though there had been no interruption at all.

"If you want I'm sure we can arrange for you to visit the other homes. I mean it. It might well be helpful. If you can spare the time. But I don't think you need to see them before you actually get started. Now let's move on to the rest of the house."

There were more portraits on the landing, including a black-and-white shot of a young boy in long shorts and a huge smile standing by a river. "Gone but not forgotten," said the inscription, and below it, the date, the seventeenth of May, 1949. I remembered Elizabeth Maurier's brother, dead at nine, a grief and an inspiration to the bereft. Opposite it hung an enormous photograph of Lizzy sitting at what appeared to be the high table at a formal college dinner. Beside her sat the man I'd seen in the picture downstairs, the man with the cane. A waiter hovered at the edge of the shot, a large dish in two white-gloved hands. Lizzy had a glass of red wine in one hand and wore a white blouse and a black gown over it. She was turning towards her neighbour, an earnest expression on her face as he held forth.

Lizzy was leading us towards a room at the far end of the landing, but it took us past what looked like the master bedroom, and as I looked in I saw two figures bent over, looking at something on the floor. The wall behind them was marked, black and red smudges on the cream background.

"Was there a fire in here, too?" I asked as we walked past. The figures straightened up and turned towards me as I spoke.

I recognised one of them. Detective Inspector Martins. DI Olivia Martins, of Westminster CID, was in charge of the investigation into the murder of Elizabeth Maurier.

I'd met DI Martins. I'd had a highly unsatisfactory interview with her immediately after my return from Manchester, during which she'd pestered me for details of my relationship with the late Elizabeth Maurier and repeatedly demanded to know why Elizabeth Maurier had called me so many times in the week prior to her death. She'd called me in a day later for a second interview, during which she'd asked me exactly the same questions in a slightly different order. I had little to offer on either occasion; I hadn't answered Elizabeth's calls. And DI Martins had been reluctant in the extreme to answer any of my questions about the murder and her investigation. She knew my reputation, she told me. I *interfered* with police investigations. She didn't want me *interfering* with hers.

"What the hell are you doing here?" she asked, that sharpness in her voice that never seemed to leave it. She emphasised the *hell*, as if it had been paradise before I'd shown up and turned everything infernal. I shrugged and gestured ahead of me, towards Lizzy, who'd stopped outside the room she'd been intending to show us and turned in my direction.

"I'm sorry, DI Martins," she said, one eyebrow raised, one arm angled pertly between shoulder and hip. "But you did say I could use the house. So I'm using it. Mr Williams and Mr Brooks-Powell are my colleagues."

I happened to be looking towards Brooks-Powell as she said the word "colleagues", and from the lines that briefly creased his forehead I could have sworn he was fighting the same battle I was to hold back an expression of absolute incredulity. I hoped I was doing a better job of it.

The other officer walked towards me, her hand outstretched. She was young – very young, I thought, early twenties, which meant she must have been good at her job to be out of uniform already.

"Detective Constable Colman," she said. "Like the mustard."

"Sam Williams."

I shook her hand. Her boss had turned back to whatever she'd been looking at on the floor. Lizzy and Brooks-Powell had disappeared, presumably into the room at the end of the landing, and it was just me and the two officers. Those scars on the wall intrigued me. Martins had been as unfriendly as I'd come to expect, but this was an opportunity I couldn't pass up.

"So was there? A fire, I mean. In here."

Martins ignored me. I could almost feel the hostility radiating from her back. Detective Constable Colman shrugged and bent down alongside her boss. I gave it five seconds and went to join Lizzy and Brooks-Powell.

They were in a second bedroom – Lizzy's own bedroom, when she stayed, which was infrequently enough before her mother's death and not once since, she told us, with a gentle shudder. There was nothing of interest at all; no photographs, no childhood memorabilia, nothing to set it apart from a good clean uninhabited room anywhere else. Lizzy proceeded to take us into the lounge, the drawing room and, on the second floor, three further guest bedrooms, all clean and blank and entirely uninteresting.

On the way back past the master bedroom I noticed that DC Colman was alone. I could hear a voice from downstairs – DI Martins, on the phone, and not happy, from what I could hear. I tried to remember whether I'd seen her happy even once, even for a moment, and realised I hadn't. I stood in the doorway and coughed, and DC Colman turned and smiled at me.

"This is where she died, you know," she said.

I nodded. It had all been in the press reports, the fire in the study and the death in the bedroom. Something struck me, suddenly, and I spoke quietly. I didn't want Lizzy to hear.

"There wasn't a sexual element to the crime, was there?"

Colman stared at me, and shook her head.

"No," she said. She glanced at the damaged wall, and then back at me, her eyes narrowed, appraising. She had short blonde hair and a little button nose that didn't go with those serious eyes. She was cute, I decided. But young. Far too young.

"No," she repeated. "This is where the writing was."

I hadn't heard about any writing. The press had kept that quiet, if they even knew. I nodded, casually, but Detective Constable Colman wasn't buying it.

"You didn't know about the writing."

It wasn't a question. For a second or two I considered lying, but Colman had me pegged, I was sure of it. I went for a sheepish smile, instead, the one Claire had told me was the reason I got away with being mostly useless most of the time. Colman muttered something under her breath, something unclear that definitely opened with an "f", and stared at the floor. Apparently the sheepish smile wasn't good enough for the Detective Constable.

"I'm sorry," I said. "You don't have to say anything else. I'll go and join the others."

That *sorry* was real enough. Young Colman had the misfortune of working for a DI who I was convinced, from my limited experience, was a cast-iron bitch. She was at the start of her career, maybe on her first case, and she'd already blown sensitive police information to the four winds. I hoped she wouldn't pay for it. I flashed her a smile, turned and walked away, and I'd made it halfway down the corridor when she called me back.

She had that narrow-eyed look on her again, but there was a grin perched underneath.

"Here it is, Mr Williams," she said. "What I tell you goes no further than this room, OK?"

"OK," I replied. It wasn't like I had a team of eager colleagues ready to share the news with, whatever it was. My girlfriend was a journalist, and Colman probably didn't know that, but my girlfriend was wrapped up in other things and hardly talking to me, so she wasn't the threat she might have been. Colman was standing beside me, looking at the damaged wall at the far end of the room.

"She was killed right here. Smashed on the head in the study, where the fire was, dragged in here and stabbed to death. And then whoever did it used her blood to write on the wall."

Blood. Elizabeth Maurier's blood on her own cream walls.

"What did he write?"

"He? You seem pretty sure it's a guy."

"Fair point. What did they write, then?"

"They wrote *no one will hear.*"

"No one will hear?"

She nodded.

"Anything else?"

"No. No more words. But there was one other thing."

Colman was frowning now, and the grin was long gone. Whatever she was about to tell me, she wasn't sure I should know. But it didn't stop her.

"They cut out her tongue. It was found on the floor next to her. They wrote *no one will hear,* and then they used the same knife they'd stabbed the poor woman with to cut out her tongue and leave it lying beside her body. While she was still alive. What kind of a sick bastard does that, Mr Williams?"

I wondered, for a moment, whether she was accusing me, but only a moment. She wasn't accusing me. She wasn't really asking a question at all. She was just making the kind of observation she couldn't make at Westminster CID, because she didn't want to look green or stupid or anything else that would have her back in uniform by the end of the shift. I opened my mouth to say something sympathetic, and stopped.

There was someone in the corridor. Just outside the room. I turned and walked out, Colman half a step behind me, and there was Lizzy Maurier shaking her head, the tears rolling down her face, and beside her DI Martins wearing the look of someone who's just had a bag of shit thrown at them. Behind them both was Brooks-Powell, head tilted to one side, inscrutable as ever.

There was a silence, Lizzy sobbing mutely and staring at me, me looking between Lizzy and Martins and wondering whether Lizzy had known all these details before she'd overheard them, Colman looking at me, blank-faced, like she was expecting me to come up with a solution there and then, and Martins staring at Colman and looking very much as though she'd decided what she was going to do about that bag of shit and Colman wasn't going to like it.

"I'm sorry," I began, but Martins raised a hand and stopped me in my tracks.

"What are you playing at, Constable?" she asked. It was like I wasn't there, me or Lizzy or Brooks-Powell, just the DI and the DC, only she hadn't said "Detective". Just "Constable." Colman took up where I'd left off.

"I'm sorry, ma'am. I didn't realise. I thought he knew."

I didn't know Martins well, but I knew her well enough to be sure that wouldn't wash.

"You thought he knew? You thought he FUCKING KNEW?" she shouted. I wondered whether she realised it was a lie, whether she understood Colman had been well aware of my ignorance. I wondered, too, why the young DC had chosen to enlighten me, why she had chosen then and there, and me, and then my attention was drawn to Lizzy, still crying, louder now. I took a step towards her, but as I approached she edged back and seemed to shrivel still further. I turned instead to Martins. This might have been our mess, mine and Colman's, but the DI was only making things worse.

"Ease off a bit, will you? This woman's just lost her mother! Can't you see she's upset?" I said. It was the wrong thing to say.

"Of course she's upset, Williams," thundered Martins. "You're talking about her dead mother. What did you expect? Confetti and fucking cake?"

Lizzy turned and fled up the corridor to the bedroom she hardly used. The door slammed shut behind her. I waited for a moment, and addressed Martins again.

"Look, Detective Inspector, it's done now. I'm not going to say a word about it, so it's not like it actually matters. Everyone's on edge, Lizzy most of all, and it doesn't help people screaming at each other in her house."

"*Not like it actually matters?*" parroted Martins in a hideous, pompous parody which left me wincing. "I'm glad you think so, Mr Williams. I'm glad we've got an expert like you on board. I expect you'll crack this one in minutes, what with your decades of experience solving difficult murders. I'll be sure to take your opinion on board when I'm deciding what to do with Colman here."

I gave up playing nice with DI Martins. There wasn't any point.

"That's fine," I said. "You do what you have to. I assume you're familiar with the clean-up stats when the police don't even have a suspect a week after the murder? Guess you've got your work cut out for you, DI Martins. But no need to take it out on everyone else."

Before she could say anything, I turned and walked away. I caught a glimpse of her face, cheeks flushed, mouth set. Behind her Brooks-Powell had returned his head to the vertical and was smiling. I wondered what Claire would have made of it, looked forward to telling her about it later and hearing her laugh, and then remembered we weren't in a telling-and-laughing place right now.

I knocked on the door to Lizzy's bedroom and waited for her quiet "come in" before I opened it and stepped inside. She was sat on the bed, her face dry, three crumpled tissues and an iPad beside her.

"Sorry," I said, but she shook her head.

"It doesn't matter. I knew about it, the police did tell me, in confidence, of course, but hearing about it all over again – well, it just hit me, all of a sudden, like I was hearing it for the first time."

I sat down beside her as she went on.

"I was at home when they told me she was dead. They turned up at nine in the morning, two of them, a liaison officer and that woman, Martins. I thought it couldn't be anything important, I didn't realise the significance of the liaison officer. I was making tea when she suddenly came out with it, all of it, the blunt instrument and the knife and the writing and the tongue, and then there was tea and broken china all over the floor and I spent the next fifteen minutes staring at the floor and clearing it all up because I couldn't face them. I didn't want to see them in my house. I didn't want to hear their voices. And they kept asking me questions, they didn't understand that I didn't care. I don't care. I don't care if they catch him. I don't care if he kills again. That's their job. My mother's dead. That's the only thing I care about."

She'd seemed so together at Willoughby's office, when that fat bastard had sprung Elizabeth Maurier's last surprise on me. Only now did I see how hard that must have been.

"Is there anything I can do?" I asked. "I can make you some tea, if you want. Or coffee. I promise not to break anything."

She smiled, weakly, and shook her head.

"It's OK." She pointed at the iPad. "I'm on with the grief circle. They'll sort me out. They understand. They've been through the same thing and come out the other side. I don't know what I'd do without them."

I nodded, placed an arm on her shoulder and squeezed, and stood up from the bed.

"But Sam," she said, as I turned to go. "Thank you. And

please thank David for me too. I think this will really help me, working with the two of you."

I nodded again. So this was the reason. This was the point of it all. Make Lizzy Maurier feel better. It was as good a reason as any.

"I think it would be nice if we could kick things off on Wednesday," she continued. "Dinner at my place. Does that work for you?"

"Yes, sure," I replied. "I look forward to it."

That was a lie, of course. But not as much of a lie as it would have been a couple of hours earlier.

5: The Board

MARTINS' WESTMINSTER CID team was based in a narrow grey office smeared like meat paste between a taxi firm and one of those places that sell tickets for West End shows at ten times face value to gullible tourists. It struck me that there was probably enough going on next door to keep Martins busy all year round, but fate had thrown her into my life, and I was the poorer for it.

I paused on that thought and tried to rewind it. I was here to apologise. It was her investigation. It was her job. I had a reputation for sticking my nose in and I could see why she might not want that nose on her patch. She'd wound me up the previous day, and I'd let loose, because she'd been rude to me from the start and treated her DC like something she'd just scraped off the bottom of her shoe. But this was CID, not kindergarten. If Colman couldn't handle a bit of abuse from her boss she wouldn't last very long in the job, however smart she might be. And I was used to people being rude to me, police officers in particular, Detective Inspectors pretty much invariably. It came with the territory.

And, I realised, I'd made a mistake. I hadn't spotted that mistake until I'd gone straight home from Holland Park and told Claire what had happened. I told her about Brooks-Powell, who was only human after all, she'd been right about that (or at least Adrian had); I told her about my run-in with Martins, I even told her about the writing and the tongue after she agreed not to write about it. And I told her about little Lizzy Maurier, poor Lizzy Maurier, crying into her iPad and worshipping her mother's memory like the High Priestess of Elizabeth Maurier.

Claire listened, nodded, and when I finished, she turned

to me with half a frown and said "So it sounds like you're going to do it, then? You're working with Lizzy and Brooks-Powell?"

"I'm not sure," I said, and then I realised I *was* sure and it was done. I'd argued with the DI and then gone and said *yes* to dinner and Elizabeth's bequest out of pity and because I didn't know what else to say. It was too late, and there was nothing I could do about it. I gave myself a mental kick, and then returned my focus to Claire, who'd said more to me in those two questions than she'd managed for the last two days.

"It's probably the right thing, you know," she continued. Maybe everything was better. Maybe I'd been forgiven whatever unknown sin I'd committed.

"Maybe it is," I replied. "Maybe it'll do some good." I couldn't imagine what good it might do, but imagination had never been my strong point anyway.

She nodded. "Oh, by the way. Jonathan mentioned something."

"Yes?"

"He was wondering whether you might be able to say anything. On the record. About Elizabeth."

"Why would I do that?" I asked, with a touch more aggression than I'd intended.

"Well, it's already out there. Look."

She picked up her laptop and brought it over to me. There was a photo – Lizzy and I, stood outside Willoughby's office, talking; another of the same scene with the vultures rushing past, Lizzy and I obscured among their dark coats and golfing umbrellas. A further two shots, David Brooks-Powell's back as he rang the doorbell at Elizabeth's townhouse; mine, too, my face half-turned towards the camera. Hanover must have been ready with the camera the moment I responded to his shout.

The text was fairly innocuous. Hanover had written it

himself; *Real World News* was "alternative media", disruptive (by which they meant deliberately controversial), not the sort of outfit that would foot the bill for a journalist *and* a photographer. I wasn't named and neither was Brooks-Powell. Lizzy was, but as the victim's daughter she'd hardly have been difficult to identify. There had been a murder; there had been a will; these people were involved. A hint that one of the bequests had been a little out of the ordinary; a reference to *Tulkinghorn*, the gossip column from the *Law Society Gazette* I hadn't looked at in fifteen years. Not a great deal to say, not a lot to speculate on, either. Hanover hadn't even tried.

I looked up *Tulkinghorn*, scanned through the last few columns, found the one I was looking for. No more in there than there'd been in Hanover's piece. Still, it gave me something. I had an idea who'd been talking to the press.

"I don't think so," I said, finally, when I'd finished reading through the three short paragraphs a second time. "It just doesn't seem in very good taste."

Claire grinned. "Think you're some kind of expert in good taste?"

"Well, I picked you, didn't I?"

"Everyone gets lucky once in a while, Sam Williams."

She was whistling – actually whistling – as she strolled to the bedroom, for a nap, she said, and for a moment I found myself thinking everything really was OK. She didn't really care whether I obliged her editor or not, she was just passing on a request. And it wasn't like anything I had to say would stop the press. Everything was fine, I thought, everything was normal, and then I remembered Lizzy Maurier's dinner and her mother's bequest and the fact that there was nothing I could do about it.

I spent the next fifteen minutes conjuring up ideas, escape routes, running halfway down them and then crossing them off as another impossibility or implausibility hit home. Fifteen increasingly depressing minutes, and then I gave up and called Maloney. I explained the situation, and listened to him clicking his tongue against his cheek for thirty seconds before I said "Well? Any ideas?"

"Come for a drink," he replied.

The Mitre was more Maloney's sort of pub than mine, dirty grey walls and a carpet so old the cigarette burns hid most of the pattern. I wondered how a place like this could survive on the fringes of Islington, with its Lebanese restaurants and Brazilian bars, and then I saw the paltry handful of change I'd got back from a twenty for two pints of lager, and I figured they didn't need more than me and Maloney to break even for the night.

Maloney had been a client, back when I'd set up on my own. He'd been a gangster, of sorts, a local crime lord of the Robin Hood variety, if Robin Hood had run a drugs operation on the side. I'd done the job he'd hired me for, and I'd thrown in a little extra, too: the news that someone he trusted was running dirty drugs and underage girls and generally soiling an operation that Maloney had been trying to clean up. We'd become friends since. Maloney was a mine of information; if he didn't know something he could usually find it out soon enough. And he'd got me out of trouble more than once – his sort of trouble, not mine, the sort that needs false documents or untraceable phones and maybe a tough guy or two.

I'd been waiting ten minutes when he showed up, and he didn't apologise, just grabbed his drink and sat down and fixed me with a look that said I owed him that drink and I'd be buying him plenty more before the night was out. He was a heavily-built guy with a heavily-built face and a nose that had knees and fists written all over it; he looked like what he was, or at least, what he had been. Maloney had gone straight, he was at constant pains to remind me. A bona fide businessman, not that he'd ever specified what the business was. He finished the drink before he said a word, holding up a hand to stop me when I opened my mouth to start talking. He slid the glass towards me and pointed to the bar, and I got up and paid for a second, knowing he was watching me for signs of resentment, anything he could mock me for later. I made sure I gave him nothing.

"So, your old mate Brooks-Powell," he said, when I returned. He wore a smile nearly as big as his face. He knew my history with Brooks-Powell. He'd been one of my first clients after Mauriers.

"Yep," I said, and told him everything, the same story I'd given him on the phone, with a little more flesh on the bones. He stopped me when I got to Martins.

"This the DI?"

I nodded.

"She's your way out, Sam. She doesn't want you getting in the way, right?"

"Yeah, she made that clear enough."

He took a long drink. He was close to finishing his second pint. I got up to for a third but he held out a hand, waved a finger at me. "So you make sure you don't get in her way. You play nice. Let her set the rules. You see what I'm saying?"

I shook my head. I didn't. He continued.

"Remember that bloke? What was he called? You told me about him. Barrister. You know."

"I've worked with a lot of barristers, Maloney. I'll need a bit more than that."

"Then I'll need another drink, smart arse. Off you go."

This time, at least, he handed me a fiver before I got up. It wasn't enough, but it was something,

"Steelforth or Greyforth or something like that," he said, before I'd set the drinks back down.

I laughed. "You mean Wentworth, right?"

He nodded, his face deep in his glass.

"What about him?"

"Do what you did there."

I started to ask why and how and what on earth he was talking about, and then I remembered. And I smiled. Maloney was worth the drinks.

It had been before I'd left Mauriers, something I must have told Maloney about years later. A case – a dull one, and there were more than enough of them to go round. For every framed murderer or high-profile whistle-blower there were a dozen idiots and crooks with enough money to get Elizabeth Maurier batting for them. She needed the money – the high profile cases didn't tend to pay. The details of the case were fuzzy, but I remembered I hadn't wanted it, even more than I usually didn't want dull work, probably because there was something tasty in the offing and I needed to be free if I had a chance of swiping it from Brooks-Powell's gaping jaw. I couldn't just go to Elizabeth and tell her; she'd have handed me the next half dozen rich idiots as punishment for trying to beat the system. So I went about it a different way.

She'd already appointed counsel – our barrister, our client's barrister. I didn't remember the client's name or the crime he'd been accused of, but the barrister was a tall floppy-haired man called Wentworth who wore bow-ties in the pub and had a laugh like a horse. I'd seen him at the White Hart, a stone's throw from the office, him and his friends. I'd seen Brooks-Powell wander over to him, serious, ingratiating, seen Brooks-Powell offer to buy him a drink, seen Brooks-Powell remind him that they'd been at school together, that Wentworth had been head boy in Brooks-Powell's first year. The guy hadn't remembered him; of course he hadn't. He'd probably spent that year buggering every last one of the thirteen-year-olds. No reason one should stick in his mind any more than the others.

I'd tracked him down one night – it hadn't been hard, there were three or four places they drank, his crowd, and I'd found him in the second. I'd sat and listened to them talk, and tried to hate him, but despite the laugh and the tone of the voice I'd found myself thinking he was a relatively normal man, after all, even warming to him, which made what I was about to do all the harder.

Didn't stop me doing it.

As he'd stepped away from the bar clutching three full glasses I'd turned, as if I hadn't noticed him, and caught him in the kidneys with my elbow. The drinks had gone. The pub had fallen silent. He'd turned to me, a look in his eyes not so much of anger as of exasperation, and shaken his head. No doubt he'd been expecting an apology and three fresh drinks. No doubt that's what I'd have given him, in normal circumstances. But these circumstances weren't normal.

Instead I'd shaken my head right back at him, looked him square in the eyes – which was difficult, since he was a good four inches taller than me, but I did as well as I could – and told him he was an ignorant fucker and if he couldn't carry his drinks he shouldn't be allowed to drink them. I'd made sure he got a good look at my face, and then I'd turned and walked out of the pub.

Elizabeth had arranged the case conference for the following morning. I had half an hour with the files, and then I was to meet the client. And the barrister. He'd walked in, Wentworth, laughing at something Elizabeth had said, he'd greeted the client, who he'd already met, and then he'd turned and seen me and his face had been a picture of shock and disdain.

We managed the next twenty minutes as well as could be expected. Efficiently enough, I supposed, although I made sure there were enough awkward silences that Elizabeth wouldn't fail to notice the atmosphere. I gave it five minutes after they'd gone, and then I went to see Elizabeth and apologised.

"Sorry about that," I'd said. "Hope it doesn't make things too difficult."

"What's the problem between you and Wentworth?" she'd asked, which made me smile, since she'd never bothered asking the same question about me and Brooks-Powell. Maybe we just hid it better.

"He doesn't like me. That's all. Had a little run-in the other day. My fault as much as his, probably," I lied. "If it does make things difficult – "

"Get out," she'd interrupted. "I'll speak to Wentworth."

An hour later she'd called me back in and kicked me off the case. Wentworth had, apparently, been gracious and said he'd be more than happy to work with me if I could work with him. But the case was too important to let personal matters intervene.

The case meant fuck all. But the client was rich. I got thrown onto the next case, the one I'd wanted all along. When I bumped into Wentworth a few weeks later I apologised and bought him a drink, and during the course of the next half hour he confided in me that he did remember Brooks-Powell from school, because all the boys had called him *Dolly*. He didn't remember why.

I didn't think I'd be buying Martins any drinks, but I owed Maloney a few right now. I could see what I had to do. Because we were getting in the way, me and Brooks-Powell and little Lizzy Maurier. We didn't want to cause any trouble, but we were stepping on Martins' shiny steel-capped toes. I didn't want to step on Martins' toes, and I didn't want to work with Brooks-Powell, and if I played humble enough with the DI, she might order us to back off. I'd make the suggestion myself, if it came to it, *I'm sorry for breathing, ma'am, if it helps you can order me and the nasty blond man to steer clear and I'll be more than happy to comply.* The mere idea of it left a bitter taste in my mouth, but not as bitter as the prospect of weeks, maybe months cheek-by-jowl with Brooks-Powell. I bought Maloney another drink, and we chatted about this and that, and when I got home Claire was asleep and I was drunk and breezily confident I wouldn't have to worry about Elizabeth Maurier's memoirs any longer. And first thing next morning I was standing outside Westminster CID practicing my apologetic face and trying to push back every angry thought about DI Martins.

Half an hour later I'd given up practicing and the angry thoughts were back with friends. I'd told the greasy-haired young man at the desk behind the main door who I was and who I wanted to see, and he'd asked me to take a seat and he'd let Detective Inspector Martins know as soon as possible. Then he'd disappeared down a narrow corridor, leaving me in a tiny anteroom with no chairs in it apart from the one he'd just vacated.

I took his chair and waited, and waited, and waited some more, and thirty minutes went by and I started to entertain myself by imagining the damage Martins and Brooks-Powell could do to each other if they were locked up in that room, with Willoughby and the caviar, but also a variety of sharp implements and a motive. Any motive would do. As the thirty-fifth minute clicked past, the front door opened and Detective Constable Colman walked in, saw me, frowned, turned to look behind her, turned back and gave me a stare and a grin.

"What the hell are you doing here, Williams?" she asked. "Things got so desperate you're moonlighting for CID?"

I explained the situation, skipping over the bits about kindergarten and how much I detested David Brooks-Powell, and focussing on how important it was that she and her colleagues be allowed to proceed with their work unimpeded by a pair of lawyers and a bereaved poet. The frown was back on her face – I couldn't be sure, I didn't know the woman well enough to judge her mood from her expression, but if I'd been forced to guess I'd have said she was disappointed. And then the disappointment cleared, if that was what it had been, and she smiled again and told me to follow her.

There was something else. Another look, a flash of something I couldn't quite put my finger on, between the disappointment and the smile. Shrewd. Calculating. Not what I'd have expected of Detective Constable Colman, with her button nose and her tender years. But I'd been wrong about people before, I remembered. Just last month I'd spent hour after hour for nearly a week with Serena Hawkes, a brilliant and beautiful solicitor who turned out to be helping the very people who'd just framed my client for murder. She'd died, that brilliant solicitor, she'd put a bullet in her own head, and after she died it emerged that she'd been threatened and forced into everything she'd done, and I'd spent a good part of every day since going back over my conversations with her and spotting the signs I hadn't noticed at the time.

It might not have hit me as hard as it had done if it weren't for the fact that getting under a person's skin was supposed to be the one thing I was good at.

I followed Colman down the corridor her greasy-haired colleague had taken, up a flight of stairs and round a corner, and suddenly I could hear it. Phones ringing, phones falling back into their cradles with a smash, chairs dragging, and the voices: the questions, the insinuations, the guesses and pleas and angry shouts. The hum of a police station in full working order.

There were more people in here than I'd expected, twenty, twenty-five detectives crammed in between desks and files and a printer so old it probably had a setting for papyrus. I heard Martins before I saw her, a high-pitch full-volume stream of expletives, the sort of thing my acquaintance with Roarkes had taught me to expect of DIs. Whoever she was shouting at, they had the good fortune to be at the other end of a phone instead of in the room with her, but that didn't stop her pointing with her free hand, gesturing as if she were preparing to stab that finger into her hapless victim's eye.

Behind Martins was a board, and on the board were four photographs.

Each photograph was of a body.

Above and to either side of each photograph was a series of words – names, dates, locations, body parts.

And below each photograph was a short sentence.

It took me a moment to spot Elizabeth Maurier, lying in a pool of her own blood in her own bedroom, a knife beside her, and beside the knife a small red *thing* that could only, I realised, be her tongue.

So these were photographs of murder victims at the scene. Murder scenes undisturbed. The root of any investigation.

There was her name. The location. *Elizabeth Maurier. Holland Park. Tongue.* The date. *25 November 2016.* Below that, the sentence. *no one will hear.*

All this I knew already. But there were other photographs. Other bodies in other pools of blood. Other words, places, dates.

Paul Simmons. Sutton. Eyes. 25 November 2016. no one will see.

Alina Singh. Epping. Nose. 26 November 2016. no one will smell.

Marcy Granger. Tooting Bec. Fingers. 26 November 2016. no one will touch.

Two days. Four bodies. Four pools of blood.

6: The Collateral Damage

I COUGHED AND started to gag. Detective Inspector Martins looked up from her phone and saw me, and her expression shifted from furious to volcanic in the blink of an eye. She slammed down the phone and took three steps towards me, and if I'd been thinking straight I'd have turned and run right then.

I wasn't thinking straight. I was drowning in pools of blood and flailing through severed organs. I found myself focussing on the green and gold strands of tinsel that flanked the boards as if death were just the final Christmas present. Martins was approaching like the angel of death herself, and for one crazy moment our eyes met and I found myself thinking she was the killer and I was moments away from a very bad ending. Then she was standing in front of me and shouting, and it wasn't me she was shouting at.

"What the FUCK is HE doing in HERE?" she bellowed. Colman, who'd asked a very similar question just minutes earlier in a far friendlier tone, took a step back. Martins didn't give her a chance to answer. "Get him OUT!" she bellowed. "Get him the fuck OUT of my office. Get him OUT of my life! I don't want to see his face again!"

I'd been on the receiving end of similar opinions before, but usually with more reason. The blood had drained from Colman's face – clearly she hadn't been expecting an onslaught of quite this severity. It wasn't her fault, I remembered. It wasn't really mine, either. I was here to apologise and to step aside, to make Martins' life easier. I opened my mouth to explain, and she turned to me and held out a hand to shut me up.

"Seriously, Williams. Are you going to be under my feet the whole way through this investigation? Can I expect you in my living room when I get home tonight?"

"Look," I began. "I don't want to get in your way. I just want to help."

"Help? How the hell are *you* supposed to help *me*?"

She wasn't the angel of death any more. She was a rude bitch who needed a little cutting down to size. I reached for the knife.

"I've done this sort of thing before, you know. I'm not just one of those bloody lawyers who makes you want to tear your hair out. I've helped the police crack cases that were a lot harder than this one, and they've been grateful for it."

Now she was smiling at me, a thin strip of white tooth on blood-red lips that was somehow nastier than the abuse. I didn't know where that *harder than this one* had come from, I had no idea how hard this case was, but it was out there now and I had the feeling she'd home in on it.

"They've been grateful, have they? Do go on. Please."

"Roarkes. Detective Inspector Roarkes. Last month, up in Manchester. You must have heard about it."

She laughed. The laugh was even worse than the smile, a knowing little hoot that had me glancing around for the nearest way out.

"Oh yes. I heard about that. Arrested the wrong man, let him nearly kill himself, all the suspects dead, the bloke's lawyer, too, and a police officer stabbed to death in the police station while Roarkes was supposed to be protecting him. I'm sure everyone was *very* grateful for your help. I'm sure it's done Roarkes the world of good, not that he was exactly flying anyway. Roarkes was yesterday's man before Manchester. Now he's last century's. If that's the kind of *help* you're here to offer, I think I can do without it."

I gave up. I wouldn't have helped Martins now if she'd got down on her knees and begged me. And she hadn't finished, either.

"So, DC Colman, I want this man out. Take him away. I'm going to make a call. If he's still here when I've finished you'll be putting your uniform back on and cursing the day you ever heard my name."

"Yes, ma'am. I'm sorry, ma'am. I just didn't think," muttered Colman. I had the feeling she was cursing that day already. It wouldn't have surprised me if most of the officers in the room cursed the day they'd first heard Martins' name on a weekly basis. But that didn't make her any easier to swallow.

Colman took me by one arm, gently, and led me back the way we'd come.

We went for a coffee. There was a café three doors down, a dingy little place with steamed up windows and bored cabbies at every table. We drank our coffees in silence, and then Colman went back to the counter. I picked up my phone; there was a voicemail from Maloney, asking how it had gone. As I put my phone down I glanced up and saw a face I recognised, sitting a couple of tables away and staring right at me.

Rich Hanover. *Real World News*.

He saw me register him and walked over, standing above me with a sheepish grin on his face.

"Sam Williams, isn't it?" he asked. I didn't bother wondering how he'd found out. I picked up my coffee and took a sip.

"Anything to say? To our readers? Ex-colleague of Elizabeth Maurier. Golden years. Big cases. Don't want to rock any boats. Come on, mate. Nothing difficult. Just a bit of puff."

"Sorry," I said, putting my mug down slowly and deliberately. "I have nothing to say."

He shook his head and walked away, picking up a coat as he passed his table, letting the door slam shut behind him.

Colman was back a minute later with a bacon sandwich.

"Sorry," she said. "I can't think straight until I've eaten."

I looked at the clock above the counter, and then back at Colman. It was nearly eleven. A little late for breakfast. She wiped a smear of brown sauce off her lower lip.

"Big night last night. Needed some bacon."

"Right. Did you see that?"

"See what?"

"That journalist. He was there outside Willoughby's office."

"Hold on," she said, mouth still full of bacon. "Who the fuck's Willoughby?"

"The lawyer. One who read the will. And he was outside Elizabeth's house, too, when I met you and your boss."

She frowned, then nodded.

"Yeah, I remember. So what?"

"So I think he might be following me."

She tried to laugh, found herself starting to choke on a lump of meat, swallowed it down. "Following you?"

I nodded.

"This place is three doors down from a major CID unit. Half the customers here are journalists. They'll be waiting for us at the George by lunchtime. You're just the collateral damage."

I hoped she was right. It made sense. She took another bite of her sandwich, chewed and swallowed it down.

"So what do you reckon?" she asked.

"I reckon your boss is an A-grade bitch."

She nodded and took another bite.

"That's not in dispute. I mean, what do you think about the case."

She'd put the sandwich down and fixed me with that same shrewd gaze I'd thought I'd seen earlier, and suddenly it hit me. All that *yes, ma'am, I'm sorry, ma'am, I just didn't think* was just a front. Colman had been thinking from the moment she'd seen me sitting there waiting at the front desk, and she hadn't stopped thinking for a second, even while she'd been walking me into a room full of sensitive information that hadn't been made public, even while she'd been cowering – or pretending to cower – under her boss's brutal onslaught.

"You let me see all that on purpose, didn't you?" I asked, even though I already knew the answer.

She nodded and took another bite from her sandwich, but didn't say anything.

"Why?"

She smiled at me.

"Because Martins pisses me off, and I thought this would be a good chance to piss her off back."

"Really?" It didn't seem likely. There must have been easier ways of getting at Martins without putting her own career in jeopardy.

She shrugged.

"Well, I don't like the way she's doing things. I don't agree with keeping all this quiet. There's a serial killer out there and no one knows. We should be out there making this public, getting information, building up links between the victims and the locations, but if we can't let on there are any links it makes our job a hell of a lot harder."

I nodded. I could see that. Knowing precisely when and what information to release was one of the hardest parts of the job, Roarkes had told me, getting the balance right between the flood of useless shit that would come in the moment the story hit the airwaves, and the fragment of gold that might be buried in all that shit. Martins had a good-sized team, by the look of it, but when the press got hold of a serial killer line every single officer in that room would be fielding calls round the clock from the drunk and the short-sighted and the forgetful, the confused and the malicious, and, if they were lucky, the man or woman with the fragment of gold.

But four people had died, and fifteen days had gone by without an arrest. I wondered, briefly, whether it was just four, whether there had been more in the intervening days, but if there had been then surely they'd have been up on that board leaking their blood onto the floor. Four dead, and nothing since. Martins needed help. The taxi driver who'd driven the killer from Epping to Tooting Bec. The passer-by who'd asked him for a light and noticed something strange about his face or his clothes. The hardware store clerk who'd sold him knives and ropes and wondered what he was planning to do with them. The public might be a pain in the arse, but Martins needed them.

I realised I'd been sitting in silence, nodding, for close to a minute. Colman had that look trained on my face, sharp, entirely aware of everything that was going on and probably most of what I was thinking. I could see how she'd managed the jump into CID so young.

"OK," I said. "But you know I'm not going to go running to the newspapers, right?"

"Not even your girlfriend?"

I smiled. She smiled back.

"But yeah, I know," she continued. "I don't expect you to leak this, and if you did I'd probably end up losing my job, but I think you might be able to help anyway."

"What did you have in mind?"

"I don't know, to be honest. Whatever you did for Roarkes. Seems you're quite an unusual lawyer, Sam Williams. One who finds answers instead of trying to hide them. I thought we could do with someone like you on our team."

I didn't like where this was going. I took a deep breath and prepared to disappoint her.

"Look," I said. "I'm sorry. But this isn't my thing. I'm

not a cop, as Roarkes is always trying to tell me. I'm just a lawyer."

"Not exactly sinking under your caseload, are you?" she replied, quick as lightning.

"How do you know that?"

She shrugged again.

"Martins had us looking into you. Digging stuff up. Said she wanted some dirt in case you got in her way. She really doesn't like you, Sam. Thinks you're a loose cannon."

I didn't need Colman to tell me that. And I didn't need to be any deeper in Elizabeth Maurier's death than I already was. I was about to tell her Martins was right, to tell her to steer clear of me and anything I've touched or looked at or been near if she wanted a decent career and a long life, I was forming the words when the door chimed and a man walked in. Colman looked up and frowned.

"What is it?" I asked.

I turned to follow her gaze. He was young – younger than me. Better looking, too. Three days' stubble, I reckoned, dark under his dirty blonde hair. Sharp suit. Police, I thought. He looked around the café for a couple of seconds until his eyes fell on Colman, then on me, then back on her. He didn't look happy. He beckoned her over, a single eyebrow conveying both the instruction and the disappointment that he'd found her there, with me.

"Sorry," she said. "Won't be a minute."

They stood there by the door, whispering together. She nodded a bit, shrugged a lot, looked like she was agreeing, but not completely. He shook his head at her. She shrugged again. He turned and headed out, glancing back at her as he went, and even though she wasn't looking in my direction, I could have sworn she winked at him. He was grinning as he disappeared onto the street.

"Well?" I asked.

"He's giving us ten minutes."

"I don't understand."

"That's Larkin."

"Super. Tell him I hate his poetry."

She didn't laugh. "Tommy Larkin. DS. One of the good guys."

"So good he's giving us ten minutes? What's that all about?"

"Martins' orders. If you're seen anywhere near the station or anywhere near one of her officers, you're to be pulled in. Arrested. For interfering with the investigation."

I snorted, but she wasn't smiling.

"She means it, you know. Larkin would have pulled you in just now, but, well."

"Well?"

"Well, he wants to get in my pants, doesn't he? So we've got ten minutes." She glanced at her watch. "Eight now. What are you going to do, loose cannon?"

"I'm sorry," I said. Larkin's intervention had made me all the surer that getting out was the right move. "But the only reason I'm involved at all – the only reason you've even met me – is this bloody memoir. I'm not exactly thrilled to be working on that, either, but it looks like I'm stuck with it. This serial killer thing is different, though. I don't want anything to do with it. You heard Martins. I might have cracked the case up in Manchester, but it wasn't wine and roses. Roarkes won't be putting that one down on his list of favourite jobs, believe me. Listen to your DI Martins. Listen to your DS Larkin."

A frown appeared. Shrewd was gone, disappointed was back. I hated to let her down, but the last thing I wanted was to get dragged into this Maurier mess and make an enemy of Martins. DC Colman had played her cards and lost.

"You surprise me, Sam. After what you've just seen. Four bodies, Sam. Three more families, going through what

Lizzy Maurier is going through right now. Don't you want to help?"

"I've already told you, DC Colman. I don't help the police. When I try, people die. Forget what I said to Martins, inside. She just got my back up. Believe me, you don't want my help."

She shrugged. "That's a shame. And it's Vicky, by the way."

"I'm sorry, Vicky."

A sigh, and another shrug. "OK. Never mind. I'll get back to looking at Elizabeth Maurier's diary on my own."

I gave her my best shot at a rueful grin, stood up and extended my hand. I was already through the door when it hit me. I turned, walked back in and sat down at the table. Colman hadn't moved. She was watching me, expressionless, but somehow slightly smug.

"What diary?"

She tapped her chin, squinting at something invisible on the table between us, and made a play of thinking about it.

"I thought you weren't interested, Sam."

"Don't play games, Colman. Vicky, I mean. What diary? I'm supposed to be working on a memoir. We were supposed to have all her papers. No one mentioned a diary. So what are you talking about?"

"Does this mean you're going to help?"

"No. It means I'm here about the memoirs, and I need Elizabeth Maurier's diary if I'm going to do my job."

She nodded, slowly.

"I'll see what I can do about getting you a copy. It's evidence, see. And you've seen what Martins is like. Doesn't like you, doesn't like the press, doesn't like anyone she can't put a gag and a lead on. She'd cut out everyone's tongues herself if they let her. You want a definition of "control freak"? Look under *M*."

She smiled at me and continued.

"Thing is, Sam," and here she dropped her voice so I had to lean in to hear her words, "thing is, there was an appointment in her diary. For the night she was killed. Just one word."

I waited. She was watching me, silent, waiting herself. She needed me to ask.

"And?"

"Connor."

"Who the hell's Connor?"

"Beats me, Sam. Not mentioned anywhere else. No one's got a clue."

I sat back and searched my brain. I'd known Connors, first names and last, I'd been at school with one, I'd dated another, there was a sergeant in South West London with the same name who liked me about as much as Martins did. But none of them had anything to do with Elizabeth Maurier. Colman was watching me, expressionless again. I felt a weight settle on me, a sense of foreboding, the certainty that I was being manipulated just as Serena Hawkes had manipulated me one month earlier. I'd missed the signals back then, and people had died. I didn't want the same thing happening here. I didn't want anything to do with Maurier or Connor and I certainly didn't want anything more to do with DI Martins.

But along with the weight, there was a tingle. This Elizabeth Maurier business was messy and unpleasant and wouldn't pay enough to keep me in coffee. I'd gone to Martins that morning with the intention of digging myself out of it. But now, with Colman, with the board, with the elusive diary and the mysterious Connor involved, it was turning into something else entirely. Something interesting.

"So what do you say, Sam?" she asked, after an age. "You in?"

I breathed out, heavily, and nodded.

7: Lonely Den

I'D FORGOTTEN THE golden rule of dinner engagements: always find out who else is going. "Dinner at my place," she'd said, to "kick things off", and fool that I was, I'd thought she meant the three of us. Not that Brooks-Powell's presence would have brought a golden lustre to the evening, but it might have helped.

There was no Brooks-Powell.

I'd arrived fifteen minutes late: no Brooks-Powell. Still, I thought, he swims in the kind of circle where half an hour's nothing and even an hour's not worth apologising for. But now there were cold starters on the table with glasses of expensive white wine beside them, seventy minutes had gone by, and there was no sign of the bastard. She hadn't invited him. He wasn't coming.

Lizzy had called me that afternoon; I'd recognised the number and let the call go straight through to voicemail. If I'd answered maybe I'd have realised it was going to be just her and me. Maybe she'd have let something slip. But I didn't, and all she said was her address, which I already knew, and the time I was expected, which was burned into my brain like an execution date, and not to bring anything with. I hadn't planned on bringing anything with. She spoke with a light, breathy voice that reminded me of Elizabeth, and I wondered as I listened whether that was a conscious affectation or just something she'd absorbed without knowing it.

She lived three streets away from her late mother's Holland Park residence, on the fringes of Notting Hill. The flat was a smaller version of Elizabeth's house, cream on the walls, oak in the kitchen, which was where we were sitting down to quails' eggs wrapped in smoked salmon, two tiny nests of them perched in the centre of two huge white plates. Two glasses. Two plates. Definitely no Brooks-Powell.

She'd opened the front door with a big fake smile, panting like she'd run from the other side of London at the call of the bell, but I'd heard the slow footsteps and the long pause while she steeled herself to let me in. I'd assumed she was bracing herself for a repeat of my feud with Brooks-Powell, but she didn't need Brooks-Powell to make the occasion any more awkward than it already was.

As well as the cream and the oak there were boxes, I noticed, as she led me past her open bedroom door to the living room. There were boxes in the corridor, boxes in the bedroom, too, perched around the unmade bed like stepping stones for a midget tenant. I picked my way down the corridor past a couple of boxes beside the armchair to which she'd directed me, and asked the obvious question.

"So what's with all the boxes, Lizzy? Are these related to the memoirs we're working on?"

She'd shaken her head and pointed to a black folder resting on a coffee table in the middle of the room.

"That's it."

It was a thin folder. Forty, fifty pages inside, maximum. I could hardly believe my luck. I could get through that in a couple of days, write it up in one more, and wash my hands of the whole thing.

Lizzy must have seen the look on my face, because she was shaking her head and smiling.

"That's not everything. That's just the list. A directory, you could call it."

I tried to smile back at her, as though I were relishing the prospect of a long-term, in-depth analysis of her mother. I couldn't be certain I'd pulled it off.

"I'll show it to you in due course," she said. "And the actual documents, most of which I've got round here. But

I want to flick through them first and make sure there's nothing too…"

I waited for her to complete the sentence, and eventually she did.

"Controversial."

She flashed an awkward little grin. I couldn't imagine what she was worried about. Elizabeth Maurier had lived ninety-nine per cent of her life in the public eye, and from what I knew of her, the other one per cent would be a model of propriety. I doubted there were any whips and chains hiding in the Maurier files.

Lizzy was still talking.

"Once I've had a first look at everything we can start work in earnest. I'd suggest working here. We can make my flat the centre of operations. Keep all the records here. You won't have a problem with that, will you?"

I nodded, obligingly, but I didn't like it. There was something claustrophobic about Lizzy's flat, for all the cream and high ceilings. Something narrow and dark. No Christmas decorations up, no tree, not that we had anything particularly eye-catching back at our place. Perhaps things would improve when the boxes were cleared away. Perhaps the boxes weren't going to be cleared away. Perhaps they were a permanent fixture.

She offered me a gin and tonic and I gratefully accepted. Sat back down in our armchairs, she opened with a new theme.

"I must say, I was quite taken aback by David's comments the other day."

I tried to remember what she meant. Not the dust and the fingerprints; that was just plain funny. No, it was what he'd said before we'd even begun, sat round that oak table. *Why do we actually need to do this?* I'd been taken aback, too, but I doubted it was for the same reasons. I'd been surprised and impressed by how honest and straightforward the guy was being. Of course, there was probably something else underneath it, some longer game I wouldn't understand until I came crawling out from the ruins of what I'd missed. I looked down at my own hands, took a sip of my drink, and glanced back up to find Lizzy watching me, waiting.

I might have agreed with Brooks-Powell, in this instance, but I didn't owe him a thing. I nodded.

"You're right," I said. "I was surprised, too. Not just the indelicacy, but the fact that he didn't see it the way you and I do."

I smiled as I wound up the sentence, and fought back a creeping sickness at the back of my throat. *The way you and I do.* I didn't like the person I was pretending to be, but worse than that was the realisation that I might have more in common with Brooks-Powell that I'd suspected.

The smile stayed on and the bile stayed down. I might not be fooling myself, but at least Lizzy was buying it. She took a long, deep drink, nearly half her gin and tonic in one gulp, and smiled back at me.

"Because I am right, aren't I, Sam? This *is* important. The woman she was. It has to be remembered, and remembered properly, not just in a bunch of obituaries and court records."

It hit me again, while she was talking. The way she'd put it, back at Elizabeth's house. *This is all there is left of her.* I'd wondered then whether she was talking about herself as much as she was her mother, and I felt it again now, clearer still.

Somehow we got through another two gin and tonics each, without seeming to talk about much at all, and then we were in the kitchen and the quails' eggs were coming out of the fridge. I'd last eaten them in the nineties, and even then they'd been retro. Lizzy Maurier didn't seem to have left the twentieth century, but it wasn't time that was pulling her back. She'd chosen to live three streets away from her mother's London home. She'd chosen to work in Oxford, fifteen miles from her mother's country house. Her mother's name reflected onto her the whole time, in small. It was as if Elizabeth had always intended to leave behind nothing more than a faint imprint of herself. Lizzy Maurier, I realised, had never really left home.

The eggs and the sauvignon blanc were followed by a beef stew and some expensive-looking red wine. The food was surprisingly good and the wine tasted fine, but neither did much to improve the company. Lizzy was drinking hard, matching me two glasses to one, and when the bottle was empty she simply opened another. The wine did something strange to her. It opened her up, but only as far as she let it. I could see some pretty choice insults going Brooks-Powell's way, and I wouldn't have minded hearing them, but each time she bit them back half-formed.

Somewhere towards the end of the stew she fell silent and I realised that she'd been steering the conversation the whole time, with my contribution limited to the occasional *tell me about it* or *you're not wrong there*. The tinkle of cutlery and the crunch and splash of tooth and saliva seemed horribly magnified now she'd finally stopped talking, and I could only bear so much of it. After thirty seconds or so I snapped.

"So Lizzy, tell me about the poetry? I know you're a professor and that's serious work, but I can't believe you've given up writing your own stuff."

She put down her knife and stared at me, chewing furiously and swallowing down a lump that wasn't ready for it. Her face went pale, and I expected a fit of coughing and tried to remember if I'd ever actually seen the Heimlich manoeuvre, but instead she just shook her head at me.

"No, no, put all that behind me a long time ago. I mean, childish things, right? It wasn't important and it didn't earn any money, and let's face it, it wasn't exactly Milton, was it?"

I cast my mind back. She'd shown me some of her poems, sat beside me waiting while I read them and tried to work out what the hell she was talking about and what I could say to her when I'd finished. Just words, I remembered, long words and too many of them in each line, like she was trying to make a point, like she was trying to fill up the space for the sake of it. And all the names, Greeks and Romans I'd never heard of, talking trees and fiery chariots, a million things happening at once that seemed to have nothing to do with one another. I was no expert on poetry, and I hadn't been back then, either, but even I could tell this was amateur hour.

She was waiting. For a few seconds I tried to work out why, and then the fog of wine cleared and I realised she'd asked me a question. It wasn't one I could really answer. *No* meant her poetry was worthless. *Yes* was telling her she was wrong, and an evening listening to her views on Brooks-Powell's dissent had reminded me that Lizzy Maurier wasn't a woman who took contradiction well.

I tried a shrug. I wasn't sure it would be enough, but she gave a short, tight smile and carried on talking.

"And look, if I'd dedicated myself to writing poems I'd hardly be able to do the stuff I'm doing now. I've spoken all over Europe and the States, I've got forewords in the definitive editions of Spenser and Sidney, I'm a professor at the most prestigious university in the world. I hardly think a few lines of doggerel would be worth sacrificing all that for."

I'd swallowed the mouthful I was on already, but I went on chewing to give myself time to think. I'd seen her, at her mother's house, glaring at those portraits of herself like she was her own worst enemy. I'd got the distinct impression she wasn't happy about her career. And here she was

73

singing its praises.

And the words. *The most prestigious university in the world. A few lines of doggerel.* I didn't know Lizzy that well, but already I had a feel for the way she spoke, and this wasn't it. It was someone else.

Of course.

It hit me so hard and so suddenly that I had to reach for my glass and take a slow, measured drink just to keep from blurting it out.

Elizabeth Maurier had always belittled her daughter's verse. From what I'd read, she'd probably been right to, but she might have been gentler in her critique. Lizzy was an intellectual who loved all the Greek and the Shakespeare and the names no one else had ever heard of, she'd been like that years ago and it was clear she was still like that now, but back then she'd had something else, too. An urge to write, an urge to create, a need to get something down on paper that wasn't just her take on something someone else had written centuries ago. She'd bowed to her mother's pressure, and resented it, and now that mother was dead and Lizzy Maurier was free.

Only she wasn't.

She'd never be able to admit it, I realised. To admit that she'd silenced that urge and spent a decade doing work she didn't really care for after all. That her mother's view of her life had become her life. That she could go back, now, and start again, if she wanted to, but that would mean rewriting the past. It was easier to pretend that everything was fine, that her mother was right, had been right all along. That dancing to Elizabeth Maurier's tune, living and working in her shadow, had been the right call.

And for all that to work, for the gargantuan self-deception to take hold, Elizabeth Maurier had to loom larger than anything real, had to be nobler and greater and more perfect than she'd ever been in real life. If the idol that was Elizabeth Maurier fell from its perch, Lizzy Maurier would have to take a long hard look at herself, and I didn't think she'd like what she'd see. So the memoirs *had* to be completed and Lizzy *had* to be in complete control, had to filter out any impurities that might endanger her sterile, make-believe world.

I felt air where there should have been wine, coughed, and realised I'd drained the glass. Lizzy was looking at me curiously. I'd been down in that glass too long. I tried to think back to what we'd been talking about before I'd gone silent. Her poetry. Dangerous ground. I changed the subject.

"So tell me the truth, Lizzy. Why did your mother want me working on these memoirs? You, I can understand, even Brooks-Powell, although I still think it was a strange choice. But me? We hadn't spoken in ten years."

She gave a short, serious nod, stood and walked around to my side of the table. She leaned in towards me, and for one horrible moment I thought she was about to kiss me. Instead she reached for my empty plate. She spoke as she cleared the table, slowly on both counts, which might have been because she was thinking about what she was doing and saying but was probably because she'd drunk three gins and the best part of two bottles of wine.

"She liked you, Sam. She admired you. She always admired you." She paused, for a moment, set down the plates in the sink, turned to me and smiled. "She thought you and she would end up working together again, one day. Hoped you would, at least. She had the greatest respect for your ability, even after the trouble. I never heard her speak about you any way other than kindly."

After the trouble.

Lizzy couldn't know about that. Not the truth of it.

There were three versions of *the trouble*. There was Sam Williams, thrown from grace, kicked out of Mauriers for unknown reasons and left to fend for himself.

That was the version the public knew, if they cared to find out.

There was Sam Williams, unscrupulous dealer in suspect fees and tainted police officers in disreputable pubs. The Sam Williams who got results, even if he never quite said how. The Sam Williams whose methods were exposed by David Brooks-Powell and condemned by Elizabeth Maurier. And thrown from grace, as above.

That was the version the insiders knew. Half the legal community, and, no doubt, Lizzy Maurier.

And then there was the deeper truth. Sam Williams, hotshot genius with a photographic memory and a nose for the right angle, who'd freed a man who'd served twenty years for a murder someone else had committed. The Sam Williams who'd turned, at the moment of his victory, and looked at Bill and Eileen Grimshaw watching the release of the man they'd spent twenty years blaming for their child's death. The Sam Williams who'd been haunted by those faces every night for a decade, who'd let his career slide without much caring and hardly put up a fight when Brooks-Powell turned the screws and Elizabeth Maurier applied the coup de grace.

Not many people knew that version of *the trouble*. Claire knew. A friend or two. And Elizabeth Maurier herself, as it happened, but she wouldn't have told her daughter.

And yet Elizabeth had dragged me back in. She'd have known, if I was working on her memoirs, that I'd have to relive that case. The case that made my name and broke my spirit in same moment. The case I'd spent years trying to forget. Hardly the action of someone who liked me.

I changed the subject once more. I'd walked into that one. I was more cautious this time.

"Oh, Lizzy, have you heard about someone called Connor?"

She screwed up her face and gazed at me, thinking, and I realised I wasn't going to get much out of her. She was drunk enough to forget her own name, let alone a word in a diary she'd probably never seen.

"No," she said, after a pause long enough to eat the desserts she'd either forgotten to make or forgotten to serve. "No, but the name rings a bell. I think the police might have asked me about it."

"OK," I replied. I was about to go on, to ask her about the diary and whether they'd kept that from her, too, but something about her face stopped me. The eyes were flickering, open and shut, the mouth trembling. She was, I realised, trying to hold back tears. Connor, the police: it had brought it all back. She stood, stumbled and grabbed the back of a chair to right herself.

"I just need…" she began, paused for a sob, went on. "I just need to get online. The grief circle. They can help. Whenever it hits. They understand."

I took her arm and helped her out of the kitchen and back down the corridor to a dark, narrow study with papers scattered on every surface, including the tops of two more of those boxes. Three thick lever-arch files with dates on them sat atop a third.

A fourth box, however, was open. I glanced inside, as she brushed more papers off a chair and took a seat at a makeshift desk (two more boxes, a tablecloth draped artfully over them) with a small and expensive-looking laptop on top. Books. The box was full of books. I reached in and pulled two out, identical paperbacks, an amateurish cover featuring a woman facing an aged image of herself in a mirror against a solid black background. Lizzy was tapping slowly on the laptop, and I chanced another look in the box. More of the same. Dozens of them. Hundreds, if the other boxes were the same.

I remembered. I remembered Elizabeth's fury, the

shouts we'd heard behind her closed door, her daughter's look of horror as she emerged and saw us all slink guiltily back to our desks, what we had overheard written all over our faces.

Her "slim volume", Lizzy had called it. Her own poems, published at her own expense. She had drawn on her inheritance (her father had died when she was still a girl, her portion of the estate held in trust; she had worked secretly and cleverly on the trustees to engineer the release of the funds). She had opted for a good-sized run with the most expensive cover and trim she could find, and it was clear to everyone but her that she'd been exploited by the vanity publisher she'd been so delighted to sign with – *Gordon's just so excited, he's expecting enormous demand*, she'd said, breathless with excitement herself. When it was all over she'd spent a great deal of money, and Elizabeth had been incandescent with rage, angrier than I had seen her before or since, far angrier than the sunlit autumn afternoon on which she'd fired me for tarnishing the reputation of her firm. Lizzy, I recalled, had sold not a single copy, had, at her mother's insistence, sent every last one to be pulped. At least, that's what she'd told Elizabeth.

But here they were. Released from the past. For all that Lizzy had buried and belittled that part of her life, she could not forsake her "slim volume".

Lizzy was sobbing again, great slow heavy tears like the raindrops before a storm. And tapping away on her machine at the same time. I left the poetry – it wasn't like I was going to sit there and read it – and took up position behind her, with a good view of the screen. I coughed, loud and deliberate – sneaking a look inside her mysterious boxes was one thing, but I didn't want to intrude on her grief without her knowledge. She turned and gave a weak smile.

It was a chat room. I didn't know what I'd expected,

when she'd spoken of her "grief circle", perhaps some online equivalent of a student bedroom, candles and incense and overuse of the word "love", but it was just a chat room after all. Black background (of course) with a hint of a floral pattern, like an undertaker's wallpaper; blue and grey boxes for users to post and comment. *TCGilly* spoke of waves of grief, crashing in and receding, each time a little less intense, each return a little slower to come. *FatherMac* advised Lizzy to "take each day one by one, and each will be easier." *StillHere* talked of death and rebirth and cycles of life. *Therese* invited Lizzy to remember happier times. All of them repeating the old, time-worn clichés, all of them apparently unaware that everything they were saying had been said a million times before. I watched for a few minutes as Lizzy tapped away, faster and faster, replying individually to each comment, each reply creating its own thread. Maybe that was the point. Maybe getting lost in a hundred new conversations, each heading in a slightly different direction, maybe that was enough.

She knew I was there, still – or had she forgotten? I coughed again, twice, but her gaze wouldn't shift from the screen. Her fingers were moving so fast now it was impossible to track her words without watching the screen – clearly the alcohol hadn't impaired her typing ability. I gave up watching and went to the kitchen, poured myself another glass of wine, and returned to the living room and the armchair. I sat back and closed my eyes and let everything flow through me, the grief circle, the *trouble*, the poetry. Elizabeth Maurier. But every image was overlaid with four others, four bodies, four pools of blood, four sets of severed organs. I hadn't mentioned Martins' board to Claire – she was back to ignoring me and walking out of the room as soon as I entered, or turning up the volume on the TV so she didn't even have to hear me try to get through to her. I'd done what I could to get her talking, yet again. I'd even resorted to trying to rile her, telling her to get on and do something before Jonas Wolf died of old age. She'd ignored that, too. I hadn't mentioned the board to Rich Hanover, either, although that would have been the easy way to achieve Colman's aims. Hanover had emailed me just a couple of hours after I'd seen him in the café to ask whether I'd reconsidered my position on talking to him about Elizabeth. I'd ignored him the same way Claire was ignoring me, a sad, lonely cycle of passive aggression. Hanover hadn't mentioned the other victims in his email, just Elizabeth, so I assumed he didn't know about them. But I knew. I'd done what I could to forget about that board and bury those images. But nothing could help me do that. Not even Lizzy Maurier.

Some time later – I didn't think to check precisely when – Lizzy walked in and I woke with a jolt. The tears had dried, but the face was still pale and the eyes wide. There was a glass in her hand, the rich amber of whisky or brandy. She started talking before I'd fully come round, pausing only to sip on her drink and holding out her free hand when she did so, to forestall interruption.

"She was a wonderful woman, though, Sam, wasn't she? She was wonderful. So clever. So full of achievement. Her brother died, did you know that, when she was a child, and she didn't let it destroy her, she just went on and did what she could for everyone else, she fought so hard, I wish she could have fought at the end, I wish she could have fought for herself."

The words came fast but slurred. She was drunker than she'd been before I'd fallen asleep.

"And they cut out her tongue, can you believe that, they cut out her tongue and they put it on the floor next to her, apparently they did that before she even died, she'd have seen it, she'd have died looking at it, her own tongue on the floor next to her, who would do something like that? Do you know the myth of Philomel? Of course you do. You probably read it at school, didn't you? Ovid?"

I didn't know what kind of school she thought I'd gone to, but we certainly weren't reading Ovid at mine. She carried straight on, either ignoring my shrug or taking it as affirmation.

"And then, there's Titus Andronicus, I've edited one of the latest versions of that, one of the more disregarded plays, very underrated."

That one I'd heard of, at least, if only because I remembered an old English teacher telling us that if we wanted to be entertained by sex and violence we should stop listening to "gangster music", as he put it, and pick up this particular Shakespearean tragedy. Severed heads. Children baked in pies.

"They all have one thing in common, Sam," she continued. The pitch and volume had increased, a shrill whistle into a head that was already starting to ache. "A woman is raped and then her tongue is cut out to prevent her from identifying the rapist. Tereus, in the original. Philomel is prisoned in this lonely den, she says, and then she weaves a tapestry which tells the story of what's really happened, and she and her sister, they kill the son, his son, Tereus' son, they feed him to his father, and then Philomel turns into a nightingale so she can sing, finally. And the silence is broken. But my mother never got to sing. And her tapestry, that was everything else, everything else she did, that was her life. That's what we're doing now. Weaving her tapestry. She was a wonderful woman, Sam. But."

She stopped, finally, and looked at me, for so long I found myself fidgeting under her gaze. It seemed she was waiting for a response.

"But what?" I asked.

She waited, again, and when she spoke it was slower,

quieter, more measured.

"I'm not stupid, Sam. You know that, at least. Don't you?"

I nodded. Disturbed, certainly. Unpredictable. But not stupid. Definitely not stupid. She went on.

"I know what everyone says. I know what they think of me."

I doubted any two people thought the same thing about Lizzy Maurier, but I kept my thoughts to myself.

"I can see it, when they look at me, when they mutter. It wasn't just Elizabeth Maurier who got her tongue cut out. That's what they're saying, isn't it?"

She was watching me intently, her eyes unblinking, and I tried not to flinch or cover my mouth or do anything that suggested I knew what she was talking about. Surely Martins hadn't told her about the other murders? But there hadn't been another tongue, had there? Unless there were more bodies and more limbs Martins didn't know about. I frowned and tried to look blank and hoped Lizzy was drunk enough not to see the deception.

"It's me, isn't it? It's me they're talking about. I had a voice. And it was silenced," she said.

It was her. Nothing to do with the bodies. Nothing to do with Martins. Just Lizzy Maurier and her poetry and her insistence on seeing significance and connection where there were just coincidence and words. Elizabeth Maurier's tongue had been cut from her dying body. Lizzy Maurier had been told to stop wasting the family fortune on poems. No significance. No connection. And now the tears were back.

"I need to go to bed, Sam," she said, and looked away from me. I picked up my coat from the floor, where it had fallen when Lizzy stumbled against the chair it was hanging on. I turned back towards her, to offer a consoling word or even a hug, and she reached out and dragged me in to her, hard, desperate.

"Put me to bed, Sam. I need you to put me to bed."

Put, I thought. Not *take*, which would have been unambiguously dangerous. But this was still uncertain ground. *Put me to bed.* I took her by the arm and led her down the corridor to her bedroom. I glanced at her, as we stumbled past boxes and bounced off walls together. Drunk, her face had lost its tightness and her eyes their disconcerting intensity: she wasn't unattractive, with her petite features, her dimpled chin, her long dark hair. But she wasn't for me. Not with Claire at home, if you could call it home, if you could call us lovers any more, it had been so long; not with Lizzy the way she now was. Drunk was one thing. Drunk, in mourning, unstable: even the worst of me wouldn't stoop that far.

I wondered if I was reading too much into her request, but as we reached her bed she pulled me towards her again, her mouth opening in invitation. I turned at the last moment, a quick slip and roll, and pushed her gently down until she was sitting on the bed. I wasn't imagining it. I wondered why, whether anyone would have done, whether it had to be me, whether this was why Brooks-Powell hadn't been invited to dinner. If it was me, it was nothing to do with looks or charm. Probably a final revenge on her mother, who had apparently spent her last weeks trying to get close to Sam Williams without success. Lizzy had unfolded, before me, had come as close as she'd come in years to breaking her silence. But this particular act took two, and I wasn't dancing.

"Can't blame a girl for trying," she muttered, and smiled sheepishly at me from the bed. "And mother would probably have approved, this time."

She fell back and into sleep in seconds. I tugged the duvet from beneath her and draped it over her, wondering all the while what the whole evening had been about and how once again I'd misread signals and misjudged intentions. And what she meant by "this time".

On the way out I stopped in the study and pulled out the lever-arch files. They were heavy and it was raining, but I had a thick coat and there was a taxi rank at the end of the road. She'd told me she planned to show me the documents, after all. Of course, she'd intended to screen them all first, but I doubted there would be anything worth screening.

And if there was, all the better.

8: Pain

I SHOULD HAVE known it wouldn't be so easy. I should have known he'd be there, Rich Hanover, standing across the road leaning against his bike under a yellow streetlamp that picked out the raindrops on his hair.

"Sam!" he cried, as if we were old friends and he hadn't been expecting to see me. I ignored him, fastened the top button of my coat, and turned away. But within a second he was there, in front of me, walking backwards, dancing, almost, grinning and firing questions at me. I hadn't drunk as much as Lizzy Maurier, but I'd drunk a lot, and Rich Hanover dancing in front of me was doing strange things to my head.

"Something, Sam?" he said, and I shook my head. He stopped walking, forcing me to stop, too, to turn to the side, slowly and deliberately on the narrow, slippery pavement. He stuck with me, mirroring my every step. I saw his lips move but couldn't understand the words.

"Morning sherries?" he said, or at least that was what it sounded like. I shook my head again and kept moving. The taxi rank couldn't be far now.

"A couple of cavorting beneficiaries?"

This time the words were clearer and I stopped, confused. He stepped up to me and grinned.

"You and Lizzy Maurier, mate. A couple of cavorting beneficiaries. Do you like that? Came up with it myself. Sounds like a decent headline, right?"

"Fuck off," I replied, and started walking again, Hanover always just a few steps in front. *Tantalus*, I thought. In reverse. It wasn't just Lizzy Maurier. I remembered some of that classical stuff too.

"Oh come on, mate. I'm just messing with you. I

wouldn't write that kind of shit. At least, not if you give me something decent instead."

I stopped again and took a breath. I needed to end this. "Listen, Hanover – "

"It's Rich."

"Fine. Rich. Whatever you want. But this," I gestured behind me, at the world at large, at the half of London I was walking away from, at Lizzy's flat in particular. "This isn't important. This isn't even interesting. This is a private matter between me and a woman who's still mourning her mother. With no cavorting involved."

I tried to smile as I wound up, something friendly, conciliatory, but I sensed more of a grimace on my lips.

"Right," he replied. "Got you. Just a private matter. Not interesting. You and Elizabeth Maurier's daughter alone in her flat while your girlfriend's tucked up in bed at home. Alone. At least, I think she's alone. What do you reckon, mate?"

I took another step, a bigger one, and turned and used my right arm and Lizzy's files to force a path by him so that I was finally past him, in front of him, nothing but clear, journalist-free air between me and the end of the street.

"I hope you left her alive, though, Sam."

He'd stopped. I was five, six paces past him. But now I stopped too, and turned.

"Lizzy Maurier. I hope she's OK. Not dead. Not like that last one."

He was walking towards me now, slowly, and I had a sense again of danger. Of unpredictability.

"What was her name? Ended up out of the window with a hole in her head. Serena something, right? Has Lizzy got a hole in her head too, Sam?"

He'd reached me as he finished speaking and I acted without thinking, the files dropping to the ground and drawing his gaze downwards, my left hand pulling back and then flying forward in a hook to the side of his face, my right following with an uppercut that he managed to lean away from and ended up scraping along his cheek. He grabbed onto my coat as he took a step back, stumbled, released the coat, reached down and steadied himself with one hand on the slick dark pavement. He looked up at me. I couldn't read him. Couldn't see what he was saying, what he was thinking.

I picked up the files and shook the rain off them, and then I turned and strolled away to the taxi rank.

When I walked through the front door and into the living room half an hour later Claire didn't even seem to notice. She had the television on, volume turned right down, a three-quarter gone bottle of red on the table and an empty glass beside it. I closed the door behind me, louder than usual, and she turned slowly towards me.

"Hi," she said. It's not easy to slur a single syllable, but she managed it.

"Hi you," I replied, and sat down beside her. She smiled. First smile she'd given me in a while, and sure, she was drunk, but I wasn't complaining. I wasn't thinking about Rich Hanover, either.

"So how was the evening?"

"Shit," I said, and her smile got a little broader. "It started awkward and went downhill from there. If I never see Lizzy Maurier again it'll be too soon."

The smile was still there, but her attention had drifted back to the television. Another news broadcast. She'd switched the subtitles on, sitting there alone with her bottle of wine and roomful of silence. More boats. The words flashing along the bottom of the screen counted dead in the hundreds, day by day, month by mounting month. Claire had been watching the news more and more lately, not just the refugees and the wars but the accidents and arguments and the petty domestic murders. She just sat there and watched, usually without the wine and with the sound on, but she never spoke about it. I wondered if it was becoming another obsession. I stood and shrugged off my coat, and she turned and frowned at me.

"What happened to your coat?" she asked.

"What?"

"Look." She pointed to one of the pockets. It was torn almost away from the coat, hanging there in space, a sad, stray bit of cloth.

"Must have been Hanover," I replied. She frowned again. "The journalist, the one from *Real World News*. He was waiting for me outside Lizzy's place. And I saw him earlier, too. In a café. It's like he's stalking me."

"What happened, though? Why would he tear off your pocket?"

It wasn't until I'd explained what had happened that I remembered this wouldn't sound as straightforward as it really was. Claire was a journalist. She believed in the rights of journalists to ask questions. To piss people off. I tailed off and waited for her to say something.

"So you hit him?"

I nodded. "He had it coming. You heard what he said."

"Maybe. He does sound like a prick." I nodded. At least she wasn't on his side. "But you could get into all sorts of trouble, you know."

I laughed. "Doubt it. He's the one who's been stalking me. He's not going to get much sympathy if he complains."

"You need to take this a bit more seriously."

I laughed again. "Come on. He's not even a proper journalist. Just some dick with a phone and a moped. He's not going to win the Pulitzer Prize following me about, anyway."

"For fuck's sake, Sam. It's not funny."

She stood and faced me. She was glaring at me, now,

and any sense that there was anything funny at all in the situation was gone, sucked from the room by that thin set mouth and those angry eyes. She needed careful handling, I could see it, I should have seen it, it would have been obvious to anyone with eyes of their own.

But I was still drunk, and angry. It wasn't Claire I was angry with, but she was there and Hanover wasn't.

"Why don't you slap a fucking smile on your face for once, Claire? Forgotten how?"

She took a step back, and I saw Rich Hanover in her place, reaching forward and down, something on his face I couldn't read. And then it was Claire, again, and she was smiling after all, and all that anger I'd been feeling had evaporated so fast it was like it had never been there at all. If I'd been drunker than I was I might have thought everything was just fine.

But I wasn't that drunk.

"Did she smile for you, Sam?" she asked.

"Who? Lizzy?"

She shook her head. Still smiling.

"Your lawyer. Your pretty lawyer. In Manchester. Shame you can't piss off back there and see the fucking smile on her fucking face, Sam. Not so pretty now, I'd imagine."

I stared at her. My mouth had fallen open, my face blank, idiotic, not that it mattered. I saw her above me and realised I'd sat back down. There was a ringing in my ears, as if it had been me that had been hit, not Hanover, as if Claire had thrown a punch or two alongside the words.

Neither of us spoke.

After a minute she sat down beside me. I'd managed to close my mouth by then, but little else. She reached out to touch my face. I thought about backing away, pushing her hand away, but I thought too slow, and before I could do anything her fingers were on my cheek.

"I'm sorry," she said, and like that, the ringing was gone. I shook my head.

"It's OK."

"No it isn't. I shouldn't have said that. I don't even *think* that. I've never thought that. I shouldn't have wanted to hurt you."

I'd asked what felt like a million times in the last few days, but this seemed a better opportunity than any.

"What's wrong, Claire?" I said, and she took her hand from my face and sighed, looked down at the hand, turned it one way then the other. I waited.

"It's the case," she began, and corrected herself. "The story." She stopped and raised her eyes to meet mine.

"Go on."

"I'm – I suppose I'm stressed." She laughed, a short, bitter laugh. "Ridiculous, isn't it? It's not like I've got anything to be stressed about. It's not like I can bring them back to life."

"It's not ridiculous," I said. "It's important."

She shrugged. "Thank you. I used to think it was important. I don't know any more. I can't get anywhere. I'm stuck. I don't know what to do about it."

"Tell me."

She fixed me with a look I couldn't quite figure out. Appraisal, in part. And something else. She did nothing for a moment except breathe, deep and loud. Deciding.

"Wolf," she said, finally. "Jonas bloody Wolf. He did it. We know he did it, right?"

"Well, the evidence – " I began, but she stopped me with one hand in the air and a shake of the head.

"Forget the evidence. We're not in court now. We know he was involved, right?"

I nodded. I had the sense that she needed to be doing the talking now, not the listening. She continued.

"And no one's interested. The police won't take it on."

She paused, and I wanted to ask her why they wouldn't take it on, if she'd stopped pushing them and why, what they'd said to her about it, but I let the silence grow instead, and waited for her to go on. "As for Thorwell – he's useless. He won't let me print. I know I don't have enough to print yet anyway, but he wants me to look at other things. I said to him I do that, I write his shitty little articles about hats and exam results and whatever crap they want me to look at, I can carry on doing that, that's what he's paying me for. But at the same time I want him to guarantee that when I've got enough, he'll make the space for me. And he won't. It's all *maybe* and *depends what you've got*. I've told him what I've got. I've told him what I might get, if he gives me the time and the confidence to get it. Says he can't guarantee anything. Says he can't take any risks."

She paused. There was an opportunity here, to ask her what Thorwell was talking about, what risk he was running, and to remind her she wasn't just talking to herself. But there was a more important opportunity, too: to let her say more, say everything she needed to say and hadn't said in all those days of staring at the television and snarling at me. This was it. The heart of it all. The story. The fucking story. I waited.

"He's my editor. He's supposed to have my back. He said he'd have my back, our backs, all of our backs, when he took over. Like fuck he's got my back. I mean, what the hell am I supposed to do, Sam? What would you do?"

She paused again, but this time she'd said my name. She'd asked me a question.

"Sit tight," I said, and saw her face fall and realised that was nonsense. *Sit tight.* Useless. "I mean," I continued, "look. Just carry on. The police might not be helping now, but that doesn't mean they won't. Thorwell won't print now, but that doesn't mean he won't, eventually, when you've got more to give him. It'll crack – and you know, maybe it won't. Maybe it won't crack. I'll tell you what I'd do." I was warming to it, now. "I'll tell you what I've learned. What I learned from Manchester. Don't get too close. Keep some distance. Don't make it personal. Treat it like a job, and when you win it'll be a job well done, and if you don't it's just a job. Either way, you don't give up on it. You're a professional, Claire. You're a bloody good one. Keep working."

She nodded as I spoke, quiet, thoughtful. She waited for a moment, after I'd finished, and then muttered something so softly I couldn't make it out.

"Sorry?"

"Not too personal. That's what you're saying, right? Don't make it too personal."

"Yes." I had to tread carefully, I knew that, because all that time working on one thing made it personal, even if you didn't want it to be. "Yes. Exactly. I know it means a lot. It's two years' work. It's all those hours travelling all over the country and talking to prosecutors and police, tracking down witnesses, poring over papers and pictures, I get it. It's part of you. Just make it a small part."

She nodded again, and took another deep breath. I waited, because it looked like she had something else to say, but after a while she looked up at me, a weak smile on her lips, and said "So tell me, how was Lizzy Maurier? How was Brooks-Powell? Still evil?"

"Not evil," I replied, slightly taken aback by the change of topic but prepared to go with it. "Just absent."

"What?"

"He never showed up. Just me and Lizzy Maurier and her dainty little quail eggs and runny stew. Not really my cup of tea."

I felt a little guilty as I spoke; the stew had been decent enough, after all, probably the best part of the evening. But Claire didn't need to know that. I pushed on. If she wanted to know, I might as well tell her. Maybe we were back to bouncing things off one another.

"And the woman's mad, Claire. I mean, granted, she's been through a tough time. But she has this grief circle, this bunch of people sitting at their computers typing out the same clichés a thousand times over and congratulating one another like no one's ever said this stuff before."

Claire was back to looking at her hands. I tried to read some expression into the chunk of head and fraction of face I could see, but there was nothing. On I went.

"And she's determined to make it all about herself. She knows her mother kept her down, she doesn't make any secret of that, but she won't admit that's a bad thing. She's determined to make a hero of Elizabeth. I think she wants to convince herself she's led the life she was supposed to lead and everything's OK. And then there's the obsession with the tongue thing. You know, her mother's tongue. She's going on about Greek myths and Shakespeare tragedies like there's some kind of hidden meaning in the fact some sick bastard cut out Elizabeth's tongue. I've forgotten the names. Terry and Pylon, something like that."

I was lying; even drunk I'd remember a pair of odd Greek names from an hour earlier. But I figured Claire would have heard of them; would find my mistake amusing; would let it lift her, suddenly and magically, back to life. It almost worked.

"Terry and Pylon?" she laughed. "What's that, War of the Worlds meets eighties sitcom? Tereus and Philomel, that was what she said, right?"

I nodded; she was looking at me again now, the smile back on her face, and for a moment I thought I'd broken through. An argument, a long, painful monologue, some counsel, a joke. It wasn't as much work as I'd thought it would be. I imagined us in bed in five, ten minutes' time, I imagined my hands on her body, I imagined myself inside her – for the first time in nearly a fortnight, I realised with a start, which was the driest of dry spells for us.

"Yeah," she continued. "You're right. She sounds like a fucking idiot."

And with that, she turned back to the television. I'd almost forgotten the television was on, silent, running sad pictures of the real world and the horrible things that had happened to the people in it. I wasn't having it all end there.

"That's what I thought. I mean, what kind of person turns their mother's murder into a fucking Greek myth?"

The back of her head moved. A nod, I hoped.

"And she's got boxes full of poetry, shit she wrote years ago that Elizabeth made her give up." I was getting desperate now, jumping on anything that would just keep the conversation moving without falling into a hole I couldn't drag it out of. "She says she hates the stuff and she loves her job but why's she kept it all, why's the flat full of it?"

Claire sighed, and turned back to me, and I had a sense that even though I had her attention again, it might have been better if I hadn't.

"Look," she said, "I get it. The devil didn't turn up. Elizabeth Maurier's daughter's a nut job. You've walked into an Agatha Christie story and everyone's trying to turn it into something else."

Again, she turned away. Again, I persisted.

"An Agatha Christie story?"

"Family murders, wills, crazy people, books, obsessions," she replied, still facing the television. "I wouldn't be surprised if a fat guy with a big moustache turns up and cracks the case. And the thing about the tongue."

She stopped. I fought back an urge to ask her what the hell she was talking about, and waited for her to continue.

"*A Pocket Full of Rye*. That's it. Maid gets killed, peg on her nose, to match the nursery rhyme. Reminds me of that.

Don't know why. I'm off to bed. Don't wake me."

She stood, with surprising grace and balance, switched off the television, and disappeared into the bedroom. I watched her go and realised there was still some breaking through to be done.

9: Small Steps

I WOKE AT seven, head surprisingly clear, full of a curious and unaccountable optimism. I'd slipped into bed after an hour of sitting on the sofa trying and failing to make sense of my day. Claire was sound asleep on her side, lying on the edge of the bed with her back turned towards the middle. She'd pulled the duvet around her like a shield, not that she needed one with those thick winceyette pyjamas. I lay there listening to her breathing and imagined life without her, without the sudden freezes and rages of the last week or so, but I couldn't. Even at her worst, Claire was something I needed.

Still, I wouldn't have minded her out of those pyjamas.

When I opened my eyes hours later she hadn't moved, lying there and breathing gently, as far as she could get from me without falling out of bed. I carefully picked myself from under the duvet and crept to the kitchen, where I made myself as strong a coffee as I dared and sat down with Lizzy Maurier's files.

They were arranged chronologically. I started with the most recent, figuring there might be some clue there as to why I was really involved in this. I'd gone along with Lizzy's line the previous night, *she liked you, she admired you,* but I hadn't bought it any more than I bought her line on herself. If Elizabeth had reasons for dragging me into her posthumous cheer squad, for reuniting me with a man she knew I hated and her own freak of a daughter, maybe they'd be in the files.

They weren't. I skimmed back from the latest item, a few days before she died. Press cuttings about art exhibitions. She'd been a patron of some gallery or other, I remembered. One of her many noble causes. There were notes stapled together which on inspection turned out to be shopping lists; there were receipts and invoices, short paragraphs describing dreams, a scribbled draft of a note asking a contact for help finding work for the son of a friend. There were no emails, but the woman I remembered had stuck rigidly to pen and ink whenever she could. Elizabeth Maurier, it seemed, had kept everything, and the police had been through it all, and as I journeyed back through the final months of her life, through the weeks in which she'd tried incessantly to get hold of me, I found myself conspicuous by my absence. Not a single mention.

Which meant that for all it seemed these files were her life in full, they weren't. There was something else.

There was the diary, of course, but I hadn't heard a thing from Colman since our chat at the café and I wasn't sure I'd be getting anything useful out of her. I scanned again, the same notes, the same few months. No Sam Williams, and no Connor, either. It wasn't like she'd shied away from the personal. I found a short note written to the memory of her husband, on the anniversary of his death three months before her own. She spoke of her worries about Lizzy, of whether she'd done the right thing by their daughter, thoughts that still gnawed at her years after they'd first drawn blood, doubts that the Elizabeth Maurier I'd known would never have revealed in public. As vague as it was, there was a nakedness and candour that startled me. Emotional honesty wasn't something I'd associated with her.

I gave up looking for obvious trails and started again, a third attempt, this time digesting every word and consigning every detail to that bit of my brain where they'd slumber in steel-trapped isolation until I chose to recall them. That was the way it was supposed to work, of course; that was the way it had once worked. I realised, as I flicked past the second week before her death and into the third, that this was the way I'd got things done before the Grimshaw case, before everything had gone sour. Use the material. No preconceptions. Use the material and find the thing that jarred. It was a cold way to work, but it had brought results. I hadn't done anything like this in years, and I wasn't sure I could do it any more. For one thing, that steel trap wasn't as solid as it had been. I'd found myself, over recent months, forgetting things I wouldn't have forgotten ten years earlier. The date of Claire's parents' anniversary. The precise mix for the perfect vodka martini. The words my own mother had used when I'd informed her that I was leaving Mauriers to set up on my own.

But I hadn't tried anything like this in all that time, either. Perhaps, I reasoned, it was all about use, a machine that had grown rusty through neglect but could be sharpened and burnished to a bright fiery point once set in motion. And Claire was still asleep and Colman hadn't called and the Hasina Khalil case was stalled and it wasn't like I had anything else to do, anyway.

Halfway through week three I found something, not a revelation or a jar, more a curiosity. I locked it away and continued, hoping for further reference to it, but there was nothing, and no more curiosities, either. I shut the file – I'd gone through six months, which I felt could count as a heavy morning's work by recent standards – and returned to it.

Elizabeth Maurier had described one of her dreams. Again, not something I'd have associated with the woman, but it seemed it was a regular habit of hers. She mentioned a man called Derek Case on a number of occasions, and the name rang a bell, so I flicked through one of the earlier files until I found it. An old friend of her mother's, it seemed; an aristocrat and dilettante who'd made a habit of interpreting his friends' dreams back in the fifties, at some of the more unusual Maurier soirees.

But Case wasn't the curiosity. In this particular dream she had been standing in a large white room. At the other end of the room, a man had stood and smiled at her. She omitted any mention of his features – perhaps he had been featureless, or so forgettable as to defy the waking recall. But his hands had been moving, up and down and side to side, movements of finesse and detail, and the whole time he had carried on smiling at her. She could not see what he was doing with his hands, what he was holding or folding or creating. She had found herself walking towards him, and slowly his activities had come into sharper view.

The man was working with thread. Gossamer-thin, as she put it, fine, almost invisible, or perhaps entirely invisible other than to her sleeping eyes. He was still moving, carefully, eyes on her the whole time but with small, precise movements that suggested a lifetime of practice. She drew closer, unable to see what object he was weaving.

And then – she could not recall why – she chose to stop. Only, she could not. She continued to move, walking jerkily towards him, unable to bring herself to a halt.

Only when she was within touching distance of the man did she see it. He was weaving a web, a brilliantly complex network of node and thread with lines crossing and extending in all directions. Some of those lines were looped around her, around her arms and legs, her neck, her fingers and feet. As she gazed down at herself – it was unclear at this point whether she was just looking down at her torso and legs, or had left her body entirely and was watching from above – it became apparent that the thread was everywhere, was wrapped around her so thoroughly that she was all but cocooned. And the man continued to smile, wider and wider, drawing her closer and closer in no little fear until she woke, suddenly, cold and afraid, and, she wrote, required a large whisky before she felt able to go back to sleep.

Curious, in itself, but still not what had caught my attention. Elizabeth had made no detailed attempt to deconstruct the dream; there was no mention of the ubiquitous Mr Case in this fragment. But underneath it all she had written a single sentence, and it was this that had caught my attention.

I do feel a little guilty, it said, *about ignoring Dr Shapiro*.

The name meant nothing to me. But the jump, from the surrealism of the dream to what I assumed was a flesh-and-blood human being, had seemed striking. I'd be looking up this Dr Shapiro.

I opened up the laptop and hit a few keys, but it was old and slow to wake up. Slower even than Claire, who dragged herself into the kitchen while I was making another coffee.

"Morning!" I called, with a brightness I didn't feel; I'd been lost in Elizabeth Maurier and her dreams.

"Hmmm," she replied, and shuffled over to take the cup I was offering. The winceyette had been complemented by a greyish dressing gown that had seen better days and a pair of slippers with semi-detached soles that slapped forlornly at the floor every time she took a step. I turned to look at her, properly, and she glanced at me and then away again, but the glance lasted long enough to appreciate the extent of her hangover.

She looked awful. I'd seen Claire in some pretty bad states, I'd held her hair back as she vomited a day's worth of food and a lifetime's worth of tequila onto the floor inches from a toilet bowl, but I hadn't seen her look like this, pale with odd blotches on her face and bags under her eyes that could have done for a week's skiing. I toyed with the idea of reviving our conversation of the previous night, but there was no point. I knew what the problem was, what had turned her from a normal woman into a zombie on a hair trigger. We'd been through it. She knew what I thought. It would crack or it wouldn't. More work, small steps, that was the answer. Small steps, and distance. Instead I asked her, quietly, if she wanted some paracetamol, and she nodded gently, a fraction of a nod, as if anything stronger might sever her neck. I poured her a glass of water and handed her the pill, and watched as she knocked it back and returned to the bedroom without a word, closing the door behind her.

I finished my coffee and opened that door a crack. She was face-down on the bed, sleeping, but not happily; twitching and jerking every now and then as if she were trying to shake off a curse. I backed out and returned to the computer.

Ten minutes later – before I'd found out anything about Dr Shapiro other than that there were several hundred Dr Shapiros in England alone – the house phone went off. I answered on the third ring.

"Hello, is Claire there?" asked a smooth upper-class voice I didn't recognise.

"Who's calling?" I replied.

"It's Jonathan, at the Tribune," he said, and I realised with a start that it was Thursday, Claire's one day at the office each week, only she wasn't fit for her own kitchen let alone the noise and chaos of the newsroom.

"She's not very well," I lied, "can I ask her to call you when she's feeling better."

"Please do. It's nothing urgent. And do send her my best wishes for her recovery."

He'd seemed pleasant enough, I thought, but he'd been parachuted in from an American magazine owned by the same proprietor, over a number of long-serving and well-qualified Tribune stalwarts, and from what Claire had said the previous night he wasn't proving the most reliable of editors. I decided not to wake her. Whatever Jonathan Thorwell wanted to talk to her about – and I suspected it might be something to do with her role at the Tribune – she'd be better off hearing it after she'd had more sleep.

I finally tracked down the right Dr Shapiro after realising that he might have had some involvement with Elizabeth's work. I was right, or at least, I was on the right track: Dr Ian Shapiro had been a forensic psychiatrist who had examined and testified in the cases of dozens of people accused of crimes at the nastier end of the spectrum. He had retired four years earlier, following the rather public discrediting of certain of his methods that had led to the conviction of a Tyneside rapist. The conviction had been quashed and the man had walked free, only to rape – *again* was the word the newspapers weren't allowed to print – three weeks later. I remembered the case, although not Shapiro's name. There were no obvious links to Elizabeth Maurier that I could see, but it wouldn't have been unusual for her to come across someone like Shapiro in her day-to-day work.

Dr Shapiro was living in Norfolk and chaired the board of governors of the local primary school, which meant tracking him down was easier than it might have been. I winkled his home telephone number out of the cheery-sounding school secretary – past halfway through the working week and already looking forward to four o'clock on Friday, I guessed – and found myself speaking to the man himself before Claire had stirred again.

Ian Shapiro ("don't call me doctor, dear boy, those days are long gone") spoke softly and slowly, with a tendency for pauses so long that I kept checking my phone to make sure we were still connected. I cut straight to the chase: I'd come across his name in Elizabeth Maurier's notes, which I was reviewing in order to compile her memoirs; could he tell me anything of her and the nature of their relationship?

"Ah," he said, and then stopped again for nearly a minute. "Yes. Elizabeth Maurier. Remarkable woman. How is she?"

So he didn't know. I guessed Ian Shapiro wasn't the type to keep up with news and current affairs in his retirement; Elizabeth's murder had been all over the television, radio and press. I had the sense of a man who tended his garden, grew his own vegetables, ignored the outside world. I didn't relish bringing it to his door, but he had to know.

"I'm afraid she's passed away, Ian."

"Oh," he said, an exhalation fraught with meaning I couldn't decipher through the phone. "Oh," again, after a mercifully short pause. "I had no idea. I hope it was painless."

"I'm sorry to have to tell you this, but Elizabeth was murdered."

This time there wasn't even an exhalation, just a long unbroken silence that seemed not so much an absence of sound as a real, solid thing. There was no noise from the street outside, nothing from the bedroom, not even a crackle down the line. I imagined the sounds Dr Shapiro was hearing, wind through a wheatfield, the drone of bees, the lowing of a distant herd. For a moment I could almost hear them myself. And then he was back and the silence had gone.

"Well, I must say, that comes as rather a shock."

I'd thought he would ask for details, given his background, but he didn't; those days, as he'd said, were long gone. I waited again, just in case, and this time he came back with something I wasn't expecting.

"If you'd like to talk about her," he said, "feel free to drop by. I'm a little out of the way, and I'm not sure there's much I can tell you, but it's probably best we talk face to face."

I was on the verge of arguing the point, since a trek into the depths of East Anglia wasn't high on the list of things I'd planned for the next week or so, but I stopped myself. I could spare the time, and it might do me good. Perhaps I could even persuade Claire to join me. I agreed to his suggestion and we fixed on Saturday morning – two days' time – for my visit. I warned him that I might not be alone, and he laughed and assured me that he'd be very much alone, and would relish the company.

Claire finally emerged as I was taking down directions and saying goodbye. She looked better than she'd looked earlier, but only marginally. A shower and some more coffee might help, I thought, and went to get the coffee started.

"Feeling any better?" I asked as I walked past, kissing the top of her head. She shrugged and offered a weak smile.

"A little."

"Thorwell called."

She sighed, like someone who'd been cornered by the boss on the way out of work and had an extra shift landed on them.

"What did he want?"

"Wouldn't tell me. Wants you to call him back. I told him you weren't well."

She smiled again, and collapsed onto the sofa. When I brought her the coffee two minutes later she was already asleep.

The ringing of the phone twenty minutes later brought her back to life; I'd tried to catch it before it disturbed her, but it was ringing six inches from her head with a sound that would have woken half the dead Mauriers and possibly the living one a few miles west.

I answered with the standard "Hello?"

"Hello," echoed a voice in an accent I couldn't place. "I am sorry to bother you. Please could I speak to Claire?"

"Can I ask who's calling?"

"Please tell her it is Viktor."

I'd never heard of any Viktor, but Claire was awake and sitting up with one hand stretched out for the phone. I gave it to her and returned to Elizabeth's notes, listening to her murmurs and short, broken sentences with half an ear.

"Who's Viktor?" I asked when she'd finished.

"Tanya's dad," she said, and I nearly dropped my coffee. Tanya was one of Claire's murdered girls, not that she was Tanya at all, really. Tanya was the name Claire had assigned to "Girl A, Blonde", on the basis that someone early on in the investigation had thought she might be Russian.

"Only," she continued, "her name's not Tanya after all. It's Yelena. And she's not from Russia. She's Ukrainian."

Close enough, I thought.

"I can't believe you found him. I didn't even know you were looking. That's brilliant work."

She looked up at me – those bags hadn't shrunk much, and it seemed the act of raising her eyes was costing more effort than it should have done – and shook her head.

"I didn't. He found me."

I shrugged.

"Either way, that's got to be good news. You've got a relative now. More to put in front of Thorwell. More pressure on the police to prosecute, right?"

"Hmmm," she said, and went back to staring at her coffee. I was surprised she hadn't mentioned Viktor when we'd talked the previous night; I was surprised she was taking the whole thing so calmly. Finding a relative could only help. I looked at her and wondered and decided she was working on that distance I'd told her she needed. Good move, I thought, and I was about to say it out loud when she got up and walked into the bathroom. A moment later I heard the shower kicking into life.

I returned, slowly, to the Maurier files. There was so much I hadn't known about Elizabeth, but little of it would be of interest to anyone reading her memoirs, if we ever wrote them, and none of it would help DC Colman. I skipped back a little, and started seeing names I knew only too well.

Little Bill Badman. Pierre Studeman. Edward Trawden.

All clients. Each one a victory, for Mauriers and for me, personally. Or so it had seemed at the time.

Badman was a dealer. Low-key and small-time, but not small enough to escape the notice of others who weren't so low-key and didn't want to be small-time themselves. He'd managed to get himself beaten up outside Camden police station, beaten so badly he was lucky he'd lived. He was luckier still that he found Elizabeth Maurier and she was lucky she had me on the case and I was still young and fresh and actually cared what I was doing, because what I found earned him quarter of a million in compensation and a mass of good publicity for the firm. I had no idea what Badman was up to these days, I'd always assumed he'd burn through that quarter million in a year or two and be back on the streets and his regular rotation between police station and hospital until he found a hole he couldn't climb out of.

Studeman was the last case I'd worked on at Mauriers. Studeman had the misfortune of having the couldn't-give-a-fuck-any-more Sam Williams acting for him, but even that Sam Williams could get the right results, for a fee. By then I'd stooped about as low as I could, paying off police officers for tips on procedural errors that might get my client out of jail. I'd wondered, at the time, whether I was paying them for the tips or paying them to get those errors made in the first place, but tried not to dwell on it. As it turned out, it didn't much matter. Someone talked to the wrong someone else, and Brooks-Powell, who'd hated me since we'd both started at Mauriers, went running to Elizabeth like a good little puppy. Elizabeth told me if I left quietly, without a fuss, she wouldn't feel obliged to tell the police and the Law Society. Going solo had never been my plan, but I didn't have a choice.

And Trawden. Trawden was what turned young, fresh Sam Williams into that couldn't-give-a-fuck-any-more Sam Williams. Edward Trawden was serving forever-and-a-day for killing young Maxine Grimshaw, who'd lived next door to him on a cosy Warrington cul-de-sac, but Trawden had never stopped telling everyone who'd listen that he was an innocent man. Robbie Evans, a convicted paedophile and killer, was said to have claimed he was Maxine's killer, and might have coughed up to it in court if he hadn't been stabbed to death in prison. It didn't matter. Elizabeth Maurier took on Trawden's case. I sifted through the files. The police insisted Evans had been a hundred miles from Warrington when the murder took place. I put him on the scene, right day, right time. In court two weeks later, Trawden walked, and I punched the air, silent, victorious. And then I turned and saw the parents, Bill and Eileen Grimshaw. This was no victory for them. They'd sat there in court listening to it all, the whole thing, the nature of the injuries, Eileen's discovery of her daughter's body, the street cordoned off, the lights and the tape, the journalists and the forensic tests. Twenty years to bury it, and we'd dug it all back up again. If this was justice, I'd thought, why did it have to hurt so much?

I shut the files, which had shed no new light on those cases, closed my eyes on the living room and its miserable excuse for a Christmas tree, and pushed myself back a decade. That moment had killed it all for me, the thrill, the ambition. I'd not exchanged so much as a word with the Grimshaws, but for all that, I was too close. So I built up a distance. I didn't care. I won cases, but I won them the easy way. Better to keep the pain at bay. I'd let that slip, in Manchester. That hadn't worked out so well.

The phone rang, and it was Brooks-Powell on the other end. As if he'd known I was thinking about him, about our mutual past. And how had he even got my number?

"Listen, Williams," he said. That was the preamble. *Listen.* "I've been thinking. Lizzy was right."

I wondered what he was referring to. Surely not her obsession with her mother and the memoirs? I kept my mouth shut and let him continue.

"I'm not going to pretend we haven't had our difficulties, Williams. But we need to put that behind us. So I was wondering whether you'd like to come to dinner tomorrow night."

That was unexpected. I waited, again, and he came back with "Williams? Are you there?"

"Yes," I said. "I'm here. Yes. That'd be lovely."

That'd be lovely? What was I thinking? Who was I kidding?

"Bring your wife," he added, and before I could think I'd replied.

"My girlfriend. We're not married."

"Fine. Bring your girlfriend. We're in Kensington. I'll text you the address. Come around seven if you can."

After I'd hung up I found myself listening to that short closing speech, with its *fine* and its *bring your girlfriend* and its *we're in Kensington*, and hunting down traces of that superior Brooks-Powell I'd so detested. He was still there, I decided, for all the eye-rolling I'd found so amusing. I turned on the television – more news, it seemed the whole world was just one sad tale after another – and wondered what the following night would bring. Claire walked in – showered but back in her dressing gown – and I was about to tell her about our dinner date when she marched up to the television and turned it off. She turned to me and said "How can you think with all this bloody noise?" and strode straight back into the bedroom.

All this bloody noise, I thought. You could write those words on my gravestone. As if on cue, the phone rang again.

"Hello?" I said, expecting another Ukrainian or news editor or bastard.

"Hello, Sam," came the reply, and I felt the breath catch in my throat.

I hadn't heard that voice for a long time. I found my mind racing ahead of me, searching for some other voice, some similar voice, anyone it could be but the person I knew it was. I didn't speak.

"Sam?" he continued. "It's Edward. Edward Trawden. I think you and I should have a chat."

10: How The Other Half Live

"HELLO, TRAWDEN," I replied. It felt inadequate, but I couldn't think of anything else to say.

"How have you been, Sam?"

There was a hint of concern in his voice. Was it genuine? I remembered him, in the pub, celebrating his release, "Here's to Robbie Evans," a twisted little grin on his narrow mouth, but he'd been in prison for twenty years by then. For all I knew he'd been a sweet, mild-mannered gentleman before he'd gone in; for all I knew, the last decade outside had turned him back into one. He'd asked me a question, I realised, and I hadn't answered.

"Not so bad. You?"

"Excellent. Just excellent."

Had I detested Trawden the way I remembered it, or was that just something that had been added after I'd seen the hell the Grimshaws were in? And it wasn't even Trawden who'd put them there. There was that toast in the pub, that was real, I could hear the words as if he were whispering them in my ear right now, but he had all the reason in the world to think of himself back then. And perhaps, I reasoned, he'd been toasting Evans' confession. Not the murder. I cast my mind back to earlier meetings with him, the interviews, the preparation. He'd been pleasant enough then, I thought.

He was waiting for me to say something.

"So what brings you to my phone?" I asked, with a sunniness I wasn't feeling.

"Well, I think you know that, don't you?"

I waited for him to go on. I hadn't worked out how I felt about him, but I wasn't going to make the conversation easy.

"It's Elizabeth, Sam. Elizabeth Maurier. The late. Your ex-boss. My redeemer. Turns out we're in the same boat, you and I."

"Eh?"

I'd decided to let him talk, to draw out the silences and see where they led, but the word slipped out before I could stop it.

"Your good friend and mine. Detective Inspector Martins. Has that charming lady been trying to make things difficult for you?"

I wondered how he knew, where he got his information, but this time I managed to stop my tongue before it gave me away. I waited. Trawden didn't seem the slightest bit put out by my reticence.

"Well, Sam, I gather she has been. I gather she wanted to talk to you. About various calls you'd received from *la grande dame*? I'm in the same position. A few calls from her ladyship and suddenly I'm a *person of interest*. The interest, thankfully, didn't last long, and I presume the case is similar for your good self, but it reminded me, Sam. It reminded me of you. Of what you did for me."

Had he spoken like that in the past? All those linguistic trills, those verbal twists and turns? Had he been a client now, or a witness, I'd have been trying to find something underneath all that cleverness, the darkness the dazzle was meant to obscure, but some people, I knew, just spoke like that. Perhaps Trawden was one of them. Perhaps he was someone who adapted. Another trick he'd have learned inside. Be the man you need to be at the time. Play to your audience.

"Anyway, Sam, I think you should come to see me. There's someone I'd like you to meet. I think you'll find him interesting. He might even be able to help you find some work."

Trawden was an unusual character, that was undeniable.

And he wanted me to meet someone *interesting,* but he wasn't saying who. I was intrigued, so much so that I forgot to tell him I didn't need his help.

"OK," I said. "When and where?"

"This afternoon. I'll send a taxi for you. Don't worry, I've got your address."

And my phone number, I thought. It seemed half the world had my phone number today. Claire was right. There was too much bloody noise.

By the time Trawden's taxi arrived I'd at least managed a rapprochement with Claire. And more. She emerged from the bedroom dressed – in yesterday's clothes, I noticed, but that was an improvement on the dressing gown – and walked purposefully towards the sofa, where I sat waiting for whatever inexplicable onslaught she was about to deliver. Instead she smiled, leaned in and kissed me, and even muttered "sorry" on the way back up. I didn't know what she apologising for, really, or what had prompted the change of mood and how long it would last, so I sat quietly and smiled back at her as she pottered about the kitchen in silence.

"Are you OK?" I said, as she pushed a mug of coffee into my hand and sat down beside me, her head resting lightly on my shoulder.

"I'm fine. Drank a bit too much. Sorry about earlier. Can't blame you for the headache. You weren't even here."

I laughed, and then remembered what had happened while she'd been sleeping. "Brooks-Powell called."

She sat up sharply and looked into my eyes, incredulous. "Seriously?"

"Seriously. Invited us to dinner tomorrow night."

"Think he's planning on poisoning us?"

This was the old Claire. She *was* back. Distance. The guaranteed cure for all ills. I let out a slow breath of relief and shrugged.

"There are easier ways to get rid of me," I said. "He lives in Kensington. He was at pains to point that out. I said yes, but I can always cancel if you don't fancy it."

She frowned, that deep, furrowed face of concentration I'd fallen in love with months ago, and pushed a stray blonde strand away from her face.

"Don't do that. I've always wanted to dine with the devil. Bring the long spoons."

I laughed, and she leaned in and kissed me again. As I lifted my face away she grabbed my head and pulled me back in, and the weight of all those days of tension seemed to lift so suddenly I found myself wondering whether it had been there at all. Even the Christmas tree seemed brighter, somehow – spritely and impish rather than forlorn and prematurely withered. She took my hand and guided it to her breast, and the three hours it had taken her to finally get dressed were undone in seconds.

I wasn't complaining.

I was still putting on my trousers when the buzzer sounded and I was informed, in an unexpectedly refined accent, that my car had arrived. I cast a long look back at Claire, sprawled naked on the sofa with a look on her face that suggested the taxi had interrupted what would have been an afternoon to remember, and cursed Trawden's timing.

The accent wasn't the only surprise. Instead of the dirty local cab I'd been expecting, there was a gleaming Mercedes and a grey-haired, middle-aged gentleman in a dark uniform beside it opening the door for me and announcing "Your car, sir." It had been a while since anyone had called me sir. The Mercedes was clean inside, with a faint aroma of whisky and cigar smoke, which was nice, but still not as nice as the sofa and its occupant upstairs.

"Where are we going?" I asked, as we steered in cocooned silence around Highbury Corner and towards the heart of London.

"Pall Mall, sir," came the reply. "It shouldn't take too long."

"That's nice. Any chance you can lose the prick behind?"

I'd noticed him as we pulled away from the kerb, Rich bloody Hanover on his tiny bloody bike. He was wearing a helmet so I couldn't see his face, but I knew it was him and I hoped there was a bruise or two on it.

"I wouldn't worry, sir. He won't be getting in where we're headed."

I wondered where that might be, what was on Pall Mall and why Trawden would choose to meet me there. It didn't seem like his sort of place. But I was learning new things about lots of people these days, or at least learning there were things about them I'd never have suspected. Perhaps Trawden was moving up in the world. Perhaps he'd been there a while.

I sat back in silence and watched London slide by. It was raining, the streets teeming with umbrellas and heavy coats, the sky an unbroken greyish white that cast the city into a sombre grandeur somehow magnified by the gentle hum of the engine. This, I recalled, was how Elizabeth Maurier had liked to travel; she had cars enough, and a valid licence, but for journeys outside London she had always preferred to let someone else do the driving. Journeys to the families of clients in Milton Keynes council estates that looked like war zones. Journeys to the fringes of the city where owl-eyed barristers sat at home with great piles of paper and awaited their audience with the great lady. Journeys to her Oxfordshire home, where I'd once been picked up from the village railway station in a slender bullet of a car with Elizabeth beckoning from the back seat, smiling in a black dress bought specifically for the occasion.

We drew to a halt outside a palatial building at the corner of Pall Mall and one of its lesser tributaries. The door opened beside me and there was Trawden, standing and smiling at me.

"Sam!" he cried. "It's been too long."

I took a few seconds longer to extricate my limbs from the car than I really needed, staring all the while at the man in front of me. He'd aged, certainly, but not by much; he seemed taller and somehow grander than he had when I'd last seen him, although this was probably down to the suit and tie he was wearing. The hair was grey – I tried to remember if it had been grey ten years ago, but I couldn't quite picture the detail. The smile was slightly lop-sided, lifting half of his face and leaving the rest behind as if it were still contemplating its mood and didn't yet want to commit to an expression.

He held out a hand; I took it and saw he was looking at me and shaking his head.

"This won't do," he said, and walked around the car to exchange a few words with the driver. The driver nodded and produced a small suitcase from the seat beside him, to Trawden's obvious relief.

"Here," said Trawden. "It's not normally the done thing, but you can change in the car. They won't let you in wearing denim."

In where? I thought, as I opened the case and found myself gazing upon a full set of clothes – suit, shirt, tie. There were two pairs of identical shoes in different sizes. I wondered for a moment what I was letting myself in for, whether I should allow myself to be dressed by a man towards whom my feelings were ambivalent at best, but then I remembered the intriguing *someone* I was to meet, and the vague promise of work. I retreated back into the cocoon and emerged five minute later holding a small black bag with my own clothes in it, and attired more suitably for wherever it was we were going. As I closed the car door and glanced up I locked eyes with Hanover on the other side of the street. The helmet was gone. He stood there, phone in his hand with the camera aimed at me, at us, Sam Williams and Edward Trawden dressed to the nines outside a Mercedes on Pall Mall. I decided I didn't care.

"The Reform Club," announced Trawden, looking me up and down with notably more appreciation than he had shown first time round. "Thank you, Collins, you can go now."

With that the driver nodded and merged seamlessly into the traffic. Trawden took my arm – I hesitated at the contact, but put up no resistance – and led me up a set of stone steps to an impressive black door guarded by a smiling, uniformed gentleman with a paunch and the face of a heavy drinker.

"Mr Trawden, sir. Please come through. Lord Blennard is waiting for you and your guest in the Coffee Room."

Trawden stopped and moved to the side, waiting for me to step in front of him, but I was frozen to the spot.

Blennard. I'd assumed Trawden was introducing me to a dodgy cop or a friend in a spot of bother, and if the Reform Club was an unlikely setting for that, it was an unlikely setting for anything involving me or Trawden or pretty much anyone I knew. But Lord Blennard made sense.

Charlie Blennard. I'd never met the man, of course, but his name had been tossed around the office at Mauriers like loose change. *Charlie says he doesn't think it'll get through the first reading. Charlie has a fascinating line on the Home Secretary. I'm off to see Charlie for lunch, so don't expect me back before tomorrow*, the last with a sly little wink that had me wondering on more than one occasion whether there was more to Elizabeth's relationship with the old politician than wine and reminiscence. Charlie, Lord Blennard of Holden. The Man Who Would Be King. I roused my limbs and stepped inside, looking back over my shoulder to see Rich Hanover standing at the bottom of the steps and realising that was as far as he was going to get.

The Coffee Room was more than the name suggested. A vast expanse of marble, pillars like elephants' legs supporting the gallery, burgundy leather as far as the eye could see. A Christmas tree that looked as if it had been lifted whole from some ancient forest towered over an undergrowth of tables and chairs. Trawden's hand was at my back, steering me gently towards a table at the far end of the room with a single occupant. I'd have recognised that face anywhere.

And then I was in front of him and shaking his hand. He'd hauled himself out of his leather chair as we approached, and on his feet he was taller than I'd expected, lean, a broad smile on a broad, lightly-lined face, a sense of huge power and energy compressed into a human form.

"Sam Williams? Delighted to meet you at last. Glad Collins got you here in one piece."

"Me too," I replied, an adequate response to both his comments. "Nice place you've got here." He gave a quiet chuckle as he turned his attention to Trawden. Before I knew it we were seated and a black-clad waiter had pressed a menu into my hand – more burgundy leather.

"I hope you haven't eaten, Sam," said Blennard. "The food here is quite excellent, as Edward will no doubt attest."

Trawden nodded. I shrugged. I'd bolted a microwave chicken chow mein at eleven in lieu of breakfast. A decent meal wouldn't kill me. Blennard was still smiling at me, and now we were all seated and he was no longer towering a foot over my head, there was so much in that smile I hadn't seen. A sense of inclusion, comradeship. And a depth, too, in those dark brown eyes – I tended not to notice eyes, particularly not the eyes of octogenarians, but there was something compelling about Blennard.

He'd been a powerful man, at one time. A key member of that select little coterie that had been mentored and drilled by Elizabeth's father. A handful of cabinet positions, but never any of the major ones; Blennard had a tendency not to toe the line on the big calls, the foreign wars, the clampdowns on immigration, the sort of thing that endeared him to Elizabeth Maurier and the rose-tinted dreamers who frequented the Reform, I assumed. He'd resigned from his post on points of principle on more than one occasion. And, it suddenly struck me, he'd been one of those rare voices that championed Trawden. He'd probably brought the case to Elizabeth's door. There was one connection brought into the light, at least.

"I suppose you're wondering why you're here," he said as I flicked through the menu.

"Well, it's no Kensal Kebabs, but it'll do." He chuckled again, and I continued, keen to get past the laughter and to the point. "You were a friend of Elizabeth's. I don't mean to be rude, but you could have summoned me any time. You've picked now, after she's died – been killed, I should say. After I've been appointed to work on her memoirs. That's supposed to be confidential, but I can't believe you wouldn't know it already. Anyway. That's why."

He nodded.

"Indeed. I knew her for most of her life, you know. Remarkable woman."

Remarkable woman. Dr Shapiro had said the same thing. And it was true, I supposed. She had been. And now she was dead, and nobody, it seemed, wanted to leave her alone.

"Yes," continued Blennard, although nobody had said anything for him to agree with. "Yes, I remember her as a child, as a teenager, I remember when she started that firm and the years building it into the extraordinary institution it became."

The kind of extraordinary institution that got itself on the front pages for all the right reasons, but worked hard to hide the bullying and viciousness that went on within its own four walls. I wondered if Blennard knew all that, knew about my own personal history at and after Mauriers. He'd gone silent, and I looked up, wondering whether it was my turn to speak. He was staring at me, a look of concern on his face, and I realised I was frowning as thoughts of those final days at Mauriers coursed through me.

"I think I'll have the sole," I said, and Blennard nodded approvingly. He might have nodded at me and said *Yes* to himself, but he hadn't taken me up on the subject of the memoirs.

"Excellent choice. You are a man of taste, I see. Elizabeth never mentioned that, even though she spoke of you often."

Here we go, I thought. Another one trying the same line. With Lizzy it had been plausible, just about; she at least knew me, my name might have cropped up. But Blennard? Why on earth would my name have reached his noble ears? Lizzy had wanted something out of me, my cooperation on her mother's memoirs. Blennard, I realised, wanted something too. I wondered if it would come out over lunch. I looked past Blennard, around the room, men reading newspapers and tucking into their lunches and leaning back with glasses of expensive wine, all men, all content in their own little corner of the nineteenth century, and realised that if it did come out, it would be on Blennard's terms. And it would come slowly. I'd have to wait.

I'd had enough of waiting.

"So really," I asked, dodging the compliment. "Why did you want to see me, now? What can I do for you?"

He smiled.

"You're a man who gets to the point, Sam. I like that."

I returned the smile, but stayed silent. After a moment he continued.

"The fact is, Elizabeth Maurier played a huge role in my life. As did you in hers – don't deny it, Sam, you must have done, for her to have entrusted such a significant task to you after her death. I needed to meet you. That's all."

It was convincing. It explained why he'd chosen now, of all times, to meet me; he wouldn't have realised how important I was to Elizabeth until he'd heard about the memoirs. I hadn't realised myself. Yes, convincing enough, and almost the whole story. Almost. I'd given him the chance to tell me everything, and all I'd got was almost. If I was going to find out what was missing, I might, I realised, have to wait after all.

We drifted into reminiscence, nothing surprising, nothing to give any of us away. Elizabeth's travels, her work, her husband ("fine man," said Blennard, and then moved onto more interesting topics). Her daughter.

"Ah, yes, poor Lizzy," he said, when I mentioned that we were working on the memoirs together. I saw him catch Trawden's eye, and frown, slightly, and then change the subject again, to a party he had been at with Elizabeth at which the Foreign Secretary had drunk too much port and engaged in a highly public and remarkably colourful argument with his wife. I'd tried to force things, and Blennard wouldn't have that. His place. His time. His terms.

"Dorothy was with me then," he said, and fell silent, and I remembered her then, his wife, dead in her fifties from breast cancer while Blennard was at the height of his power. Elizabeth Maurier had missed a court appearance for the funeral – had sent Brooks-Powell in her place, to my disgust. I wondered whether there had been children – I couldn't recall any, but I'd had little reason to keep track of Charlie Blennard's personal life even while I'd been working for his friend.

The silence lasted just a second or two, and was followed by more reminiscence. He worked hard, Blennard, choosing topics I could engage in and people I either knew or would have heard of. And he was brilliant, too; charming and witty, with a modesty that seemed genuine underpinning it all. Another person might have played on his success, and I'd have bristled, but he was too clever for that. Instead he twisted things, put himself in our shoes, Trawden and I, gave the impression that he was privileged to have met and worked with so many fascinating people and done so many fascinating things, that luck had put him in the right places at the right times, and those places and times were no more his than ours. He radiated charisma, and I could see how influential people might fall under his spell. I was falling under it even as the food arrived.

He was right, of course; the sole was excellent, as were the wine and the pudding. The conversation continued, hardly blunted by the food, both Trawden and I adding our own asides and anecdotes from time to time. The time we'd hit a pothole on the way to Oxfordshire, her chauffeur unable to change the tyre, her refusing to let me so much as look at it but instead insisting I stay there with her, in the back of the car, drinking port until someone arrived to rescue us. The time she'd stood outside court and waited patiently while a journalist fired question after question at her, each ruder and more objectionable that the last, and finally replied by quoting his own editor back at him in terms that put her firmly in the right. I had my stories. Trawden had his, too. But there was no doubt who was running the show. Back and forth we went, Prime Ministers and criminals, judges and warlords. And the Mauriers. Always the Mauriers, Elizabeth, her parents, her daughter. *Poor Lizzy*, again and again, and I found myself agreeing and then wondering why. It wasn't Lizzy who'd been brutally murdered. Again, Blennard must have noticed my frown;

"She did rather grow up in her mother's shadow," he pointed out. I couldn't disagree.

As our plates were removed he sat back and favoured us both with one of those enormous smiles.

"I hope you've enjoyed the meal, Sam."

I nodded and thanked him for his hospitality.

"I just wanted to tell you that if there's anything I can do to help, if I can be of assistance in any way, do let me know. Here's my card. Alas, I have to be at Westminster in twenty minutes, so I must leave you. But please, feel free to contact me at any time."

He stood and walked away. *The Man Who Would Be King.* The press had come up with that, one of the broadsheets, but it wasn't quite right. He'd never been Chancellor or Home Secretary, Defence or Foreign Secretary. He'd had a seat at the table, but halfway down, in among the Under Secretaries and Ministers. He'd made it to Attorney General, but he'd never have risen any higher, and from an hour or two in the man's company I didn't think he'd have wanted to. It wasn't entirely false, that repositioning, that notion that he'd had it all thrust upon him. He was too much of an outsider for anything else.

And now he'd gone, and I'd failed to get anything out of him, anything real, and he'd left me sitting at a table with Edward Trawden, talking quietly, a man who made my stomach turn, but who had been surprisingly good company over lunch. I turned Blennard's card over and over in my hand, and finished my coffee. I was drained of conversation, and Trawden seemed almost as lost for words as I was, which suited me just fine.

"I've got to go," I said. I didn't bother making up an excuse. Everyone seemed to know my business as well as I did, anyway.

Trawden extended his hand, and after a moment's hesitation, I took it. Perhaps he wasn't so bad. He was an innocent man, after all. He didn't deserve the taint of a crime he hadn't committed.

But why, if that was the case, did I still feel so uneasy?

PART 2: TAPESTRY

11: Notorious

GETTING TO SLEEP that night was harder than it had been for a while. Claire lay beside me, snoring gently – there had been no repeat of our earlier activities, but she'd seemed pleased enough to see me and keen as a greyhound to know what had happened at lunch. I had the feeling she was slightly disappointed by what I had to tell her, but Blennard would do, his presence, his buying me lunch, his inviting me into the hallowed halls of the Reform Club. At least she wasn't obsessing over her story, her girls. She'd taken my advice. She'd built some distance.

I hadn't, though. I couldn't sleep. I couldn't get Trawden out of my head.

What was the man really like? He'd greeted me like an old friend, comfortable and in control, but at The Reform, after Blennard had left, he'd seemed as awkward and unsure of himself as I was. Was that real? Was he just moulding himself to the image he was presented with, the feelings I was projecting? He had, I reflected, grudgingly, always been open and honest, but that was in his interest: he'd wanted the truth, and all of it, because that was his route out of jail. I'd met him a handful of times before his release, always with Elizabeth, sitting beside her, taking notes and interjecting only occasionally with a question of my own. She'd seen him without me more frequently, but had rarely come back with any information of interest. And when it came to getting him out, it wasn't anything Trawden had said or done that had provided the key. It had been the files on Evans, it had been my photographic memory and doggedness and refusal to give up on the lost cause that Robbie Evans' second-hand confession was said to be. I'd asked Trawden, before I'd left, why Elizabeth had called him, but he wasn't sure. He hadn't been able to speak to her before her death, a source, as he put it, of unending regret. When I'd first mentioned the memoirs during lunch he'd nodded, as if everything were falling into place; it made sense, he told me afterwards. Elizabeth Maurier wanted to set everything down, wanted her life documented. The fact that she had died shortly afterwards was nothing more than coincidence, of course, but the fact that she had tried to speak to Trawden was an entirely logical piece of the whole. She wanted his recollections, to test them against her own, to probe for gaps and ensure everything was known. That was all.

And this had drawn us together, Trawden and I. This search for the whole. He was probably right, I decided.

My thoughts drifted onto Blennard. He'd dazzled me over lunch, on his home ground; I wondered whether he'd have had the same effect elsewhere. Hours later, at home and in the dark, the notion returned to me that he *had* wanted something, that he hadn't just summoned me to offer some vague *assistance* and ply me with wine and Dover sole. Whatever it was he was after, it hadn't come out. There was more to Blennard than met the eye, I decided.

I lifted my head and glanced past Claire's sleeping form to the luminous green digits on the clock radio. It was a relic from the nineties but seemed older, a seventies vision of the future with numbers ticking inexorably on to the moment of doom. I couldn't see any doom coming my way. The trouble was, I couldn't see much else, either.

It was 1am.

By half past I'd given up, crept delicately from the bed, and set to work on the Maurier files I'd looked at earlier that day. This time I started at the beginning – there must have been earlier files, but the ones I'd grabbed happened to open with my own tenure at the firm.

The Little Bill case brought back some memories. I'd been with an unusual girl at the time, a beauty with a history of domestic violence and, it turned out, an addiction to it as well. It hadn't lasted. It might not have stuck in my memory at all, Little Bill or the girl, were it not for the fact that Trawden had followed straight after.

The files were light on Trawden, which surprised me given how important he'd been to Elizabeth's reputation. The barest facts, and not even them when it came to how we actually found the truth. *I.* How *I* actually found the truth.

Robbie Evans had been dismissed as a solid lead because a tired lawyer or police officer had sorted through his history – Evans was dead by then, his claim to Maxine Grimshaw hadn't come to light until long after he'd bled out his last in the prison showers – and misplaced a date. Evans had spent a short stint as a glazier for a local firm in Bangor. I could see the words on the page even as I recalled them twelve years later. I could see the witness statement from Casey Donohue, who worked at the Ford showroom at the end of the Warrington street the Grimshaw house backed onto. She'd been interviewed by the police because she'd come running to the house when she heard Eileen Grimshaw screaming. She'd heard the scream because she'd taken a long walk that afternoon, and she'd taken a long walk because she was having an extended lunch break, and she was having an extended lunch break because the whole showroom was shut for three hours while some Welsh bastards (her words) fitted a massive new glass front and no one had bothered telling her a bloody thing about it or she'd have organised a lift home.

According to the records, Evans' time as a glazier had ended a year before the murder, but I didn't believe in coincidence, and I was right. The records weren't. Casey Donohue put Evans on the spot, and the rest fell smoothly into place.

None of this figured in Elizabeth's notes on the case. She mentioned Evans; without him there was almost nothing to say. She mentioned my *assistance*, which was putting it mildly, but there'd been little point in seeking recognition for a job well done even when she'd been alive. Trawden was exonerated; Trawden was freed; onto the next. If Trawden meant so little to her, why had she tried to speak to him before she died?

That thought took me back to the phone call and the sudden realisation that perhaps she hadn't. If the whole point of the day's machinations was to get me in front of Blennard, for reasons I still hadn't established, then it was entirely feasible that Trawden had made that phone call up. He'd claimed that Martins had been on his case, but that could just as easily be another corroborating detail without a basis in reality. Everything he'd told me might well be one hundred per cent bullshit, and I knew how to find out.

I glanced at the clock before I made the call. Half past two. But Colman had wanted my help, had said *any time of day or night*, I remembered the exact words and how I'd been thinking, as she uttered them, that she might come to regret them. I felt a sudden surge of energy that decided it for me – there was no way I was sleeping before I'd spoken to her, and there was no way I was sitting around till dawn, searching through Elizabeth's files for a hidden unicorn until it was safe to call.

Colman answered on the eighth ring, by which time I'd normally have given up, but I'd decided I was speaking to her now come hell or high water and we were still a long way short of that. She sounded breathless, which suggested she'd had to run for the telephone.

"Who's this?" she asked.

"It's Sam. Sam Williams."

"Oh, right." She was still breathing heavily. I heard some

muttered words, faint, too far away from the phone to be the person who'd just answered it, and it occurred to me that most people keep the phone close at hand, at night, if they've any intention of answering it at all.

"Sorry I woke you," I said, deciding then and there that I hadn't.

"Don't worry about it. I wasn't asleep."

"Have I interrupted something?"

"Yes," she laughed, "but I wouldn't worry about it. He's not exactly Don Juan."

"Hey," said the voice I'd heard in the background, now clearer and closer. "I can hear you, you know."

"Shut up and keep yourself ready," replied Colman, to her unseen lover, but still audible enough. "I haven't finished with you yet, sir. Now then, Sam, what can I do for you in the middle of the dark and gloomy fucking night?"

"Trawden."

I waited. *Sir*, she'd said. DS Larkin. Tommy. He hadn't wasted his time. Neither had Colman.

"Name rings a bell," she replied. "Child killer, right?"

"He was exonerated. I worked on it, with Elizabeth. Says she tried to call him before she died. Says Martins spoke to him about it. Is he making this stuff up?"

"I don't know," she replied, after a moment's silence. I had no idea what was going on at the other end of the line, but I doubted it was considered reflection. "But I can find out. Think it might be helpful?"

I paused in the instant of thinking "Yes" and realised that whatever came of it, even if Trawden had made the whole thing up, it would probably come to nothing. I doubted it had anything to do with Elizabeth's murder and I doubted Trawden's motives, or Blennard's, would be interesting enough to justify the lack of sleep on my side or interrupted pleasure on hers.

"Possibly," I said. "I'm not sure."

"I'll see what I can find out, then. Speak tomorrow."

I set the phone down and looked up to find Claire looking down at me and shaking her head.

"Bit late for making calls, isn't it?"

I opened my mouth to reply, but she continued before I could get a word out.

"Don't worry. Really. You've got calls to make, make 'em. Just keep the noise down. Don't wake me up, OK?"

"OK," I said, and watched her stumble back into the bedroom, still half asleep. I sat there staring after her for a minute, and then went to the kitchen and made myself a coffee. It was, I realised, going to be a long, dull night, just me and Elizabeth Maurier's files.

I woke to the sound of the kettle and lifted my head slowly and painfully to see into the kitchen. Claire was up. She was washed and dressed, and she was whistling. She turned and saw me, and walked over with a smile.

"Coffee's coming. Looks like you're going to need it."

I gaped at her.

"It's eleven o' clock, Sam. When did you finally get to sleep?"

I shook my head. "Not sure. I was looking through the files."

"I know. You must have dropped off midway through, because there were papers all over the floor."

I looked down. Nothing there, nothing on the sofa, either, except an unpleasant-looking patch of drool I must have left there overnight. She saw me searching the room from my semi-supine position, and pointed to the kitchen counter.

"I tidied them up. Spent half an hour creeping around you like a cat, but I reckon I could have let off a bomb and you wouldn't have noticed."

She smiled again. I joined her.

"Thanks."

She returned to the kitchen and I watched her, the thud in my head slowly dropping gear until it was a ghost of the pain I'd woken with. I'd slept with my neck twisted into the side of the sofa, I realised, and this was the result. It hadn't been worth it. Nothing useful in the files. I reached for my phone. Nothing interesting there, either. A voicemail from Brooks-Powell reminding me about tonight, the time, his address.

"Did you find anything?" asked Claire, sitting down beside me with her own coffee. That faint coconut smell washed over me, her shampoo, the scent that was entirely her to me.

"Nothing much," I replied. "Nothing I didn't already know, anyway. Unless Lizzy's been hoarding the good stuff somewhere else this is going to be a very thin memoir."

She nodded, leaned over and kissed me on the cheek.

"You'll get there, lover boy. You always find the good stuff in the end."

I sat back, smiled, and drank some coffee. *Lover boy* was what she'd called me back at the start, the expression she still used from time to time to remind me, I thought, that we were more than just two people who happened to share a flat.

"I hope so," I replied.

"And what about your mysterious phone call? Who was that?"

"Colman. The DC, the one who's working on the Elizabeth Maurier case."

Claire nodded. "And? Did she have any great insights at half past two in the morning?"

I studied her face as she spoke, looking for signs of anger or resentment, but if that was what she was feeling she was hiding it well.

"No. Not this time."

The words had slipped out before I'd thought about them, and she was onto them like a shark.

"This time?"

I reached for my coffee. I needed a moment to think. Just a moment, though, because this was Claire. She was a journalist, true, but whatever I'd said to Colman about confidentiality – and I wasn't entirely sure where we'd left that particular detail – Claire was the one person I trusted.

"There was something," I replied, setting my empty cup down on the coffee table and turning to her. "At the police station."

I watched her eyes widen and her mouth fall open as I went on to tell her about the board, Martins' reaction to my presence, Colman in the café afterwards, the obscure name in the elusive diary. When I'd finished she sat back and exhaled, and asked me what Colman had said when I'd woken her in the middle of the night. I grinned and explained that I hadn't woken her at all, but I did appear to have interrupted something a little more active than sleep. She started to laugh, and then the phone rang, and she picked it up and disappeared into the bedroom, closing the door behind her. I picked up my coffee, clambered awkwardly to my feet, and wandered over to the kitchen. The files sat there like yesterday's leftovers, a meal I'd hoped to enjoy but had got little out of. I owed them another look, but I reckoned it could wait.

Fifteen minutes later Claire emerged and handed me the phone.

"Maloney," she mouthed, and I put the phone to my ear.

"Hello, mate, what's new?" he asked.

"Nothing much. Oh, except I had lunch in The Reform Club with a Lord yesterday."

He laughed. "Yeah. Claire told me. And what's this I hear about the pair of you going to Brooks-Powell's for dinner tonight?"

He'd been talking to Claire for a long time, I realised. Not that there was anything wrong with that. They'd always got on well enough. It just seemed unusual. I realised Maloney had fallen silent and was waiting for me to say something.

"So what's up with you?" I asked, finally, ignoring the question about tonight's dinner.

"Just wanted an address for Roarkes. Thought I'd send him a card."

That was normal enough, too. Maloney and Roarkes might have sat on opposite sides of the law, but they'd always had a grudging respect for one another. So what if my gangster friend was writing letters to my police officer friend? So what if he was talking to my girlfriend, too? I had to stop jumping at shadows, I realised. I scrolled through my phone for the address and gave it to him.

"Cheers," he replied, and that was the moment for me to kill the call and forget about it.

I've never been very good at forgetting things.

"So what did Claire have to say, then?"

"Why don't you ask her yourself," he shot back, quick as a bullet. I shut my mouth on the *fuck off* that was coming to a boil in there and opted for silence instead. After a few seconds he backed down.

"Not a lot, really. Just venting. Think it does her good, talking to someone other than you."

I wondered what she was paying Adrian for if it wasn't talking. At least Maloney was free.

"Anyway," he continued, "I reckon she could do with a night out. Or an afternoon. Forget it all. Get away from everything for a few hours. What do you think?"

"I'll have to check my diary," I said, wondering whether Maloney could hear the sarcasm through the line.

"Your diary ain't what counts, mate. I meant me and

Claire. I'll take her to the Mitre, not one of them poncy places you like."

I stopped, stunned.

"Really?"

"Why not?"

I cast about for a reason, and couldn't find one. If Claire wanted to spend the afternoon in a filthy run-down boozer watching Maloney throw expensive beer down his throat, then fine. She was a big girl. She could look after herself.

Which was what she promptly did. I looked up and she was standing in front of me wearing a smart cream duffel coat and a smile.

"I'm off now," she said, bent down to kiss me, and left before I had a chance to ask where.

I heard a voice in the distance and realised I was still holding the phone and Maloney was still talking.

"Sorry," I said. "What was that?"

"What about this article, then? Got you good, that fucker."

I paused, waiting for my brain to tell me what he was talking about. My brain remained silent.

"What are you on about, Maloney?" I asked.

"Not seen it? Get on that website. What's it called, you know, *Big News* or something?"

"*Real World News*?"

"That's the one. You're the star of the show, mate. The notorious Sam Williams. Have a read."

He was gone before I had a chance to ask anything else, and I waited, fuming, while my laptop connected and then disconnected from the internet three times before the right page would load. When it finally did, I found myself wishing it had never connected at all.

Bad Luck or Bad Lawyer?

That was the headline. Underneath there was a photograph of me and Trawden standing just outside the door of the Reform Club. I was looking back over my shoulder, and because I was looking down – I'd spotted Rich Hanover at the bottom of the steps, and I was at the top – the image was one of superiority, not helped by the suit and tie or by my self-satisfied smile as I realised Hanover wouldn't be able to follow me in.

The photograph had its own caption. "Sam Williams dines at London's exclusive Reform Club with sinister ex-prisoner Edward Trawden, who served decades for the murder of a child before Williams managed to secure his release." I supposed, if you put it like that, it didn't sound great. And then the article, which pulled together a whole heap of unrelated facts – my meeting with Lizzy, Elizabeth's murder, Trawden, my "assault on this journalist, in connection with which I am currently taking legal advice", and the "tragic affair in Manchester, during which, among several violent deaths, a lawyer with whom Williams was said to be extremely close took her own life."

I didn't come out well. I sat there fuming and wondering what I could do about it and what Hanover's lawyer would tell him about the so-called assault. I had punched the man, I supposed. The assault, like everything else in the article, wasn't actually untrue.

Just misleading.

I couldn't do anything, I decided. Hanover didn't have enough to have me arrested or sue me. Maloney might have read the thing but he'd be in shallow company. In audience numbers, *Real World News* wasn't exactly the BBC.

I tried to put it out of my mind.

The afternoon passed uneventfully, my fruitless rereading of the Maurier files interrupted only by a call from Colman, whose opening comment was "Beating up journalists isn't a bad idea, but try to keep it quiet next time."

Maybe I'd been wrong about those audience numbers.

She wasn't calling just to taunt, me, though. She'd done some digging. Elizabeth's phone call to Trawden was real enough; he hadn't made it up. There had been three calls, it emerged, but Trawden had the same line I did: they hadn't spoken, the calls had gone to voicemail, he'd have called her back eventually, if she hadn't gone and died on him. Trawden had no idea what Elizabeth wanted to speak to him about, and the police didn't either, but they weren't concerned either way. According to Trawden they spoke once or twice a year anyway, just catching up, never an important matter to discuss. I had, I realised, been jumping at shadows again. Blennard was on the level. Trawden was on the level. The phone call wasn't even a dead end, because there wasn't a road to follow. That spark that had awoken in the café over Elizabeth Maurier's diary was down to a dull glow. Vicky Colman and her delightful boss could carry on digging into Elizabeth Maurier's death. The only thing that concerned me was her life.

Claire showed up shortly before six, just as I was starting to worry that she might have forgotten our dinner engagement and wonder whether calling her would be taken as charming or overprotective. She breezed in clutching a pair of shopping bags and wearing a Santa hat over that duffel coat.

"I know, I know," she said, catching my inadvertent glance at my wrist. I'd lost the watch months back, but the habit persisted. "I just need to get changed. I'll be ready in ten minutes."

I didn't doubt it. One of Claire's many admirable qualities was the ability to transform in the briefest of times. Not that she needed much transformation right now.

She disappeared into the bedroom, and then the bathroom, and emerged seven minutes later wearing the sort of clothes where naming them doesn't do justice. Pale woollen jumper. Black leather trousers. Blonde hair and those eyes and *that* smile. A year, I thought, a year and change we'd been together, and I didn't see myself wanting that to end. Not soon. Not ever.

Claire was in a good mood. I was in a good mood. Even the prospect of dinner with the Brooks-Powells couldn't dent that.

12: Crystal

WE KEPT UP a decent conversation on the tube, whispering about Lizzy Maurier and grinning over what we'd find at Brooks-Powell's place. The trains were running smoothly, and the light drizzle that had been coming down when we went underground had dried up by the time we resurfaced. Everything, in fact, was fine, until the moment we turned a corner and found ourselves outside the address Brooks-Powell had given me.

Rich Hanover had beaten me to it. There he stood, grinning, in front of his bloody bike and behind his bloody phone. He held it up for a minute while I tried to position myself between Claire and the lens. Whatever this was, it wasn't her problem. I turned to explain it to her, but she shook her head and said "Don't worry. I read the article. Man's a prick," and a moment later I heard an engine gunning and Hanover was gone.

We turned our attention to the house. I'd always known Brooks-Powell would do well for himself. He'd come from money, he wasn't a bad lawyer, for all that I'd willed him to be the worst, he knew a thing or two about getting to the top. I'd been expecting a smart flat in a smart block with an underground car park and a gym no one used.

There was no flat. There was no block. Instead there was a four-storey mansion set back from the road, with what looked like a hundred windows staring back at us as we stared in. Lights on in most of them. I couldn't imagine Brooks-Powell giving much thought to the electricity bill. The wrought iron gates that opened silently as we approached must have cost what I made in a good year.

The theme continued inside. The door was opened by Brooks-Powell himself – I'd been expecting an army of servants or at least a butler, but there he was in the flesh, jacket and tie and the same old sardonic face. He looked pale. He'd always looked pale, I reminded myself. And its severity had always surprised me.

"Thanks for coming," he said, and introduced himself to Claire, who responded with a half-smile and a brief nod of the head. Whatever else was happening, she hadn't forgotten everything I'd told her about the man.

He took our coats and showed us into an ornate living room with chandeliers and a grand piano and, half-reclined on a sofa big enough to house a family of four, a woman in a black dress who I assumed was Mrs Brooks-Powell.

She had her back turned to us as we entered, and stayed like that for long enough that I started to think she hadn't heard us come in. Her husband had left, with our coats. For all I knew the room he was putting them in was fifteen minutes' walk away. I found myself staring intently at that back, at the triangle of white flesh sliced neatly by the sheer black dress, and then she moved her head, turned towards us, and rose, a thin smile etched across her face like a scar.

Another blonde, I thought, but as different from Claire, in her woollen jumper and leather trousers, as one could imagine. The dress accentuated the pallor of her cheeks; below each ear hung a crimson drop that finished the job. Mrs Brooks-Powell was as close to bloodless as made no difference. Perhaps that was her husband's doing; perhaps they were drawn to one another, these pale, elegant creatures.

There was also, I thought, something familiar about that face.

She was walking towards us, and I hadn't moved. Claire, seeing me motionless, stepped past me and extended her hand.

"Claire Tully," she said, a warmth in her voice that might or might not have been real. "It's so kind of you to invite us."

The wraith smiled again and took the proferred hand.

"Nonsense. It's a pleasure to have you. Melanie Golding."

I started forward, my own arm already outstretched.

"I thought I recognised you," I said, before I could stop myself, and she nodded, eyes cast to the floor as she shook my hand. Now the house made sense. The money made sense. Melanie Golding Asset Management was big enough that even I'd heard of it. And its founder and chief executive wasn't one to shy away from the cameras.

She turned again, and for a moment I thought that was it, she'd done her bit, introduced herself, and now she was going back to staring at the walls or whatever it was she'd been doing when we arrived. But instead she sank back into the sofa and patted the cushions either side of her.

"You must be Sam Williams," she said as I sat, and I realised I'd forgotten to introduce myself. "I've heard so much about you."

"Oh dear," I replied automatically, and she laughed, a surprising, full-bodied laugh that pulled her out of the ether and grounded her.

"I wouldn't worry, Sam. You're in decent company. David doesn't have a good word to say about anyone these days."

I wondered about that, about *these days*, about whether that was a reference to my case against Mauriers, his humiliation and departure from the firm, whether it was the slow, relentless uphill gradient of middle age, or something else entirely.

"Seems he and Sam have more in common than they'd care to admit," said Claire, and Melanie turned and favoured her with a smile, and then, to my astonishment, she reached out with both her hands and gathered Claire's right hand into them.

I stared, transfixed. Claire was gazing mutely at the hands, the strange trio, the one-potato-two-potato weirdness of it all. I edged forward on the sofa so that I could see Melanie's face; the smile was still there.

"So pleased to meet you, Claire. I don't know what's going to happen between these two men, but I hope they can keep it between themselves. Does that sound fair to you?"

Another brief nod from Claire, the same she'd offered Brooks-Powell on our arrival. She was playing a role, I decided. Whatever happened, fireworks, reconciliations, friendship or hatred, she would be above it all.

"Eminently," she replied.

"Excellent," said Melanie, and then stood abruptly and called out to the unseen presence of her husband. "Come on, David! Aren't you going to offer our guests a drink before dinner?"

There was a moment's silence, and then the disembodied voice of David Brooks-Powell, floating in the semi-darkness.

"With you in a minute," it said, and his wife sat herself back down with a groan.

"Useless," she muttered, quietly but distinctly enough for both of us to hear. "He's been useless since that...well, you know."

I knew. And I knew the part I'd played in it. But I wasn't apologising for getting my long-overdue revenge, any more than Brooks-Powell had apologised for all the trouble he'd caused in the first place. I glanced at her and realised I must have been playing out my feelings on my face, because she was smiling softly at me and shaking her head.

"Don't worry," she said, and patted me on the shoulder. "It'll all work out for the best."

I doubted that. I smiled and nodded back at her and thought that everything turning out for the best was about as likely as a friendly chat with DI Martins.

Just as the smiling and nodding were entering awkward territory Brooks-Powell strode in, a bottle in one hand and four champagne glasses dangling from the other.

"Some fizz, I think," he announced, looking pleased with himself. He set the glasses down on a sideboard and started pouring before any of us had a chance to demur. At least he hadn't given us the vineyard and vintage, I thought, and then he did. Rare and expensive, no doubt, but it meant nothing to me.

I smiled and said "Thank you", and found I rather liked the champagne after all. But after the first few sips there had to be words, conversations, questions, recollections. Everything I'd dreaded. I answered the questions politely, and asked a few of my own, safe questions, about the house, how long they'd lived there, whether Brooks-Powell had heard anything from Lizzy Maurier or the police. It wasn't easy. Tight work, finding that safe narrow space with his job (which I'd cost him) at one end and her work (which was probably paying for everything) at the other, with a dead woman overhead and a court case underfoot. And I was onto my second glass of champagne, which didn't help. Claire was ahead of me and sipping on a glass of Chablis. I told them about Rich Hanover's presence outside the house. They hadn't heard about the latest article, which made two people in the world who hadn't. And they didn't care about Hanover. Melanie, at least, would have been used to the unwanted attentions of the press.

We moved into the dining room, Brooks-Powell, Claire and I. Melanie was in the kitchen. There were, I realised, no Christmas decorations. Each to their own.

"Has she cooked dinner, then?" I asked, unable to mask my surprise.

"Not just a pretty face," he replied, with a grin. "Not just a rich one, either. Melanie won't be long. She plans everything out to the second. Or at least, she tries to."

The grin had faded by the time he'd finished talking and we'd taken our seats. A vast oak table in a vast oak-panelled room with crystal in the chandeliers and crystal glasses and, for all I knew, crystals hidden in whatever it was Melanie was about to serve us. Claire sat opposite Brooks-Powell. I was beside her, opposite Melanie's empty chair. Between us we occupied no more than a quarter of the table.

A moment's silence followed, broken by Claire's "You have a beautiful house, you know." She leaned forward as she spoke, a hint of breathlessness to her voice, and I realised with a start that she was flirting with him. With *him*. With David Brooks-Powell. While he shrugged and thanked her, I took a moment to work out how I felt about that.

Fine. I felt absolutely fine. For all the difficulties we'd been going through lately, for all the confusion I'd felt over her long conversation and planned drink with Maloney, jealousy wasn't an issue. She could flirt all she liked.

Melanie entered the room with two plates and a smile, which vanished as she spotted the near-empty wine bottle in the middle of the table.

"More wine, David," she snapped, and returned to the kitchen. Brooks-Powell shook his head, slowly, and strolled off in the other direction. They came back at the same time, more plates and another bottle. Claire picked up her glass the moment it was filled and took a long gulp. Anything, I supposed, to take the edge off the atmosphere. I was rather enjoying that edge. Not that I objected to Brooks-Powell's expensive wine, either.

The starter was home-made crab tortellini, and as we settled in and started eating – it was good, a lot better than quails' eggs – the edge began to fade. Brooks-Powell asked Claire about her journalism and she answered, guardedly at first, but slowly warming to her theme until the full tale of the murdered girls spilled out. I quizzed Melanie on the state of the economy and pretended to understand more than a tenth of what she said. I glanced over to Brooks-Powell as his wife was telling me about the long-term implications of the recent OPEC quota agreement, and Claire was going into fine detail on Yelena's newly-discovered background. He was nodding and frowning in all the right places, inserting questions and prompts that went beyond the usual *please, go on*. I wondered whether I was doing as good a job of feigning interest as he was.

But even murder and oil pall after a while. The conversation waned before the tortellini, and we were left with the tinkle of cutlery and the noise of a piano in the background. I hadn't noticed the music until that point; the speakers were invisible, no doubt built into the walls.

"Rachmaninov," said Melanie, as if reading my mind. "I'm a huge fan. This is Richter's famous 1959 performance of the second concerto."

The strings had swept in. I wasn't familiar with the second concerto. Or any of the other concertos, for that matter. I nodded, much as I'd been nodding at OPEC. It was interesting music. Intense. Certainly not relaxing. We had fallen silent again, the four of us, each concentrating or pretending to concentrate on what we were hearing. I picked up my fork and it occurred to me that eating now, at this moment, when the music was all, might perhaps be an unforgiveable faux pas. It also occurred to me that I didn't care.

Brooks-Powell stole my thunder. I'd been watching him, as we were listening in silence, as I'd prepared to dive back into the tortellini, no matter the consequences. He'd tuned his expression neatly into Claire's history of the dead girls, a light, interested frown gracing his brow, but now those lines had deepened and there was nothing light or interested about them.

"For Christ's sake, Melanie," he said, and then he noticed us all staring at him and hastily rearranged his features into a smile. "Rachmaninov? For dinner? Can't we have something a little lighter?"

The smile wasn't fooling any of us. Melanie's voice was tight as she replied, tight and high, as though it were on the verge of shattering.

"Certainly, dear. What would you prefer? Something we can all join in? Some musical theatre, perhaps?"

I set down my fork. Claire picked up her glass, drained it again, reached for the bottle and poured herself another. Brooks-Powell just sat there, the smile still in place, staring at his wife. This went on for fifteen, maybe twenty seconds, and then Melanie shook her head and walked over to a cabinet in the corner of the room. A moment later Rachmaninov abruptly ceased, to be replaced by the more familiar tones of Jarvis Cocker.

The remaining tortellini were consumed; the conversation resumed, Claire taking the initiative by reminiscing over her university days, listening to Pulp in pubs and clubs and not remembering any of the night before the morning after. I sensed Brooks-Powell would have a clearer memory of his own misdemeanours, but Melanie jumped whole-heartedly into the subject with a tale or two of her own. Nothing outrageous; nothing too risqué; just enough to soften her in my mind. We'd all been young once, I thought. Well, all except her husband.

I pondered on that as Melanie cleared the plates away and returned with fresh ones piled high with boeuf bourguignon that smelled of thick, meaty heaven, and Brooks-Powell disappeared in search of a "decent" red, and Claire smiled at me and dragged her fingernails across the side of my thigh. She was definitely drunk, now, and in a good mood, but it was Brooks-Powell I was thinking about. He was unhappy, I realised. Perhaps he'd always been unhappy. But this marriage – I'd been watching it for less than two hours and it didn't make for pleasant viewing. I doubted living it would be any nicer.

The food tasted as good as it smelled, and Brooks-Powell's red was more than decent, even I could tell that. But ten minutes into the main course Claire spilled a glass of it down her jumper and Melanie leapt from her table in horror, staring at her husband with a venom that suggested he had poisoned a guest rather than merely furnishing one with the means to stain a jumper.

After a minute's ineffectual dabbing, her expression changed. Mournful, now, and sympathetic; the demise of a pet, perhaps; the death knell on a promising career.

"Let me see if I've got something you can wear," she said, and the two of them disappeared from the room, leaving me alone with Brooks-Powell.

13: Locusts

WE SAT THERE, the two of us, diagonally opposite from one another, and I found myself unable to supress a smile. He was looking at his plate, but then he glanced up and saw me, and frowned, and asked me what I was grinning about.

I shrugged. There was no reason to lie.

"If anyone had told me a month ago that I'd be sitting in David Brooks-Powell's house having dinner with him, I'd have told them they were mad. And now look at us."

He gave a short laugh and lifted his glass.

"Fair point, Williams. Fair point."

He stood to top up my wine, and when he sat down again it was in his wife's place, opposite me.

"So what do you think of all this?" he asked.

It could have been anything, but I knew what he was talking about. Elizabeth Maurier. Lizzy Maurier. The past waking and swarming into the present. I remembered something about locusts; how they'd disappear, sleeping or living underground for years or even decades, and then suddenly return like a plague, all at once, in their millions. Buried, but not dead. I told Brooks-Powell, and he nodded and said "Cicadas."

"What?"

"Cicadas, not locusts. But I take your point. I tried to put it all behind me too, you know. Not just last year. But further back. The things I did. The kind of person I was. I know you won't believe me, but I'm not the same man. Haven't been for years."

He was right; I didn't believe him. But it was the closest thing to an apology I was ever likely to get from David Brooks-Powell, so I wasn't dismissing it entirely. I found myself nodding with a rueful smile, and wondering what *things* he was referring to, whether he meant me, whether he regretted it, whether it kept him awake at night. I doubted it.

But still. He was trying to be honest, and I'd had a glass or two of wine. Without warning the desire to reciprocate in some way swept through me, so fiercely and so unexpectedly that it felt as though something had happened outside my mind, as though someone had entered the room and spoken my thoughts aloud.

We were, I remembered, supposed to be working together. It was time for a leap of faith.

"Can you keep something to yourself?" I said, and he nodded, and then checked the nod. "It has to stay between us, David."

I'd said his first name without thinking, and saw his eyebrows slide upwards in ill-concealed surprise.

"Whatever it is, I have to tell my wife, Sam." He smiled. "There are no secrets between us."

I thought perhaps there should be. However their relationship worked, it didn't seem to be working well. But that was their business, and what I'd been planning on telling him was something I'd already told Claire, possibly against the instructions of DC Colman. If I couldn't trust an evil lawyer and his fund manager wife, who could I trust?

Claire and Melanie bounded into the room a moment later. Claire was still wearing the jumper, but the stain had disappeared. I stared at her, at it, at where it had been, for a full thirty seconds before the sound of giggling drew my gaze back up.

"I told you he'd be confused," said Claire.

"I had the same top," explained Melanie. I must have let my surprise show, because she laughed again and went on. "I don't always wear little black dresses, Sam."

Brooks-Powell stood and returned to his place; we finished our food – outstanding to the last forkful – and I offered to help clear up.

"Nonsense," said Brooks-Powell, and carried everything away himself. I wondered whether I ought to reassess them, David and Melanie, what with the comparatively normal clothing and the home-cooked food and David Brooks-Powell on washing-up duty. But then I remembered that edge. Perhaps they'd just had a row. Perhaps there was something deeper.

When he'd returned from the kitchen I decided it was time for that leap of faith, and told them about DI Martins' board. I told it straight, very matter-of-fact, nothing inessential, but the deaths and the wounds and the organs and the blood, they were, I thought, essential, and I'd be a liar if I didn't admit I rather enjoyed the open mouths and gasps the tale drew forth. When I finished there was a moment's silence, and then Melanie asked me to go through the words and the wounds again.

I counted them off on my fingers. *Tongue, no one will hear. Eyes, no one will see. Nose, no one will smell. Fingers, no one will touch.* Even without the photographic memory, I wouldn't be forgetting that little list. I looked back up at Melanie, expecting more shock and disgust, but instead she was frowning in thought. Claire and Brooks-Powell were silent.

"It doesn't work," said Melanie, finally, and we all turned to look at her.

"What doesn't work?" I asked.

"The words. They don't fit. Eyes, see. Nose, smell. Touch, fingers. They all go together. Eyes are the organ of sight. Nose is the organ of smell. Fingers are the organ of touch."

"Skin's the organ of touch, dear," interrupted Brooks-Powell, and his wife shook her head at him impatiently.

"Well we should be grateful he didn't skin that one, then. But fingers will do. They do *touch*, right? They feel. They're *part* of the organ."

Claire, who'd remained silent, was suddenly nodding. "Yes, yes. I see it," she said. I looked at Brooks-Powell and he looked back at me, mirroring my own blankness.

"Don't you get it?" continued Melanie, with a hint of impatience. "For *no one will hear* he should have cut off her ears."

"Or she," said David, but this time she ignored him entirely.

"Or, if the point was cutting out the tongue, he should have written *no one will taste*. I mean, that's what the tongue does, right? Taste?"

At that, I felt Claire's hand on my leg again and remembered she was drunk. I was glad all the talk of severed organs hadn't dampened her mood. Melanie was still talking.

"It's almost like he's trying to trick us. Don't you think?"

"Yes," nodded Claire, excitedly, her fingers still lightly tracing up and down my thigh. "Yes, that's it. It does feel like that." She gave a sharp and sudden squeeze and I held back a gasp. "David, would you agree?"

Brooks-Powell merely nodded, and then changed the subject entirely.

"So how was your dinner with Lizzy?" he asked, turning towards me. "I overheard her asking you, at her mother's place."

"You wouldn't have wanted to be there, believe me," I replied, and explained everything that had happened, or almost everything. That "*Put me to bed*" stayed firmly under wraps. Brooks-Powell remembered the poetry, too.

"Awful, wasn't it? I remember she made me read one of them, once. Nonsense. I've read a lot of pretentious crap in my time but her stuff took the biscuit."

I couldn't disagree.

"Thing is, that's what she's saying herself, now," I continued. "But I don't think she believes it. I think she's forcing herself to accept it because otherwise she has to admit her mother made her give up something she loved. And it's all the same thing, she has to pretend her mother's some kind of god, because if she doesn't and there's any suggestion the great Elizabeth Maurier could have been wrong about anything, then perhaps Lizzy shouldn't have given up poetry, and perhaps she shouldn't have become an academic, and perhaps she's wasted the last ten, fifteen years of her life."

Brooks-Powell nodded, then grinned and said "But she was right about the poetry."

I grinned back.

We span around the topic, Brooks-Powell and I, with Claire and Melanie silent for the most part but occasionally dropping a flash of insight into the conversation. We span carefully, though; all the leaps of faith in the world couldn't make Elizabeth Maurier and her daughter a comfortable subject for the two of us. There were too many mines to avoid. I told them about the stew and the quails' eggs, my realisation that Lizzy had never really left home, the boxes, the grief circle – that produced a guffaw from Brooks-Powell which provoked its own reproving glare from his wife. Brooks-Powell wondered aloud whether there might be something Platonic in Lizzy's relationship with her mother, whether Lizzy was nothing but the shadow Elizabeth had projected onto the wall of a cave, a blurred, insubstantial version of the real thing. I nodded sagely, as if I knew what he were talking about, and brought up Connor, the mysterious entry in the mysterious diary that no one seemed to know anything about. I owned up to taking Lizzy's files home and what I'd found while going through them, including the mysterious Dr Shapiro and our less-than-conclusive telephone call. Claire was no longer squeezing my thigh, but when I mentioned my planned visit to the man, she kicked me hard in my shin in the short silence that followed.

I took the hint, grateful she wasn't wearing heels. It seemed Claire's interpretation of good manners demanded that I invite Brooks-Powell to come with me.

"Want to come along, David?" I asked. "I'm going tomorrow morning. I doubt there'll be much coming out of it, but you never know."

Brooks-Powell looked thoughtfully at me. He didn't fancy a day stuck with Sam Williams any more than I fancied a day stuck with David Brooks-Powell, but neither of us could say it out loud. I wondered whether he'd be getting a kick too, and winced on his behalf. I'd noticed the four-inch heels on Melanie's feet when she'd first stood up.

"I'm tempted," he began, finally, and convincingly enough that I almost believed him. "But I've got enough on my plate, to be honest. Why don't you take this one and let me know if there's anything we need to follow up on?"

And there it was. A perfectly innocent comment, one I'd have made in much the same way had our positions been reversed, but my reaction was instant and visceral. Brooks-Powell was talking down to me, acting like my boss, belittling me by throwing a crumb of independence and authority my way, as if it were his to throw. He'd been like that from the start, his assumption of superiority worn so lightly than nobody other than me even seemed to notice it. And my jaw was set, my fists clenched, my mind racing with decades-old slights.

He was watching me still, and he must have noticed my expression, because he spoke again before anyone else could interrupt and asked me how Lizzy had been when I left. I waited a moment and turned over my options, and decided there was nothing to gain by being offended and even less to gain by showing it.

"Not great, to be honest. And she had this thing about the tongue, about her mother's tongue being cut out, she had the weirdest notions about it all."

I explained her theory. Her idea that it was all about her, the tongue, that everyone knew it, that we were all talking about her, about her tongue, about her silence. Lizzy Maurier at the centre of everyone else's universe.

"And the stuff she was saying, some of it you wouldn't believe. Greek myth. Shakespearean tragedy. Tereus and Philomel."

I glanced to my side and saw Claire grinning at my pronunciation. At least I'd got that right. I continued.

"And there's this tapestry – I don't know the details, but she was drunk anyway, so it probably doesn't matter. There's this tapestry that the woman weaves, Philomel, to tell her story, but Elizabeth didn't get to weave her tapestry, that's what Lizzy thinks, when she's not thinking that it's *her* tapestry and *her* tongue. So that's our job, David. Weaving Elizabeth Maurier's tapestry. You any good at weaving?"

Brooks-Powell was nodding at me, slowly, the considered slow nod of the man with weighty things on his mind, but I could see a hint of a smile, too. He knew I'd been angry – he might not have known why, but he'd seen the anger all right – and he knew I'd pulled back and saved us both an embarrassing scene.

"It's an interesting notion," said Melanie, leaning back on her chair and staring at the ceiling. "I mean, this tongue thing. If it weren't for all the other victims and the other body parts, I'd almost be inclined to go along with it. The transformation myth. Procne, Philomel, the nightingale. The severing of a tongue is such a resonant gesture, isn't it? I mean, if you know the stories, you can't do something like that without recalling them." She looked back down, at three faces turned towards her wearing expressions of surprise shading into horror. "Not speaking from experience, of course," she concluded, with a smile.

"I suppose," added Brooks-Powell, "she's decided she's the one who gets baked in a pie, too. When she's not having her own tongue cut off. What a mess."

So Brooks-Powell knew it, too. And Melanie. And Claire, of course. The Shakespeare and the Ovid and the rest of it. They'd all been to the *right school*, I thought, and felt my face go tight again.

"I'll tell you what's wrong with that girl." Brooks-Powell was still talking, eyes not on me and my angry jaw but on Claire, who was smiling back at him. "She's repressed. That's all it is. Totally repressed."

His wife snorted. I didn't blame her. *Repressed* was a little facile for David Brooks-Powell, and whatever else his faults, being facile wasn't one of them. A brief silence fell, another in an evening too often punctuated by them, but Claire's smile hadn't dropped a fraction. Behind that smile, drunk as she was, I thought I could see her thinking.

"Have you told David about Trawden?" she asked, brightly and without warning, and the three of them leaned forward, grateful for the change of subject.

"He called me yesterday. Asked me to meet him. So I did. Lunch. With him and Lord Blennard. At the Reform Club."

I was watching Brooks-Powell as I spoke, scrutinising his face for the slightest reaction. All he did was nod.

"Charlie?" he said, still nodding. "How is the old fellow."

Of course he knew Blennard. They'd probably buggered each other behind the quad. I felt myself sinking, the alcohol and the anger and – I couldn't deny it, not to myself – the jealousy, sinking to a point where I'd say something I couldn't take back. I tried to haul myself back up. So what if he knew Blennard? He'd been at Mauriers a lot longer than I had; Blennard had been a close friend of Elizabeth's. It would have been strange if they hadn't met.

As if reading my mind, he continued before I could say anything.

"I've met him from time to time. With Elizabeth, of course. Never took me to the Reform, mind. Just the pub, or her office. Smart fellow."

"He's got a brain all right," I replied. A smile flew across Brooks-Powell's face, there and gone again. I'd dragged myself back up again. This time, he'd helped. "The food was good, too. Thing is, I wasn't really sure what they wanted. Blennard offered to help. I wouldn't mind his help, but I don't know what he's planning on helping with."

"What about Trawden?" asked Brooks-Powell, and his wife shuddered beside him.

"Never liked him. Not that I've met him, of course," she said, "but what I've read. What I've seen on TV. You can be not guilty of murder and still be a frightening, horrible man."

Brooks-Powell gave a short low laugh. "My fault, I'm afraid. I really couldn't stand the man. Didn't trust him. Seems I've infected the wife."

I remembered his dislike of Trawden. I remembered him passing me in the office, asking how I was getting on with my child-killer, strolling jauntily off before I had the chance to compose a suitable riposte.

"Yes," I said, and considered whether I should go on. Claire was still smiling at Brooks-Powell. I went on. "Yes. I thought that was just jealousy. You know, because you didn't get the case."

He laughed, again, this time louder and longer, and I wondered if I'd been too direct, but when he spoke the words were fair and reasonable and the voice much the same.

"You're right. I was jealous. Biggest thing Mauriers had done for years, and everyone wanting to carry Elizabeth's bags. We were all after that case, you, me, Alison, even

Elana. Remember Alison and Elana?"

I hadn't. I did now. It hadn't just been me and Brooks-Powell, back at the beginning. There were four of us, all starting at Mauriers in the same month or two. Had they still been there when I left? I tried to picture them. Alison, a giant of a woman, an athlete, a university hockey player and a beer-drinker and a laugh like a horse. Elana I could hardly see. Small and dark and quiet. You're supposed to look out for the quiet ones, but I never had.

"So yes. I hated the bastard, because you were working on his case and I wasn't. Doesn't mean I wasn't right," concluded Brooks-Powell, and fixed me with a glare. But underneath the glare, he was smiling.

"I think you probably were," I said, and there was another silence, but an easier one.

"It was difficult, wasn't it?" he asked, eventually. Melanie had stepped outside to *take a look at dessert*, whatever that meant, and Claire was busy with her wine.

"What was?"

"Being open. Back then," he replied. "Being honest." Melanie had come back, and Brooks-Powell stared at her as she took her seat. "I mean, let's just say mistakes were made, right? Everybody makes mistakes. You just have to live with them. You just have to try to get on."

Melanie was pouring herself a glass of wine and politely ignoring us, but he hadn't taken his eyes off her as he spoke. I understood why. If he was going to bare his soul, or the closest thing he had to one, if he was going to take another step towards an apology, then he wouldn't be wanting to look into the eyes of the man he'd wronged. I'd have done the same, in his place, if I'd had the guts to do the baring at all.

"Enough of the serious stuff," said Melanie, suddenly. "Apple crumble, anyone?"

We didn't leave for another three hours, during which the *serious stuff* faded into the background and the silences faded with them, or if they were there, we were too drunk to notice. For all the high finance and Rachmaninov, Melanie Golding was entertaining, a well of amusing anecdotes, in most of which she came off worst. Brooks-Powell – I was struggling to think of him as David, but managed to say it from time to time – was a decent host, liberal with the wine and the spirits, delicately guiding his guests back to the conversation when it seemed we might be flagging, not above sharing an embarrassing story of his own, to my surprise. Claire, of course, was full of embarrassing stories and rarely shied away from telling them. The only one who didn't was me, but the last ten years of my life had been one long embarrassing story and there wasn't much in it to laugh about. So I contented myself with laughing at the others, which they didn't seem to mind, and then suddenly Claire was whispering something in my ear about a taxi and it was half past one and we were saying goodbye, and before the door closed on them I was kissing Melanie on the cheek and shaking Brooks-Powell's hand and saying "Thank you" and *meaning it.*

In the taxi, with the quiet murmur of the radio and the lights of London sailing by, I wondered whether Claire was still in the thigh-stroking mood. I put my arm around her and drew her towards me. She looked up and smiled, and as I prepared to kiss her she said "She was right, you know."

I stopped myself. "Right about what?"

"About misdirection. The victims. *No one will hear* and *see* and *touch* and whatever the hell they won't do, because they're dead now and they're not likely to do much of anything at all. But she's right. There's a difference with the Maurier one. It feels wrong. It's like –" she paused, her face creased with concentration. The mood, I realised, had shifted decisively. I waited.

"Did you ever read *The ABC Murders*?" she asked.

I shook my head. I'd never even heard of *The ABC Murders*.

"Another Agatha Christie. Not *Pocket Full of Rye* this time. There's a bunch of murders. And they're all linked. Only it turns out they're not. There's just one important murder. The others are only there to hide it. It's like hiding a tree. Where do you hide a tree?"

"I don't know. Where do you hide a tree?"

"In a wood."

My mind was moving slowly, but I thought I could grasp what she was driving towards.

"So," I said, "so you're telling me someone murdered Elizabeth Maurier and then murdered a bunch of other people just to throw the police off track?"

She nodded, and then shook her head and laughed.

"I'm being ridiculous, aren't I? It doesn't sound very likely. But your friend David's a tricky one, isn't he?"

Another sharp turn. Drink, I remembered, did that with Claire. She'd run with an idea until she had another one.

"I suppose so." I didn't know where this idea would lead. I wasn't sure I wanted to find out, handshake or no handshake.

"You do realise he's gay, don't you?"

Of all the things I might have been expecting, that wasn't even on the list. I couldn't think of a decent reply, instead stammering out "But he's married!" in, I realised, a somewhat affronted tone of voice.

"Like that means anything. Of course he's gay. Remember Melanie took me upstairs, to get the jumper – oh that reminds me, I left mine there, I was going to get it washed and return hers, we'll have to sort that out some other time. Anyway, I went upstairs and they've got separate bedrooms."

"That doesn't mean anything either," I said, my composure part way to recovery. "Couples do that. Sometimes," I added, in case Claire decided it might be a good idea.

"Yes, but remember what she said about musical theatre?"

It rang a bell. I thought back. The start of dinner. The sharp little exchange about Rachmaninov. Yes.

"And there was something else," she continued. "At the end of the meal. He was talking about the past, and making mistakes, and just having to live with them. He was looking at her the whole time. He was talking about *them*, about their marriage, how it had all been one big mistake but they had to live with it. It was like we'd walked in halfway through someone else's private conversation. He was apologising and admitting it and begging her not to leave him, that's what he was doing."

I smiled at her and shook my head. Sometimes I wondered whether Claire might have a little too much imagination for a journalist. She looked up at me, a frown spreading across her face as she registered the expression on mine.

"Sorry, Claire. It's a great idea, but it's not right. He was looking at her because he didn't want to look at me, and the reason he didn't want to look at me was that it was me he was apologising to."

The frown flipped into confusion, followed by incredulity.

"What?"

"All that stuff. Mauriers. When you went upstairs to get changed he came halfway to saying he was sorry. That little scene at the end of dinner, that was three-quarters."

"Are you serious?"

"Why shouldn't I be?"

"So you're going to ignore the separate bedrooms and

all that niggling between them when we arrived, *he's useless* and *aren't you going to get drinks*, and the Rachmaninov stuff, that's all just coincidence, is it?"

I shook my head again, realising even while I did it how patronising I must have looked. But I couldn't stop myself.

"No. It's not coincidence. They'd had a row. Couples have rows. We're having one now. Doesn't mean I'm gay."

"So it all has to be about you, does it?"

Now it was my turn for confusion. I ran through what she'd said and started to form the words to my reply, but I didn't get past opening my mouth before she went on.

"You really are a selfish bastard, Sam. Whatever's going on, whatever the problem is, it's always about you. You don't listen, you don't notice things, you don't see what's happening to other people even when it's happening right in front of you. It's always just the biggest noise, the loudest shout, the hottest case, and what the effect might be on you. What was it you told me? *Don't get too close?* Fucking hell, Sam. You can't even get outside your own head." She'd built up the volume, but now she sighed and spoke quietly. "It might come as some surprise to you, but there is a world outside Sam bloody Williams. Quite a big one, as it happens. If you spoke to Adrian you'd understand."

For a moment I wondered what she was talking about, how she'd got from Brooks-Powell being gay to this, how she'd managed to drag her wretched *life coach* into a conversation about dinner, and then it clicked.

Serena Hawkes. She was bringing up Serena, again. The lawyer in Manchester. The woman I'd spent hours each day with, the woman who'd sat in my car and poured her soul out to me, the woman who'd sat opposite me over a chicken jalfrezi and all but told me the truth.

And I hadn't seen it. *Right in front of me*, as Claire put it, and I hadn't seen it at all. I hadn't seen it, and Serena had blown the back of her head out right in front of me, and I didn't need Claire reminding me of the fact every time she wanted to hurt me. I was more than capable of reminding myself.

"That's not exactly fair," I began, reasonably enough, I thought, but Claire ignored me, leaned forward and asked the driver to turn the radio up. The news report had just begun. Murder all over the country, economic turmoil all over the world, court hearings, witnesses and deals, elections in places the powerful didn't care about, wars in places they did. And Serena Hawkes had died and I hadn't seen it coming.

We arrived back at the flat ten minutes later, as the preview of the weekend's football began. I unlocked the front door and shook my head, unseen, as Claire pushed past me and straight into the bathroom. I sighed, unheard, as she locked it behind her. I undressed and stared at the ceiling until she fell into bed beside me in her pyjamas and turned onto her side, her back towards me, breathing slow and deep and far too even for sleep. I began to drift, images of the evening tumbling through my brain, images of Serena Hawkes, handy-sized portraits of corpses in pools of their own blood. Words flew in and around the images, birds on the wing, words like *Tongue* and *Ovid* and *Poem* and *Misdirection*, phrases like *Right in front of you* and *It was difficult* and *Put me to bed* and *Her mother's shadow*, and as the images began to blur and the words began to run together, I saw it.

No one will hear.

Elizabeth Maurier had died leaving something unsaid.

14: A Nice Drive in the Country

I WOKE BEFORE six. Claire lay beside me, still on her side, still facing away, still sleeping. My head was clear; despite the late night and all the wine, there was no pain, just a gentle thirst and a more urgent need to relieve myself.

I visited the toilet and made myself a coffee and listened to the cats fighting outside and the early vans and lorries dragging the city into the light.

Elizabeth Maurier had died leaving something unsaid.

I wondered whether it was too early to call Brooks-Powell or Lizzy. I wondered whether I should call them at all and decided probably not. It was a hunch. An idea, insubstantial enough to walk through and not even notice you were doing it. If it firmed up, I'd make the calls. If it didn't, I'd watch it dissolve into nothing and no one else would ever know.

Six o'clock. I sat down with the Maurier files and flicked through them once more, hoping to stumble across an answer that had eluded me the first three times, but the only thing that stood out was her strange dream and its teasing little accompaniment.

I do feel a little guilty about ignoring Dr Shapiro.

Half past six, and Claire stumbled from the bedroom in those winceyette pyjamas, stretched and threw a forlorn little smile my way.

"I'm sorry," I said. "Did I wake you? I'll get you a coffee."

She ignored my question, took the coffee in silence and turned the television onto the news channel. Maureen Davies was anchoring. The Welsh one with the unconvincingly blonde hair. An American economist called Pauline Adams tried to predict the future course of global interest rates. Sergeant Paul Jenson of the Metropolitan Police Immigration Enforcement Liaison Unit explained the scope of the British role in preventing illegal mass migration in the Mediterranean. An angry woman named Bernadette wanted to let everyone know that the countryside was dying and it was the Government's fault. After a while Claire picked up the remote control and muted the volume, but she didn't get up or do anything. She sat there, cradling her cup and staring at the screen, until I reminded her that I'd be driving to Norfolk later and asked if she felt like coming with.

"Forecast is decent," I said. "Sunshine. Nice weather for a drive in the country, I thought."

She shook her head.

"I don't think so. Think I'll just stay here and sit tight."

"Right, then. Think I'll get ready and head out."

She smiled at me and turned back to the television. That was it. A second's worth of smile. I wondered what I needed to do to get her attention. I could strip off all my clothes and stand in front of her until she noticed me, but that coffee was still hot. I could tell her about my last-minute flash of insight into Elizabeth Maurier, but I had the feeling she'd heard enough about the Mauriers for a lifetime. I could say something nice about Adrian Chalmers, but then I'd have to spend the rest of the day washing my mouth.

I checked the clock on the oven. Not yet seven. The darkness was shading towards grey; even on a day that promised sunshine, not much of that would reach our particular street, with a London smog blunting any rays that made it past the high-rises. Dr Shapiro and I had agreed on Saturday morning, and we hadn't specified a time, but whatever Norfolk was like today it couldn't be much worse than this. Google was telling me two hours thirty for the drive. I took a quick shower and threw on jeans and a sweater that had once been black, but had faded over the years until it resembled the scene outside the bedroom window. Claire wasn't coming. Claire was hardly speaking. She offered her cheek as I went to kiss her goodbye, murmured "Drive carefully," and turned back to the television, which was now running trailers for the evening's big shows. By twenty past seven, I was on the road.

He was behind me before I'd hit the end of the street, pulling out between two cars and edging closer until he was no more than four feet away. The road was wet – it had rained overnight – and I thought briefly about slamming on the brakes and seeing what happened to that little green bike and the asshole riding it. And then I remembered where I was going and thought it might be better just to waste his time.

He stuck close for three miles but started to slip back after that. It must have been clear I was heading out of London by then. He gave up after four miles, veering to the side of the road and disappearing from my rear-view mirror as I turned a corner. I supposed he'd figured it out. A bike like that had a tank so small you could fill it with one good piss. Wherever I was going, he'd have to fill up on the way, and I wouldn't be waiting for him to catch up and follow.

The Fiat was still in good order, after all the miles and hurt I'd put it through, and the roads were mercifully quiet. London still hadn't fully woken, its workers sleeping off the excesses of the office Christmas parties or gathering their strength for a Saturday on the High Street. As I hit the heart of the suburbs the light gained in strength, and by the time the first big patches of green began to appear the sun was blinding me every time the road bent east. I wondered how far Hanover's bike could get on one tank. He'd made it to Mayfair without stopping. He'd made it all the way to Brooks-Powell's place in Kensington and Lizzy's flat in Notting Hill. London was probably in range, all of it, within reason. Norfolk would be a whole lot of steps too far.

Something occurred to me, and then floated out of reach before I could catch it. I was tired. Whatever it was, it would come back later.

I skirted Cambridge and Ely and slowed as I approached King's Lynn. Dr Shapiro's home wasn't far from here, he'd said, overlooking the Wash. I took a right through villages that still didn't seem to have woken, even though it was well past nine, and eventually the line of brilliant blue to my left grew and separated itself from the sky until it became the clear and unambiguous sea.

Dr Shapiro lived in a village called Holme, a few minutes past Hunstanton, which I'd heard of, even if I couldn't remember when or why. Desolate windswept dunes occupied the few hundred yards between his cottage and the sea. Despite the wind and the cold, I found him sitting in his garden drinking tea, beckoning me on as if it weren't quarter to ten on a December morning and we weren't within spitting distance of the North Sea.

But the garden was sheltered, hedges cleverly set so as to soften the worst of the wind whilst still permitting a decent view. Dr Shapiro had left his French windows open, so I had a clear line of sight into the uncluttered kitchen of what looked like a good-sized fisherman's cottage built of flint and sandstone. And Dr Shapiro himself was bigger than I'd expected, too, a broad welcoming smile, an ample figure perched carefully on a small garden chair.

I shook his hand and exchanged pleasantries, and sat down opposite him while he poured tea and asked me how the journey had been. I complimented him on the view, and he thanked me, and then, without much by way of preamble, he said "I suppose you want to talk to me about Edward Trawden."

I must have betrayed my surprise, because he smiled broadly again, and explained that Trawden had been his connection to Elizabeth Maurier, "May she rest in peace."

I hadn't known that, but then, Shapiro hadn't really given me much opportunity to ask when we'd spoken on the phone. As if sensing my thoughts, he shrugged apologetically.

"My wife died last year. I do like a little company. And truly, I find explaining things on the telephone rather trying. I prefer to speak face to face. You can see so much more. You can see when to stop, when to go back, when to go on. On the phone, it's all silences and missed signals and bad interpretations. I like a face."

"That's fine," I said. I remembered those silences from our call earlier in the week. "It's a pleasure to be out of London." And I meant it.

"So. Edward Trawden. I did tell Mrs Maurier, you know. All those years ago. And I remember your name, Mr Williams."

"Sam. Call me Sam. Only the police call me Mr Williams."

"Sam it is," he replied, smiling. "Quite brilliant, they said you were. Of course by then I was already on my way out. They forced me out, eventually – you know about that, I presume?"

I nodded. He went on.

"But even if they hadn't I don't think I'd have gone on much longer. I was out of touch. I don't mean *they said I was out of touch*, I mean I really was. These things move on. The brain may be ancient but its study is young."

"They say much the same about law," I said, and he smiled at the interruption.

"Yes, I suppose you're right. The old order changeth, yielding place to new. There were fishermen living here, once, in this very house. There haven't been fishermen in this village for decades." He stopped, turned, gazed at the sea and didn't stop gazing at it until I cleared my throat, and then he jerked around, remembering, suddenly, that he wasn't alone. "But where was I?" he asked. "Oh yes. Trawden. Interesting man, that's for certain. Probably the most fascinating case I had the privilege to work on. Not that any good came of it."

"So when did you work on Trawden? I don't recall your name on the original case files."

"No." He shook his head, emphatically. "No, the trial work was all done by Michael Slater, but he retired soon after, so when it came to parole hearings and the like, they turned to me. I had to examine him, to see if he was fit to be returned to society, but there was never really any prospect of Trawden making parole. Those examinations were a waste of time, in that sense, but they do like to make sure every box is ticked before they say no."

I nodded at that. Shapiro went on.

"And the thing was, he was a fascinating man, quite possibly a genius, and he didn't mind talking to me, so I made a point of speaking with him whenever I found myself in the same prison."

"Belmarsh?"

"Well, Broadmoor first. The hospital. By their standards he was the very picture of normality. After he was discharged he spent some time in Wakefield before he was transferred to Belmarsh."

It sounded like Shapiro had followed Trawden's prison career closely, and I wondered why his notes had been absent from the appeal papers.

"And Elizabeth Maurier?"

"Ah, well, that's the thing. I'd come across Mrs Maurier once or twice before, and I had enormous respect for her ability. So when I heard she'd taken on the appeal, I thought it would be a good idea to speak with her, to share my findings. I visited her at her house in the Cotswolds."

A series of images flashed through my mind again. The

house. Elizabeth, welcoming and gracious. Black-coated waiters with canapés and champagne. The gardens on a clear and moonlit night.

"And I told her everything I knew about the man," he continued. "I suppose I wondered why I was never called to testify at the trial, but it wouldn't have made any difference in the end. It was all about the actual evidence, wasn't it? All about that Evans chap. The hard facts."

I nodded. I was the one who'd found those facts. After that, it wouldn't have mattered if Trawden had confessed right there in the courtroom. He was always walking. I drank the last of my tea and shivered – the wind had grown in strength, cutting through the hedges and my coat and my skin right into my bones. Shapiro noticed the shiver and stood.

"Let's go inside," he said. "The fire's lit."

Behind the kitchen was a snug, furnished with two deep leather armchairs, wood on the floor, a thick red rug on the wood, and the promised fire smouldering gently in a small iron stove. The world was entirely absent; we could have been anywhere; it could have been night time outside.

Once we were settled and Shapiro had added a little coal to the fire, he continued with his narrative.

"Edward Trawden, as I mentioned, was a truly fascinating case. Putting aside his innocence of the crime for which he was convicted, Trawden is a master of control. He can filter noise and create it, he can manipulate the cleverest of people, people who think their actions are entirely their own, people who think their thoughts are entirely their own. And he's a chameleon, too. He can be whatever you want him to be, whatever works at the time."

I thought back to the Reform Club, to his awkwardness after Blennard had left, and the sense I'd had, later, that the awkwardness might not have been his after all. Shapiro went on.

"To him, the world is divided into useful idiots and enablers and victims – those were his terms, by the way," he added, noticing my sceptical frown, "and by 'victims' I refer not to the poor Grimshaw girl, who was of course murdered by Evans, but to those individuals who may actually see what Trawden is doing but are powerless to prevent it."

"But how would he do that? I understand what you're saying about manipulation, but how could he force people to do what he wants when they're aware of it?"

Shapiro shrugged. "Allies help, of course. The useful idiots and the enablers. Information, too."

I pondered that for a moment, before I realised what he meant.

"Blackmail?"

"Not that I have anything concrete, you understand. Not that he ever actually said it, in so many words. But that was certainly the impression I got from the man."

I sat back in my chair and Shapiro followed suit, each of us looking into nothing, thinking and remembering. None of this mattered, of course. Trawden was a conspiracy theorist's dream, at first the darling of those, like Blennard and Elizabeth Maurier, who were always looking for the innocent abused; subsequently an obsession of those who claimed he had been the murderer all along and sought to redeem Evans from the charge. Evans was dead by then, though, and they were wrong. I'd seen the evidence. There were no shades of grey. Evans had been there, Evans had killed Maxine Grimshaw, and nothing Shapiro could tell me about Trawden would change that.

"He was, I suppose, a megalomaniac," he said, softly, still gazing straight ahead. "Better than everyone else. Above them. Do you recall his background?"

He'd turned to face me, and I shook my head. I'd never delved into Trawden's past; Elizabeth had insisted it was irrelevant, and she'd been right.

"Grammar school, then Oxford," he said, and I found myself raising an eyebrow. My own path from childhood. A very different outcome. "But he didn't last long at Oxford. Too clever to do any actual work, so they kicked him out after the first year. So sure of himself, so sure he knew what everyone else was thinking. And curiously, that was his weakness. He could not, for the life of him, comprehend the notion of a breaking point; that the individual human being, in situations of extreme emotion or danger, happiness, fear or grief, might not act in the way the rational human being is supposed to act. I admit I was fascinated by this. I even created games to play with him, to explore it further. Games of *if* and *if* and *if*, and then what. And he never managed to get beyond the input. Never allowed anything to derail the logical progression, however extreme the circumstances."

"I'm not sure I follow you," I said, because Shapiro seemed to have wandered into abstract thought, and I was floundering in a sea of concepts and semi-meaningful words.

"I'll give you an example, then. I posited a kidnapping. A child is taken, the parent is warned to say nothing, or the child will be harmed. 'What will the parent do?' I asked Trawden, and his response, once he'd made it clear that he was not a kidnapper and that anything he had to say on the matter was purely theoretical, was to ask me 'Does the parent like the child?' I assured him that yes, the parent did like the child, and he informed me with some certainty that the parent would remain silent."

"That doesn't sound unreasonable," I pointed out.

Shapiro smiled grimly and nodded. "And it isn't," he replied. "But that was just the starting point. The silence. After the silence there are the deeds. Money, to begin with: the parent has to pay a large sum to the kidnapper, and

Trawden asks the same question, 'Does the parent like the child?', and I give him the same answer, 'Yes', and the parent, of course, does precisely what the kidnapper asks. Again, not unreasonable. And then the parent has to steal the money from a stranger. Same question, same answer, same conclusion. The parent has to steal the money from a friend, a relation, a spouse. Same question, same answer, same conclusion. The parent has to hurt an adult stranger. The parent has to hurt a child. The parent has to kill. On it goes. 'Does the parent like the child?' 'The parent likes the child.' 'The parent will do as the kidnapper requests.' No doubt in his mind, no hesitation. At the final stage the parent has to abduct and murder another child, not a stranger, the son or daughter of a friend or a loved one, and the questions and answers come like clockwork."

Shapiro sat back and watched me as I took it all in. A hideous, inevitable progression, a trail from silence to murder, with Trawden apparently unaware of the gulf that separated them. He waited a moment, but I had nothing to say. An interesting insight into an unusual mind. Nothing more. He continued.

"He simply could not conceive of that breaking point. It was all just switches, just circuits, logic gates at each decision point, no doubt in his mind that the current would keep on flowing, that the fuses would never blow. And that's ironic, in a way. Because Trawden himself does have that fuse. His own circuit isn't quite so straightforward."

I sat forward, suddenly intrigued, and Shapiro smiled at my belated show of interest.

"The way I analysed it, Trawden was – is, no doubt, because it's not like these things are likely to fade away – a sociopath. An extremely clever sociopath. To his way of thinking, he is so far above the rest of mankind that we are little more than insects. It's a mania. And when the mania is at its strongest, he reacts in ways that even he might later regret. For instance. In the kidnapper game, he would answer as the parent, as I've described. But from time to time he would switch. He would play the part of the kidnapper. He would describe unimaginable things, the torments he would inflict on his victims, and he would do it with a smile. And then he would stop, suddenly, and the smile would fade, he would bury his face in his hands for a moment, and when he came back up the smile would be back, and he'd be telling me it was all nonsense, and he'd been merely teasing me. But he hadn't been. He'd gone too far. He'd trusted too much in his own invulnerability, and realised it too late."

"That's definitely interesting," I told him, and it was, but only academically. I wondered now whether that had been Elizabeth's interest, an abstract, theoretical one, nothing to do with the reality of crime and prison and exoneration. And Shapiro was no fool. He knew precisely what I was thinking.

"You're right, Mr Williams. It's fascinating, but that's as far as it goes. Back then, of course, he was a convicted murderer, and I assumed that his mania had played a part in that murder. He'd killed the girl because he could, because it didn't matter, she didn't matter, he could do whatever he wanted and never face the consequences. A calculated action, not a random crime of passion, but calculated on assumptions based within his mania. And later, of course, he'd realised he'd gone too far, possibly he'd even regretted it, but it was too late. That's what I thought, and I was wrong, because it was Evans, and you proved it."

I opened my mouth to object, although there was little to object with, but he held up a hand to forestall me.

"It's perfectly fine, Mr Williams. I was wrong. Even the most brilliant can be wrong, and I can assure you, I've never made the mistake of considering myself brilliant. And Mrs

Maurier knew. She listened to me, with that same look you're wearing now, and told me my ideas were certainly *fascinating* and that there might even be an element of truth in them, but that the mind and the law were two very different things and as sure as I might be that Trawden was mad, she was equally sure he was innocent. And in the end, she was right."

He stopped, finally, eyes still fixed on me as they had been throughout his long speech. And then he smiled, again, and apologised for dragging me all the way from London to listen to an old man's reminiscences, and offered me more tea, or perhaps something a little stiffer, but I was about to start on a long drive and suddenly anxious to be home and see Claire. I bade him farewell, and ten minutes later I was on the road.

I'd wasted my time, and the clouds had begun to mass while we were inside. Dr Shapiro might have been brilliant once, for all he said he wasn't. But now he was an old man with nothing to do but dwell on the past. The sun seemed to burn through the clouds every time the road veered towards it, the mirror image of my drive earlier that morning, and I stopped in a layby a few miles north of Ely to rest my eyes.

I pulled out my phone to check for voicemails, but there was no signal. Instead, there was something else, something in my head. An idea, that notion that had come to me earlier and faded before I could get hold of it.

Rich Hanover had followed me halfway out of London, earlier. Before that, he'd followed me to the Reform Club. But outside Lizzy's, outside Brooks-Powell's – he'd been waiting for me there.

I closed my eyes and saw him, in the café down the street from Martins' station. I saw him watching me, and I knew. I smiled to myself and opened the door.

There was a hint of a hill or two here, and I left the car

in the layby with the occasional lorry blasting by, and set off on foot, following a footpath veering gently upwards and disappearing into a copse that blocked any further view. It had been warm in Shapiro's snug when we'd entered, stifling by the time I left, and I'd jumped straight into the car with hot air blasting the windows to wipe away the mist. I wanted to see Claire – her apathy was nudging at me more than it had done this morning – but I needed cold fresh air more.

The path was surprisingly steep, and I was panting by the time I reached the first of the trees. What had promised to be a shady grove proved little more than a handful of stunted oak and dogwood, huddled at the top of the slope. I glanced behind me – the road was hidden by the contour of the hill – and walked on through the trees.

The wood was over almost before it began, and as I cleared the final oak the land dropped away before me and a vast plain appeared. Field after field, every shade of green and brown, flat as far as the eye could see. A village or two, spires scattered among the fields; a town in the distance, a grey blur squatting on the earth.

The view could hardly have been more different, but I found myself thinking, again, about Elizabeth Maurier's country house. I'd made a habit, when I was driving there alone, which I usually was, of stopping on the way, heading off the main road at Burford and driving deep into the Cotswolds. I'd drive for ten minutes, twenty, once as long as half an hour, and find a spot, stop, and walk until I could no longer see the road.

It wasn't like I was even that keen on walking, or the countryside. But something about those drives and that destination compelled me to stop and get out of the car and push my feet against something softer than tarmac and less forgiving than carpet. There was one particular spot I'd frequented several times – not by design, because I couldn't have found it on a map if I'd tried to. But I'd driven until the perfect location presented itself, the site most suited to my mood, a layby for the car and some decent trees to wander into, a hill just steep enough to obscure the road but not steep enough to leave me tired and stained with sweat. I'd climb that hill, and stop, and a feeling would come over me that try as I might I could never explain. Everything, suddenly, had made sense. Everything could fit into my mind, at once, my car and my shirt and my job and my flat, Elizabeth Maurier and David Brooks-Powell and whichever girl I happened to be seeing at the time, my friends and my family, my hunger or thirst, my past and my future, all those things that took a lifetime to see and more than that to comprehend, they were all there, clear and tangible in the glow of the beech leaves and the slow descent of the willow.

For a moment, looking out at the East Anglian flats, I remembered it again. I didn't feel it; I didn't even come close. But I remembered it. I hadn't thought about those drives for a long time, hadn't been near the Cotswolds in years. A different place, different trees, but the same silence broken by the same wind. I'd forgotten that feeling.

I stood looking into the brown and green until a cloud passed overhead and I realised that it was the middle of December and I was standing on top of a hill. I'd left my coat in the car. I trotted back through the trees and down the slope to the road to London.

15: A Lonely Death

THE FLAT WAS empty when I returned. I drove round the block twice before I parked, but there was no sign of Hanover. I'd left Shapiro's house at eleven and made it back for half past one, hoping I'd be able to get something out of Claire. I didn't really care what that something was, anything from a fuck to a fight would do. But even as I turned the key in the lock I could tell there was no one behind it.

There was no note, either. Not, I reminded myself, that there was any rule saying she had to leave one. Claire was a big girl. She could go where she wanted. She didn't have to tell me. But I couldn't shake the feeling something was badly wrong, something more than just her and her story, more than just me and her mother. Maybe she was right. Maybe I was so self-absorbed I couldn't see anything that didn't hit me directly. Maybe Serena Hawkes wasn't just bad luck. And if that was the case, could I blame Claire if she was sick of being hooked up to a man so obsessed with his own little world that you had to shoot yourself in the head just to get him to see things your way?

There were no voicemails on my mobile, but the answerphone on the landline was flashing. I pressed play and heard, for the first time, the voice of Adrian, the *life coach*. He was asking whether Claire was OK. He hadn't heard from her in a while. There was something about that voice I didn't like, something I'd almost expected, a hint of grease, a drop of oil smothering the words. Someone like that could say anything and it would always sound the same. My index finger hovered over the delete button, but in the end I withdrew it and dialled Claire's mobile number instead. It went straight through to voicemail. I killed the call before the beep came. I wanted to leave a message, I wanted to say something, but I couldn't think of the right words.

So instead I sat down on the sofa with the files I'd plundered from Lizzy's study on the table in front of me, and tried to work out if anything Shapiro had told me could shed any light on Elizabeth Maurier's dream.

I stopped after twenty seconds. It was too obvious. Shapiro had thought of Trawden as a master of manipulation; in her dream, someone had been pulling Elizabeth Maurier's strings. And not pulling them figuratively. If Trawden was the faceless man, then where had he drawn her to? Had he drawn her at all? Had the idea merely been planted in her mind by Shapiro's warning, a set of ideas no more grounded in reality than Trawden's conviction had been, waiting to be recalled in a moment of vulnerability? Awake, Elizabeth would have given little credence to any of it. *I do feel a little guilty about ignoring Dr Shapiro.* Nothing more than that. She'd ignored him, recalled him, and continued to ignore him. She had the facts at her disposal. Evans was the killer.

Elizabeth Maurier was dead and Trawden himself had spent so much time under the microscope there wasn't a part of him that hadn't been identified, labelled and filed away. I turned my attention to the others. Evans had been killed in prison, stabbed with a makeshift knife in the showers by another prisoner who'd decided that Evans' particular crimes rendered him unfit to breathe the same air as the rest of them. Evans' own killer was hardly a model citizen himself – it wasn't easy to find a model citizen in Pentonville – but in the hierarchy of evil, the murder of a child trumped a gangland killing.

And Evans wasn't particularly interesting, either. A Welsh paedophile with one death under his belt before he'd popped up in Trawden's life, the only thing that had brought him to our attention was his claim to have murdered Maxine Grimshaw, a claim no one bar his cellmate had ever heard him make.

I recalled the cellmate. Hussein Akadi. A vile little man who was serving his own time for manslaughter. The man he'd killed had been his best friend, he'd insisted at his trial. He'd grabbed the knife in self-defence, never intended to do more than frighten. The jury bought the best friend line, but not the self-defence; there were drugs involved, after all. With Akadi there had always been drugs involved. I'd never liked to make snap judgments on people, because when I did the wrong things tended to get snapped up. But in Akadi's case, those tiny shrewd eyes and that horrible, ingratiating smile, it was difficult not to. The man he'd killed might well have been his best friend. I doubted Akadi would have cared.

It had been Akadi's repetition of Evans' claim, a few weeks after the Welshman's own demise, that had reopened the Grimshaw investigation. It had snapped shut again when it looked like Evans had been a hundred miles away from Warrington on the day of the murder, and it had taken my own diligent investigation of the facts to prise it wide enough for Trawden to crawl to freedom. Akadi, I realised, would be out by now, would have been out for a few years if he hadn't done something stupid, and I didn't see Akadi as the type to do anything stupid. He hadn't been enjoying his time inside. Once out, he'd have wanted to stay there.

I opened up my laptop and clicked on the browser, realising as I began to search that I was logged in as Claire. She must have been using my laptop. Hers temperamental these days, slow and bad-tempered, prone to shut down without warning. She'd been looking for answers around words like *trial* and *witness*, and it hit me that she hadn't given up on her girls entirely, and that not giving up was fine. Work was fine. It was obsession that wasn't. I wondered, briefly, whether that might apply to me, too, and then I shook my head and typed in *Hussein Akadi*. I narrowed the search with *Trawden* when half a million hits came up, and filtered again for English language. The first few items were news stories from back in 2005, the BBC and a couple of the national dailies. There was nothing new there – I'd read all these at the time, anyway – but I flicked through them anyway in the hope of finding my own name. I did, eventually, a "Ms. Maurier, assisted by Sam Williams" buried deep in the penultimate rambling paragraph of a poorly written *Warrington Gazette* feature from the week after the trial. I shut down the page and moved onto the next.

The next was an article from Maurier's own website, again from 2005, which gave me a little more prominence, but still, I felt, not quite enough. I hadn't really noticed any of this at the time. I'd been content to bask in Elizabeth Maurier's reflected glory and my own certainty that it had been me that had cracked the case, me, not Elizabeth Maurier or Trawden himself, and (most gratifyingly) not David Brooks-Powell in any way at all. I'd assumed that Elizabeth felt the same way, that this was just the way things were done, the partner taking all the credit and the junior associate getting a word or two in the dregs of the more detailed press releases no one would ever read. I was wondering whether I'd been right about that when my phone rang and I picked it up and answered and said "Claire?" before I'd had a chance to register the number on the display.

"Nope," said a voice I recognised but couldn't place for a moment. "Interesting that you don't know your girlfriend's number," it continued, and the name and face slotted home.

"Hello Colman," I replied. "How's Don Juan?"

She laughed. "It's Vicky. I told you. And Don Juan's

been sent packing. Not man enough for me."

I wondered how dumping a superior officer would play out for her at work, and decided to let it go. I wasn't going to pry into Colman's love life, however clear the invitation.

"So, Vicky, what can I do for you on this bright and shiny Saturday?" I asked, throwing her own style back at her.

"Got anywhere?" she asked, and for a moment I wondered what she was talking about. It hit me half a second later, the bodies on the board. How soon we forget.

"No, not really. I'm looking into Trawden, but I don't think there's anything there. And I've already been through the files I got from Lizzy Maurier. I've got to be honest, Vicky, I don't think I'm going to be much help."

I paused, expecting a denial, but she said nothing, so I went on.

"Any luck getting me that diary?"

"No," she shot back, sure and fast, like I'd just asked for a date with her mother. "No, and I reckon we can wave goodbye to that. Martins is on the warpath. I think someone saw us in that café, Sam. Someone who wasn't Tommy Larkin. She's told me I'm not to speak to you under any circumstances."

"Good to see you're following orders again."

She laughed. "Yeah, well, that's why I wanted to call, really. To warn you. She'll be in touch."

I shivered at the prospect. Dealings with DI Martins were the last thing I wanted. A call from her ranked right up there with dental surgery.

"Thanks for the heads up," I said, flat and weary, thinking maybe it *was* Tommy Larkin who'd told Martins about Colman and I. A simple enough step, if he was feeling bitter. I kept my mouth shut on that one, and listened to Colman trying to tell me everything would be just fine.

"Don't worry, Sam. She may be a dog with a bone, but

she's easy enough to throw off the scent. Don't tell her anything, and keep digging, right? And let me know if you do come up with anything interesting."

"Yeah," I replied. *Yeah* was how I felt right now, with a healthy portion of *Whatever* thrown in. I remembered, just as I was about to end the call, my theory about the tongue, the notion that Elizabeth Maurier had died leaving something unsaid. I set it out for Colman.

"Hmmm," she replied.

"You're not convinced?"

"Well, I'm not unconvinced. I said something similar to Martins myself, before your little showdown with her in the house. She told me to keep my stupid ideas to myself."

"But it's not stupid, is it?"

She paused, and her reply, when it came, was slow and considered.

"No. No, I think it's a decent idea, and it makes more sense than the theories Martins is looking at."

"Which are?"

She sighed. "Anatomy fetishist. Someone with some kind of sensory condition. Burglaries gone wrong."

"Burglaries gone wrong?" I parroted, stunned.

"Yeah. Even Martins had to admit that was stretching it a bit. But Elizabeth Maurier having some kind of message herself, yes, I could buy that. That was one of the reasons I thought you could help. If she's the key, then the more we know about her, the better."

I couldn't help thinking that was all very well if you weren't the one digging fruitlessly through Elizabeth Maurier's files, revisiting a life you'd hoped to forget. Colman, I reflected, had mastered the art of delegation early. She'd make a good DI. I didn't say any of that out loud. Instead, I remembered what had come to me that morning and realised that Colman would be perfect.

"Can you make a call for me?" I asked.

"Sure. Who am I calling?"

I explained what I wanted her to do. Timing was everything. I didn't want to be out when Claire got home, but I didn't know where she was or when that would be. In the end I went for that evening. Colman said I shouldn't worry, she'd do it, and she hoped I wasn't going to give up on helping her.

"Sure," I said, muttered a quiet goodbye and turned back to the screen. My phone rang two minutes later. I glanced at the number and let it go through to my voicemail.

The next hit on Akadi was from a website called *Miscarriages of Justice!* That title sat at the top of every page, blood-red, bold, with the exclamation mark tacked on the end like a knife. According to the site's author, the investigation into the murder of Maxine Grimshaw had been littered with errors from the beginning, and whilst I found the tone irritating, I could hardly disagree, at first. Trawden was not guilty, the unnamed writer asserted, could never have been guilty, should never even have been a suspect. But – and this was where the crusader and I would have to differ – Evans wasn't guilty either. Evans' conviction was merely an attempt to distract from the failings of the initial investigation by placing the blame on a man no longer alive to protest.

I'd seen all this before. Back in the day there had been hundreds making the same outlandish claims. There was something about a particularly nasty murder that brought all the lunatics and conspiracy theorists out from under their rocks.

My phone rang again. This time I checked the number before answering, but I didn't recognise it.

"Sam Williams," I said.

"Oh, hello, Sam. How are you, my dear fellow?"

I sighed, inwardly. After DI Martins, Christian Willoughby, probate lawyer, was the last person I wanted to talk to.

"Very well thank you. Busy, as ever."

I wondered if he'd buy it. Half of London seemed to know I didn't have more than an hour's paying work to fill each day. No reason Willoughby should be one of the ignorant.

"Delighted to hear it, Sam. Delighted. But I do hope, with all this important work you have, that you've been able to spare an hour or two on Elizabeth Maurier's bequest."

I tried to work out if there was a timbre there, a sarcastic tone to that *important work*. I couldn't tell. Every word he spoke came out in that same rich roll.

"Because," he continued, "it has been a week. I wonder if you've managed to make a start. I see you've been making the news, meeting old friends at the Reform Club, Sam. I do hope you're not getting distracted."

I was torn. Willoughby had my edge up – I could feel my jaw tightening even as he spoke, with his continued insistence that this was a *bequest*, that I should be somehow grateful for being thrown back ten, fifteen years into a past I'd rather have forgotten, that what I did with my life was anything to do with him at all. I wanted to let him know precisely how I felt, and I wanted to challenge him about the leak to the *Law Society Gazette*, because I was convinced he was behind it, and that if it hadn't been for the *Law Society Gazette* there would have been no Rich Hanover dogging my every step and no photographs of me outside the Reform Club for Willoughby to spot. But at the same time I wanted him off my phone and out of my life, and the easiest way to achieve that was to give him what he wanted.

"Oh, things are going very well, Christian. Very well indeed. I've had several meetings with the other beneficiaries." I looked around for a drink to wash away the taste of the word on my lips, but there was nothing within reach. "We're making good progress. It's a significant task, of course, I'm sure you appreciate that. But we've made an excellent start."

I was surprised how smoothly I'd lied, how easily I'd fallen into Willoughby's own patterns of speech. He seemed somewhat taken aback himself, if the haste with which he extricated himself was anything to go by, winding up the call with an *Excellent, don't hesitate to call if you need anything* and a couple of *Jolly good*'s that felt a little like a verbal security blanket.

The next hit on Akadi was a strange one, stranger even than the conspiracy theorist that had preceded it. Some kind of blog, I thought, although when I tried to reach what I assumed would be the home page there was nothing there at all. I navigated back to the initial page, which seemed to be a broadly accurate but oddly stilted description of the proceedings right up to Trawden's acquittal. No opinions were given, no views as to guilt or innocence or sympathy for the family or railing at the police. Instead, just a set of dates and events. *Edward Trawden convicted of murder. Robbie Evans convicted of murder. Robbie Evans confesses to Grimshaw killing. Robbie Evans killed in Pentonville Prison. Hussein Akadi informs authorities of Grimshaw confession.* And more of the same, with some smaller details in between, but not many of them, right up to the release. White text on a black background. Everything about the site was primitive, earlier-than-2005 primitive, although, of course, it couldn't have been. Another lunatic, I thought. A fan, perhaps, although of what or of who I couldn't say.

I was halfway through the next hit, another article, this time by a criminologist attempting to fit Evans into a profile she was certain would match every paedophile murderer in the western world, when the phone rang again. Again, I looked at the number; again, I didn't recognise it, but I knew who it would be and I toyed with the idea of ignoring it, of letting it ring, and letting the caller dial again, and again, time after time, fruitless and unanswered. And then I realised that wouldn't put her off, she'd just send someone round to "bring me in", and the wisest move here was the same one I'd played on Willoughby. Give her what she wanted.

"Sam Williams," I said, again.

"Mr Williams, it's Detective Inspector Martins here. I'm just calling to ask if you've remembered any useful information since our last conversation."

I didn't recall her asking me for any useful information. I didn't recall her asking me for anything much at all, once she'd decided I wasn't the murderer, and couldn't possible have been the murderer, because when the murder had taken place I'd been at the funeral of a lawyer two hundred miles away and there had been half a dozen police officers there to vouch for me. I bit back an instinctive response, a *you must be getting desperate if you've come back to me* sort of response, and answered her politely instead.

"I'm sorry, DI Martins. I haven't got anything else. I'll let you know immediately if anything does come to mind, of course."

"Thank you, Mr Williams."

She paused, and I wondered why we were being so polite, why we were pretending to have a normal, professional relationship when the last time I'd seen her she'd thrown me out of her police station. Colman had warned me about her less than an hour ago. Larkin had warned Colman that Martins would have me arrested if I interfered. I wondered when she was going to get to the point, because fishing for clues I didn't have and wouldn't have given her if I did wasn't reason enough for her to call me.

The pause went on, and I found myself desperate to fill it. Maybe this was her method, her interview technique. Just shut up and let the suspect hang himself. If so, it was working.

"I've just been working on her memoirs," I said. "Nothing particularly earth-shattering there, I'm afraid. Everything there was to know about Elizabeth Maurier already seems to be in the public domain."

I'd thrown her a rope instead of a noose. I hoped she wouldn't pull it too hard. There was nothing in what she'd actually said – there couldn't be, really, not in the words or even in the tone of voice. But it was all so transparent. She wanted to know if I was going to *interfere*. I'd just told her I wasn't.

"Good," she replied. "I mean, it's a shame you haven't found anything. You just keep working on those memoirs, Mr Williams."

And stay out of my investigation. Those were the words she wasn't saying. She didn't need to. And I didn't need to endure any more of this. She'd made her point.

"Thank you, Detective Inspector. I'll do that. Good bye."

"Good bye, Mr Williams."

I needed a coffee. I needed a whisky, really, but I was out of whisky, it was half past two in the afternoon and I'd skipped lunch, so a coffee would have to do. I took five minutes out to close my eyes and take in the hot bitterness, and returned to the computer.

After a dozen stories with nothing new in them, and a couple with plenty that *was* new but had little basis in fact, the next one came as a shock. The headline was stark enough – "Body Identified as Local Drug Dealer". The article was less than a fortnight old, and the source was the *Walsall Guardian*, a good-sized local with a decent reputation and some major national stablemates. Nothing, in short, to suggest the story that followed would be anything but genuine.

Akadi was dead. That was the gist of it. A body had been

found in a park a week earlier, nobody had known whose body it was, and now they did. "Sources" – the paper was tight-lipped on who these sources were, but that was their right – had identified the man as Hussein Akadi, a small-time drug dealer of unknown origin, who had drifted into the Midlands following a number of prison sentences for a number of different crimes. The police were happy to concur with the identification and confirm that Akadi had been dealing locally for more than three years. The date for the inquest had been set for early in January, not that there would be much interest in the verdict, from the sound of it – Akadi's friends hadn't exactly flooded forth to claim him. The journalist cited other sources – police sources, no doubt – who were all but certain the cause of death was an accidental overdose, an occupational hazard for a dealer who mixed business with pleasure. A local politician named Kevin McManus harped on about the sadness of a lonely death, about what a shame it was that society could not do more to redeem the man, for his own sake and for the sake of those who lived and worked around him. I opened another tab and looked up Kevin McManus. He was a parish councillor with big ambitions, standing for the vacant Police and Crime Commissioner post on an independent platform and a lot of cash from his construction business behind him. The money wouldn't help; the big parties had it all sewn up, the same way they always did, and anyway, Kevin McManus' business dealings had left him less than popular with certain elements of his potential constituency.

But he was right. It was a shame. I thought back to the Akadi I'd known, and I shivered. The word that came to mind was *slimy*. Always after the next thing. He'd implied – not actually asked, but implied – that he hoped to get something out of his testimony. What he'd wanted was money, but Elizabeth Maurier had pretended not to notice his veiled bargaining stance and handed him over to me, not wishing to soil her hands with the Akadis of the justice system. I could hardly blame her: if there had been anyone below me in the food chain I'd have passed the bastard right on again. But there hadn't been, so it was Sam Williams and Hussein Akadi, half a dozen meetings in the visitor's wing at Pentonville, teasing out his testimony, picking out the holes the other side might spot, steering my witness round those holes as subtly as I could. Akadi was a shark, a murderer and a drug dealer of the worst sort, but that didn't make a blind bit of difference in the end, because he was telling the truth about Evans, and we proved it. Still. It would have taken a lot more than a sensitive and benevolent society to redeem Hussein Akadi. No wonder he wasn't overwhelmed with mourners.

It was three o'clock. Not fourteen hours since we'd staggered out of Brooks-Powell's palace. I'd learned a lot since then, but I wasn't sure any of it was useful, either for the memoirs or the murder investigation. I picked up the phone to call Brooks-Powell, to tell him about Shapiro and his views on Trawden, about Akadi's death, about my own sudden revelation, as sleep had swept over me, that Elizabeth Maurier had died with something unsaid. And then I remembered who it was I was calling. Sure, we'd ended on good terms, we'd mended some bridges, we'd each taken a leap of faith. But still. He was David Brooks-Powell and I was Sam Williams and nature dictated that we be in opposing corners.

Instead I called Lizzy Maurier.

16: Forgiven

SHE ANSWERED ALMOST immediately, as if she'd been sitting by the phone waiting for it to ring.

"Hello? Who's that?"

She sounded groggy, and a little confused. Maybe she'd opted for that whisky I'd been forced to do without half an hour earlier.

"Lizzy? It's Sam. Sam Williams."

"Oh. You."

The groggy and confused were gone, and in their place was a cold hostility that couldn't have been clearer if it had been brandishing a knife and baring its teeth. I spent about half a second trying to figure out what she might be angry about, and then it hit me. That's the trouble with a photographic memory, or at least my sort of photographic memory. No problem recalling her phone number. More of an issue remembering in time that I'd left her comatose and alone in her flat and taken with me a bunch of files she'd expressly told me not to look at it until she'd had her turn with them.

"Listen, Lizzy. I'm sorry."

"What are you sorry about?"

She was testing me. I was going to have to tread carefully.

"About the other night."

"Which bit of the other night? Leading me on and letting me make a fool of myself, or stealing my dead mother's papers?"

Don't rise to it. *Don't* rise to it.

"Look, I'm just sorry, OK? We'd both had too much to drink. I wasn't thinking. I saw the files and I just really wanted to get the work started. It's important work, right?

You said so yourself. You were right. It needs to be done."

"Of course. It needed to be done when it suited you to get it done."

I started to protest, but she spoke over me.

"Listen, Sam, I get it. None of this was what you wanted. You're doing your best, but don't pretend your heart is in it."

"No – no. I'm sorry, Lizzy, but that's not it. It's really not." I knew I was lying even as I spoke. There was something driving me on here, but it wasn't Willoughby and the damn *legacy*. But that didn't matter. "I've found something. In the papers I – in the papers I took home with me. There was something about a Doctor Shapiro. Does that ring any bells?"

There was a pause, a long silence, and I wondered whether Lizzy was thinking about my question or had just given up on the call altogether. I got my answer a few seconds later.

"No. Sorry, Sam. What's this all about?"

Her voice was different now. Not the barely-conscious wreck of earlier, and not the terrier spoiling for a fight, either. I'd piqued her interest. I pushed on.

"It's pretty obscure in her notes, but I went to see him. He'd been a shrink of some sort. Did a lot of work with Trawden."

Another pause. Even through the silence I could sense that interest waning. Time for some more bait.

"And – well, I know it's not got anything to do with your mother, not really, but Akadi – remember Akadi?"

"I remember the name," she said, matter-of-fact, noncommittal. "Something to do with Trawden, and Evans, right?"

"He was Evans' cellmate. He was the one who told the police Evans had claimed Maxine Grimshaw. Anyway, he's turned up dead in Walsall."

There was a gasp from the other end of the phone, and then "Murdered? Like my mother?" when she'd got her breath back.

"No. No, looks like an OD. It was always on the cards with Akadi."

"Hmm," she said. "I think I can see what you're driving at here," and for a moment I thought I'd reeled her in. But instead she wriggled free. "You've been landed with these memoirs and now you're doing your best to make it all interesting. I get it. I do. But be honest, please. Don't play games with me."

I took a moment to figure out what to say. She might have missed the mark with the line about leading her on – that had been the last thing I intended, and as far as I recalled the last thing I'd done. But she'd hit closer to home with the rest of it. Was that all this was, the secret calls with Vicky Colman, the arguments with Claire, the half-day I'd spent driving to Norfolk and back? Was I just inventing an angle to liven up a dull job?

No, I decided. I wasn't. I wouldn't exploit Elizabeth Maurier's death just to indulge some strange, mysterious fantasy. But if I wanted to convince Lizzy, I needed something else. I considered, briefly, telling her about the board, the other victims, the body parts, but that would be wrong in almost every way – whatever state Lizzy Maurier might be in now, she wasn't ready to hear about more severed organs. And given that state, I couldn't trust her not to go running to Martins and set loose a firestorm of the Detective Inspector's fury on my head. Instead I gave her a hunch.

"Listen, I think there's something else. It's just occurred to me." I wondered if it would work, in isolation, without the eyes and the nose and the fingers, without *no one will see* and *no one will smell* and *no one will touch*. I had to take the chance. "I think your mother had something to say. I think that's the point, the words on the wall, I think she had something to say, and whoever killed her wanted to make it clear that no one would ever hear it."

I trailed off. I'd delivered my piece; there was nowhere left to go. I waited.

"OK," she said, after what felt like an hour. "OK. I'll see if there's anything here, anything at all, that makes what you're suggesting make any kind of sense whatsoever. Akadi, you say? And Trawden, of course. And this Shapiro. I'll have a look."

"Thanks, Lizzy. It's just a hunch, but there's too much that looks a little out of place." I was backtracking now, but I could afford to. I'd landed her, which meant I'd landed the rest of Elizabeth Maurier's files. I asked her about Rich Hanover, whether he'd been harassing her, too, but although she remembered the man who'd been hanging around the townhouse the day Brooks-Powell and I visited, she didn't seem to know what had happened since, and I didn't think it was worth drawing her attention to something that would only upset her. She agreed to call me back once she'd been through the material, and I returned to my laptop and the Akadi search results.

There wasn't anything else there, of course. Akadi was a footnote. His impact on the world could be measured only in the lives he'd taken, the lives he'd blighted, his own lonely death. Barely a ripple.

Roarkes called. They'd found a place in a local hospice for Helen. He sounded cheerful, as if this were some kind of cure rather than a softening of the end. It was a matter of days, now, not weeks. Roarkes never sounded cheerful, even when things were going well. I thought about pushing him, seeing whether I could drive him to some kind of honesty, some kind of emotional response that made sense, but he didn't want that any more than I did. He just wanted to tell someone, so I let myself be told and assured him I'd come and visit her as soon as I could. The usual Roarkes would have jabbed in some dig about the state of my client list and the poverty of my workload, but the one on the other end of the phone just thanked me and said goodbye. I'd only met Helen Roarkes twice; she'd seemed charming, witty and intelligent, the reverse of the picture her husband habitually painted of her, but I had the feeling this was all agreed between them, this pretend Helen Roarkes, the wife he could complain about at work and unwind with happily at home. I wondered what kind of a man he'd be without her.

There was still no sign of Claire. I tried her phone again, without success, and turned on the television. It opened on the news channel, which was too depressing, so I flicked around looking for something inane and cheerful enough to lift me. A decent action movie would have done the trick, but there was nothing, and I sat back with the sound of a home renovation programme buzzing through my ears, and closed my eyes.

It was dark when I woke, and my phone was ringing. I glanced at the time before I answered. Five o'clock. I'd been asleep nearly two hours. It was a good thing she'd called.

"Hello?" I said, that upward cadence there even though I knew who was on the other end.

"Hello, Sam," said Lizzy. "I'm just calling to let you know that I've been through the files. I'm sorry, but there's nothing about Shapiro, nothing about Akadi, and nothing about Trawden we don't already know. I don't want to deflate you, Sam, but I'm really not sure there's anything in this."

She waited for me to argue, but I didn't have the fight left in me. After a moment, she continued.

"I know you weren't making this up. And when I've got a chance to spend some more time going through everything, I'll have a proper look – I mean, all I've been able to do this afternoon is flick through. But I don't think there are any great dark secrets, Sam. I think it's all out there for everyone to see. All we have to do is put it in the right order and make it look pretty."

"I suppose you're right," I muttered. "And thanks. I appreciate your taking the time."

The home renovation programme was still on – same presenters, different owners. The same words, it seemed, *knock through here* and *a lick of paint* and *see if we can extend out here* and *sort out the windows*. I wondered if houses were like people, if these presenters could tell in an instant whether they were full of promise or full of bullshit, the way I could tell – the way I'd thought I could tell, before Serena Hawkes – whether someone I was talking to was lying to me. Shapiro hadn't been lying to me. Trawden? He'd been covering something, sure, but I doubted it was anything that concerned me. Broadmoor and Belmarsh. Twenty years. There would be plenty he'd want to hide from the outside world, from Sam Williams and Elizabeth Maurier and Charlie Blennard and the Reform Club. What had Shapiro called him? A *chameleon*. It didn't mean he'd done anything wrong.

There was one more call to make.

"Hello David," I said, when he answered, and back he shot.

"Hi Sam. How's the head?"

It was like we were friends, all of a sudden. We'd had a good time last night, but friends? I couldn't see it.

I filled him in on the trip to Shapiro's, and what I'd learned about Akadi since. He let out a long, low whistle.

"So what are you thinking, Sam? More to your chum Trawden than meets the eye?"

"I don't know. I think I'm inches away from a big fat dead end, but I'd quite like to keep driving until I hit it. Any chance you can get hold of the old Mauriers files on

Trawden? There might be something there I can chew on."

"No can do, I'm afraid. You'll have to ask them yourself. I'm not exactly flavour of the month there these days."

I had to head out shortly, so I didn't have long, but Brooks-Powell was right. He had no more chance of getting the files than I did. But when I called Mauriers two minutes later I was in for a surprise. There was a lawyer there, even though it was Saturday, but that wasn't the surprise, because from what I'd heard Mauriers had turned into the kind of firm that worked its lawyers till they dropped, like every other firm in London. The woman I was talking to – a junior associate I'd never heard of and who'd probably been knocking back her first illicit vodka and coke when I'd been at the firm – knew who I was, but that wasn't the surprise either, because it was only a year since I'd sued her firm. And she wasn't prepared to give me the files, and that also wasn't the surprise, because those files were confidential and I had no right to them whatsoever. But she was prepared to tell me that she couldn't give me the files even if she'd wanted to, because they'd been handed to Trawden's new firm four months ago.

That was a surprise.

"Which firm?" I asked, and she paused and wondered whether she should say anything.

"Hancocks," she muttered, finally, and hung up.

I tried Hancocks as soon as the dial tone returned, anxious to get things moving, and eventually managed to speak to an intellectual property partner named Julian who blustered and threatened to report me to the Law Society if I made any more outrageous demands to see private client paperwork. I glanced at my watch, or where my watch would have been if I hadn't lost it, and checked the laptop in front of me instead. Still a few minutes. I called Brooks-Powell again.

He wasn't surprised when I told him what had happened

– it was all *David* and *Sam* now, and for all the effort I thought it was going to take, I found myself drifting into it easily enough. He wasn't surprised I hadn't been able to get the files. But Trawden taking on new lawyers was news to him.

"I can't believe it," he said, for the fourth time in as many minutes. "I mean, yes, I know he was tight with Elizabeth, or had been, and she's dead now, so that link's gone, but from what you're saying he moved when she was still alive. That's, what, thirteen years with Mauriers and then he's off? And what does he need a lawyer for now anyway? Why bother going to the effort?"

I had some thoughts on that front, but they were wild thoughts and it made sense to keep them to myself. Brooks-Powell was still talking, to himself as much as to me.

"It doesn't seem like a rational thing to do. Mauriers had looked after him for years. Elizabeth knew him better than anyone. Do you think maybe that was the problem?"

A pause, during which I realised that he had been addressing me after all, and that the question he'd asked was close enough to the ones I'd been asking myself. But still. Wild thoughts. Crazy ideas.

"Maybe, David. I don't know. I'm not very comfortable with Trawden, but he didn't kill Maxine Grimshaw and really that's the only thing about him that should matter."

"Hmm," he replied, slowly, the second *Hmm* I'd received in the last few hours, but far less challenging than the one that had preceded it. "Well, whatever the answer is, it's in those files. Let's get them."

"I just tried, David. Haven't you been listening?"

"You went direct. Got to have a bit of cunning, Sam. I'd have thought you were all about the cunning."

I laughed. I was all about the cunning and Brooks-Powell was all about the diamonds and yachts. That was what we thought of one another. And yet here we were having a civilised, almost friendly conversation, the day after a reasonably civilised and ultimately friendly dinner.

"Got something in mind?" I asked.

"Not yet. But I will have by the time you get here."

For a moment I was about to object, and then I thought *why the hell not?* I needed to be out in a minute anyway, a quick there and back again. No harm in making something more of it. Claire was out and there was no way of knowing when she'd be home. If I sat here by myself waiting for her I'd just end up going through those same three files again and hitting Google for the millionth time. I didn't think we'd be getting anything out of Hancocks, however confident Brooks-Powell sounded, but I was interested to see what he had in mind.

"OK. I have to stop off on the way, but I shouldn't be long," I said. "Shall I tell Lizzy?"

"Why?" he asked, and I filled him in on my conversations with her, or at least those bits of those conversations that concerned Trawden and her mother rather than her and me.

"No," he said, when I'd finished. "The girl's a mess. I'm sorry for her, but she can't help us and she can get in our way, so I'd rather she wasn't there."

I liked his bluntness. It helped that he was right, and it helped that I'd had enough awkward conversations with Lizzy Maurier for one day. It also helped that it was his decision and his house.

I still had one awkward conversation to go, though. As I was packing away my meagre paperwork and laptop into a case and slinging a coat on, the door opened and Claire walked in.

If it had happened an hour earlier, I might have been prepared, but I'd given up on Claire coming back any time soon. Even unprepared, I had a whole list of lines, a whole series of *Where have you been* and *Why didn't you call me* and

Why didn't you leave a note and more of the same, and I stood up and took a breath to launch into them. And then I got a proper look at her face.

She looked tired.

That was all. Not sad or afraid or stressed, not anything to talk about really. Just tired. And tired was enough.

"Are you OK?" I asked. I put the case down and let the coat drop to the floor, and walked over to put my arms around her. She shrugged, and let me, but all she was doing was standing there.

"Look, Claire, I'm not going to ask where you've been. Unless you want me to. But you have to know that I'm sorry."

I didn't know where the words were coming from. They certainly bore no resemblance to the script I'd been writing in my head the whole time I'd been looking up Akadi. She turned her head to look up at me, and there it was there, that tiredness, and nothing besides.

"I'm sorry I was so horrible about your mum coming to stay," I continued. "That was wrong. I know it was wrong. And I'm sorry the story's gone cold. And I'm sorry if I've been a dick for weeks. You were right. I'm stuck in my own head, and I've got better places to be than there."

I tried a sheepish grin. Claire didn't say a word. On I went, all pretence or subtlety gone. I'd tried every approach I knew. It was time to plead.

"Please, Claire. We've got to talk about this. If there's something you want to tell me, if there's something you want to accuse me of, whatever it is, however bad, please, we've got to talk. Isn't that what Adrian would say?"

I regretted the words as soon as they were out. Claire lifted my arms from her shoulders, walked to the sofa and sat. I stood there, staring at her, my arms still stuck in the air where she'd left them. I didn't know where she been, but more important than that, I didn't know what she was feeling. She sighed, finally, and turned to look at me.

"It's fine, Sam. You're right. We needed to talk. Now we've talked. We've done it. You're forgiven."

I shook my head, picked up my coat and my case, and headed out into the cold London night.

17: Not a Murder Investigation

THERE WAS NO sign of Hanover or his bike outside the flat, and I hadn't expected to see him, either, but I still found myself looking over my shoulder as I walked and starting every time I heard a loud noise. I walked to the Three Bells, which was busy enough to render me inconspicuous as I passed through the main bar to the back bar to the beer garden, which was empty bar a handful of quiet, sullen smokers, and from there through the gate onto a completely different street from the one I'd entered by. If Hanover had been following me, he wasn't now.

Marco's was a brisk two-minute stroll from here, through light drizzle and the occasional distant shout. Marco's wasn't the kind of place you'd expect to find anyone unless they knew it – it was away from the main streets, it served nothing but kebabs, and it was filthy on the outside and dirty enough in the dining area, all of which was enough to put off the casual diner. I'd been in the kitchen, though – Marco liked company when it was quiet, and I'd spent enough time in his place for him to trust me – and back there, it was spotless. As I ducked in out of the rain and let the door slam shut behind me, I saw the place was empty apart from Marco, behind the counter, and one man sitting at a table facing away from me.

I ordered a kebab and took a seat at the table behind his, and then I waited. The kebab took fifteen minutes. I wasn't in a hurry. It wasn't my time I was wasting. When it arrived I ate it slowly, savouring every bite, and when I'd finished I called out to tell Marco it was as good as ever. The whole time, the man behind me hardly stirred. I waited another minute, and then I leaned back and tapped him on the shoulder.

"Got Colman's message, then?" I asked.

He turned, a blank face with confusion hastily painted on as he registered my grin and realised what I'd said.

"I don't – who's Colman? What do you mean?"

I shook my head, stood and walked over to his table, where I sat down opposite him. I couldn't deny it: I was enjoying this.

"Come on, Rich. It's game over. And you must realise she's not coming."

"Who's not coming, Williams?"

Williams, he'd said. Not *mate*. Not *Sam*. He might be playing dumb, but I'd got him, and he knew it. I turned and called over to the counter.

"Marco! How long's this journalist been sitting here staring at his hands?"

"'Bou half hour, Sam. Least that."

I let out a whistle. "Half an hour, Rich? That's a lot of time for nothing."

"I was hungry. I fancied a kebab."

"Just in the area, right? Marco," I turned, again. "Has Rich here actually eaten anything?"

Marco shook his head, and I heard Hanover's breath start to quicken.

"I was just deciding what to order."

I shook my head, again. I wasn't angry. Not now. Hanover had turned out to be as predictable as the rest of them, and I was determined to have some fun. "I didn't think you lot did that any more, Rich. After all the trouble. Newspapers have gone down for less. I mean, hacking voicemails? In this day and age? I thought better of you. I really did. Although is it really hacking if you just sit there and watch me key in my PIN? Does it count?"

"I really don't know what you're talking about, Williams."

I was still having fun, but I had somewhere to be.

"Look, first there was Lizzy's flat, then there was Brooks-Powell's place. They both left messages telling me where to go and what time to be there. Now I've got the fact you were here before me. I've got a message on my phone from Colman telling me to meet her here, round about now, or twenty minutes ago, anyway. You didn't follow me and you're not a regular – he's not a regular, is he, Marco?"

Marco shook his head.

"And," I continued, "Colman's CID. I mean, hacking a lawyer, that's bad enough, but listening to confidential messages from a detective? You've got balls, Hanover. I'll give you that."

"It's – "

"Are you really still trying to dig your way out of this? Listen. Listen to me. I'm not a vindictive man. All this," I gestured around, at the restaurant, at my phone, out on the table between us, "we can forget all this. You fuck off, and get out of my life, and Colman's, and Lizzy's, and Brooks-Powell's, and my girlfriend's, and everyone else I know. I don't want to hear from you again. I don't want to hear about you again. There's ten million other people in London, Hanover. Go and hassle one of them. And this, this'll all disappear. Put it down to bad luck and move on."

"Really, Williams – "

"But if you fuck with me, Hanover. If I catch even the faintest sniff of you. Your editor will not be happy. Not when he's got an angry lawyer and Press Standards on his back. Are you regulated by them, *Real World News*? I think you are, aren't you? You've got to have someone keeping an eye on you."

"I don't believe you," he said, and stood. He walked to the door, turned and looked at me. "This is coincidence, me being here when you were supposed to be meeting someone. You've got nothing on me, Williams."

The door slammed shut behind me. Marco was

grinning at me, bemused but entertained. I grinned back. For all his bluster, Hanover was rattled. He was out of the picture. He knew it, and I knew it too. I gave it five minutes, thanked Marco, and headed back out to the street.

The headquarters of the Brooks-Powell Legal Consultancy was a mid-sized room on the second floor of the Brooks-Powell residence. Back when Samuel Williams & Co. had catered to clientele more impressive than a single dubious asylum-seeker, I'd at least managed an office outside my home. But then, my home was of a different order to Brooks-Powell's.

"Come in, come in, get out of the cold," he said, even though it had dried up and turned mild, and the coat he took from me had been resting on my arm most of the way there.

"Melanie about?" I asked, and he shook his head.

"No. Away with friends for a few days. Glamorous life of the financial wizards," he added, with a grin I wasn't buying for a minute. She hadn't mentioned anything about going away when we'd been here less than twenty-four hours ago. Melanie Golding, I suspected, spent much of the year *away with friends*.

There was only one chair in the "office", one chair and one desk with a sleek-looking screen on it. Brooks-Powell disappeared to fetch something for me to sit on, and I spent thirty seconds looking around the room while he was gone. Thirty seconds was enough. Chair, desk, screen, filing cabinet (locked), white paint on the walls, one window looking onto the road and a large Holbein reproduction – *The Ambassadors*, the one with the odd-shaped skull across the bottom – opposite the window. He returned carrying a bean bag, which seemed a little out of place, but I wasn't complaining.

"Funny choice of artwork," I said, pointing at it, and he

grinned at me.

"I like it. Gives perspective." He shrugged. "No matter who you're dealing with, who's paying you or getting in your way, they'll be dead some day. And so will you."

I got the sentiment, but I still wouldn't have wanted that skull and those two miserable-looking diplomats staring at me while I tried to work. I slumped into the bean bag and tested the painting from this new angle. The skull looked bigger. Clearer. More unsettling.

"It's gone six," he said, glancing at his watch. "Still a chance we can catch someone there today." I must have looked confused, because he went on. "Hancocks. The woman I reckon we need spends most of her life in the office."

As he reached for the phone – I hadn't noticed the phone, a tiny black thing sitting almost behind the screen – it started ringing. He put it to his ear, answered, waited a moment, then hit a button and put the phone back on the desk.

"Hello Charlie," he said. "Long time no see. How are you?"

"Excellent, David. Excellent." Charlie Blennard's voice boomed out from a set of invisible speakers. "I was wondering how you were getting on with Elizabeth's memoirs."

"Oh, fine, fine," said Brooks-Powell. I opened my mouth to say something myself, but he saw me, put a finger to his lips and pointed to the screen. A hidden microphone in there, no doubt. "I was surprised not to see you at the funeral," he added, smiling at me.

"Yes, I'd have liked to have been there, but I had to be away, unfortunately. Morocco. Important business. But as long as things are progressing well with the memoirs, that's the important thing. I'd like to see them in print before I die."

"Oh, you don't have to worry about that."

"And – David, I hope you don't consider this too much of an imposition, but given how close she and I were – well, it would really set my mind at rest if I could see a draft *before* it gets published."

Brooks-Powell was nodding. Evidently he'd expected something like this. Perhaps those suspicions I'd entertained about Blennard and Elizabeth Maurier weren't so wide of the mark.

"Of course, of course," he said. And waited. I'd heard it, too: there was something about Blennard's tone, about the way he'd said those last few words, that suggested there was more to come.

We didn't have to wait long. Blennard cleared his throat, and lowered his voice a little, as if he were concerned someone might overhear him.

"And one more thing, David. I've been hearing – well, I've been hearing *things*. About your friend Sam Williams."

Brooks-Powell snorted. "No friend of mine," he said, and winked at me.

"What I've been hearing, David, is that he's taking things in directions they shouldn't be taken. Stepping on toes. Confusing matters. Now, I must stress these are nothing more than rumours, but I strongly advise you to play a straight bat here. Don't let him persuade you to do things you shouldn't do. And if you have any influence on him whatsoever, try to remind him what he's supposed to be doing here. The legacy. It's a memoir. Not a murder investigation."

"I haven't seen him lately, Charlie, but I wouldn't be surprised if he was going off on a frolic of his own." There was a chuckle from the other end of the line as Blennard registered the legal witticism. "But I haven't heard a thing about it. All sounds very cloak and dagger to me. Don't you worry. I'll steer well away from it any nonsense."

"Thank you David. I always knew you were a sensible chap. Please give me a call if you think I can be of any assistance."

They said their goodbyes, and Brooks-Powell turned to me with a frown on his face. I knew what that frown meant. There was too much at stake here, even for a millionaire whose career didn't really matter any more. There was the Brooks-Powell reputation on the line, the quality of the name, Blennard's influence was too great to risk making an enemy of him, and as a friend he could do so much good – I could hear the arguments even before he made them. I was on my own.

"What a wanker," said Brooks-Powell, the frown clearing. I stared at him, lost for words.

"Wanker," he repeated. "What was all that crap about *sensible chap*? He's hardly exchanged a dozen words with me in as many years, and now he knows who I am? *Straight bat*? What was that about?"

I thought back to our dinner, in this very house, and its aftermath, in the taxi, with Claire. Was Blennard insinuating something? Or was I reading too much into a bland commonplace uttered by someone who didn't want to go into too much detail?

"So you're going to help me get the files?" I asked, and he nodded.

"Too right I am. Us. I'm going to help *us* get the files, and *we're* going to look through them until we find out what the hell it is *Lord* Charlie Blennard doesn't want us to see. You with me?"

I nodded, and smiled at him, but a nod and a smile didn't seem enough. In the end we shook hands. And then we got to work.

18: Every Victory Is Tempered

BROOKS-POWELL KNEW the Hancocks number by heart, so they must have been people he'd had dealings with fairly recently. He asked for a Rebecca Ashcroft, and while we were waiting for the call to go through, cupped his hands around his mouth and whispered "It's bound to be her, she'd have grabbed Trawden with both hands. Anyone who got in her way, she'd have torn them to pieces. Bit like you, back in the day." He grinned. "I really don't like her." A moment later a female voice came on the line.

"Hello, this is Jenny Beech. Rebecca's secretary. Can I help you?"

"I'd like to speak to Rebecca, please."

"Who shall I say is calling?"

"Tell her it's David Brooks-Powell."

There was a pause, a couple of beeps, and then the phone went dead. A moment later, the dial tone returned. Jenny Beech had hung up on us. Undeterred, Brooks-Powell dialled again.

"I'm sorry," she said, "I don't know what happened there. I know she's in the office – I can see her from here. I'll try again."

This time we ended up back with the switchboard operator, the same one who'd answered the first two calls, who by the sigh he delivered when he heard Brooks-Powell's voice was clearly growing as frustrated with Jenny Beech as I was. But Brooks-Powell himself was the model of politeness when she came back on the line.

"I'm sorry," she explained. "It's my first day. I thought I'd figured out these phones."

"Don't worry. Is it a Garminca box and headset?"

I was impressed. The Brooks-Powell I'd worked with

wouldn't have paid any more attention to the secretarial equipment than he had to the secretaries.

"Yes, yes it is."

"OK, just press the F2 button, wait for the tone, dial her extension, and when she answers you can tell her it's me, wait for her to bite your head off, because she doesn't like me very much, and then just hit F2 again, which should put me through. If she's told you not to you can just pretend it was a mistake."

Jenny Beech laughed, a silvery little trill. Several further beeps followed, and I'd resigned myself to hearing that weary switchboard operator one more time when a different voice boomed out.

"David. What are you doing calling me on a Saturday? Bored, are you?"

"Far from it, Bex. The only thing that could possibly improve a glorious day like this one is the sound of your voice."

"Cut the crap, Brooks-Powell. What do you want?"

"Trawden."

"Yes?"

"I understand you've taken over. I'd like to see his files."

"And I'd like to see Idris Elba naked. Not gonna happen. Neither of them."

"Come on, Bex!"

"Come on? Is that all you've got? *Come on*? You want me to hand over confidential client documentation on the strength of a *come on*? I won't say I wasn't expecting to hear from you, Brooks-Powell, but I was hoping for something a little better than *come on*."

"I put this file together, Bex. You can take out anything you've added in the last, what is it, four months? My guess is that's nothing. But everything else, I damn well put there. I know it already."

"In that case, David, you won't really be needing the file,

will you?"

"Don't be like that, Bex. We can work this out, can't we? Why don't you come round when you've finished up there and we can discuss it?"

Rebecca Ashcroft gave a derisive snort. "We both know that's not going to happen. You can't get round me that way, believe me. Now why don't you piss off and make your stupid prank calls to somebody else, OK? I've got a secretary to shred, and then I'm off to Covent fucking Garden for a three hour bloody ballet. Oh come on!" A shout, loud and angry, directed at someone else in the office. "For Christ's sake, Jenny, don't cry about it. I've told you. You're staying here until you've fixed your mistakes. You're getting paid for your time. Stop bloody crying."

Rebecca Ashcroft's voice was replaced with the dial tone as she cut the call. Brooks-Powell shook his head.

"Her husband's a trustee," he said.

"Of what?"

"The Royal Opera House. He's a decent enough chap. Don't know what he ever saw in her." He rested his chin on his hand and stared at the blank screen in front of him. I gave it a minute before I asked.

"So what do we do now?"

"What would you do?" He turned to me, one eyebrow raised. "You'd figure out a way, wouldn't you?"

I nodded. We sat there in silence for a few seconds, and then something occurred to me.

"That secretary. Jenny Beech. First day on the job. Might be an angle there."

He shook his head.

"She won't have any loyalties. But she's not going to risk throwing away her job on the first day. And Rebecca Ashcroft, trust me, she'd fire her. She'd do it with a smile on her face."

I slumped further into the bean bag. Something told me

there was material in those files I'd want to see, better than anything in the papers I'd taken from Lizzy Maurier and probably better than anything in the ones I'd left behind. Maybe even something about the elusive Connor. We sat there, me on the beanbag and Brooks-Powell on the chair, his back to me once more, and I felt those files slipping further and further away.

"OK, I've got it," he said, suddenly, and I sat back up. "But it's on you, Sam. They know my voice. You're going to have to do it."

He set out his plan. I didn't like it, but there was no other plan hanging around waiting to be snapped up, and I didn't not like it enough to give up on those files. We gave it half an hour – Jenny, from the sound of it, was set for the evening, but we wanted to wait until Rebecca Ashcroft had left for the ballet. And then we called.

"Hello," I said, my voice slightly deeper than usual. I'd never met Philip Lancaster, the man I was pretending to be, and there was no reason to suspect he had a particularly deep voice, but deep seemed somehow right. "Hello, I'd like to speak with Rebecca Ashcroft, please."

"I'm sorry, she's not here. I can put you through to her secretary if that will help?"

"Thank you."

So far so good.

"Hello, this is Jenny Beech. Rebecca's secretary. Can I help you?"

Same words, same delivery as last time. Professional. Her struggles with the phone system aside, I liked the sound of Jenny Beech.

"Hello, this is Philip Lancaster." I was hoping she knew who Philip Lancaster was. It was her first day, but he was one of the most senior partners at the firm. Hopefully she'd have heard of him. She wouldn't have met him, barring extremely bad luck, because, as Brooks-Powell had just informed me, Philip Lancaster was just coming to the end of a three-month sabbatical which he'd spent on a boat, or several boats, sailing around a variety of Caribbean islands. Philip Lancaster was due back at work in just over a week. He and Brooks-Powell were, apparently, quite friendly, which surprised me at first, because I couldn't think of Brooks-Powell being friendly with anyone, even this new, improved Brooks-Powell. After a moment's thought it fell into place. David Brooks-Powell had the millionaire wife and the mansion. Philip Lancaster had the boats and the Caribbean, and, apparently, a chalet in a glamorous Swiss resort I'd heard of and associated vaguely with the royal family.

"What can I do for you, Mr Lancaster?"

She'd heard of me. Of him. I could tell from the deference with which she spoke the name.

I played it straight, at first. I was home and I needed some files to be sent round to my house. And Jenny was sympathetic, but still professional, and slightly hesitant. So I wheedled, stressing the importance and the urgency and how she'd be doing me a tremendous favour, because my wife would kill me if the first thing I did on my return from the Caribbean was to head into work on a Saturday night.

"He's divorced," hissed Brooks-Powell, but it seemed Jenny Beech wasn't familiar with Philip Lancaster's marital status, because she agreed to have the files sent over as soon as she had located them.

"They'll be in Rebecca's office," I said. "Thank you." I reeled off Brooks-Powell's address and prayed she wouldn't check that against Philip Lancaster's entry in the partnership directory.

The files were with us forty minutes later, during which we'd knocked back most of a bottle of red wine that looked expensive and tasted slightly sour. I was drinking because I wanted to, but I was also drinking out of guilt. Jenny Beech was going to be in a world of trouble come Monday. I mentioned this to Brooks-Powell, and he just shrugged and said something about "collateral damage", which was an unpleasant flash back to the old him.

We'd moved downstairs, to the living room in which Melanie had entertained us the night before. With her away, no need to remain cooped up in the *box room*, as Brooks-Powell put it, which made me wonder whether he actually knew what a box room was, or whether the boxes were just that much bigger in his world. Claire called while we were waiting, demanded to know where I was, which was a bit rich, I felt, but didn't say. I told her I was working, and she shot back with "Who is she this time?", but then stopped and apologised before I'd had a chance to deny it.

"It's OK," she said. "Come back when you're done. I'll be here. Got to go. There's a call coming through. It's Viktor."

I was worried about Claire, but that seemed to be turning into a permanent thing, a constant low-level tension that hit me whenever I wasn't worrying about something else. Right now, I had more immediate things to worry about. I felt a little bad about the stunt we'd pulled on Jenny Beech; I hoped it wouldn't blow up in her face, and tried to work out if there was any chance it would blow up in mine. But the wine helped with the guilt, and the arrival of the files washed it clean away.

We decided to divide them in half, flick through, and swap over when we were done, but we'd barely begun when my phone rang again, with a very unwelcome voice at the end of it.

"Hello, Sam."

Trawden. I hesitated before replying, as if giving away my identity was giving away anything at all.

"Hello Trawden. What can I do for you?"

"Well, a little birdie told me you've been digging, and

really, you of all people should know better."

Brooks-Powell was sitting opposite me in an armchair, with a questioning look on his face. I mouthed "Trawden" at him, put the phone face up on the table between us, and switched it to speaker.

"What exactly do you mean?"

"No need to play coy, Sam. You're after my files. I can't imagine there's anything in there you don't already know, though. And if there is, well, all you have to do is ask?"

"Ask?"

"Well yes. Just ask. I've nothing to hide. If you need some background, you know, for those *memoirs* you're working on, I'll be more than happy to assist. And between my experience and your photographic memory, I doubt we'll miss anything."

Those memoirs, again. I didn't like the way he said the word, as if he didn't believe it, as if he knew the memoirs were nothing more than a cover for something far more interesting, if it existed at all. It was there, in Brooks-Powell's living room, with Edward Trawden on the phone and his history spilling out across the sofa beside me, that I realised he was right. It wasn't about the memoirs. Not any more.

I wondered whether to deny it, to throw in a soft meaningless rebuttal or two, but I didn't think Trawden would buy it, and he hadn't stopped talking, anyway. Now he was onto the reminiscences.

"We saw a bit, you and I, didn't we? Do you remember that day in court, Sam?"

"Yes," I replied, uncertain where he was heading but not looking forward to getting there.

"Yes, it was remarkable. *You* were remarkable, Sam. I know Elizabeth got all the credit, but it was your work, your digging, that was what did the job. But then, every victory is tempered, isn't it?"

He paused, but there was no way I was jumping in now. My mouth was dry and my mind was racing – I couldn't have spoken even if I'd known what to say. *Every victory is tempered.* I knew those words. He went on.

"Do you remember them, Sam? The Grimshaws? Do you remember their faces, the look on their faces, when the judge said I was walking out of there a free man? I know we were celebrating, you and me and Elizabeth, we had reason to celebrate, but those faces – I'm not likely to forget them. I doubt you are, either. Faces like that are enough to haunt a man for the rest of his life. And you try to push them away, of course you do, and maybe you get through a day without seeing them, but they're always back at night, aren't they?"

I glanced up from the phone. Brooks-Powell was staring at me with a concerned look on his face. I was shaking.

"Anyway, Sam. Like I said. All you have to do is ask. Be seeing you."

He ended the call. I reached for the glass in front of me and drained it in one gulp. Brooks-Powell walked over to a sideboard and came back with a bottle of whisky, but I shook my head. We sat there in silence for a moment. Trawden's voice might have been sympathetic, but the words were anything but. How did he know? How could he know about the years of nightmares I'd faced, how it had ground me down until I couldn't work any more, not properly, not the way I'd worked before he'd come into my life? How could he see inside my head?

And then I had it.

Elizabeth Maurier. I'd told her. I'd gone to her quietly, months after the trial had ended and she'd moved on to other things as though it had been just another case, just another client. I'd told her, in confidence, about the Grimshaws, about the nightmares, about the way it hit me, every night, and suddenly during the day, while I was reading a file or talking to a client or eating dinner or drinking coffee. She'd suggested a counsellor, told me the firm would pay for one if my insurance wouldn't, but she'd said all that so casually, so dismissively, that I'd never got round to it. She'd given me her famous smile as I turned to leave, and she'd said something that had seemed, at the time, to sum up every disappointment I was feeling.

"Every victory is tempered," she'd said. I'd nodded back at her and walked out of the room and mulled over those words. If every success had a downside like this one, I'd thought, maybe I'm not cut out for this job.

And now Trawden had thrown those same words back at me. She'd told him everything. She'd betrayed me. I wondered whether they'd laughed at me, whether they'd sat there in the office or the pub downstairs, or even in the drawing room in her Oxfordshire house, and laughed at the poor struggling lawyer who couldn't handle a little sadness in the world.

I reached for the whisky. I'd changed my mind.

19: A Short History

CLAIRE WAS ASLEEP when I got home – it was only ten, but there she was, lying on her side sheathed in winceyette, breathing deep and slow and utterly oblivious to the drunk staggering around the flat trying not to break anything.

After Trawden's call we'd made excellent progress on the whisky, but very little on the files. Instead, I'd taken my share home and we'd agreed to get through as much as we could the following day. I stopped outside the front door and scanned the street, but everything was quiet and there was no sign of Rich Hanover or his bike. Inside, I put the papers down, undressed, and slid into bed beside Claire, thinking I'd be getting up in half an hour's time, haunted by Trawden's voice and the images from the trial, and spend the night blinking and trying to focus on decades-old legal documents. Instead I fell immediately into a deep and dreamless sleep, and woke late next morning to find a cold empty space beside me, and in the kitchen a note that wasn't much warmer.

"I've gone out," it said. And underneath that. "Your friend Blennard called. Said he'd try again later."

Blennard. Through the fog that was seeping through my brain, I remembered he'd called Brooks-Powell while I'd been there the day before. Blennard had called. Trawden had called me. Martins had called, earlier. A paranoid man might think there was something they wanted to keep me from finding.

As for Claire, I tried, as I made myself a double-strength coffee, to remember the last time we'd had a normal conversation. I couldn't. There were ups and downs, but nothing in the middle, and lately precious little up.

Everything between us seemed fragile and tense and on the verge of breaking. Sod Claire, I decided. I'd tried to meet her halfway, and then I'd kept on walking until we were nose to nose. Even after that, she wouldn't talk to me. Sod Claire. She could defrost when she was ready. I'd had enough of pushing the buttons. And sod Blennard. He was welcome to call back, but he wouldn't be getting the politest reception from me if he did.

As if on cue, the doorbell rang, and I leapt from the sofa, spilling coffee on my t-shirt in the process.

"Who is it?" I asked, as I approached.

"It's the police. Please can you open the door?"

The police? It was Colman's voice, Vicky Colman, although not the way I'd have expected her to announce herself. As I turned the handle to open the door it occurred to me she might not be alone, she might have brought someone with her, she might have brought Martins with her, which would account for her formality. But when I pulled the door open she was standing alone, frowning.

"Mr Williams?"

"Yes," I said, before I'd digested the question, and then "Yes, of course. You know who I am."

She ignored the latter part of my reply.

"Mr Williams, we've received a complaint, and I'd like to come in and discuss it with you, if I might."

"A complaint?"

"Please can I come in?"

I stood aside and watched her walk into the living room and slump down onto the sofa, the frown suddenly gone and its place a sly grin. I closed the door.

"What the hell was that about?"

"Can't risk the bitch finding out we're working together. And I thought it would be funny. You should have seen your face."

I shook my head, slowly. "Funny. Yeah. Dead bloody

funny."

"The thing about the complaint wasn't a joke, though. We have had a complaint."

"Really?"

"Yup." She stood up and sauntered over to the kitchen. "Got anything to eat?"

I pointed to the corner, where a collection of near-empty cereal packets appeared to have nested. "There's a bowl with a couple of apples in it round there somewhere, too. Who's complained?"

Ignoring the apples, she reached into a packet of corn flakes and came out with a handful. "Trawden," she said, chewing furiously. "Sorry. Haven't eaten since yesterday lunchtime."

Frustration was beginning to eat through the surprise. "Will you stop eating for a minute and tell me what's going on?"

She shrugged in mock offence and returned to the sofa, still chewing.

"Trawden spoke to his mate, Blennard. Blennard spoke to the bitch. The bitch told me to scare the living shit out of you. That's it. Short story."

I sank into the sofa beside her, thinking. I knew nothing, but even knowing nothing seemed to have people running scared. And that made me all the more determined to find out something useful.

Colman's eyes had fallen to the coffee table. She reached forward and picked up a few pieces of paper.

"These from the files? The ones you got from Hancocks?"

I nodded. She was certainly well-informed.

"You're not supposed to have these, you know," she said.

"I know." I turned to face her, uncertain where she was heading. "Gonna take them from me?"

She smiled, finally, and shook her head.

"Not bloody likely. I'm going to help you."

The following three hours were spent in silence, broken occasionally by a sigh of disappointment from Colman as yet another page was relegated to the cast-off pile with no great revelation found. Her day job would have involved just as many dead ends, if not more, but those dead ends were probably a sight more interesting than the minutiae of court reports, disclosure requests and complaints about the quality of legal representation. There was a smattering of background information, Trawden's life and works distilled in black and white, but no smoking gun.

Edward Trawden had been born in 1948, in a Staffordshire village neither of us had heard of. He'd shown early promise at primary school, breezed through grammar school, and arrived at Christ Church College, Oxford, in 1966 with the green fields and rolling hills of a brilliant destiny before him.

It hadn't quite worked out like that, of course, and I thought I could see why. Even when I'd been at Oxford, Christ Church had a certain reputation: its students were the wealthiest, the best connected – clever, certainly, but intelligence wasn't their defining characteristic. Lord Sebastian Flyte's college, in *Brideshead Revisited*, and although times had moved on and Christ Church had moved with them, I couldn't imagine its sixties incarnation being the most welcoming environment for a grammar school lad from the Potteries, even one as gifted at shifting his shape as Trawden seemed to be.

There was a letter in the file from his tutor, regretting that "it has come, finally, to this" – couching his expulsion alternately in a wistful, elegiac sadness and the formal euphemism of the university.

As we were poring over the Oxford correspondence, my

phone rang. I recognised the number, but answered anyway.

"Mr Williams," he began, without preamble. "I've been hearing things that concern me gravely."

"Fascinating, Mr Willoughby," I replied. So he'd reverted to *Mr Williams*, had he? This time, I decided, I wasn't going to let him have it all his own way.

"Yes," he said, his tone very much that of a teacher berating an errant pupil; the very tone Trawden had no doubt been forced to endure during his brief spell at Oxford. "Yes, I understand you have gone well beyond your brief in this matter."

I snorted. I couldn't help it. I had no intention of lying down and letting him walk over me, but I didn't plan to rile him, either.

"I'm sorry, Mr Willoughby, but I believe you've been misinformed." I was, I realised, unconsciously adopting his own manner of speaking. That was fine by me. "All I have done is pursue areas of historical interest that will be germane to the memoirs."

"Now listen, Williams," he replied, and the tone had changed. There was a seriousness there, a flaunting of his superior position, but underneath it a desperate powerlessness which made me all the surer of my position. "It has come to my attention that you are abusing your role as beneficiary, and in danger of abusing the bequest itself."

"Preposterous," I began, but Willoughby was still talking.

"And I must inform you that the Law Society would not look kindly upon your position should a complaint be made, Mr Williams. You would do well to act in such a manner as to avoid tarnishing your reputation."

I snorted again, and followed the snort with a full-blown laugh. "I'm sorry, Mr Willoughby, but you're clearly not very familiar with my reputation if you think there's much of it left to tarnish. And incidentally, Mr Willoughby, I'd steer clear of the Law Society if I were you, or they might take it upon themselves to find out how confidential information about a murdered woman's bequests found its way into their own gossip column. Now, if you'll leave me to get on with my work, I'll be going now."

I killed the call. A threat from Willoughby was very different from the sinister machinations of Trawden and his friends. If he'd been intending to put me off, he'd miscalculated. I felt buoyed.

That was a good thing, because Colman was becoming more deflated with each page. She'd continued leafing through the files as I sparred with Willoughby, her sighs getting louder and her frown broader. She was wearing a dark trouser suit, which didn't suit her and didn't strike me as the sort of thing she'd wear by choice, so I was guessing she'd come straight from work, or was on her way. Whichever it was, Trawden's files weren't doing anything to lift her mood.

We took a break, which meant Colman raiding the cereal again – I provided her with milk and a bowl and spoon this time – and me retreating to the shower to clean myself up. I'd been wearing yesterday's clothes when Colman had arrived, and hadn't seen the need to change if we stood a chance of making any sort of progress. That chance, unfortunately, was looking smaller by the minute.

As I stepped out of the bathroom, clad only in a ragged blue towel, the door opened and Claire walked in. I watched her take in the scene, turning from me, shrouded in the steam escaping from the bathroom behind me, to Colman, sat on the sofa with a bowl of corn flakes in front of her and a quiet little smile on her face as she returned Claire's gaze.

"Hi," I said, trying to project an air of normality into the situation. "Claire, this is Vicky Colman. Detective Sergeant

Colman. Vicky, this is Claire. My *girlfriend*."

I emphasised the *girlfriend*, hoping it would buy me points with Claire and encourage Colman to play ball, and then I remembered what I'd decided that morning. I'd done as much as I could. It was up to Claire to straighten things out.

"Hi Vicky," she said, walked over to the sofa and extended a hand. She smiled as they shook. She turned, walked to me, gave me a peck on the cheek and said "Hello, darling. I've just come back to pick up some papers. Busy busy busy!"

She disappeared into the bedroom, but before I had a chance to figure out what was going on she was back again, some scraps of paper in her left hand, another kiss on the cheek, a "Nice to meet you, Vicky" – and she was gone. I turned back to Colman, who was watching me patiently, as though I was about to come up with an explanation for what had just happened.

I had no explanation.

Instead I picked up the nearest sheet of paper from the Hancocks files. Trawden had encountered little difficulty in the years after leaving Oxford, in the short term, at least. He'd moved to London and drifted into journalism, working for a variety of local newspapers with moderate success for around a decade. He'd started as a generalist, but moved into entertainment reviews and then, more specifically, theatre, before a sudden departure from the *London Evening Standard*. No explanation was offered for that departure, and nobody seemed to have sought one, but as I glimpsed into the years that followed, I thought I could sense the outline of a reason.

After the *Standard*, he'd continued to glide naturally into theatreland. A fixture in the bars of the West End, a regular at the backstage parties and the opening nights. Nobody seemed to know quite what Edward Trawden – Eddie, as he styled himself at the time – was doing, but there he was, knowing everybody worth knowing, introducing them to one another, making ill-defined *arrangements* to the mutual benefit of all involved. The perfect environment, I thought, for someone like him, first one thing, and then another, always ready to play to his audience.

Drugs, I assumed. If he'd been supplying drugs to the cast or crew of the plays he was supposed to be reviewing, the *London Evening Standard* would have wanted shot of him as quickly and as quietly as possible. But the files were shy, drugs weren't mentioned, nothing was mentioned. A few years in theatreland and then a sudden departure from there, too, first to Stoke-on-Trent, not far from where he'd been born, and finally to Warrington, where he'd set up as an antiques dealer, operating from home, spotting deals at auction, usually from estate sales run by clueless beneficiaries who had no idea the pot or painting they were selling for a few pounds might be worth thousands. I could see him talking his way round them, the grief-stricken widows he'd have plied with tea and cake, the adult children lumbered with a skipload of useless junk that Trawden would be happy to take off their hands and allow them to return to the rest of their lives.

Trawden had enjoyed a level of success in the antiques business. Nothing stellar, but enough to earn him a semi-detached house in a quiet suburb and keep him in food and drink until Her Majesty's Prison Service took over that particular role. Less than a year after he'd moved into his new home, he was arrested and charged with the murder of Maxine Grimshaw, and there was nothing in the files that followed I hadn't seen before. I hoped Brooks-Powell was having more luck with his share of the loot.

My phone rang. I didn't recognise the number. I answered warily, expecting yet another warning from someone who thought they were entitled to tell me what to do.

"Sam Williams?" said a voice I'd thought I wouldn't be hearing again.

"Hanover? What does it take to get rid of you? What do you want now?"

"Don't hang up. I'm not calling to give you any grief. Really. I just wanted to pass on something I've heard."

I sighed. It couldn't hurt, I supposed, although I very much doubted it would help.

"Go on."

"Word is you've been rubbing the police up the wrong way. Word is, they're this close to pulling you in." I imagined him pressing his thumb and forefinger together to illustrate the point. "Want a chance to put your side?"

I thought about it, for a minute, silent.

"Sam?"

"Hang on."

It was tempting, certainly. Use the press, flush some secrets out. Piss off Martins, who liked everything so tightly controlled she could sit back and let things run themselves. But I didn't trust Hanover. And even if I did, what could I say? The only thing I really had was the board and the other victims, and if I told Hanover about all that Martins would pull me in for sure. I wouldn't even blame her.

"No," I said, reluctant but certain this was the sensible move.

"Come on."

"Look, Hanover, I can see you're doing the right thing here, so well done you, but I haven't really got anything I can tell you. If I did have, I would."

"Call me if you change your mind."

"Does this mean you're going to rip me apart in your next story?"

He laughed. "No. Not me. Not us. Someone probably will, though, sooner or later. You'll regret not having got your own side in first when that happens."

"Maybe you're right," I said, and ended the call. I turned to Colman. "Looks like your boss has gone to the press after all."

"Really?" She looked surprised.

"Not about the case. About me. Wants me muzzled."

She nodded. "Makes sense. She hates the press. She hates you. She's using one enemy against the other and keeping herself in the clear. Got to admire her, really, haven't you?"

"No I fucking don't," I muttered, and went back to the files.

An hour or so later, as I was setting down the final sheet of paper, she sighed and turned to me and said "There's nothing here, is there?"

I shook my head. I explained my theory, about the Evening Standard and the drugs, but even I knew it wasn't provable, even if it were true, and it probably wasn't useful even if it were provable.

"Right," she said, and stood. "I'm on late tonight. Gonna go home, grab some food, grab some sleep, get myself into work so Martins can string me up because I've forgotten to read her mind. Let me know if anything comes up."

I hadn't asked, I realised. I hadn't even asked the all-important question.

"Any luck catching our killer?"

She shook her head. "Nope. Not looking likely, unless someone does something to shake things up. My guess is we'll get a deathbed confession in fifty years' time from someone we could have caught last week if we'd opened this up to the public. But Martins doesn't like the public. Too messy."

I noticed the time, as she left. Five, and I hadn't eaten a thing all day. Colman hadn't left much cereal behind, but there was a giant sirloin steak in the fridge we'd been saving for a special occasion. There hadn't been a special occasion, the steak was a day away from turning bad, and there was no sign of Claire, so I threw it in the pan, finished it in the oven, and ate the whole thing in five minutes, no vegetables, no bread, just steak and mustard and a glass of cold water.

I was washing the pan when the phone rang. It was Brooks-Powell, and he was excited.

"I've got something," he said, before I could get a word out.

"What?"

"Did you know there was a link, between Akadi and Trawden?"

I thought about it, for a second. We'd asked them both, of course; Akadi was the one who'd brought the case back to life, and it was important his motives be clean. There was no connection between them.

"No," I said. "There was no link. We asked."

"Did you check?"

Again, I took a moment to cast my mind back twelve years. Had we checked? Or had we just asked them both, assumed they were telling the truth, forgotten about the details in the excitement of putting Evans on the spot on the day of the murder.

"No," I said.

"I'm emailing it through. Take a look and call me back," he said, and hung up.

I woke the laptop and sat there waiting for it to gather itself together. The email appeared two minutes later, no message, just a picture attached. I clicked.

The image on my screen was a photograph. An old photograph, judging by the graininess and wash of the colour, and by the clothes the people in it were wearing.

The photograph showed a group of people standing in front of a bar. There was a caption, over the top, neat handwriting in thick, dark ink. "Coach and Horses, April 21st, 1981. Opening night for *Life, Death and Everything in the Middle*."

I'd never heard of the play, but that didn't matter. What mattered were the people. There were seven of them, five men and two women, and it was the two men standing next to one another at the back of the group that drew my eye. The photograph had been taken decades before I'd laid eyes on either of them, but I knew them. I was sure of it.

Akadi and Trawden.

At the bottom of the photograph was another line of writing, in biro. A distinctive leaning scrawl, very different from the careful script above. A scrawl I'd seen a lot of, over the last few days. Six words in the unique handwriting of Elizabeth Maurier.

"Not relevant to defence or prosecution."

PART 3: SONG

20: Unwoven

I STOOD BACK and watched as Brooks-Powell pounded on the door. There was a bell, an obvious bell sitting there clear as day just to the side, but Brooks-Powell was in the mood for pounding.

He might, I had to concede, have a point.

I'd called him straight back, as soon as I'd read those words. *Not relevant to defence or prosecution.* And shoved in the bottom of a file half a million pages long, hidden from everyone else involved in the case. Hidden from me.

I was furious with Elizabeth. Brooks-Powell's anger took an entirely different direction.

"She knows," he said. "She bloody knows!"

"Who?"

"Who? Lizzy bloody Maurier, of course. She knows about this. She's known all along and she's been deliberately keeping this from us. She's got all those bloody boxes, all those bloody files, what have you seen, a tenth of them, a hundredth? She's got all this. She knows."

"Slow down," I replied. "The boxes are full of poems. It's her mother who knew, not Lizzy. No doubt Elizabeth thought it was just a coincidence and didn't want to muddy the waters, especially once we had Evans in Warrington on the day. But Lizzy?"

"She knows. I'm telling you. I'm going round there."

And he'd hung up.

I stood there, bewildered, for a moment, wondering what I should do next, and then I grabbed my coat and my keys and headed out the door. I typed a text for Claire as I jogged to the tube station, head bowed against the wind and rain. "Had to go out," it said. "See you later." I wiped a few drops from the screen and looked at what I'd written, and added a question mark at the end, which made it seem friendlier at the same time as asking another, more pertinent question, namely *where the hell are you?* I hit send as I sprinted down the escalator, just before my signal cut out. I didn't know what Brooks-Powell was planning, but I had an idea I'd need to be there to soften it.

I ran all the way from Notting Hill tube, and reached the corner of Lizzy's road as Brooks-Powell was heading up the path to her front door. "Stop!" I shouted, and he looked up at me, shook his head, and started pounding. When I reached him twenty seconds later he was still pounding, no let-up, no break or diminution in the blows. I was glad I wasn't that door. I was glad I was the right side of it. If Lizzy Maurier had any sense, she'd keep it shut.

It seemed she had no sense, because as Brooks-Powell was drawing back his right fist for a renewal of the assault, the door opened, and there she was, arms folded, head to one side, the very picture of the wronged woman.

"David," she said, and he took a step back, suddenly deflated. "There's a doorbell," she continued, pointing at it, and then turned and walked back inside, leaving the door open. As Brooks-Powell started to follow I reached him and put a hand on his shoulder.

"Let me do the talking," I said, quietly. He stopped and stared at me, and I could see the fight dying in his eyes. He nodded, and I followed him inside.

The boxes had gone. The flat looked the better for it, but there was still an air of neglect that didn't go with the cream walls and the shiny light fittings. Nothing I could see or smell, nothing I could put my finger on. Just an air. She led us through to the living room, pointed to the armchairs – there were two now, where there had just been one before, but with the boxes gone there was plenty of room – and sat down on the sofa, staring at us. No opening pleasantries. No offer of a drink. I sensed Brooks-Powell turning to look at me. It was time to begin.

"Lizzy, we've found something that's come as quite a surprise."

Brooks-Powell took a loud, long breath. No doubt he'd have opened with a more aggressive gambit. Lizzy carried on staring at me. I went on.

"It turns out Trawden and Akadi knew one another. Before the whole Evans thing. Back in the eighties."

She shrugged, now, as if she didn't know a thing about it and it wouldn't have mattered if she had. I waited for her to say something, but all I got was the shrug. So I continued.

"And more important, your mother knew about it. She knew all about it."

"And," thundered Brooks-Powell, already forgetting it was me that was supposed to be doing the talking, "she didn't tell anyone."

He'd managed to keep his voice down to a moderate roar, which was an improvement, but I shot him a warning look, anyway, and he gave a brief nod of acknowledgement.

"There's a photo," I said, "of Trawden and Akadi, together, in a pub in 1981. Your mother's written on it, says it's not relevant to the case. But even if it wasn't relevant, doesn't it strike you as odd that she never told anyone?"

Lizzy nodded. Her arms were still folded, a barrier across her chest. Her jaw was set. But there was something else in her eyes. A weakening. I pressed on, knowing what I was about to say would be difficult to hear, but knowing at the same time that it had to be said.

"Lizzy, this is important. Your mother was murdered. They haven't caught the killer. If you knew about this, if there's anything else you know, you've got to tell us. You've got to."

Still she sat in silence. I turned to Brooks-Powell; he looked at me, a question on his face. *Is it time?*

It was time. It was time to wheel out the big guns. I

nodded.

"Come on, Lizzy," he said. "Talk to us. It's not like someone's cut out your tongue, too."

She gasped – the first sound she'd made since she let us in. She gasped, and shook her head, and Brooks-Powell, encouraged by the response, carried on.

"Or maybe they have. I mean, look at you. I remember you, ten, fifteen years ago, you were full of life. Bursting with it. And look at you now, for Christ's sake. Why are you protecting her? She gagged you and shoved you in a box your whole life, and even now she's dead you won't climb out. But you can, Lizzy."

She was still shaking her head, but there were no tears. I'd been expecting tears. Instead, there was something else, a loosening of that jaw, a sense almost of relief. Of release.

And Brooks-Powell, having gone in for the kill, was playing it more sensibly and gently than I'd have given him credit for. He'd got to his feet and walked towards her and extended a hand, and now he was kneeling down in front of her speaking so quietly I could hardly hear the words.

"Climb out, Lizzy. I know it's hard. But you can, and you must. Climb out."

And to my amazement, she took his hand, and as he rose slowly to his feet, she rose too, until they were both standing. She turned to look at me. Now the tears were coming.

"I'm sorry," she sobbed. "I should have said something. I should have told someone. But I couldn't. Don't you see?"

I sensed Brooks-Powell about to argue the point, and jumped in before he could.

"Yes. Of course I can see, Lizzy. Of course *we* can see. But now you can. You can tell us. You can tell us everything."

She nodded. She sat back on the sofa. Brooks-Powell returned to his chair. And the tale began to unspin.

"Yes," she said. "There was something. She'd always been interested in that case, but in the last few months it was like an obsession. She called me every day, and she'd pretend to be calling about something else, but at some point she'd always mention Trawden. She'd sat on something for decades – I suppose it was this picture, I didn't know about it, truly, but I knew she was keeping a secret somewhere. She even told me as much, said there was a fact that she should probably have disclosed, but it wasn't relevant, and she still believed that. And," she turned to me, frowning, "and she's right, isn't she? I mean, whatever else we know, we know that Evans killed that girl. He was there, on the day. We know it."

I nodded. I'd known it for years. I'd been certain of it, however much I despised Trawden, however haunted I was by those faces at the trial, however uncomfortable I felt. I'd known it.

Only now, I wasn't so sure I knew it any more.

"There was this man, Shapiro, I think he was called, she kept saying *maybe Shapiro was right*. She tried to speak to Trawden, but he wouldn't make himself available, and in the end he moved his affairs to some other firm. That only made her more determined. She managed to speak to Akadi, and she claimed he'd lied to her the same way he always lied, but she'd found something anyway."

"What? What did she find?"

Brooks-Powell was sitting up, unable to contain himself.

"Connor," she said, and I felt my heart miss a beat. "There was a man called Connor. When Akadi and Evans were in Pentonville, they shared a cell."

Brooks-Powell and I looked at one another, his frown echoing my own.

"We know that," I said, and she shook her head.

"No, you don't understand. They shared a cell with *Connor*."

233

There was something in that. I couldn't put my finger on it, I couldn't figure out why it was important, but it was. I knew it was.

Brooks-Powell didn't feel the same way.

"So what?" he said. "I'm sure they shared cells with plenty of people."

Lizzy shook her head, again. "No they didn't. Not Akadi and Evans. Two to a cell, back then. First Connor and Evans, then Evans and Akadi. Except for one fortnight in the middle, right around the time Evans made his confession, when all three of them were in together. Overcrowding, apparently, but it didn't last long. Connor attacked Akadi, Connor got kicked out of the cell, and after that it was just Akadi and Evans, right up to the day Evans died."

Brooks-Powell was still frowning. I wasn't. I was starting to inch my way towards the light.

"And what, Connor knew something, from his time in the cell with them? He knew something that might have contradicted Akadi's version of the confession?"

She nodded. "Something like that. We never knew. Mother never knew. She thought she'd tracked him down, and I have a feeling she was supposed to be meeting him the night she died, but I don't know, I don't know anything, it's all so confused, it was never meant to be like this, she can't be dead."

The tears were coming, again, thick and fast. I stood and walked over to her, put a hand on her shoulder, and she turned and looked up at me and gave me a desperate, meaningless smile.

"But it's not real, is it, Sam? I mean, I know he's an odd man, Trawden. Maybe even a dangerous man. I know he's a liar. But he didn't kill that girl. Evans killed that girl. You proved it."

I nodded, again, even though the uncertainty had

grabbed itself a solid foothold and was starting to gain ground. Evans had been there. Evans was a killer, proven and convicted. That wasn't enough, not by itself. But there was more. There was the forensic evidence – I'd hardly glanced at the forensic evidence, it was all academic by that point, I doubt anyone had examined it very thoroughly, because putting Evans on the scene was enough to do the job.

"He's not a murderer, Sam," she was saying. "I'm sure of it. He's clever but there's something wonderful about him, too. Mother never saw that. But there is."

Wonderful? I wanted to explore that further, because *wonderful* was the last word I'd have used to describe Trawden, even with his strange ability to be a different person for every audience, but Brooks-Powell was focussed on the more mundane details.

"She thought she'd tracked him down, you said. Do you know how?"

She shook her head, frowned, and then nodded. "Wait here," she said, and stumbled out of the room. We heard the sound of something tearing from elsewhere in the flat – that little study, from my recollection of the layout – and a moment later she was back with a piece of paper in her hand. She stood there, unsure which of us to give it to, and Brooks-Powell answered for her by taking it from her and bringing it over to me.

"Search," it said. Elizabeth's handwriting, again. "Connor Trawden Akadi Evans Grimshaw."

I was trying to figure out what it meant, but Brooks-Powell was one step ahead of me.

"Where's your computer?" he asked, and Lizzy led us up the corridor to the study. The boxes were gone from here, too, and I wondered what she'd done with them. She hadn't sold them, that much was certain; there wouldn't have been more than half a dozen buyers in the country.

Maybe she'd pulped them, fulfilled her mother's wish, fulfilled her own promise fifteen years too late. Brooks-Powell sat at the desk and typed in the words, and a bunch of random pages – just lists of names, really – came up. But at the top of the list, not random at all, was something I recognised.

"Hit that one," I said, pointing at it.

It was the blog, the fan page, the website I couldn't quite describe. White text on black background, bare factual account of the murder and the trial and the appeal and the release. Little detail of any note. And, I realised, as I scanned the few short paragraphs again, no mention anywhere of the word "Connor".

"It's not here," I said, disappointed, but Brooks-Powell shook his head.

"Has to be here. It was the number one hit. That's a bunch of names we've fed in, there are hundreds of directories that'll have them all, so why does this one come up first?"

"But the name's not there."

"Oh, it's there," he said, turning to me with a sly grin that reminded me of the Brooks-Powell I'd known back at Mauriers. But now that grin was working with me, not against. "It's there. Probably in the metadata. We can find it, if you give me a little time."

"The what?" I asked, but he'd turned back to the screen already, tapping away, looking up, shaking his head, tapping away again, repeating the whole process. I glanced behind me, but Lizzy was nowhere to be seen. I hoped she was OK.

"Got it," said Brooks-Powell, finally, turning back to me with triumph written all over his face. "You know what happens when you highlight text on a web page, just select it to copy and paste or whatever?"

"Yeah," I said. "It changes colour."

"Precisely. And the easiest way to hide a word? Write it in the same colour as the background. So all I have to do is highlight the whole page, and – voila!"

I looked at the screen. He'd selected the complete text, every paragraph, and all the blank space above and below it. The text was now blue, the background was white, and the blank space wasn't blank any more.

Every single gap in the original text was filled. Every spare line contained the same word, over and over again. The breaks between the paragraphs teemed with it, even the breaks between individual words, in a font so tiny you could hardly read it. But it was there. Over and over and over.

The word was "Connor".

"This can't be a coincidence," said Brooks-Powell, and I found myself nodding. Someone had put that word there deliberately. Someone who knew what Connor knew, or knew that Connor knew something. Perhaps Connor himself.

"We've got to find out who runs this site," I said, and he turned back to the screen and started typing again.

"Got it," he said, a moment later. "Used ICANN."

I wondered whether it was worth asking who or what ICANN was, and decided it probably wasn't. Instead, I waited.

"Bollocks," he said, with feeling. "Look. Bloody corporate address. PO Box. It's held by a company and they're not telling who's behind that company. They're not supposed to do that."

"OK," I said. "It's not what we were hoping for. But it's a start."

"How?"

"Leave it with me."

He nodded. We left the study, wondering where Lizzy had got to, but we didn't have to wonder for long. The quiet sobs coming from the bedroom were clue enough.

"So I've done it," she said, as we came in. She was lying on the bed, her arms outstretched either side of her, the tears flowing freely down her face.

She was naked.

"I've broken the silence," she continued, as Brooks-Powell and I stared, speechless. "I've climbed out of the box. I've shed my old skin." She gestured at her body. "Are you happy now? Think I'll be happy now?"

I could sense Brooks-Powell preparing to say something, and held up a hand to stop him. Lizzy wasn't finished.

"Tereu, Tereu," she said. I remembered this. The wicked king. The rapist. Brooks-Powell knew all this already. He'd probably sucked it in with his mother's milk.

"She cut out my tongue. But she didn't bake me. That's something, isn't it? She didn't bake me in a pie."

It might have been a question, but she wasn't expecting an answer, because she went right on.

"Did I weave a tapestry of my own? Can I weave a tapestry now? Do tongues grow back? Is it too late to sing?"

She stopped, now, and looked up at us – until that moment she'd been addressing the walls.

"It's OK," she said. I thought she might be right. The tears had dried up and there was something close to a smile on her face. "It's OK. It really is."

"We can't leave you like this," I said, and she shook her head, the smile broadening enough to fool anyone that didn't know her and most that did. It didn't fool me. She might be on the way, but she wasn't there yet.

"It's OK," she repeated. "I'm not right. I've got problems. Look at me." She gestured at herself, at her naked body, and laughed. "Oh, I've got problems alright. But they're problems I know how to handle. I've handled them most of my life. I'm probably better equipped to do it now than I've ever been. And I've got the grief circle to help, if I need to."

I tensed, expecting a snort or a muttered expletive from Brooks-Powell, but to my relief, he managed to hold his tongue.

"Are you sure?" I asked.

"I'm sure."

As we let the front door fall shut behind us, my phone rang. Detective Inspector Martins. She wasn't happy, but I doubted happy was a state she was familiar with.

"Mr Williams. I've had reports of further harassment. You need to stop whatever it is you're doing."

"Detective Inspector Martins. How lovely to hear your voice," I replied. I wasn't afraid of her. I didn't know why, but the fear had dropped away. Blennard, Willoughby, Martins – everyone telling me at once to back off and back down, to drop it and step into line, to do what they were asking me to and not what I wanted to – I'd had enough of them. All of them. I'd had enough of their secrets and their incompetence and the way they allowed themselves to be manipulated so easily. I wondered who had reported this latest "harassment", and decided it was probably Trawden himself.

"I'm serious, Williams. If you don't stop it you'll be seeing the wrong side of a cell. Nice little lawyer like you? I don't think you'd like it very much in a police cell."

I laughed. I couldn't help it. I laughed so long and so hard I dropped the phone, and so uncontrollably my fingers couldn't get a grip on it when I tried to pick it up. Brooks-Powell picked it up for me, and passed it to me, and when my laughter had finally died down, I put it to my ear and explained myself to Detective Inspector Martins.

"You don't know me very well, Detective Inspector. You might think you do, but really? Leaking to the press? Threatening me with a cell? I've seen worse than that. I've seen worse than that this month. You'll have to try a little harder if you want to protect your friends, Olivia."

I killed the call. I didn't like leaving Lizzy the way she was, but she'd insisted, and I had the feeling she was right. She had problems enough. But she knew how to handle them. It was time to go home and consider my next move.

21: A Good Man

I TURNED IT over in my head all the way home, over and over, again and again. The third man in the cell. The website. Trawden. I thought back to what Shapiro had told me. The mania. The things he did that even he regretted. I remembered all that solid ground, that invincibility, the certainty that Evans had killed Maxine Grimshaw and Trawden was an innocent man.

Nothing seemed solid any more.

Suppose Evans was the innocent man – innocent of this particular crime, at least. Suppose Trawden was the killer. Suppose he'd killed in one of those manic phases, and regretted it, but it had been too late by then. Suppose he'd wormed his way out of it, decades later, and lived another decade and more as a free man until it came back to haunt him. Suppose he'd killed again, rationally, this time, without compassion or humanity or any of those things society tells us we need, but rationally, nonetheless. Suppose he'd killed to protect his hard-won freedom. And suppose, after that second killing, the mania had struck again – because it could, then, because he was free and he was better than everyone else, cleverer than everyone else, and hadn't he just proven it by eliminating his one point of vulnerability? And suppose, in the grip of that mania, he'd done something else he'd come to regret.

Suppose he'd written on a wall.

And after that? After the mania had subsided and he'd realised what he'd done, and what the implications might be, there was only be one thing a rational psychopath could do.

He'd killed again. And again. And again. Three more killings, three more bodies. He'd muddied the water and kicked over the traces, burnt all the links and buried the embers, hidden a tree in a wood and laughed while everyone looked the wrong way. And Elizabeth Maurier had something to say all along, and what she had to say was "Connor".

I turned it over and at the same time I made some calls. I'd told Brooks-Powell to go home and wait to hear from me, and he'd started to argue, and then changed his mind and nodded, and walked away. I was regretting that decision now; I could have done with someone to bounce ideas off, to tell me if I was just going round in circles or homing in on something real.

I called Roarkes. I wanted to know how he was, how Helen was, whether she was still alive.

"No change," he said, without asking who was calling, without me telling him. "No change, Sam. I don't know how long this can go on." That brief burst of cheerfulness I'd heard in him the day before had gone, and there was a hollow desperation in its place.

"I'm sorry, Roarkes. If there's anything I can do."

"There's nothing, Sam. There's nothing anyone can do."

I thought maybe Roarkes could help me with my problem, maybe it would help him start to get out from under his.

"In that case," I said, "come for a drink."

"I don't think so. I think I'll stay here."

"Come on. It'll do you good. I could do with running some stuff past you, too."

There was a short pause.

"What do you mean?"

"Oh, it's this case. The Elizabeth Maurier stuff. I'm supposed to be working on her memoirs and I keep finding things that – well, I'll have to show you, really. I'm adding up two and two and it would be good to have someone else tell me if I'm getting the right answer."

"Are you serious?"

"Yeah," I said. "Come on. I can bring it all down your way. We'll go to a pub."

"My wife is dying, Sam," he said, and I realised I'd misread him, his *what do you mean?* and *are you serious?* "I couldn't give a fuck about you and Elizabeth Maurier."

I heard the single high note of a call being disconnected and dialled his number again. I wanted to explain. I'd only meant to help. The phone rang for a minute and then went dead.

So I called Colman. She needed to know about my altercation with her boss, and she needed to know what we'd found. I brought her up to speed. *Leave it with me*, I'd told Brooks-Powell. Colman was my secret weapon. She was on shift, she had all the resources of the station at her disposal, and as long as she could keep out from under Martins' gaze she'd be better placed than anyone else to track down whoever was behind that PO Box and the website. I even tried Maloney, because he had ways of finding things out that the police couldn't. No answer from Maloney. That wasn't a rare thing. I left a message and hoped he'd finish whatever it was he was doing and deliver me something golden before Martins made good on her promise and locked me up.

But before I'd called anyone else, and again between every call I made, I tried Claire. I could have done with Claire's sideways style of looking at a problem. It had been Claire who'd cottoned onto the misdirection, the *ABC Murders*, the tree hidden in the wood. No answer from her, either.

I got home at half past nine and the phone was ringing, the landline, not my mobile. I reached it in time, hoping for Claire or Maloney or Colman, but what I got was Claire's mother.

"Hello Mrs Tully," I said. "How are you?"

"Not so bad, Sam," she said. She'd called me *Samuel* the first time we'd met, and the second, and I'd not said anything to her or to Claire about it, but the *Samuel*'s had dried up, so Claire must have sensed my discomfort and had a word. She was still *Mrs Tully* as far as I was concerned. "The rain plays hell with my bones, but that's England, isn't it?"

I supplied the expected laugh, refrained from the half-expected dig about Yorkshire, and waited for her to go on.

"Is Claire there?"

"Sorry, I'm afraid she's out. Anything I can help you with?"

"Do you have any idea where she is? I've tried her mobile, but she's not answering it."

I paused for a moment, and considered coming clean, considered telling her that I didn't know where Claire was and hadn't known much about what she was doing for days. That her daughter was flicking from low to high and back down again like a light switch, with the emphasis more on dark than light. But what good would it do?

"No, I'm sorry," I repeated. I wasn't sure what I was apologising for, but it was better than telling the truth.

"Has she been OK lately?" she asked, unexpectedly, as if she'd been reading my thoughts.

"I think so," I said, automatically.

"Oh good. Only, it's a difficult time. Fifteen years. I thought she might be feeling it."

I was lost. What was she talking about? Fifteen years of what? Fifteen years *since* what?

"Sam?"

I'd fallen silent, lost in lines of thought that led nowhere useful, and the silence had stretched too far for comfort.

"Yes?"

"Sam, you do know about it, don't you?"

Just a fraction of a second to decide this one, because if

I lied, I'd be caught in that lie by the time I'd drawn my next breath.

"No. No, Mrs Tully. I'm afraid I don't know what you're talking about. I don't know anything about this *fifteen years*. But I've got to say," I went on, the decision made and pushing me further in a direction I hadn't wanted to take, "Claire has been acting a little strange lately. Almost secretive."

Another silence, but this time the ball was in her court. I waited.

"Oh," she said, finally. "I really hadn't expected that. I'm not sure I should tell you about it. I mean, if Claire hasn't. It's hers to tell, really. Not mine."

The decision, I reminded myself, was made. No backing out now.

"Mrs Tully," I replied, firmly. "I have to be honest with you. I'm worried about Claire. I don't know where she is, and she's been out a lot lately without telling me where. It's not like I have to know. She's entitled to do what she wants. But it's not like her. And she doesn't talk any more. She just sits and watches the news."

"Ah yes. That case," she replied, and then gave a long, deep sigh. "OK. I think I'll have to tell you. It was fifteen years ago. Claire was just a teenager. Eighteen. She had a cousin. Not my side. Her father's side. Mandy, she was called. Amanda. Just fifteen years old."

There was a pause, another silence, only, I realised after a moment, it wasn't silence at all. Mrs Tully was struggling to catch her breath. Mrs Tully was crying. I waited.

"Claire and Mandy were close. Very close. Mandy's mother – that's my husband's sister, Georgie – we were all very close. They lived a couple of streets away and the girls played together from when Mandy was a baby. The age difference didn't seem to matter. Mandy's father left when she was four, but Mandy seemed fine, she was growing up to be an impressive young woman. A little wild, a little headstrong, perhaps, but always so sure of herself. I used to tell Claire, I used to say, you don't have to do everything she does, but you could be a little more like her, you know. Just trust yourself. You're a strong woman."

Another pause.

"Are you alright, Mrs Tully? If this is difficult," I began, but trailed off. It might be difficult but it had to be important, or she wouldn't be going behind her daughter's back to tell me about it. I waited, again.

"It's fine, Sam. Hold on one moment. I'm just getting myself a glass of water." Noises in the background, footsteps, a cupboard opening, a tap turned.

"That's better," she said, suddenly clear and matter-of-fact. She was telling a story. That was all. "Now, when Mandy was fourteen she became more withdrawn, spent more time alone. She still saw Claire a lot, they were like sisters, but she didn't go out with all her friends the way she had. I remember Georgie worrying about it and I used to tell her it was fine, she was just a teenager, they all go through it. God. I'll never forgive myself for that."

Another pause, but I wasn't making the mistake of filling it. A dam had broken.

"We knew nothing until it all came out, but by then it was too late. Far too late. Georgie had a partner by then, Joseph Farrell, a regular sort of chap, painter and decorator. They'd been living together for three years. And the whole time, he'd been grooming her daughter."

She took a deep breath and, by the sound of it, a deep drink. It might just be a story, but it wasn't an easy one.

"We didn't have that word back then, you know. *Grooming*. It sounds so innocent. Little girls playing with toy ponies. But that was what he'd been doing with her. Turning her into his toy. And when she turned fourteen, that's when the abuse began. He raped her, Sam. He raped her over and over again, and he'd convinced her she couldn't tell anyone about it, nobody would believe her, her mother wouldn't believe her. He'd worked on Georgie by then, convinced her Mandy's friends were trouble, and one by one she was cut off from them. The only friend she had left was Claire. And shortly after her fifteenth birthday she couldn't take any more, and she told Claire."

Another break. Another moment to take stock, even though I knew where the story was heading. I'd known from the beginning. *She had a cousin.* Past tense.

"Mandy begged Claire not to say anything to anyone. She was terrified. And Claire was a loyal friend, so she didn't, she didn't tell anyone, she didn't even tell me, but she was sensible, too, and she finally managed to hammer some sense into Mandy's head and convince her to go to the police. Fat lot of good that did."

Claire had never liked the police. I'd put that down to politics, to idealism, to a hangover from the teenage years. In one way, I'd been right.

"They didn't believe her. They were about as unsympathetic as they could be, they told her she should go home and think about it before making such serious allegations, that she could ruin someone's life over a strop, they asked if he'd grounded her or told her she couldn't see some boy and was this her way of getting him back, because if it was, well, wasting police time was an offence, they said, and anyway they didn't have the time to waste. And they sent her back home. They said they'd say no more about it as long as she didn't bother them again. So she went back home. And she went up to her room. And some time in the night."

She stopped, again, and I could hear her breathing, fast, trembling. No amount of water could stop the tears now. But she wasn't going to let the tears stop her.

"Some time in the night she killed herself. Hanged

herself. In her bedroom. They found her body the next morning. The seventeenth of December. Tomorrow. Fifteen years ago tomorrow."

"Oh God," I said. I couldn't help myself. I didn't want to interrupt, but I couldn't just sit there listening to this poor woman tell this terrible story and pretend I wasn't feeling it myself.

"She'd left a note. Told everything. Georgie didn't know what to believe. She was a wreck. Joseph Farrell moved out, still claiming he was innocent, and three years later he was caught."

"How?"

"Not for that. Not for Mandy. Someone else. He'd followed a girl home from school. Grabbed her. Tried to rape her. Failed. But when it hit the news others came forward. He'd been doing it for years. He got ten years, which we were furious about, we wanted him to rot inside, we wanted him to die in prison. We got what we wanted. He hanged himself. Just like Mandy. Couldn't handle it. Couldn't handle himself if there was someone bigger than a kid to deal with. He lasted six months, and I've got to tell you, Sam, when I heard, when we heard, Georgie came over and we drank two bottles of champagne."

"Oh God," I said, again. Fifteen years ago. Had she been trying to tell me about it? Had I been so wrapped up in everything else, had I been so absorbed with the here and now that when I wondered what was bothering her, I hadn't bothered to look at *her*, just the things around her, her job, her story, me? Had I just sat there and not noticed a thing, like Mandy's mother, all this pain going on inches away and me in my own stupid little world spouting stupid little lines like *sit tight* and *don't make it personal*?

"That was why I wanted to come down, Sam. That was why I wanted to stay. Claire's never forgiven herself. Do you understand? She thinks it was all her fault. Blames herself for persuading Mandy to go to the police. Blames herself for not going straight to me, or to Georgie, or to anyone who might believe her. She doesn't talk about it any more. She doesn't mention it to anybody, it's like she's buried it in the past and doesn't want it dug up. But I know she still feels it. I thought she'd need me."

You think you know someone. That was all I could hear, in my head. *You think you know someone.* I'd known Claire. As well as I'd known anybody. And I hadn't known her at all. I found myself casting about for things that might make everything better, sticks in the sea. I lighted on Adrian. At least she had someone to talk to, even if he did sound like a tosser. And then I remembered his message. He hadn't heard from Claire for a while.

"So where do you think she is, Sam? Why isn't she answering the phone?"

I paused, before answering. I didn't want to alarm her. But it wasn't like I had a bowlful of reassuring news to pour on the problem, either.

"I don't know, Mrs Tully. But one thing I do know is Claire's not stupid. She's clearly still feeling it. You're right. That explains her behaviour, the last week. But she's not stupid. And she won't do anything stupid, either."

"Yes. Yes. That's true." She sighed. "I think you're right. Even with the trial, and everything?"

"What trial?"

"Those people. The ones who put the migrants on the boats and let them drown. The trial. It's happening at the moment."

That was what she'd been watching. That was the news story she hadn't been able to tear her eyes off for days. Yes. It would upset her, something like that. The kind of thing she'd get fixated on. Abuse of power. Abuse of trust. Coming fifteen years after what had happened to her cousin.

"OK, I'm going to do everything I can to find her, Mrs Tully. I'll call if I hear anything. Anything at all. I promise."

"Thank you, Sam. You're a good man, I think. You'll look after her, won't you?"

"I promise," I repeated.

I spent the next five hours trying to live up to that promise. I called everyone I knew who knew Claire. I left messages with her colleagues and her editor and the night shift at the Tribune. I tried Maloney, with no more luck than I'd got earlier. I called Colman and she was sympathetic but said she couldn't do anything, since Claire wasn't really a missing person, and if she tried to put out an alert Martins would find out immediately and get it shut down. I even left a message with Adrian, and as I signed off with a falsely cheerful "Thanks, bye!" I found myself wondering whether he knew all this, whether he knew about Mandy at all, and if he did, why Claire wasn't better, or at least getting better.

Was Adrian part of the problem?

I checked her Facebook account, which she'd used precisely once in all the time I'd known her, and found the same entry on it, a "Thanks for the birthday wishes, everyone!" with a smiley face at the end and a hundred or so comments she'd never read. I even checked her Twitter feed, which was something I'd never done before, and while it was loading I closed my eyes and heard Mrs Tully's words again. *She's buried it in the past and doesn't want it dug up.* Claire and I had more in common than I'd realised.

I opened my eyes and focussed on the screen. I didn't like Twitter. Millions of angry people shouting at each other, none of them listening, I thought. And not many listening to Claire, by the look of it: her account had precisely eight followers. Her feed had a certain monomaniac obsession, one I imagined was shared by those eight: her case, her story, the murdered girls. Once or twice a week she'd tweet a link to a news article about the murders, always an old article, because the murders weren't news any more, hadn't been for years. She tweeted the links with little comment or opinion. Only, over the last week, something had changed. She'd stopped tweeting the links, and replaced them with short, simple sentences. Questions.

Tuesday: "Who will speak for Xenia?"

Wednesday: "Who will speak for Aurelia?"

Thursday: "Who will speak for Marine?"

Friday: "Who will speak for Iboni?"

Saturday: "Who will speak for Yelena?"

And today, this morning, Sunday the sixteenth of December, not a question, but a statement: "I'm not afraid of the big bad Wolf."

So Jonas Wolf had put in an appearance, too.

I remembered something she'd said, early on, when she'd accused me of playing her, of manipulating her, of trying to get her to do something she wasn't sure about.

"I don't like being groomed, Sam," she'd said. Even at the time I'd thought it a strange choice of word. It didn't seem quite so strange now.

She didn't like being groomed. Being tricked and twisted and lied to. And she wasn't prepared to tolerate it happening to anyone else, either. *Don't get too close*, I'd said, but I was fifteen years too late. This had always been close. Amongst the storm of feelings I was trying to push back down, because emotion wouldn't help me at all right now, I thought I sensed some pride. She'd lost it. Lost the plot. Lost her way and her sense of reality, adrift in a sea of memory and death. But she'd lost it for the right reasons. When I managed to track her down and steer her back to dry land, I'd remind her of that.

At three, struggling to keep my eyes open despite the gallon of coffee I'd taken in place of food, I gave up, lay down on the bed, and went straight to sleep.

It didn't last. My phone went off an hour later. I was hoping it was Claire, or her mother, or someone who knew where she was and what she was doing, but it wasn't. It was Brooks-Powell, and he was excited.

"We've been going about this the wrong way," he said.

"What?" I asked, still groggy.

"We've been hiding from them, when they're the ones who should be hiding from us. We need to go after them."

It was four in the morning, I'd had an hour's sleep, and I didn't know where my girlfriend was. I wasn't in the mood for cryptic.

"Go after who?" I asked.

"Look," he said, "we know Trawden's been lying, right?"

I thought about arguing, and then changed my mind and agreed. Trawden had been lying. We didn't know who he'd lied to or what he'd lied about, but we'd found too much to pretend he was on the level any more.

"OK," I said, grudgingly.

"And who's been helping him?"

"What do you mean?"

"Who's been covering for Trawden? Who do you think it is that's been calling Willoughby and Martins and the rest, stirring up trouble? Trawden couldn't do that himself, right?"

"Oh," I said. "Yes. Sorry. Still half-asleep. Blennard, you mean."

"Ten points to Williams. You can have a coffee when we're done."

"Yeah, about that," I said. "You haven't heard from Claire, have you?"

I didn't think there was a chance in hell, but I was going to follow every last blind alley to its end.

"Your Claire?"

"Yup. Haven't seen her all night. Her mum's worried about her. To be honest, I'm a little worried, too."

There was a pause at the end of the line, and somehow I knew that during that brief moment, Brooks-Powell had conjured up a quip about jealousy or infidelity, taken note of the seriousness in my voice, and squashed that quip back down. I was grateful.

"No, Sam. Sorry."

I sighed and turned my thoughts back to what we'd just been discussing. I didn't like Blennard, for all his charm. I didn't trust him. But I didn't like where Brooks-Powell seemed to be going with this.

"It's a little extreme, David," I said. "Blennard. What are you suggesting?"

"Remember how you cracked the Trawden case?"

"Yes, David. Using my brains," I shot back, and regretted it instantly.

"I know that. Even back then I was impressed. I couldn't stand you, but that didn't mean I wasn't impressed. No, what I mean is, why were you looking at Evans in the first place?"

"Well, it was Akadi, wasn't it?"

"That's why Evans was in the frame. But why were *you* looking at Evans?"

I took a moment to think back, but it was a blur. We landed Trawden. I landed a role on the case. And then – straight onto Evans. There must have been something in between, but whatever it was, I'd decided it wasn't important enough to stick.

"I don't remember, David. Does it matter?"

"I think so. There's a file note. In the Hancocks stuff. Elizabeth's handwriting. Record of a call between Blennard and Elizabeth. I'm going to read directly from it. OK?"

"OK."

"Right. Here we go. *Call with CB, re Trawden. I explained*

that things were going slowly but that wasn't necessarily a bad sign. CB seemed disappointed, suggested we take a look at others who have admitted the crime. I disagreed, pointed out that wasn't the way we do things here. Mauriers does not chase headlines. We'll do it slowly and carefully, but we'll pick apart the prosecution case, and if there's anything to find, we'll find it. CB took issue, said that firms had been trying that angle for twenty years and if there was anything to see, it would have come up by now. CB mentioned Robbie Evans, deceased convict with potential link to MG. I continued to disagree, but conceded we would take a look at Evans. Unlikely to be anything solid, but I will ask SW to follow the Evans angle."

Brooks-Powell had finished, and I couldn't think of anything to say. It wasn't exactly conclusive – Blennard had put us onto Evans, Evans had been the line that freed Trawden, and so bloody what? All that proved was that Blennard was looking out for Trawden and had an eye for the right angle. But still. It was another stick on a growing pile.

"There's more, Sam," said Brooks-Powell. He was speaking gently, quietly, whether that was out of deference to the seriousness of the subject or my concerns over Claire or the fact that there were just four hours to go before December's excuse for sunrise. "Do you remember who ran the investigation from the police side? When it was reopened, after you'd put Evans on the spot?"

"Yes," I said. "Detective Inspector Jones." I'd never met the man, just sent his subordinates some paperwork, and it wasn't exactly a name that stuck in the mind. But sometimes the odd little details of a case made a home there.

"That's right," he replied. "Detective Inspector Gareth Brady Jones. The late. He died three years ago."

"Oh," I said. I'd never known his forenames. Brooks-Powell went on, but he didn't need to. I knew what was coming.

"Later to become Deputy Commissioner Gareth Brady Jones of the Metropolitan Police. Friend and protégé of Lord Charlie Blennard. Member of the Reform Club, although that's not a hanging offence by itself. Jones would have been perfectly placed to make sure the investigation went where Blennard wanted it to. It wasn't like anyone cared. We all knew it was Evans, Evans was dead, no one was pleading his corner, the investigation was never supposed to be more than a box-ticking exercise anyway."

"It's still not evidence," I said, but my heart wasn't in it. Brooks-Powell was right. Blennard was in this, knee-deep or worse. "And why would he do it?" I continued, casting around for anything that would steer us away from where we were heading. "Why would Blennard protect Trawden?"

"I don't know. That's the one thing I can't figure out. What was in it for Blennard?"

I cast my mind back to Saturday. Shapiro. Went through his words. Thinking aloud.

"Shapiro said Trawden had helpers. Useful idiots and enablers, that was the way he put them. But Blennard doesn't strike me as the type. Too self-serving. Too intelligent. Blennard would know when he was being played, wouldn't he?"

"Maybe," said Brooks-Powell, but I ignored him, still thinking, still talking.

"And the other group. Blackmail victims. I don't know, David. I just don't see him fitting the profile."

"What did you just say?"

"I said I don't see him fitting the profile."

"No, not that. Before. Blackmail. Is that what you said? Did Trawden have a history of blackmail?"

"Shapiro thought so. Nothing proven."

"That's it." There was something new in his voice. Certainty. Determination. Something that said the work had been done and an end was coming. And something else, too, that I couldn't quite place. "That's it. I'll meet you there."

"Meet me where?"

"Blennard's apartment. Mayfair. Do you need the address?"

"No. I've got his card. Why? Why are we going there?"

"We're going to get some fucking answers out of Lord Charlie Blennard," he said, and hung up.

I'd placed it now, that something else. Anger. A fierce, steely anger. Claire still wasn't home and it was coming up for five in the morning, but something told me I had to get to Mayfair before Brooks-Powell did something he'd regret.

22: Relics

IT HAD JUST turned five when I arrived. I hadn't wanted to drive, because I was tired and didn't know the area, but when I'd searched my jeans pocket all I found were two pound coins. I was running low, I realised; that long-term cash problem was starting to bite. No one had returned any of my calls. Claire was out there, somewhere.

I pulled up on a double yellow line and hoped for the best. Brooks-Powell was waiting for me outside the building. In the stark illumination cast by the security lights he looked older, somehow; dishevelled, by his standards. There was a wildness in him I'd not seen before and wouldn't have believed possible.

"Good. You're here. Let's crack this bastard. And no," he said, turning to me, a dangerous smile on his face and his arm on my shoulder. "This time, I'll do the talking. It's time to get some answers."

I shrugged. I could see there was no point arguing with him. "We'll both do the talking," I said, and he nodded.

The commissionaire wasn't for letting us in. He stood the other side of a big glass door and stared at us, and I saw us from his point of view: jeans, unbrushed hair, standing there talking animatedly to each other in the night. He was an old man with white hair and a navy blue uniform, standing six feet away from the door and leaning on his desk in a manner that suggested he welcomed the support. I produced Blennard's card and held it to the glass, and he walked over, haltingly, squinted at the card, and stared back at us.

"He'll want to see us," I shouted through the glass. "Sam Williams and David Brooks-Powell. He'll want to see us."

I think it was Brooks-Powell that did it, those weighty twin barrels that couldn't possibly belong to a man considering anything untoward. He shuffled back to his desk, stared at us again, and lifted the phone.

Two minutes later we were standing at the door to Blennard's apartment. Brooks-Powell raised a fist, ready to pound, and the door opened. Blennard stood there, silk dressing gown – or was it a smoking jacket? – somehow frowning and smiling at the same time. It was a good look for someone who wasn't sure quite how to receive his guests. I reckoned he'd know soon enough.

"Come in," he said, and stood aside to let us through. There was a short, narrow corridor with coats hanging on the walls and shoes in a rack, and then a door, open to a vast, high-ceilinged living room that wouldn't have been out of place in Brooks-Powell's mansion. I fingered the last two pounds in my pocket and caught myself wondering where I'd gone wrong.

"Sit down," said Blennard, pointing to a dining area off the main room, with a long table and half a dozen leather chairs. It was poorly-lit, which was probably by design, but after the security lights and the lack of sleep, I wasn't complaining. "I suppose you've come round to apologise," he continued, when we were all seated, he at the head of the table, me beside him, Brooks-Powell next to me. "It's a funny time of day to do it in, but I won't say I'm not relieved. You both know the legal system isn't perfect. It's pulled so many lives apart. Elizabeth did everything she could to put those lives back together again. It does you no credit to sully her name and undo all that good work."

I stared at him. Was this all it was? Was it Elizabeth Maurier he was protecting, rather than Trawden? It seemed a little extreme, but so little made sense at the moment that any rationale, however stretched, was a comfort. We might, I felt, get out of this without raised voices and threats.

I was reckoning without Brooks-Powell. I hadn't noticed him standing and wandering back into the living room area. I could have blamed the fatigue, but it wasn't that; I was operating on three out of four cylinders, which was good enough by my standards. No, it was Blennard. I didn't trust the man and I'd been in his company for no more than two minutes, but already I was under his spell.

Brooks-Powell, thankfully, wasn't. I turned as he spoke, and saw him holding a clock. Glass front, wooden case, burnished metal all over it.

"Sanderson, is it? Eighteenth century?"

I turned back to Blennard, who was nodding.

"Nice piece," continued Brooks-Powell. "Worth a pretty penny, I'd imagine. Now tell me," he went on, in the same urbane, apparently friendly tone, "you don't really think we've come here to apologise, do you? You're not that stupid, Charlie. Far from it. We've come here to get some answers. And we're not prepared to listen to you leading us up the garden path and spouting on about good names and good works."

Blennard had risen from his chair. The smile was gone.

"What on earth are you talking about?" he said, and there was a crash. Brooks-Powell had dropped the clock. Thrown rather than dropped, judging by the sound and the chunks of splintered wood that now littered the living room. Blennard sat back down and put one hand on his forehead as though he were trying to keep his brain from bursting out.

"We'll ask the questions, Charlie," said Brooks-Powell. Same tone. Same dangerous smile. "I know all about you, you bastard. I've heard the rumours. You hear them, in my circle. Hear them about all sorts of people. I tend not to believe them. But this time. Well. There has to be a reason, doesn't there?"

"I really don't know –" began Blennard, and stopped as

Brooks-Powell marched over to an antique desk and started picking up the objects on it – a pen, a glass paperweight, a curious carved wooden ornament that looked like it belonged somewhere a thousand miles from Mayfair – weighing each one carefully in his hands before flinging it across the room.

"I know there's no evidence," he said. "Of what you've done. You've got them all snug in your pocket, haven't you? You've got the police running all over the country shutting people up and they think they're doing the right thing, they think it's important business and Charlie Blennard says it's very hush hush so it's got to be kosher. But the moment you drop dead it'll all come out. You can't stop that. They'll all be singing the same story and you can forget your good name, *Lord* Blennard. You'll be the next Jimmy Saville, won't you? Right?"

He turned to me, and continued. He was no longer smiling.

"You think it's easy, being gay? You think it's a simple life, Sam? Even now, when it's all supposed to be fine? Maybe it wouldn't be that bad. But bastards like this one make it next to fucking impossible."

So Claire had been right, all along. I spared a moment to worry about her, but a moment was all I had. Brooks-Powell was still talking.

"So we have to try even harder. We have to make up for this lot."

Blennard was still in his seat, spluttering, trying to say a thousand things at once. I couldn't blame him. Everything was moving so fast. What *rumours*? What had Blennard done?

"So tell me, Charlie!" shouted Brooks-Powell. "Tell me everything."

Blennard had stopped spluttering and made it back to his feet. His face was red, and I could see he was sweating.

"You're a fool, Brooks-Powell," he said, with a calmness that didn't match the face. "Your allegations aren't even absurd, they're non-existent. Rumours, whistles here and there, no one even knows what these allegations are. Muck-raking. And you believe this nonsense? Oh, go ahead," he continued, as Brooks-Powell turned to gaze around the room, hunting out more objects to break. "Throw a few more ornaments around. It'll just be more things for you to pay for. Take the Bentley, if you want. Smash that up, too." He reached into his pocket and threw a set of keys on the table. "Although you should know that I happen to have a pair of antique rifles and a shotgun just around the corner. And I believe I have the ammunition to go with them."

I laughed out loud, entirely involuntarily, hard and hoarse at the same time, and Brooks-Powell joined me. I didn't know what to believe any more. Brooks-Powell seemed so sure of himself, but I still didn't know what these rumours about Blennard actually were. I was starting to worry that Brooks-Powell didn't, either. I'd said we'd both do the talking, but I hadn't done my bit yet. It was time.

"I'm sorry, Lord Blennard," I began, "but do you really think we're going to sit here quietly and wait while you forage around for an antique gun and some ammunition and then wait for you to load it and shoot us? Come on, now. David, come back to the table. Lord Blennard, sit down. This has gone far enough. Tell us what we want to know and we'll be out of here."

Brooks-Powell returned, scowling. He had, I realised, been rather enjoying his little frenzy. Blennard sat, still red in the face, the hand back on his forehead. I worried, for a moment, that he was about to have a stroke, but then he took the hand away and shook his head.

"I have nothing to say to you," he said.

This was too much for Brooks-Powell. He walked around the table, right up to Blennard, who stared resolutely down, avoiding his gaze. And then, to my amazement, David Brooks-Powell drew back one arm and delivered a hard straight right into Blennard's jaw. Blennard jerked back, his hands already covering his face, and then a moment later one of those hands moving out, palm facing us, a gesture of surrender. And from behind the other hand a voice, quiet in its desperation.

"Alright. Alright. I'll tell you. I'll tell you everything."

My phone chose that moment to ring. I glanced down, hoping it was Claire, but it wasn't. Colman. Colman could wait. Brooks-Powell had walked back round the table and sat down, silent. We both watched as Blennard's other hand came away. There was a bruise forming already. The punch had looked good. I wouldn't have wanted to be the wrong side of it.

"It's true," said Blennard, slowly, quietly. "What you think you know. About Edward Trawden. Well, some of it, anyway. There was another man. In the cell with them, Akadi and Evans. Name of Connor."

"You're not telling us anything we don't already know," said Brooks-Powell, already getting to his feet.

"Well I'm telling you everything I bloody know so that'll have to do, won't it?" replied Blennard, suddenly and briefly himself again. The bruise was darkening even as I looked at him, even as Brooks-Powell made his way back round the table and Blennard shrunk into himself. But there wasn't far enough to shrink. Things were catching up.

"Sit down," he mumbled, as Brooks-Powell came within striking distance. "Sit back down and I'll tell you the rest. I'm an old man. I don't want to fight."

Brooks-Powell sat, beside him this time, opposite me. Poised. Blennard didn't look comfortable, but then, none of us were comfortable.

"He came to me," he said. "That Connor fellow. I didn't believe him. I always thought he was lying. I still do. He claimed they knew each other. Akadi and Edward. Akadi was a drug dealer. West End. Luvvies. Edward knew that scene. They worked together, Connor said. He came to me and he told me this cock-and-bull story and I didn't buy it for a second. Said they'd stayed in touch, Edward and Akadi, when they both went to prison. Stood there in front of me, this Connor, stinking of cheap whisky, and told me he'd shared a cell with Evans. Said Evans used to talk. Used to say he'd been there, that day, in Warrington. Hadn't killed the girl. He'd been fitting a window. He'd been excited by it, the murder, so close by. Thought he'd like to do something similar. Evans had been inspired by the Grimshaw murder, that was Connor's line. But he hadn't committed it. Akadi wasn't even in the cell at the time Evans started blabbing about this, it was just Connor and Evans, but Akadi heard about Warrington and added two and two and thought maybe he could help out his old friend. Connor expected me to believe this nonsense, to believe that somehow without the authorities getting wind of it Akadi had written to Edward and between the two of them, working from two different prisons, they'd fixed the whole thing up. According to Connor, Akadi works his way into the cell, gets Connor kicked out of it, makes up some story about Connor trying to stab him, Connor denies it, realises what's going on, but can't do anything about it. The whole story was preposterous. And meanwhile, conveniently enough, Connor's just weeks away from the end of his term and doesn't want trouble. He gets out and doesn't think any more about it, keeps his head down, only then he hears Evans has died. Stabbed in the showers. The man who did it – according to Connor, anyway – this chap was an idiot. You could get him to do anything. Connor told me Akadi was behind it, he was sure of it. And then a while later Trawden got released, and when Connor heard that, well, he said he couldn't keep his head down any longer. He came and found me – I'd been involved, you know, commenting on the case, making the odd statement here and there, so he knew about me – anyway, he managed to find me, and he told me all this, and said that was his job done, and it was up to me to do the rest."

"And you did nothing," said Brooks-Powell, and Blennard shrugged.

"Of course I did nothing. Connor was a useless street thief who had no interest in anything except my money. That was obvious. He'd come up with all this nonsense just to try and wring a penny or two out of me. He was broke, and I was rich. It was nonsense, all of it. The only sensible thing to do was ignore him."

Brooks-Powell nodded, and smiled, and said "In that case, why did you ask Gareth Brady Jones to fiddle the forensic results?"

"I –" said Blennard, and stopped. And again. "I –", followed by a pause, and the face reddening again, a deep, dark shade that blended nicely with the bruise. "I don't know," he said, finally. "It was all lies. I was sure of it. And the forensics were useless, anyway. Decades old, poorly stored, not enough to convict a man in this day and age. But there was nobody left to convict, nobody alive, at least. And I had to make sure everything went smoothly for Edward."

"Because he knew things about you," said Brooks-Powell.

"Because he was my friend!" shouted Blennard. Every time he closed his mouth, he closed it hard, tight, a show of defiance that must have been painful after that punch. "He was my friend! I told Jones to take a light touch, that was all. I mean, it didn't mean anything. Connor was a thief and a liar. Edward Trawden was my friend. I wanted justice for my friend."

He was convincing, I had to hand it to him. Even Brooks-Powell had sat back down, nodding again, but calmly, now. Justice and friendship and all those nice convenient abstracts seemed to have done the trick. But I wasn't buying it. The man Shapiro had described hadn't had friends. He'd had idiots and enablers. And blackmail victims. Blennard wasn't a friend, and he certainly wasn't an idiot.

"You're lying," I said. I found myself speaking slowly and calmly, testing each word before it came, making sure it made sense and was leading me in the right direction. "You're lying," I repeated, "and my girlfriend is a journalist, and you might not care about all your antiques but you care a great deal about your reputation, and if you don't tell us the truth, if you don't tell us what Trawden knows about you, then you'll have a very black name to go with that bruise."

I could see the defiance drain from his face. Brooks-Powell saw it, too, and took up the thread.

"That's why you've protected him, then. The rumours were true. I don't know what you did, something to do with kids, they say, but whatever it was, it's enough to get you stabbed in the prison showers like Robbie Evans. Right?"

Blennard shook his head, but it was a sad, slow shake, and when he spoke, the voice matched it.

"It's not fair," he said. "You don't understand, what it was like, then. You," he turned, now, to face Brooks-Powell. "You think it's so difficult now? Imagine what it was like back then. When it was a crime. And yes, you've kept things quiet, I never suspected a thing about you, but then, what have you got to lose? A few cheap sniggers from people not worth knowing? Can you even imagine if you faced losing not just your name but your liberty, maybe even your life, the way things were?"

I didn't understand where this was going, but Brooks-Powell, by the look of him, did. His hands were over his mouth, the realisation of something dawning. Something he hadn't been expecting. Blennard went on, looking down, at the table.

"It was so long ago. I mean, yes, the boy was young, but so was I. And for heaven's sake. It wouldn't even be illegal, now. It wouldn't raise an eyebrow."

I couldn't take this any longer. I hated it, being the one person in the room who didn't understand.

"What?" I shouted. "What the hell happened that was so bad you had to cover for a murderer all these years?"

Blennard looked up, looked at me, nodded. And began.

"It was 1966. Indira Ghandi had just been elected in India. Wilson held on over here. England won the world cup. Ian Brady and Myra Hindley were convicted. I was a thirty-year-old masters student and he was an eighteen-year-old undergraduate and it wasn't like I was even teaching him. Yes, he was young. But he wasn't *that* young."

"Where did this happen?" I asked, even though I knew the answer already.

"Christ Church. He was only there for a year. Afterwards, after he'd been thrown out, he got in touch with me. Wrote me a letter. There was a photograph with the letter. I was rich. I came from a well-known family. I'd thought at the time that I was in love with him. I'd hoped he was in love with me – he'd certainly claimed to be. But I realised then that he'd planned the whole thing. He'd seduced me. He'd blackmailed me. From that moment, I was his. What have I done? What have I done?"

A silence fell over us, each of us taking it in, realising how wrong we'd been, how close to right, how the smallest lapse could lead somewhere no one could have imagined it would. I knew the law on this, I remembered it the same way I remembered every statute I'd read and most of the regulations and judgments. Sex between men had been illegal until 1967. Even then, it was illegal for men under the age of twenty-one, right up to 1994. The age hadn't come down to sixteen until 2001. Trawden had lured Blennard into a nothing of a crime, and for fifty years he'd owned him.

The silence was broken by a sob. A great, thick mammoth of a sob. And then another, and another, until they were coming so fast and Blennard's face was so red that for a moment I worried he wouldn't be able to breathe. I moved towards him, a ghost of a movement, hardly a movement at all, but it was enough for him to jerk away and raise a hand. He'd had enough of us, of me, of Brooks-Powell. Between us, we'd broken him. I felt bad about it, but it was something that had needed to be done. Brooks-Powell's hands were still over his mouth and the bit of his face I could see was as white as a blank page. He hadn't got past the feeling bad.

My phone rang, again. Colman, again. I'd been glancing at it periodically; she'd called, earlier, and texted three times asking me to call her back. Nothing from Claire. We were, I thought, as good as done with Blennard. I answered the phone.

"I've found him!" shouted Colman, before I could say a word. "I've found Connor. I've been trying to get hold of you for ages!"

"Any news on Claire?" I asked, and she stopped shouting long enough to answer me.

"No, I'm sorry. But listen. I traced the company. That website. The PO Box. Traced the shareholder. Got the address. Little village called Redbourn out in Hertfordshire, right by the M1." She reeled off the street name and house number. "I checked the electoral roll and would you believe it, the name on it is *P Connor*. Checked the utility companies and got the same result. I've been trying you all night and I couldn't wait any longer."

The whole time she was talking I hadn't got past that *No, I'm sorry*, hadn't been able to stop thinking about Claire and what she might have done, or what might have been done to her, all the way through everything Colman had said right up to the end. The signal wasn't great, fading in and out, the end of one word and the beginning of the next cutting out entirely from time to time so the part of my brain that might have been digesting what she was saying was busy just trying to hear it. And the bigger part of my brain was focussed on Claire, the whole way through. Right up to that *couldn't wait any longer*. Something about that, about the way she said it, jerked me back to her.

"What do you mean?"

"I'm there now," she replied. "I'm going in."

"Who have you got with you?"

"No one. It's OK. I called him. Connor. He agreed to talk. He's expecting me."

"Don't go in," I said, and noticed Brooks-Powell standing beside me, crouching down as if to hear what I was hearing.

"Where is she?" he asked.

"Connor's house," I said. "Hertfordshire, somewhere. Apparently he's agreed to talk to her." And then I noticed another sound. Or the absence of it. The sobbing had stopped. I looked up and Blennard was shaking his head, frantically, mouth wide open in horror.

"No," he said, finally. "It can't be."

"Hang on," I said, to the phone, but there was so much static I wasn't sure she could hear me, and then, to Blennard, "What do you mean?"

"It can't be Connor."

"Why not?"

"Because Connor's dead. He died years ago."

The last thing I heard, before the line went dead, was a tinkling noise that sounded very much like a doorbell.

23: The Centre of the Web

FOUR TIMES I tried to call her back, once that line had died. Three times I was informed, by a recording of a woman with a maddeningly calm voice, that my call could not be connected. The fourth time I didn't even get that.

I sat and looked around the room, at the faces of Brooks-Powell and Blennard. Brooks-Powell, my enemy, my ally, married and gay and behind everything I thought I'd known, a mystery. Blennard, the titan, the thorn in the side of government after government, face red and bruised and tear-streaked, his life a lie, a story spun with guilt and fear for threads.

I picked up my phone again and dialled the number for Martins. For all I'd tried to avoid any contact with the woman, she needed to know about this. It was six in the morning, but she answered on the first ring.

"Williams," she said. "I think it's time you came in."

"Came in?"

"There have been reports of a disturbance. In Mayfair. I understand you may be on the scene. I've been toying with the idea of sending uniform round to get you, but I think Lord Blennard can take care of himself. But whatever it is you've done, you've gone too far. Next time I see you, you'll be under arrest and in a cell. I told you to stop. You wouldn't listen."

"No!" I shouted. "*You* need to listen! Colman's in danger!"

"Colman?"

"Yes."

"Police Constable Vicky Colman, my former detective, relieved today of her duties within CID?"

"Yes!" I shouted, again. "Her. I don't care if you've

kicked her out of CID and she won't care either soon because she'll be too dead to know it. She's gone to an address in Hertfordshire and I'm convinced she's in danger."

"And I'm convinced you're wrong and you're just trying to deflect attention from your own activities, Mr Williams. So be a good boy and come down to the station, before I change my mind and send uniform after you."

She killed the call, and I turned to look at Blennard.

"You know her," I said. "Call her. Convince her it's real."

Blennard just shook his head. I wasn't sure he'd have been able to talk much sense into her on a good day, but he'd been mute since he'd told us about Connor's death, and the way he'd been opening and closing his mouth like a fish suggested he wasn't fit for any kind of conversation now.

"Come on," I said, and grabbed Brooks-Powell's arm. "We're going to Hertfordshire."

It took forty-five minutes, in the Fiat that was still parked and mercifully unscathed on the double yellow lines outside Blennard's building. The commissionaire had given us a searching look as we'd left, and I wondered whether it had been he that had tipped off Martins, or whether Blennard had done that all by himself when he'd been alerted to our presence. It didn't really matter now. Blennard wouldn't be making any more complaints about the two of us.

Brooks-Powell was silent. I asked him if he was OK, twice, and both times he turned to me and nodded, still pale but less so each time. And pale was his normal state, anyway. I passed him my phone and asked him to try Colman and Claire every five minutes, and every five minutes he dialled their numbers, listened for a moment, put the phone down and shook his head. I had him try Roarkes, too, fuck the time, fuck the dying wife, I had a missing girlfriend and a detective walking into a murderer's trap, but he didn't answer, either. Not the first time. Not the second, either. On the third try I heard the ringing stop and a shout from the other end of the line, followed by a long beep as the connection died.

"He told me to fuck off," said Brooks-Powell.

"I heard," I replied.

We got there just before seven, a small terrace at the end of a row of cottages on the fringes of a village that was picture perfect, until we opened the car doors and heard the boom of the M1 traffic racing by half a mile behind us. Connor's house – Trawden's house, really, there was only one person I was expecting to open the door when we rang the bell, and it wasn't Connor – was the only one in the row with any lights on, but there was life in the others, too, as the furious barking from behind several front doors informed us. I offered up a silent apology for waking the residents of Redbourn so early on a cold Sunday morning. Brooks-Powell's arm halted my progress as I marched towards the house.

"What's the plan?" he asked, and I realised I didn't have one.

"Make sure Colman's OK," I said, for want of anything else. He didn't move his arm.

"And after that?"

I thought, for a moment.

"Force him to confess," I said, finally, and Brooks-Powell snorted a brief, mirthless laugh.

"How do you think we'll do that?"

"The mania," I said, and smiled. Brooks-Powell frowned at me. "He's ruthlessly rational, right?"

"Right. That's why he won't confess. Not a chance."

"Except when he's manic. Look, when he killed Maxine

he wasn't rational, was he? When he killed Elizabeth he might have been, but when he wrote that message on her wall? No. Manic. We get him there."

He nodded, slowly. "OK. I'll follow your lead."

He stood behind me as I rang the doorbell and heard again that tinkle that had been the last sound out of Colman's phone before the line went dead. I could see why it had gone dead, too – I'd had just the one bar of signal as I approached the door, and none as I stood there and steeled myself. I glanced behind me – Brooks-Powell was still there, wearing the expression of someone waiting for life-changing news. There would be no hammering on any doors this time.

As I'd expected, it was Trawden opening the door. I glanced at his hands, searching for a knife or a gun or anything that would tell me what I was in for, but one hand was empty and the other held a china teacup.

"Come in, Sam. And you too, David. Please. I'll get the kettle on. I'm sure you could do with some refreshment. You've had a long night, I'd imagine."

Without thinking, I followed him into a cosy room with a fire in the grate, a sofa, three armchairs. One of the armchairs was occupied by a large grey cat, which eyed us suspiciously as we entered. The sofa was occupied by Vicky Colman, a china cup in her hand, too, and, to my immense relief, very much alive and apparently unscathed. No thanks to Martins. I glanced to my side to confirm Brooks-Powell had followed me in, and we sat ourselves down in two of the armchairs. Colman looked up at me and smiled, a small, strained smile that didn't sit well on her face.

"Are you OK?" I asked, and she opened her mouth to say something, but then Trawden was back, all smiles and bonhomie, and whatever it was Colman had been about to tell me died on her lips. I hoped it wasn't important.

"Tea? Coffee?" he asked. Brooks-Powell shook his

head, and I asked for a coffee, black, three sugars. I didn't want a coffee, not really. But I wanted to hear what Colman had to say.

When he returned to the kitchen I asked her what had happened.

"Nothing," she replied. I tried to read her – she was good at hiding things, I knew that much already, but I'd seen her cunning and her disappointment beneath the mask before. Now I could just see confusion, and tiredness. "He was waiting for you to get here. Said you wouldn't be long. And then, just small talk, what's on the telly, what it's like living in the country, what Martins is like, as a boss, all that. I tried to ask him what was going on, why he was posing as Connor, the website, all that, but he just kept saying to wait, *all will become clear*, he said."

I could hear a whistle from the kitchen, an old-fashioned kettle approaching the boil. "I'll do the talking," I said, and she looked at me like I was mad.

"No you won't."

"I think –" I began, but she cut me off.

"There's three of us here, and only one of us is a cop. You just stay quiet, OK?"

She turned to Brooks-Powell, as if for support, but he shook his head.

"Sorry, Colman," he said, "but I think he's right. There's three of us here, and one of us might be a cop, but this is something new. We're amateurs, all three of us. Sam's just been playing the game a little longer."

She stared at him, then at me, for a moment. Then she nodded, and Trawden was back with the coffee and that smile, again.

"So," he began, shooing the cat away and seating himself in the one remaining armchair. "You've tracked down Paddy Connor. Excellent work. I congratulate you."

"Thanks," I replied. "What with all the blackmail and

manipulation of evidence and perverting the course of justice, you haven't made it easy for us. I'm feeling quite proud of myself."

I wasn't. Not really. I was feeling scared and out of my depth, and Trawden's air of calm had knocked whatever certainty I'd had right out of me. I hadn't known what to expect when we got here, but sitting down having a coffee with a nice fire warming my back wouldn't have been anywhere on the list.

"Now then, Sam. It's all very well making accusations, but you need evidence to back them up. I don't think you've got that evidence."

"We've had some very helpful conversations, in the last twelve hours," I replied. I'd started on the offensive. I might need to change tack, but now wasn't the time. "We've heard some interesting things, Edward. I'm sure the people we've been talking to would be more than happy to repeat those things to the police."

Trawden shrugged. I'd used his first name deliberately, to show him his sense of ease and familiarity wasn't getting to me, to show him I could give as good as I got. But saying *Edward* hadn't produced a flinch. None of it had.

He sighed. "I'm sorry, Sam."

"What for? Have you poisoned the coffee?"

"No," he laughed. "Nothing quite so crude from me, if you don't mind. No, Sam. I'm sorry you've wasted your time. Lizzy Maurier can say what she likes to the police. She was half-deranged before her mother's death, and that unfortunate incident seems to have finished the job. Her testimony would be no more convincing than my cat's."

"Perhaps," I countered. "But Lord Blennard has had a bit to say for himself, and I suspect he'd cut a respectable figure on the witness stand."

He blinked, and shrugged again. "An angry man. A desperate man, obsessed with his own sins, his youth, all those failures that could so easily have been monumental achievements had he applied himself properly. Had he not chosen to hate himself his entire life."

It was a good answer; however impressive Blennard was, I had little doubt a decent defence barrister could tear him to pieces on the witness stand. And it wasn't like either of them, Lizzy Maurier or Charlie Blennard, had told us Trawden had killed Maxine Grimshaw. On the contrary. In their world, he was an innocent man, a man who'd just needed a little help proving that innocence. Although I wasn't so sure about Blennard. That repeated *What have I done?* – there was something in that, a realisation, perhaps, that he'd gone further than he'd ever admitted to himself in order to protect his name.

But none of that mattered. What Lizzy thought, what Blennard thought, what Trawden said, the shrug. None of it mattered. What mattered was the blink.

He'd blinked. Not one of those involuntary, hundredth-of-a-second meaningless blinks everyone does every minute of the day. This one was brief, certainly; if I hadn't been staring right at him, I wouldn't have noticed it at all. But it was the blink of a man who has just had something thrown at him, the blink of a man protecting his eyes and what lay behind them, the blink of fear. It had come, and it was gone, and with anyone else I might not have thought a thing about it. But it had come when I'd mentioned Blennard, and part of me was wondering whether Trawden hadn't been thrown by that. Whether he hadn't seen, just for an instant, his world come crashing down, undone by his own miscalculation. Whether he hadn't recognised his old failure, the failure to see that at a certain point, with the right stimulus, a man on the edge might do something Trawden didn't expect him to.

I put that blink in my armoury and sipped on the coffee, and listened as Trawden told us all what a lovely village it was and how delightful the neighbours had been, although, he said, he didn't care much for the dogs. More of a cat man. I looked round at Colman, sitting quietly drinking her tea, glancing at me occasionally with narrowed eyes that seemed to ask what the hell I was doing and why I was doing it. Brooks-Powell stared blank-faced into the fire, no doubt turning Charlie Blennard over and over in his head until he found somewhere he might fit. Neither of them could see where I was heading.

But they hadn't seen the blink.

Trawden was explaining the characteristics of the different three pubs the two-hundred-yard High Street had to offer when I interrupted him.

"How did Connor die?" I asked.

He stopped, and looked at me with a frown.

"I understand it was liver failure. Hardly surprising, with that sort of person, Sam. Now, as I was saying, the Bell is very popular with the younger crowd, it's not really my sort of thing, but the landlord's a pleasant enough —"

"How did Akadi die?" I asked.

"The inquest hasn't yet taken place, as far as I'm aware, Sam. The Feathers has a pool table, which is quite nice, and I've tried my luck against some of the locals. No hustling out here. None of us are very good, and everyone knows the players who are less bad than everyone else —"

"How did Evans die?"

He gave a sigh, a muted sigh of exasperation, and shook his head as if disappointed with a favourite student.

"Do you really believe this line of questioning is going to get you anywhere? I've already told you. You have nothing on me and you won't get anything on me. That being the case, we might as well make the most of you all being here at half past seven on a Sunday morning in December and try to have a pleasant hour or two before you decide to go home. What do you think, David?"

Brooks-Powell continued to stare at the fire.

"David? Aren't you enjoying our little chat? Or would you rather be at home with your glamorous and immensely wealthy wife?"

Brooks-Powell shifted his head, slightly, and said "Fuck off". Trawden gave a mock flinch, and went on.

"I suppose she isn't there anyway. I suppose she had to get away. I suppose she has needs, David. Needs you, of all people, can't really fulfil."

There was no reaction. Trawden frowned, then smiled, hardly bothering to disguise his surprise. He'd picked the wrong time to go after Brooks-Powell. A few hours earlier and it might have worked. But after what we'd heard at Blennard's place, after what Brooks-Powell himself had let slip, there wasn't anywhere left to push him.

"How did Maxine Grimshaw die?" I asked, in the brief silence that followed, and Trawden sighed again, but didn't answer. I wasn't leaving it there. I wasn't settling for – how had he put it? – *a pleasant hour or two*.

"That was a mistake, wasn't it? The others, they were calculated. Elizabeth Maurier, and the other three?"

He looked blankly at me, but then, he would have done.

"You do remember their names, don't you?" I asked, and he continued to gaze at me. "Paul Simmons. Alina Singh. Marcy Granger. You do remember them? Or did you ever even know them?"

Nothing. I pressed on.

"They make sense. Sick as it is, they make some kind of sense. They had to die, because otherwise your plans might not have worked. Otherwise, you might have wound up back in prison. But Maxine Grimshaw? That wasn't something you'd have done in the cold light of day."

He stared at me. Just stared. Took a sip of tea. Stared again.

"No, Sam," he replied, finally. "I wouldn't have done

it. I wouldn't have done it because I am not a murderer and I am not a paedophile, and the fact that I am not a murderer and I am not a paedophile is now a matter of public record, thanks to your sterling efforts twelve years ago. For which, Sam, I will always owe my heartfelt thanks."

He smiled, again, and it occurred to me that when I pictured Trawden it was always with a smile on his face, that whatever else shifted, whatever other guise he wore, the smile was as close to a fixture as it got, and that I'd never once trusted it. There was always a sense of something behind it. The horrors he'd witnessed in prison, I'd thought, twelve years ago. The natural defence of a shy man thrust into the limelight. Nerves – the normal, everyday nerves that normal, everyday people have in abnormal situations. Now I saw something different. I saw calculation. I saw tactics weighed against strategy, moves considered, played out, in the mind's eye, rejected, accepted. And I saw the possibility that his strategy and his tactics and all his moves could be undone, in an instant. If the right moves were made against him.

"You're good at this, Edward," I said, flashing his smile back at him. "You're very good indeed."

"At coffee?" He shrugged. "It's just instant. I'm glad you like it."

"You know what I mean. You're clever. You know what people want, what they fear – isn't that all there is, really? If you know what a person's after and what they're afraid of, if you can seem to offer one and protect from the other, or to withhold and inflict at will – well, you can control a person, can't you?"

Trawden frowned, cocked his head to one side, as if he were giving serious consideration to my question. He wasn't, of course. It was an act. Everything was an act, with Trawden. If only I'd seen that twelve years earlier.

"I suppose you're right. In theory," he smiled. "In

theory, of course, because I don't believe real, functioning adult human beings can be pushed around like that. Too complex, Sam. Too many variables."

"And I suppose that would be true," I shot back, "if the targets – victims, I should say – if they were just people chosen at random. But what if they weren't? I mean, people are complex, yes, but people with particular fears, particular desires, specific vulnerabilities? People like that can be distilled into their one weak spot, can't they, Edward? People like Akadi want money. People like Blennard, they just want safety, security, protection, they want to be free from the fear of exposure. And people like Lizzy Maurier? What do they want, I wonder? What does Lizzy Maurier want?"

I was thinking back, as I said it. Thinking back to what she'd told us, earlier, in her living room. *Wonderful*, she'd said. That there was *something wonderful about him*. And even as I asked the question, I had the answer. I pressed on, before Trawden could respond.

"She wanted to break away, didn't she? She wanted to break out from under the shadow of her mother. And who better to help her do that than you, Edward? Who better?"

He laughed, suddenly, a high-pitched, uncontrolled laugh that jarred, that made Colman sit bolt upright and rattle her china teacup on its saucer, that drew Brooks-Powell's gaze from the fire and etched a frown across his face. I ignored the laugh.

"The thing is, Eddie" – I was pushing it with that *Eddie*, I knew, but it seemed the right way to go – "you think you know what these people are going to do. You look at the – what was it you said? You look at the *variables*, and you make your adjustments, and you get it right, ninety-nine times out of a hundred. You push them to a point – to a wall, I suppose – you push them all the way there, and that's very clever, I applaud you. And they don't say a thing, the whole time. They're silent. If they've got something to say, well, *no one will hear*, right?"

I looked at him. The smile was still there, but it seemed somehow stretched. Painted on. Perhaps it had always been like that. Perhaps it had taken all this to see it. I went on.

"Only, at a certain point, your calculations stop working. You think you know what they'll do, but you're wrong. You don't know what people will do when they break. When they're pushed too far. You didn't know Lizzy would talk. You didn't know Blennard would talk."

He blinked, again. On *Blennard*. Twice on the same name. It wasn't a coincidence. Mixed in with the anxiety and the sheer exhaustion, a bubble of excitement rose inside me. There was a chance this was going to work. There were all kinds of things wrong with the plan, not the least of which was that I had no idea what would happen if I drove a psychopath to mania.

But I'd cross that bridge when I came to it.

24: The Silent

"HOW IS LIZZY?" he asked, suddenly, a perfectly friendly question in a perfectly friendly voice. "How is lovely little Lizzy?"

I waited. I looked at Brooks-Powell, who returned my gaze and then glanced down to his right hand, which had formed a fist and was pressing hard against his left. It had worked on Blennard. He raised his eyes back to mine, questioning, and I shook my head. He shrugged. I turned to Colman. The excitement was past. She hadn't been with us to Blennard's apartment, hadn't heard everything we'd heard, and now her eyes were drooping and occasionally snapping wide open as she remembered where she was. She was drained, shattered, all of us were shattered, all except Trawden, who looked between us, into space, wistful. He was pushing us all, moving us around the board, picking us up and putting us back down where he chose.

Suddenly, I was fine with that. If he thought he was pushing me it might be easier to push him, to pick him up and put him down in that place where he was so certain of his superiority he slipped up and made a mistake. The place he'd been in when he killed Maxine Grimshaw – because I was sure of it now, as sure as I'd been that he *hadn't* killed Maxine Grimshaw twelve years earlier. The place he'd been in when he'd looked down at Elizabeth Maurier's body – murdered not in mania but in cold, calculated reason – and then looked up, seen the wall behind her, and decided to leave a message. But I realised, as I looked at Brooks-Powell and Colman, that he'd rather punch Trawden into mania than push him, and she didn't know the plan anyway. I'd be pushing by myself.

"Lizzy's fine," I said. "As well as you could expect, after

all you've put her through." I didn't want to talk about Lizzy. It wasn't Lizzy that made him blink.

"Lovely little Lizzy," he continued, as if I hadn't even spoken. "Lovely, lyrical little Lizzy. Did you ever read that poetry, Sam? Her *slim volume*? Did you ever fight your way through it? It might have been small, but it felt like pushing your way through mud, I thought. That's probably how they felt in the trenches. At the Somme. Push your way on. Right at the guns. Just shoot me. Just kill me. Anything to get out of this mud. Is that how you felt, Sam?"

I laughed, in spite of myself, and Brooks-Powell joined me. Colman sat up suddenly, again, looked down at her teacup, and set it carefully on the floor by her feet. Trawden was still watching me, so I shook my head. I hadn't enjoyed the poem I'd read, but I hadn't hated it quite that much. It didn't matter what I did or said, anyway. Trawden wasn't waiting for an answer.

"I felt sick, Sam. Encouraging her. I'd only been out of prison a couple of months, but we'd met a few times, at the house, in Oxford. She showed me her poems. She was so proud of them, and it was so obvious what her mother thought, but she didn't get it, Lizzy, she really believed that if she could only get them published, Elizabeth would finally understand her. And yes, Sam. I encouraged her. I told her what to do, who to speak to, how to get round the trustees. How to get the money. Awful poems. Just awful. A crime against good taste, but needs must, I thought. It was so easy. Have you seen the inscription?"

I shook my head, again, and he stood, walked over to a bookshelf and came back holding a book. *The* book. That cover, the woman and the mirror. He opened it to the first page and handed it to me.

This book is dedicated to freedom, it said.

I handed it back, speechless.

"Freedom," said Trawden, and laughed. "Two peas in a

pod, we were, that's what I told her. I'd won my freedom. Her poetry would earn Lizzy hers. An escape from that box. And when it backfired, as it was bound to, when Elizabeth pushed her back in that box and sealed it up, well, she had to do something else. Something Elizabeth would hate, even if she'd never know. I made sure I was on hand. It was even easier than the poetry."

I felt sick. I remembered now what she'd said in her flat, after dinner, when I'd put her to bed and turned away. *Can't blame a girl for trying. And mother would probably have approved, this time.*

This time.

I'd been right, then. He'd taken this poor, half-broken girl, he'd pushed her with that awful poetry until she was almost beyond repair, and then he'd finished the job. He'd seduced her and he'd slept with her, and he'd allowed her to think of him as her revenge against her mother. I remembered how she'd been, then, always nervous, always ready to retreat, and I wondered if he'd been her first, if she'd been poisoned by him, if he'd been her only. I wondered if Elizabeth had ever known, and decided she hadn't. Not until she died. Perhaps Trawden had told her, as she lay there, looking at her own tongue, feeling the life drain away. Perhaps he'd taunted her, when there was nothing left to lose and nothing she could do about it. Perhaps it had been his own confession that had pushed him into mania.

Perhaps he was approaching the same point now. That was what I was hoping, after all. To drive him into a mistake. If it happened, it wasn't going to be a happy journey getting there.

"As for not knowing what people will do when they break, well, you're right there, I'm afraid," he said. Still smiling. "An army of the world's top shrinks wouldn't be able to predict a trauma response with a decent level of accuracy, and I'm no shrink. But there are ways to mitigate that, Sam. There are random elements, of course, but there are measures one can take to manage the risk. To hedge, if you will. And as any trader worth his salt would tell you, the most effective way to manage your risk is to keep a close eye on the market."

I frowned. He'd made sense, until now, but he seemed to be heading somewhere I couldn't follow. He continued.

"So that's what I do. I keep a close eye. I *monitor*. I have various ways."

His head tilted towards me, his smile broadened. He was waiting for me to say something. I declined the invitation, waited, and eventually he gave a gentle shake of the head and went on.

"And monitoring isn't so difficult. You just have to be there at the right moment. At the moment of danger. Of distress. Of *grief*."

He emphasised that final word, that *grief*, and I saw at last what he was driving at and felt myself shrink, slightly, in revulsion. All those times she'd run to her laptop, all those times she'd taken refuge with her fellow-sufferers, at her lowest, at her most vulnerable.

"I must say, I did rather enjoy being FatherMac. Rather like being at a funeral. All those commonplaces, all that trite, meaningless sympathy. The clichés just flow, don't they? And the amazing thing is, they work. This nonsense, it actually makes them feel better. So whatever you may think of my motives, Sam, consider this: I have been an influence for good. I have helped poor little Lizzy Maurier take her first steps in her new, motherless life. I do hope they've been in the right direction."

While he was talking I was wondering whether we'd done the right thing coming here. Colman seemed to be in no danger. And Trawden was ahead of us, so many steps ahead it was as if he'd planned out every move, every variable, decided in advance precisely what we would do and been there to nudge us gently onto his preferred course. There had been that blink, earlier, two blinks, at Blennard, but he seemed to have got over that, and if I was waiting for a mistake, it looked like I'd be waiting a while.

"What about Connor?"

I looked round, in surprise. Colman had been sitting so quietly, almost asleep, I'd almost forgotten she was a participant in all this. Trawden seemed surprised, too, but pleasantly so, if his grin was anything to go by.

"Whatever do you mean, my dear?"

"I mean the name. The man. What happened to him? Why did you take on his identity?"

"Ah, of course. You're wondering if any offences have been committed. I suppose it's possible they have, but I'm not sure it's illegal to do as I have done. If anyone had ever asked, I would have come clean. But living under another name? Artists and writers do it all the time. Why shouldn't I? And the fact remains, I was – I am – a far better Connor than he ever was. Do you know anything about him?"

She shook her head.

"He was a street thief," said Trawden. "A worthless criminal with a tendency towards violence and hardly space in his head for a brain. He spent five years in prison, and if there had been anything worth saving when he went in, prison ruined it. When I heard he had passed away I couldn't resist the opportunity to become him. I must admit, it has been fun, being Connor. And useful, of course. With the website and the shareholder records and everything else. It enables me to see if anyone is getting close."

"Close to what?" I asked, wondering if perhaps he was on the verge of a slip, and he smiled.

"Well, let's take an example. An entirely hypothetical situation, you understand, Sam?" He paused, expecting some kind of response, so I nodded. "Then say," he continued, "for instance, one's old lawyer – not you Sam, don't worry. The monkey, not the organ-grinder. But if such a person were digging into things that didn't concern them, if such a person dug deep enough, if such a person finally found their Connor, then who would they really meet?" He smiled again, broadly, and gave a deep, ironic bow. "Why, me, of course!"

"So you killed her," I said, and Trawden shook his head.

"Come now, Sam. How foolish do you think I am?"

Not foolish at all, I thought, and that was the problem. I took a sip of coffee, glanced at my wrist, and remembered again that I'd lost my watch. Some things don't stick in the mind. But the coffee was cold and light was beginning to filter through the net curtains. We'd been here an hour, maybe longer, and all I'd got was a pair of blinks. I yawned – the tiredness hadn't really hit me till now, and stretched, and looked for somewhere to put my cup of cold coffee.

"Allow me," said Trawden. As he stood and approached me, one hand out, the picture of civilised urbanity and reason, I felt something bubbling up inside me. I felt hatred. Hatred for what he'd done to the Grimshaws and the Mauriers, for the others, murdered and mutilated for something that wasn't much more than a game. For the lives he'd taken and the lives he'd ruined. For the man he was, laughing about it, mocking those who tried to bring it to an end. For what he'd done to me, twelve years ago, sitting in court and taking it all in, and more recently, spinning his threads faster and faster and closer and closer until I was nothing but another fly in his web. He took the cup from my hand and he must have seen something in my eyes, because when he returned from the kitchen he was shaking his head.

"Don't do anything stupid, Sam. It wouldn't do you any good."

"I don't know what you're talking about," I said, even though I knew perfectly well what he was talking about. I could have stood up, reached him in half a second, wrapped my hands around his throat in another half. Brooks-Powell would have helped me. Colman wouldn't be quick enough to stop us. I could have broken his neck. And I wanted to.

He shook his head again, and smiled.

"That's fine. Just – well. As I say. Don't do anything stupid. Not with the lovely young officer here."

He turned his smile on her, now, and again I wondered what they'd been talking about before Brooks-Powell and I had arrived. They'd been here nearly an hour, just the two of them. Had it really just been tea and the weather, the Bell and the pool table? Or had he taunted her, too, dropped hints about organs and words on walls, enough to hit home, but not enough for more than discomfort and a certainty that would be as good as useless in court.

"You are a pretty young thing, Detective Constable Colman. I hope you don't mind me saying it. Something of the classic beauty about you. The nose. A Gallic belle, I feel. And you seem intelligent, which is, after all, the more important attribute in your line of work. You'll go far, if you learn when to get involved and when to step away. I'm sure Detective Inspector Martins will be an excellent teacher."

Colman shrugged. It was probably the best move, a shrug. She'd been with the man an hour or two and already figured out the wisest course was not to engage with him. I'd been haunted for him by more than a decade, and I was still learning.

"No, Sam," he said, turning back to me, the smile gone, a serious, almost wistful expression in its place. "I am not foolish. Not at all. Far from it. I have wandered and fought, I have struggled and returned. Like Ulysses, I am become a name." He laughed, another high, shrill burst. "No, not a name. I am become two. Or three, even. Yes, three. No," and he looked down at his hand and counted off his fingers. "No, it's four. I am become four names."

He looked back up at me and smiled, pleased with himself. Four names. I tallied them. *Trawden. Connor. FatherMac.* I couldn't think of the fourth, but I was surprised there weren't more. Trawden seemed to enjoy these games.

He laughed again, more of a giggle this time. Brooks-Powell was still staring at the fire, which was dying now, the embers glowing red on the grate. Colman sat back, impassive. I wondered what was going through her mind, whether this would change her, how she would deal with Martins when it was all over.

"Christie," said Brooks-Powell, suddenly, and three pairs of eyes turned in his direction. "Christie," he repeated. "It's like another fucking Agatha Christie book." I'd told him Claire's theories, the *Pocket Full of Rye* and the *ABC Murders.* "Nice little village, fire, tea in china cups. I'm half-expecting an old lady to stroll in and clear everything up."

Trawden's laugh was higher still this time, and went on for an uncomfortable ten seconds or more. "You don't know how right you are," he said, when it had subsided. "*Why didn't they ask Evans?* Because he was dead!"

That laugh, again. Brooks-Powell and Colman were looking at me, at each other, nervous, uncomfortable.

I was feeling a different kind of apprehension. I was wondering if this was what I'd been aiming for, if Trawden had basked so long in his own brilliance he was heading for a fall. But I was nervous, too. If I was right about Trawden, those falls were usually accompanied by someone else's death.

"Now, you have to understand, I'm not admitting anything," he said, more calmly now, but still speaking faster than he had been. "None of this horrible murder and death. So many deaths." Faster and faster, now. "Even Akadi. He did so much for me, and he, too, had to die. Was

I there when he died? Yes, of course I was. Did I watch him die? Well yes, I did that, too. Did I kill him? Far from it. I even tipped off the authorities about his body. But I didn't kill him. People die, Sam." He'd turned back to look at me, his gaze fixed on my face. "They die. Girls die. Girls die and their relatives grieve. You know all about that, Sam. All about it."

There was something there, I was sure of it. I wasn't sure I'd call it mania, but then, I didn't really know what I'd call mania. He was less controlled, in his delivery, than he had been until now, than he'd ever been in my company. It was quite possible that inside he was as calm and collected as he'd been when he'd offered us tea and coffee. I hoped he wasn't. And taunting me about Maxine Grimshaw and her parents? I thought we'd moved beyond that.

If that was what he was talking about. Suddenly, I wasn't sure. Suddenly, I had a sense that there was something else. Was it Serena? How long had he been watching me? Had he been there, at her funeral, watching me talk to her sister?

"The funny thing with you, Sam, with all of you, is that you seem to know your Christie – which surprises me, by the way, I wouldn't have seen any of you as the type – but for all that, you don't understand her greatest gift."

I stared back at him, trying to keep all expression off my face. This was the Trawden show. I didn't know what was coming, but I didn't want to interrupt it.

"Misdirection, Sam. Oh sure, you see the obvious ones, the bodies hidden among the other bodies, but you don't seem to understand the point of the noise."

"The noise?" I cursed myself the moment the words were out. I'd decided not to engage, and I'd lasted less than a minute.

He favoured me with an approving tilt of the head. "The noise. It always leads you the wrong way. Like a magician. He shows you his hand, you want to be looking at the other one. But you never are. The noise is just a hiding place. Cut out the noise, and you can hear the silence. And silence, of course, is where the truth hides."

That sounded familiar. I wondered where I'd heard it before. It sounded like the sort of thing Claire would say, the sort of thing Adrian Chalmers would tell her and she'd believe. I was worried that there was something I wasn't seeing. A connection between Trawden and Adrian Chalmers.

Four names.

It hit me suddenly and without warning.

Four names.

How had Claire found Adrian Chalmers? I'd always assumed she'd contacted him. Could it have been the other way round? Trawden was still talking, but I wasn't listening to him, I was trying to remember Adrian Chalmers' voice, the voice on the answerphone message I'd picked up, the oily sheen that floated on its surface. It didn't sound like Trawden, not the way Trawden was talking now, but Trawden was a chameleon. Trawden could be anyone he wanted to be. On he went, and I could hardly take in a word, suddenly full of Adrian Chalmers and the awful possibility that Trawden had been pushing Claire around his board the whole time.

"Do you remember *The Mysterious Affair at Styles*?" he said. "Poirot's first adventure. You're supposed to look at the beard. But the beard is just the noise. The beard is what they want you to see. It's everything that isn't the beard that's important. I almost wish you could see it. I almost do. But you never will, Sam. You'll never listen to the important things. You'll never see what's happening right under your nose."

"If there was anything there it would be a moustache, not a beard," said Brooks-Powell, and I snapped back to the present and rejoiced, briefly, that he was still capable of a comment like that. Trawden chuckled. I stared at him. He'd fallen silent. He seemed to know everything. How did he know?

"Serena Hawkes," I said, finally, praying that was all, and he nodded.

"Yes. Exactly. Perfect example. Following all the noise, and not listening to the quieter things happening right in front of you. But that's not all, Sam. That's not all of it."

"What? What else? What are you talking about?" I asked, my voice sounding as if it were coming from somewhere high and distant. I'd carried a picture of Adrian Chalmers in my head, a round face fringed by short curly hair, stylish but subtle glasses, a ready smile and an earnest, sympathetic tilt of the head. I tried to solidify it, to merge it with the voice I'd heard, but I couldn't. All I could see was Trawden. All I could hear was Trawden. This wasn't a game any more. It was a hunt. And I didn't feel much like a predator.

"You were very restrained, earlier," he said, smiling again. "I thought you were about to beat me senseless. I could see it in your eyes, you know. But you held back, and that's admirable."

I nodded. Something was coming. Trawden continued.

"I wonder if everyone else will manage to be quite so restrained, though."

I looked around the room. Brooks-Powell wasn't staring at the fire any more, and that was something, but the man who'd smashed up Blennard's antiques was gone. And Colman was still struggling to keep her eyes open.

"Not them," said Trawden.

"Then who?"

"Hello?" he said. "I am sorry to bother you."

His voice had changed. Another tone, a familiar tone. Not Adrian Chalmers, and I felt my blood start to flow again, my heart begin beating. But the relief was short-lived.

I'd heard this voice before. My brain rifled frantically through memories, voices I knew, people I had spoken to.

"Hello," he repeated. There was an accent, suddenly. European. "Please could I speak to Claire?"

The pounding in my chest was so loud I was surprised no one else could hear it. Or maybe they could. Maybe they were all as transfixed as I was.

"They will get away with it, Miss Tully." He pronounced *Miss* as *Meess*. "They are animals. What they did, to my poor Yelena. Nobody should be treated like that."

It was clear. Everything was clear.

I'd been looking in the wrong places. It was Serena Hawkes, all over again. Only this time, it was a lot closer to home.

Four names.

Trawden

Connor.

FatherMac.

Viktor.

What had he said to Claire? What had he done to her?

"We are the same, Miss Tully." It was Trawden's face, but the accent and the tone had changed the man. "We fight for those who have no voice. For the silent. We fight against those who silence them. They are animals. And now they are protected. Who will speak for my daughter, Miss Tully? They must be avenged. They must be heard, Miss Tully. I am in Ukraine. I can do nothing. It must be you. You must speak for them. You must speak for them and avenge them, Miss Tully. And then, perhaps, you will finally speak for your cousin."

Trawden stopped, his eyes fixed on me, and without warning burst into peals of laughter, waves rolling in on me while I tried to take everything in. I stood. Brooks-Powell and Colman wore identical expressions of bewilderment. I didn't have time to explain. I strode through the room and out of the door and I didn't look back.

25: Sig

I WAS THREE miles down the M1 before I realised where I was and what I was doing. I kept one eye on the road and rang Claire's number again, not caring who saw me. It didn't matter. Anyone watching would have been hard-pressed to make out the phone, given I was topping a hundred miles an hour and the Fiat was shaking uncomfortably. I'd had one close shave already, on the way out of the village, eyes on the phone, veering round a corner on the wrong side of the road and only jerking back a foot or two away from an enormous black coffin of a car heading right for me.

No answer.

I tried again, with similar results. I had no idea where Claire was or what she was doing, but I knew whatever it was, it was happening now. Trawden wouldn't have told me if I wasn't already too late to stop it. And wherever she was, she wasn't bleeding out her last in Redbourn – Trawden was too clever for that. The M25 was coming up and I had a decision to make. Round London, or into it.

Into it. I veered back into the right-hand lane and kept going. The sun was up, now, flashes of bright gold reflecting off the remains of an overnight downpour I hadn't noticed. It was half past eight.

I needed something to keep me going. Something to keep me from panicking. I turned on the radio in time for the news bulletin.

Martins had finally caved. The murders were the top story; the police were linking four killings over a twenty-four-hour period in four different parts of London. The locations were revealed, but not the names. Not the details, either, but I could see why Martins had chosen to keep those cards close to her chest. Let the public digest the deaths, first – the "horrific murders", as the newsreader referred to them – and drip-feed the rest later, if later was needed. It wouldn't be. We knew who'd killed those four people. We knew who'd killed Elizabeth Maurier. Who'd killed Paul Simmons. Who'd killed Alina Singh. Who'd killed Marcy Granger. Who'd removed ears, eyes, nose, fingers. Who'd left messages on walls and sent the police scurrying hither and yon like mice in a maze, drugged and heading the wrong way. We knew who'd done it, and I knew that for all that, we'd never put him back behind bars. Trawden wasn't one step ahead of me. I'd been arrogant to presume it. He was playing a completely different game.

Martins was on the radio now, the woman herself, those same sharp vowels, that same false depth. Appealing to the public. Opening the floodgates. She must be hating this, I thought, and found myself smiling. I held the smile in place a second longer than I felt it. Another thing to keep my mind occupied.

After Martins and the murders, the people-smugglers. The trial, the one Claire had been obsessing over. They'd overfilled their boat, to make a little more money. They hadn't bothered maintaining it, to save a little more money. And as a result, nearly three hundred refugees had drowned, and that wasn't even the worst of it. The worst of it was that this or something like it was happening almost every day somewhere in the Mediterranean, and every time the bastards running the show got away with it.

Only this time, those bastards weren't operating out of the back of a market stall in Beirut or Cairo or Mogadishu or Khartoum. This time they were operating out of the back of a pizza joint in Leicester, and a low-rent shipping business in Toulouse, and a courier company in Rome. This time they were caught, the six who hadn't slipped the net in time, and they were on trial in London's Central Criminal Court, and half the world was watching. Claire wasn't alone, at least. It seemed like I was the only person who wasn't obsessed with the case.

That thought comforted me, for a moment. She wasn't mad. Anyone with an ounce of compassion and an interest in current affairs would have been following the trial. The newsreader was still on the same story – it was a big story, and today was a big day for it, because the star witness for the prosecution would be appearing this morning. His evidence was expected to be little short of sensational. His name was Jonas Wolf.

I managed to keep control of the car, and that was no mean feat given that my first reaction, when I heard the name, was to let go of the steering wheel and close my eyes. I felt the drag of the wheels on the strip that told me I was heading for the central reservation, the strip that separated an everyday drive from a fiery death, and heard the hum that went with it, and I opened my eyes and grabbed the steering wheel again, and hit the brakes, too, because the traffic was slowing in front of me as I neared the city and the end of the motorway.

Jonas Wolf.

It explained everything. Finally. It was as if someone had just switched on a light, and suddenly all those mysteries that had been plaguing me for close to a fortnight were gone.

Claire had implicated Jonas Wolf in her own story. He'd been involved, she didn't know how, but she knew he'd been involved. He'd helped import those girls, the five of them, and he'd helped distribute them to people who'd raped them and killed them and not given them a second thought.

And the police hadn't been interested. "Oh yes," they'd said, every last one of them, every detective sergeant and detective inspector and police constable and even the superintendent she'd eventually hounded into returning her calls. "Oh yes. Leave it with us. We'll get back to you." And they hadn't got back to her, or if they had, it had been with apologies and excuses. They couldn't go after Wolf. No one could tell her why.

And now I knew. Wolf was the star witness in an A-list trial. No doubt he'd been promised immunity. I wondered how long Claire had known, and the answer was there as soon as the question had crossed my mind. Since the beginning. Since I'd come back from Manchester and she'd been different, somehow, distracted and obsessed and angry and sad. The man talking on the radio was Sergeant Paul Jenson of the Metropolitan Police Immigration Enforcement Liaison Unit. I'd seen him on the television. I'd watched her watching him and not saying a word. He'd phoned her – the name suddenly struck home. He'd phoned the day Elizabeth's will had been read, the day everything had started, he'd phoned and I'd answered and passed him onto Claire and she'd been shouting at him as I left for Willoughby's office.

He'd been telling her Wolf was off-limits.

She hadn't told me any of this. I'd asked, and she'd come up with words that seemed to explain it all, but it had never really made sense. Why wouldn't the police take on Wolf? What was Thorwell so afraid of that he wouldn't publish? I'd listen to her half-explanations, I'd waited for her to say more, and – I remembered it now, I could see her as if she were sitting beside me in the car – she'd been about to say something, about to say everything, maybe, but I'd told her not to get too close. *Don't make it personal.*

So she hadn't. She hadn't told me Wolf was about more than the girls he'd helped kill. She hadn't told me Wolf was her cousin's last word, a different man from the one who'd driven that cousin to take her own life, but still the final stop on a fifteen year journey she'd been determined to keep to herself. She hadn't told me how Wolf had got away.

297

I knew where I was heading, at least. The traffic was slowing, but I'd spent many a long day at the Old Bailey and I knew some back roads. I'd be there by nine. What I'd do when I got there was another question entirely.

My phone rang. It wouldn't be Claire. I knew it wouldn't be Claire. I just hoped it wasn't Martins.

It wasn't.

"Sam," said Maloney. There was something in his voice I didn't recognise. Urgency. Fear, even. Fear wasn't a word I associated with Maloney.

"Can't talk now," I said. "I've got a problem."

"I know," he replied, and I nearly dropped the phone. "Look, don't blame me, OK?"

I felt something in my gut, a lead weight, a sense of dread almost physical it was so solid and unambiguous.

"What do you mean?"

"It's Claire. She's been round. I took her to the pub on Saturday and we had a blast, she opened up, you know, all about Mandy. She'd already told me about that, when we spoke the other day, but I got the full story on Saturday. She's been hurting, Sam. She's been really hurting."

I didn't say anything. Everyone knew about her cousin. Even Trawden knew. He'd tracked down her obsession through Twitter and milked her for more by playing Viktor. Maloney knew. Everyone knew except me. And all this – Trawden was right. It had happened under my nose, and I'd ignored it, or thought it was something else, I'd followed the noise and looked for the obvious and all the time it had been right in front of me, and at the very moment it was about to reveal itself I'd said *don't make it personal*, and it had scuttled back under its rock. It was my fault. All of it. I cried out, in frustration or anger or self-loathing or fear, or a mixture of all four, but Maloney was still talking. I stopped cursing myself long enough to listen.

"Yesterday she came over. I wasn't expecting her, but I

made her welcome and we drank some good scotch and she let it all out again, Mandy, but also that trial and that bastard Wolf. We had a good session, you know, hit the pub in the middle and came back to mine for more scotch afterwards."

Maloney had finally wound down his operation, but he'd held onto his base. Half a dozen ex-council flats in a block in the back end of Tottenham. Over the years, he'd turned them into the centre of a crime ring that dominated half of North London, and when he'd had enough of that, he'd simply turned them into a nice place to live. Claire would have been comfortable, at least.

"Thing is," he continued, "we drank a lot and I don't remember everything."

He paused, and I waited for what was coming. If he'd had sex with my girlfriend I'd be angry, sure, but I'd also be relieved. If she wanted to take out her anger by screwing my friend, I could live with that. It could be worse. The Claire I knew wouldn't have done anything like that. But I was starting to realise that the Claire I knew wasn't even half the picture.

"So I checked around this morning and I realised one of my pieces was missing."

He paused, again, and I tried to figure out what he was talking about. He clarified things a moment later.

"It's an old Sig. She took a couple of magazines, too. She took the right ones, so I think she knew what she was doing. I think she planned this. And I think I know where she's going."

"The Old Bailey?" I said. "I'm on my way. I'll be there in twenty minutes."

"I'll meet you outside the courts."

"OK."

"And I'm sorry, Sam."

"Don't be. She'd have figured out a way, somehow or other."

"We'll stop her, Sam. We'll make it."

I killed the call and swerved down a side road as I noticed a line of brake lights blinking on in front. I'd ignored all the bus lanes and the odd red light already. I'd be lucky to keep my driving licence when all this was over.

I was driving past the court nineteen minutes later and remembering the one thing I'd always hated about the Old Bailey.

Nowhere to park.

I cruised around the side streets for a couple of minutes, wondering whether I should just ditch the car somewhere and run. But I didn't want to attract attention. There were police outside the courts, more than usual, and a television news crew or two. A car where it shouldn't be would have them swarming all over it within seconds.

Part of me thought that would be a good thing. The police would have more luck getting to Claire than I would. Maybe they'd get to her before she did anything stupid, like putting a bullet in Jonas Wolf in front of half the world's media. But if they did, they'd have her with a gun and intent and motive and a whole lot more, and I was still hoping I could get to her myself. Stop her. Reset everything from zero.

Maloney had called, twice. He'd managed to get himself driven to the spot and dropped off, and he was running around like a crazy man trying to pick out one woman among fifty thousand commuters, every one of them anxious to be where they were heading and not interested in getting out of his way.

I drove around three times. The news came on. Martins and the murders. The trial – the day's proceedings were due to start in an hour, which meant witnesses could be arriving any time now. It was a handgun. It was small, she could be anywhere. Not inside, though. She wouldn't have got a gun into the court. The trial story was interrupted by some breaking news. A shooting, in a village. I half-listened, still keeping an eye on the road and an eye on the pedestrians and a fraction of each of those eyes on the lookout for somewhere I could ditch the car and join Maloney in his fruitless search. Half the village had been sealed off, said the radio. There were reports of casualties. Locals had never experienced anything like it. I was driving past the court again, the fourth time, still no sign of her. The village was on the outskirts of London. It was called Redbourn.

I flashed back, suddenly, to the car that had almost run me off the road as I drove away. The enormous black coffin of a car.

It was a Bentley, I thought.

I stopped the car, right there, right outside the court, and I felt my head drop until it hit the steering wheel, and the noise went right through me, the drone of the horn as my forehead pressed into the panel, the drone climbing through the mess outside and all the rest of the noise, obliterating everything in a single blaring note. I didn't move. They'd be edging towards me, I thought, armed police, there would be cameras aimed at the car and commuters stopping and pointing at me and wondering what had happened to the man in the Fiat, whether he'd had a heart attack or a mental breakdown or any of those terrible things that happen to other people.

I didn't care. Let them come, I thought. It was over. Everything was over.

The passenger door opened and someone slid in beside me and closed it behind them. I lifted my head from the steering wheel, but I didn't look round.

"You can't stop me," she said, softly.

I looked up. People were pointing. A gaggle of police officers, five or six of them, were staring in our direction, but they hadn't yet made a move towards us. I didn't dare turn to look at her.

"I know why you're here, Sam. I appreciate it. It's kind of you. But it's too late. I have to do this."

I put the car into gear and started moving off, slowly, because I didn't want to frighten her into jumping out. The police officers turned away and went about their business. I turned a corner and pulled up on a double yellow line. And finally, I turned to look at her.

"I'm sorry," I said. She opened her mouth to reply, but I put a finger to her lips and went on.

"I'm sorry I wasn't there for you. I'm sorry I didn't listen. I'm sorry about all the noise. I'm sorry I didn't understand what you were trying to say. I'm sorry."

She nodded.

"You know what this is all about, Sam?"

I nodded back.

"You know about Mandy?"

"Yes. Your mother told me."

She paused, her face wrinkled into a frown, that look I'd grown to love in her.

"There are so many of them, Sam. So many people who never get heard. So many silences. Mandy was silenced. Those girls, all of them, they were silenced. Xenia. Aurelia. Marine. Eboni. Yelena. Nobody would listen. Even Thorwell wouldn't listen. He's supposed to be my editor. He came in and told us all he'd help, everyone would get to write what they wanted to write, it was a new world under Jonathan Thorwell, but when it came down to it that *everyone* didn't include me. Not while there was a trial going on. We couldn't interfere. Things had to take their course, apparently. It wasn't important, apparently. Not next to this bloody trial. I couldn't bring them back to life. That's what they said. That's what Jenson said. You see? They even tried to silence me. Somebody has to cut through it all. Somebody has to break the silence, Sam."

"And you couldn't tell me," I said. It wasn't a question. She looked away and spoke.

"No. It was the past, my past, Mandy and everything, and I'd never wanted it to turn up here, now, with you, I'd never wanted any of it. But it was here and I was trying to deal with it and then you said *don't make it personal*, and that was just what Thorwell had said, you know that? The same words. The exact words he'd used."

She turned back towards me, and I shook my head, and suddenly she was crying, sobbing, great fat tears rolling down her cheeks, and she was in my arms, and there were people pointing at the car again, but they were just pointing and moving on, a curiosity, nothing more. She shook and buried her head in my chest and cried some more.

"It's OK," I said. "I'll listen to you. I promise. We'll cut out the noise. We'll deal with the past. We'll do it together. But not this way."

She looked up at me, her face wet, and she smiled.

And nodded.

I started the car, pulled out into the traffic, and headed for home.

26: It'll All Turn Out For The Best

I'D BEEN SPENDING too much time at funerals lately, I realised. It wasn't an activity likely to lift the spirits. There was something different about this one, something resonant and intense. All funerals are about missed opportunities. This one felt more so.

I hardly knew a soul there, but that sort of thing had never bothered me in the past. The sun shone out of a blue sky while the rest of the country tucked into their Christmas leftovers and wondered when their guests would start to think about going home. And I was in the Cotswolds, at the funeral of a man I'd hardly known, a man it had taken me years to realise I'd hardly known, and feeling like I'd lost a friend.

David Brooks-Powell's family hailed from a village a few minutes east of Cheltenham. Not a million miles from Elizabeth's place. I hadn't known that. There was so much I hadn't known.

David Brooks-Powell was dead.

There was nothing particularly unusual about the ceremony, or the burial. Melanie Golding stood by the graveside clad in black, and accepted the condolences of the mourners with grace and good will. *It'll all turn out for the best*, she'd told me, when we'd first met – almost the first thing she'd said to me. Now we were greeting one another at her husband's funeral, all forced smiles and swollen eyes. His parents held each other's hands and nodded at the other mourners, and every now and then, when they thought nobody could see them, they turned to one another and wept, soft, bewildered tears down tired and uncomprehending faces. The minister spoke of David's career, his family, his love for his wife. Ex-colleagues gathered in little knots and shook their heads in confusion. Rich Hanover stood alone and stared about him as if he didn't really understand what was going on. I'd been right about that unpredictability and that mutability, but I hadn't imagined them leading him here. Hanover had surprised me with a calm, reasoned account for *Real World News* of what had happened in Redbourn, an account that trod a firm path away from sensationalism. He'd surprised me with a well-researched and glowing obituary. He'd surprised me with a message on my phone telling me he'd be coming to the funeral, but not as a journalist. He'd be coming to pay his respects. Now he stood and stared and looked like a man who was only now learning what death really was.

And I stood with Police Constable Vicky Colman, newly expelled from CID, and wondered whether anyone had really known David Brooks-Powell at all.

Colman had called just as we got home, Claire and I, by which time I'd managed to get hold of Maloney and explain. Claire was still crying, but in among the tears that smile showed up from time to time, so I felt we were through the worst of it. But I knew we were the lucky ones. I knew something had happened in Redbourn. I couldn't get it out of my head, the Bentley coming towards me and the newsreader's announcement: *there have been reports of casualties.*

I managed to get Claire into bed and comfortable, with a cup of tea, all using just one hand. The other was pressing the phone to my ear. The reports had been right.

Two dead. One injured. *Reports of casualties.*

Blennard had shown up at Trawden's house raging and barely comprehensible. At first Colman had thought he was just drunk and angry, and then he'd let his coat fall open and revealed the antique shotgun he'd brought along with him. After that, she said, things had got a little confused, but one thing was clear: he'd come to kill Trawden.

If only he'd succeeded.

Colman had tried to talk him out of it and Trawden had stood there frozen to the spot, finally confronted with a turn of events he hadn't foreseen. Eventually Blennard had tired of Colman and pushed her out of the way, raised his weapon, pointed it at his victim. And Brooks-Powell had chosen that moment to intervene, rising from his seat to approach Blennard and telling him this was stupid and there had to be a better way.

He might have been right, but he was too late. Blennard had already pulled the trigger. The lead that made it through Brooks-Powell caused Trawden some damage, but not enough to kill him. Brooks-Powell wasn't so fortunate. Colman had leapt across the room to Brooks-Powell, realised he was already beyond saving, and looked up in time to see Blennard, gun pointing vertically at his head, blowing his own brains out.

She'd escaped with a few scratches from the debris. Blennard was dead. Trawden was injured – quite severely injured, it turned out, with lacerations to a number of important organs that would keep the surgeons busy for weeks. Trawden was hurt, but being Trawden, he'd left no evidence. As far as the rest of the world was concerned, Trawden remained an innocent man, a martyr to an establishment that had tried to destroy him. And now a martyr twice over.

And David Brooks-Powell was dead.

Claire had stayed behind in London. There had been no question of her going to the funeral, because there had been no question of her leaving the house in the ten days since everything had fallen apart.

I kept telling myself it could have been worse. At least she wasn't in a police cell. At least she hadn't been sectioned. I'd told Colman what had happened – she had to know, she'd been wondering why I'd left Redbourn in such a hurry and with such fortuitous timing. So she knew all about Claire and the Sig, although I'd kept its provenance to myself. She'd kept a number of details to herself, too, and out of her official report, including my earlier presence at the scene of the shooting. She'd driven Brooks-Powell there herself, that was the story she was telling. Yes, I'd been at Blennard's, earlier that morning. I'd been at Blennard's and I'd left, and I was out of the picture. Maloney would say whatever I needed him to say. No doubt Martins would struggle to make sense of it all. I didn't care.

Colman was out of the picture, too, in her own way. Martins had no interest in Colman's "theories" on Trawden. She couldn't prove it, she'd disobeyed direct orders, and her actions had led to the deaths of two civilians. She was lucky, Martins claimed, that she wasn't being thrown out of the police force entirely. But for their part, CID could do without loose cannons.

And Claire was at home, at the flat. Her parents were looking after her. Her dad had finally shed the bow-tie but couldn't resist acting like he was the true expert in his daughter's care, that he knew more than the doctors or his wife or me, that we should all defer to his fucking wisdom. They were staying at a cheap B&B just around the corner, they'd come down the day it had happened, and Mrs Tully hadn't complained about London once. She was being medicated – Claire, not Mrs Tully, although we'd all made the same weak joke about how we wouldn't mind some of what Claire was having ourselves, and watched the smiles fade from each other's faces as we remembered there was nothing funny about any of this. The doctor hadn't asked for the details, even though I'd had a good story all worked out; I'd just told him about recent events awakening a childhood trauma that made it impossible for her to sleep, and he'd tapped out a prescription for some pills that kept her calm, most of the time, and dozing for at least part of each night. The first three nights I'd woken to find her side of the bed empty, and found her in the living room watching the news with the sound switched off. Each time I'd brought the duvet into the living room and curled up beside her, covering us both, not saying a word, and each time she'd fallen asleep before I had. After the third night, she'd stuck to the bedroom.

She seemed to be improving. That was the other thing I kept telling myself, every time I took myself away from the other mourners to take a look at my phone and see what time it was and work out how long I'd been away from her. She'd been smiling more, engaging in conversation more, showing an interest in other things. She'd asked how Helen Roarkes was doing and I'd told her *just the same, just the same,* which was a lie, but I didn't think she was ready for the truth. Roarkes had called me on Boxing Day with the news. I'd seen his number on the phone and leapt to it, pleased he'd finally relented, and only realised as I was pressing the *answer* button that there was only one reason he'd be calling me on Boxing Day. I'd apologised, before he had a chance to say anything, and he'd told me to forget about it, that some things were more important than a stupid bloody row.

Helen had died on Christmas morning. Roarkes spoke with his usual stoicism, the way he talked about everything he couldn't do anything about, but I didn't think there was anything real about that stoicism. The funeral – another funeral, my life seemed peppered with them – wasn't for another week, but I'd arranged to pay him a visit in two days' time. I'd see how stoical he was face to face.

But Claire was improving. We'd reduced her dose on Christmas Eve, and again this morning. Claire was improving.

Colman had taken her demotion well, all things considered. She'd hated Martins and was glad to be out from under her, even if that did mean a return to the more mundane tasks she thought she'd seen the back of.

"I was too young for CID, really. They didn't take me seriously there. I'll have another crack at it in a year or two," she said. She was smiling. There was something believable about that smile, something very different from all those smiles I'd been exposed to over what seemed like half a lifetime of smiles hiding lies and fear and misery and secrets. Some of those secrets had come out. Some of them, I realised, as I saw Melanie Golding nodding away to the "loving husband" part of the eulogy, never would. But Colman's smile looked real enough to me.

"They won't know what hit them," I replied, and tried to smile back. I wasn't sure I'd managed it, but at least she'd seen the effort.

Lizzy hadn't made it to the funeral – she was *indisposed*, she said, and I believed that, too. There was a lot for Lizzy to get her head round. I had the feeling she'd be indisposed for a while. So she'd not come in person, but her poetry had, a verse composed for the occasion, not – mercifully – read to the congregation, but posted to the family and left discreetly among the flowers for those who might want to read it. I hadn't wanted to read it, but I'd felt obliged. It was an odd piece of work, a banal, almost jaunty rhythm building and then disappearing into a forest of disjointed images. It was clearly personal, and it rang with a strange, unsettling power that had me wondering whether Lizzy Maurier might be a poet after all, and too late to do anything about it. There were references to books and plays, and some of them I recognised, but they weren't in there just for the hell of it. They were in there to be torn apart. This was Lizzy Maurier saying goodbye to a lifetime of being caged by other people, and finding her own voice at last. This was Lizzy Maurier learning the truth: words alone weren't enough. Not now.

A woman was heading towards me, as I said my farewells to Colman, who had three days leave and was heading straight from the funeral into Wales for a short break with her latest lover. The woman walking my way was, I thought, in her early thirties. I hadn't noticed her talking to anyone else at the funeral; perhaps she was as much a stranger as I was. She wore glasses and short, bottle-blonde hair that stood out sharply against her dark suit. I glanced behind, to see if perhaps she was making for someone else, but she stopped in front of me, her face creased into a frown.

"Excuse me," she said, "but are you Sam Williams?"

I nodded and extended my hand.

"Jenny Beech," she continued, and I took a step back and tried not to let my surprise show.

"Right," I said, when I'd regained my composure and we'd completed an awkward handshake. "Yes. Of course."

"I suppose you're wondering why I came," she replied. A smile had broken out from under the frown.

I struggled again, for a minute, and then found myself smiling back at her. "Yes. Yes, I am. After what we did to you, David and I. Well, I wouldn't have thought you'd want anything to do with either of us."

"He sent me this." She reached into her handbag and produced a letter – a short, handwritten note on A4 paper. "Together with the biggest bunch of flowers I've ever seen."

She passed the note to me, and I read it, and handed it back. Another nail in the coffin of the David Brooks-Powell I thought I'd known.

"Don't worry," she said. "I'm staying at Hancocks. I'm moving team, though. That Rebecca Ashcroft is the worst boss I've ever had."

She laughed, and I joined her, and then she made her excuses and left. She had to be back in the office first thing, she said. She didn't want to get stuck in the rush hour traffic.

I shook my head, as she walked away, and smiled. The note had been short and to the point, something I was starting to realise had been Brooks-Powell's style all along.

"Sorry we got you into trouble," it said. "But you don't want to work for those bastards anyway. I've got enough work to keep an assistant busy. Come and work for me."

His phone number was on the bottom of the page, next to his signature. He must have arranged for it to be couriered to her on the Sunday morning, before he'd dug out the photo of Akadi and Trawden. Before he'd pounded on Lizzy Maurier's door and forced the truth out of her. Before we'd learned about Connor. Before he'd smashed up Blennard's ornaments. Before he'd been driven to Redbourn in the passenger seat of my old Fiat.

Before he'd died.

That crazy dash into London ten days earlier had earned me three points on my licence, which wasn't exactly welcome, but meant I could still drive, and the route home took me east past Burford. I couldn't resist the temptation to turn off and try to hunt down one of the old spots I'd visited on the way to Elizabeth's house. I drove north for twenty minutes, and suddenly there it was.

It was like the last fifteen years had never happened. I stopped the car in a layby that hadn't changed in all that time, and darted across the road, not that I needed to dart, because traffic was light here, as it always had been. The path was fairly dry, which was good, because I was wearing smart clean black shoes which wouldn't have coped well with a muddy ascent. I picked my way slowly up and into the trees, and tried to remember what it had been like, what *I'd* been like, all that time ago.

The parties at Elizabeth's house, with all those famous

names and the food and the drink, the double staircase she'd descend at the appropriate moment like a heroine from Jane Austen, the candles reflecting in the silverware. The intrigue at work, the gossip and the jockeying for the best clients and the most exciting cases. The bitterness when I lost and the excitement when I won. The opportunities. Where I might be living next year and what I might be earning and who I might be dating and what I might do to beat Brooks-Powell.

I reached the top of the hill. The oak, the beech and the willow. The sun disappearing into the west, the hills bathed in that strange and deceptive light, the mist lying in pockets that turned the whole landscape into something part earth, part sea, part sky.

Claire was improving, but I was afraid something had broken inside her. Elizabeth Maurier was dead. Helen Roarkes was dead. David Brooks-Powell was dead.

I reached inside my mind for something to comfort me, something to remind me that there was still some good to come out of all of this, but all I found there was Lizzy Maurier's poem, and that was little comfort.

I recited it anyway, quietly, muttering the words to the breeze and imagining them taking flight over Oxfordshire and Gloucestershire, and bringing some solace to someone else. All they brought me was sadness and regret.

The shadows of the trees lay like cold fingers on the earth. I shivered and pulled my coat tight around me, and watched the sun sink behind a hill. Then I turned and walked back to the car. Claire's parents would be in need of a break soon. Looking after her was hard work. But I could do it. I could do it better than anyone else. There was plenty of hard work to come.

But Claire was improving.

A Message From the Author

Did you like it?
You liked it, didn't you?
You did. Don't play coy.
You liked it so much you're heading right over
to my website at www.joelhamesauthor.com
to fill in your details and join my reader group
for exciting offers and free books and the
benefit of my wit and wisdom. Such as it is.

If you did enjoy this book, please consider
taking a look at my other books, or leaving a
review on Amazon. Reviews are like gold
dust, only better. I can tell people how great it
is as much as I like, no one's going to believe
me. You, on the other hand, have impeccable
taste, and are as honest as the day is long.

Also by Joel Hames

DEAD NORTH

Two dead cops and a suspect who won't talk.

"intelligent, intricately woven" - S.E. Lynes
"It's going to leave me with a thriller hangover for some time." -
John Marrs
"a white-knuckle, breathlessly-paced read that also has heart." -
Louise Beech
*"A pacy thriller, rich in voice and with gratifying degree of
complexity."* - John Bowen

Once the brightest star in the legal firmament, Sam
Williams has hit rock bottom, with barely a client to his
name and a short-term cash problem that's looking longer
by the minute. So when he's summoned to Manchester to
help a friend crack a case involving the murder of two
unarmed police officers and a suspect who won't say a
word, he jumps at the chance to resurrect his career.

In Manchester he'll struggle against resentful locals, an
enigmatic defence lawyer who thinks he's stepping on her
toes, beatings, corrupt cops and people who'll do anything
to protect their secrets. On its streets, he'll see people die.
But it's in the hills and valleys further north that Sam will
face the biggest challenge of all: learning who he really is
and facing down the ghosts of his past.

*He's working someone else's case and he's in way over his head. But
sometimes you need the wrong man in the right place.*

THE ART OF STAYING DEAD

A prisoner who doesn't exist.
A lawyer who doesn't care.
A secret buried for thirty years.

Meet Sam Williams. Lawyer, loser, man on the way down.
Sam's about to walk into a prison riot. Meet a woman who
isn't what she seems. And wind up on the wrong side of
some people who'll stop at nothing to keep him quiet.

**Sam thought things were going badly yesterday. Now
he'll be lucky to see tomorrow.**

*Read what Amazon customers are saying about The Art of Staying
Dead...*

"A brilliant read for thriller action readers"

"The suspense is perfectly timed and believable, the
atmosphere and characterisation spot on"

"The well-thought-out plot moves along at a relentless
pace"

"A pacy thriller with a rich seam of laconic humour"

"Engaging, fast-paced and genuinely thrilling"

VICTIMS – A SAM WILLIAMS NOVELLA

The trick is to save one without becoming one

Young lawyer Sam Williams is riding high. He's got a job
he loves, a girl he wants, and the brain to win out every
time.
But Sam's about to find out that he's got enemies, too.
And figuring out which one wants to hurt him most isn't
as easy as it seems.

*Victims introduces Sam Williams, hero of international bestseller
The Art of Staying Dead and Dead North, ten years younger than
we last saw him, and a lot less wise.*

CAGED – A SAM WILLIAMS SHORT

Promises come with consequences.

Binny Carnegie doesn't want her *notorious* night club shut
down. Lawyer Sam Williams wouldn't normally care, but
it's his job to fix Binny Carnegie's problems.
Fixing this particular problem might be more trouble than
it's worth.

*Caged is another snapshot of Sam Williams, hero of international
bestseller The Art of Staying Dead and Dead North, back in his
formative legal years at Mauriers.*

Please note that Caged is a short story, not a full length
novel.

BREXECUTION

There are thirty-three million stories on referendum night. This one has the highest body count.

Dave Fenton sleeps by day and drives a taxi by night. As the counting commences in the most important vote in Britain's history, one passenger leaves something in his cab.
Something secret.
Something explosive.
Something so dangerous there are people who will stop at nothing to get it back.

From Downing Street to the East End via the City and a whole bit of the country that isn't London at all, BREXECUTION is a fictionalised account of the closing days of June 2016. Politicians, bankers, cabbies and crooks - some will win, some will lose - and some won't make it past the first day of Brexit.

From Joel Hames, author of international bestseller The Art of Staying Dead, comes a thriller you'll want to put your cross on.

BANKERS TOWN

The number 1 bestselling financial thriller, "A real page turner - a hugely enjoyable, often funny, always intense thriller of a book"

"This time everyone else had their ducks lined up and every last duck had "Alex Konninger" written in bold marker-pen on its forehead. If I didn't crack this fast, those ducks would be shot, shredded and rolled into pancakes before you could say hoi sin sauce."

Everything's going rather well for Alex Konninger. He's drifted his way into a big-money job in a top-tier bank, and if he doesn't always play by the rules, he's hardly the only one. Alex doesn't know it yet, but he's got a problem, a whole army of problems, in fact, and they've all picked this week to jump on him. He's losing control, his past is about to catch up with him, and he doesn't know who he can trust, because someone wants him out, and it looks like someone else wants him dead.

In a world of bonds, bodies and blackmail, not everyone will make it to drinks on Friday.

Welcome to Bankers Town, the explosive thriller from Joel Hames

Acknowledgements

THIS BOOK HAS had a difficult journey, from its genesis, in the dark, on a ferry midway between France and England when the notions of silence and manipulation wrapped themselves around classical myth and became the character of Lizzy Maurier, to the point at which I delivered it to editors and beta readers knowing, as I pressed send, that I was delivering something markedly different from most of my previous work. *No One Will Hear* is still a Sam Williams book, and I'm confident that his friends and fans will enjoy it as much as they have enjoyed Sam's previous expeditions. But it's also, and more than anything else I have written in a long time, a Joel Hames book, marking a stage at which I have given freer rein to my own interests and obsessions than at any point since *Bankers Town*.

Gratifyingly, those editors and beta readers did precisely what I had hoped, and it is due to their kindness and expertise that this book has been allowed to complete its odyssey and reach the light of day. Thanks are due in particular to those individuals listed below.

John Bowen, whose advice and skill in writing and marketing and design have been critical to any success I've met with.

Joanna Franklin Bell, whose brilliant editorial knowhow has torn my books to shreds and rebuilt them word by painstaking word.

Tracy Fenton, founder of THE Book Club on Facebook, blogger and blog tour organiser extraordinaire. Helen Boyce, indefatigable admin and contributor to TBC, but more than that, a tireless and remarkably effective evangelist for authors and books of all types. These people are the best friends to authors and readers that any of us could hope for. The whole team at TBC are due my thanks and the thanks of many an author.

Ray Green and Rose Edmunds, fellow Mainsail writers, for all their help.

And finally: my wife, Sarah, with whom twenty-three hours a day still somehow isn't enough. My children, Eve and Rose, for making so many of those hours shine. And my parents, Valerie and Tony, for everything they've done for me over the decades, and for supporting my endeavours as an author.

Printed in Great Britain
by Amazon